What readers are saying about
the Hunter Rayne highway mysteries:

"A great take to bed read for anyone who loves crime fiction in a traditional fashion."

"Those were the best mysteries I've read in a long time! The characters were awesome and so there that I somehow think they are in my life ..."

"The dialogue is well written and smooth and ... there are well thought out and believable twists. The pacing is good and the lead characters are likable, flaws and all ..."

"I'm with [Hunter] on every page, and I can smell the cold mountain air, see the snow chalets and ski lifts, and feel his frustration as yet another mystery evolves. Hunter is an ordinary guy, the people he meets are the same as we run across every day, and we're right there, in the scene, every inch of the way."

" ... Hunter Rayne would make a great TV detective, driving around the country in his rig visiting different states and helping to solve crimes. He is that interesting of a character."

Also by R.E. Donald

SLOW CURVE ON THE COQUIHALLA

ICE ON THE GRAPEVINE

SEA TO SKY

a Hunter Rayne highway mystery

R.E. Donald

PROUD HORSE
PUBLISHING

Cover © 2013 Hunter Johnsen

First print edition 2013 by
Proud Horse Publishing,
British Columbia, Canada
ProudHorsePublishing@gmail.com

First digital edition published December 2012

PUBLISHER'S NOTE:
This is a work of fiction. Names, characters, places and incidents either are the product of the author's imagination or used fictitiously and any resemblance to actual persons, business establishments, events or locales is entirely coincidental. This story is set in the year 1997.

PRINTED IN THE UNITED STATES OF AMERICA

For the Hunter brothers from Teulon, Manitoba.
We'll never forget you.

Being apart and lonely is like rain.
It climbs toward evening from the ocean plains;
from flat places, rolling and remote, it climbs
to heaven, which is its old abode.

Rainer Maria Rilke

CHAPTER
ONE

The DC-10 started its descent. Just as the captain had predicted, it was caught in a layer of turbulence and began to lurch from one rung of cloud to the next, rocking in between like a deranged teeter-totter some fifteen thousand feet above the ground.

Mike Irwin clenched his teeth as his wife clutched at his forearm, resisting the urge to shake her fingers loose. "Calm down, Kelly," he said, not for the first time, trying not to sound as irritated as he felt. "We're all buckled in for Chris'sake. Look at the stewardess. Doesn't even bat an eye." He nodded in the direction of the flight attendant making her way up the aisle toward their row of seats with a black trash bag, collecting plastic cups and napkins. He threw back the last of his scotch and soda, wishing there was time for one more.

Mike was on the right aisle, with two-year-old Corenna between him and her mother. The little girl was picking her nose. "Let go," he said to his wife, pulling his arm out of her grasp. He leaned toward the little girl and gently pulled her hand from her face, held it up to his lips and made smacking sounds against her fingers. They were cool and sticky and smelled of the cookie she'd just eaten. Corenna giggled. "You're not scared, are you, monkey?" She shook her head, smiling, proud of his approval.

The plane dropped again, and Mike's stomach lurched. Corenna squealed, then burst into giggles again. "That's my girl," he said. "Just like the 'throw me' game, isn't it, monkey?" He smiled and stroked her hair. He loved the feel of her, soft and smooth, and the way she looked at him with those large liquid eyes. Her tiny teeth were white and even. "That's my girl," he repeated.

Mike looked up and his smile vanished. From the seat to Kelly's left, his five-year-old son Jordan searched his mother's face with worried eyes, his mouth open like some kind of moron. Mike wanted to reach over and shake the kid, tell him to buck up, not be such a wuss. His first-born son was nothing but a momma's boy. As if reading his mind, Kelly shot him a reproachful look and gave Jordan's skinny shoulders an awkward hug.

"Lighten up," Mike said, and looked beyond them, out the window. He saw a wall of mist, tumbling from grey to white and back to grey again. The plane was dropping through the cloud cover on the descent to Sea-Tac Airport. He shouldn't have let Kelly make the arrangements but he'd been so busy at work getting ready for the conference, he hadn't had time to see to it himself. "We should have flown directly to Vancouver and rented a car," he said. "What the hell were you thinking?" He shook his head. "If I'd known you were going to make such a big production out of it, I would've gone alone."

Kelly bowed her head and her face went slack. It was her hurt look. She looked that way a lot and he was getting pretty tired of it. He married her because she was young and sexy and he enjoyed being with her, but always acting hurt was affecting her looks. He should have known. If she was attracted to him because he was an older man and she thought he would protect her, that meant she was weak. He had thought that would be a good thing, to have a submissive woman, but it wasn't. It turned him off.

No wonder he still thought about his ex-wife as much as he did. Alora was more of a match for him; a woman with strong spirit, she got mad instead of hurt. Funny, though, that imagining his ex-wife submitting to him was what turned him on. Although she'd only ever shown him anger and not fear, he knew that his ex-wife was afraid of him — why else would she keep moving and changing her phone number? — but still he fantasized about actually seeing that fear in her, touching it and smelling it, feeling it quiver in his hands and beneath his weight.

"We haven't seen your parents since last Christmas," said Kelly, tucking her hair behind her ear. It was blonder than the last time she'd had it done. Very SoCal and Mike liked it. He couldn't remember if he'd told her so. "Your mom's really excited about seeing the kids," she said.

There were a few seconds of turbulence, which shut his wife up and made her grip the armrests until her knuckles turned white. Jordan grabbed her right arm with both of his dainty hands. Mike looked away, leaned back against the headrest and nodded to the flight attendant as she passed their row of seats, sure that she'd say no if he asked for another drink.

"If I wanted to see more of my parents, I wouldn't live two states away from them," he said, still looking up the aisle.

The turbulence subsided into small jiggles and Kelly relaxed a little. "You'll be busy with your conference, Mike. The kids and I can spend time with your mom and dad. You said yourself we should take advantage of the free hotel." She patted Jordan's arm as he settled back into his seat.

Mike grunted. "Why the hell are we driving up from Seattle with them? They could've just met us there."

"They have a van. We can visit on the drive up. It'll be fun."

"Like hell."

"You said we wouldn't need a car once we get to Whistler. The hotel's right in the little village and you can walk to the ski hill, right?"

"Don't whine. That's where Jordan gets it from." He pointed at his son. "Don't you talk like your mom does. Ever. Understand?" The kid had a picture book on his lap. He wouldn't look at Mike, just lowered his eyes and pretended to read. Mike snorted. Was there any point trying to change the kid? Defective. Too many genes from Kelly's side. At least, from Kelly's mother's side. Kelly's father had been a Marine, had served with Mike's father and proven himself in Vietnam, fought in close combat and survived to talk about it. Kelly's mother had OD'd on sleeping pills and left her twelve year old daughter to be raised by her father. He'd heard his own parents whisper about the woman and knew that she'd been too weak psychologically to cope with a soldier husband.

Mike thought about the time his parents had come down to LA and stayed at the house when Corenna was a newborn. He had thought it would be a good idea, having his mom there to look after Jordan while Kelly recovered from the delivery and got into a routine with the new baby. Mike spent one day at home visiting, then escaped to the office for as many hours a day as he could until they left. There had been tension, more than he'd expected. It pissed him off. It was none of his mother's business, or his father's, what happened in his house between himself and his wife, between himself and his son. He didn't need anyone reproaching him, however diplomatically, for how he managed his own family. Next time they came, he'd booked them into a nearby hotel. Kelly had suggested renting a chalet at Whistler so all of them could stay together, but Mike nixed that idea in a hurry. Separate rooms. Separate floors.

And there was only one way he'd be able to stand the 230 mile trip from Sea-Tac to Whistler in his father's Dodge van.

"Remember", he said, reaching across Corenna and squeezing his wife's upper arm to get her full attention. "I'll have to drive."

There was something about the woman at the corner table.

What attracted Hunter Rayne's attention was that the woman didn't attract attention. Here in a five star hotel at a top-rated ski resort, an adult playground where men and women sporting year round tans and wearing Ralph Lauren sweaters came to show themselves off, she was obviously not playing the game. She couldn't hide that she was attractive, although her nose, her chin, her cheeks were a little too full to be called beautiful, but she downplayed her looks by using almost no makeup. Her hair was unremarkable:

medium length, medium brown, not styled but not unruly. She wore a bulky patterned sweater the color of cedar bark that hid the shape of her body, so she seemed part of the heavy wooden furniture and textured walls. She didn't appear shy or awkward; on the contrary, her face showed intelligence and self-assurance. She appeared to be reading a paperback novel, but her eyes skimmed the room without changing the tilt of her head. He had seen the server top up her Irish coffee mug with decaf, and she sipped from her mug every now and then, sometimes checked her wristwatch.

Hunter had done enough undercover work himself during his twenty-odd years as a member of the RCMP to recognize the signs. She was waiting for someone, but he knew she didn't want whoever she was waiting for to notice her. It amused him to watch her watching the room. More than that, it helped take his mind off the reason why he was here, kept him from being aware that he was totally out of place, and kept him from wishing he hadn't decided to come. He looked down at his faded jeans and cowboy boots, not good in snow but the only boots he had without steel toes. *What's a guy like me doing here at a fancy hotel in the mountains?*

Why was he here at the Coast Peaks Hotel waiting to meet a woman he hardly knew? He guessed that he was here because he felt it was the right thing to do. He needed a break from months on the road, driving a big blue Freightliner tractor pulling a loaded trailer up and down the west coast of North America. He hadn't 'dated' — if that was the right word for it — in the years since his divorce. At first it was because he thought Christine would change her mind, then it was because he still hoped she would, and finally it was because … he wasn't sure. Maybe just because it was easier not to. He was healthy, red-blooded, unattached, and he was often lonely, sometimes bored with himself. He seemed to be searching up and down the highways for something he couldn't name or describe. He often thought back to the early days of his marriage to Christine, the mother of his two teenage daughters. It seemed to him that the man he was then was a stranger to the man he was now, twenty years, several thousand challenging days, and countless misunderstandings ago. Possibly

Alora Magee was part of that unidentified something he was searching for, but if he had a good excuse to leave Whistler right now, he would.

The watching woman had noticed him watching her. She looked again at her wristwatch, then at the pub's entrance, as if to say, 'See, I'm waiting for someone.' He followed her gaze to the doorway and there was Alora Magee, lawyer from Los Angeles, an acquaintance from last summer who seemed to be attracted to him and wanted to get to know him better. He'd liked her, but would probably never have seen her again if she hadn't made the first move. It started with 'Do you ski?' Then 'I'm coming to Whistler in February. How would you like to show me around?'

She looked good. Her hair was short and glossy, a brown so dark it seemed black beside the cinnamon colored suede of her jacket. She wore dark jeans that showed off her slender hips, and a soft ivory sweater, against which hung an asymmetrical rock of amber on a leather thong. Hunter stood up and cleared his throat, then remembered his mother's lessons on manners and made his way past a few crowded tables to greet her. "Hi, you made it," he said, offered her his arm and escorted her back to his table. "How do you like Whistler so far?"

She stood on tiptoe and brushed her lips across his cheek. Her lips were soft as a baby's breath and a rich vanilla scent lingered beside his nose. "Hey, handsome," she said. "Good thing you're here to support me. After two days on the slopes I can hardly walk." She leaned against him, warm and soft and not heavy at all.

He remembered how refreshing her cheerful, confident manner had been when he met her in Los Angeles. She acted as if they were friends already, and he went along with it. "Glad to be of service," he said with a smile, waiting as she slid into the booth before sitting down across from her. So this is how it's done, he said to himself. Just pretend you know each other better than you really do.

They talked about skiing at first. He hadn't skied for several years, he told her. Not since he broke up with his wife. He used to take his girls skiing on the North Shore mountains, the ones you could see across the inlet from Vancouver. He thought, but didn't say, that they used to have family skiing days more often when the girls were younger. What happened in those later years? Could he have spent so much time away from home, even as a detective with the RCMP, that he had no time for skiing with his family? He knew the answer. He spent a lot of what used to be family time with Ken, trying to keep his best friend sane, trying to keep him from drinking, trying to keep him from doing what he eventually did do. By the time Ken was gone, it seemed too late to recapture the family life they'd had.

She ordered a martini. "Dirty," she told the waiter.

"What's that?" Hunter asked her. "Beer for me. Labatt's Blue in the bottle, if you have it," he said to the waiter.

"A little olive juice in it," she told him. "I don't know why I order it that way. Maybe just for a conversation piece."

"It worked, didn't it?"

"I guess…" Her voice died abruptly. Her face had flash-frozen into a fixed mask, mouth slightly open, eyes wide, with a glint of panic in the pupils. Hunter followed her gaze to a large round table across the room where a man was pulling out a chair facing the entrance for himself, and motioning his female companion to one on the opposite side of the large empty table. He was a fit, well built man but the way his turtleneck sweater bulged softly above his belt showed he was past his athletic prime. He wore a light leather jacket and slacks. His companion was an attractive young woman, tall and slender but lacking the healthy glow of the skiers around her, as if she were recovering from an illness. She wore no coat. Hunter assumed they were guests at this hotel, same as Alora. The woman settled into her seat and smiled, but the smile seemed forced, almost pained, and she half turned to watch the entrance, as if expecting someone else to arrive. The man pulled a menu across the table and opened it, ignoring his companion.

Alora drew her breath in sharply and seemed to recoil. She raised her hand to the side of her face and leaned in toward Hunter's shoulder. "I've got to go," she said in a hurried whisper. "Come with me." Her other hand fumbled along Hunter's arm, and squeezed his wrist. "Please."

Hunter nodded. He knew she'd had a good reason for changing her phone number last summer, and assumed it was a stalker, although he hadn't asked her, hadn't wanted to pry, and right now was not the time to ask. He glanced over at the watching woman and sensed that her attention, too, was focused on the man in the leather jacket. Hunter slapped a twenty on the table and got to his feet, standing between Alora and the man who seemed to scare her. He kept that position as they walked toward the entrance. She shrank into herself and kept her head down and turned away, her upper body frozen as if she were carrying a cup brimful of scalding tea. She almost walked right into a little girl, less than three years old, who stopped short and was bumped from behind by a boy a couple of years older.

"Alora? Is that you?"

Alora jerked upright and gasped. Behind the two children stood a woman of about sixty, with a confused frown on her face. She was a pleasant looking woman, well groomed and wearing a ski sweater, black pants and moccasin boots. There was an older man at her right elbow, with a strong, narrow face and a military hair cut, a look of surprise on his face. "We startled her," he said, putting his hand on the woman's shoulder. "Hello, Alora." Neither his voice nor his face held a smile. The two of them, husband and wife, were clearly not pleased to see her. The children looked up at the cluster of adults in confusion.

"Well, well. Look who's here."

Hunter heard the voice and felt the presence of the man behind him but didn't turn around. He kept his hand on Alora's elbow and could feel it start to tremble as she turned to face the voice. "Mike." She nodded, her voice firmer than Hunter would have expected, then acknowledged the two older people in turn. "Beth. John." She took a deep breath before saying, "Nice to see you", which was obviously a lie.

"It's been a long time," the woman called Beth said. She smiled sadly and sighed. "I hope you've found what you were looking for," she said, unable or unwilling to hide the bitterness in her voice, and bent to the children. "Let's go find your mom," she said, and led them into the restaurant. John, the older man, nodded to Alora and started to follow his wife.

Hunter stepped back so he could see the man Alora had addressed as Mike. The man tried to stare Alora down with an acerbic smile, but she wouldn't look away. He didn't even acknowledge Hunter's presence. "Nice to meet you, Mike," Hunter said, offering his hand, and Mike seemed to notice him for the first time. He sized Hunter up, eyes moving from his sheepskin jacket to his jeans and boots, but didn't reach for his offered hand. Hunter noticed that the older man had stopped just behind Mike's back and half turned around to watch.

"You fucking her?" said Mike, his eyes back on Alora.

Hunter felt heat rise up his neck and into his face. He usually had a long fuse, but men like Mike had a way of shortening it. "Say that again," he said, low and even, "and I will knock your teeth down your throat." That forced Mike to turn away from Alora and face Hunter.

The older man behind lifted his hand. "Mike," he said. There was a note of warning in his voice.

"Not your business, Dad." Then to Hunter, "You're lucky my family's here. Watch your back, cowboy." The words smelled of alcohol. He nodded to Alora. "I'll be seeing you," he said. "We've got some catching up to do."

Alora turned and began to walk away. "You hear me, bitch?" Mike raised his voice after her.

Hunter took a step toward him, but Mike's father had grabbed Mike's arm and yanked him around. "What the hell do you think you're doing?" he asked.

Mike shrugged off his father's hand. "I said it's not your business," he said, took one last look at Alora's retreating back, and sulked his way back to his table. Hunter and the older man watched as he yanked out his chair and sat down, waving off his wife's questions, then grabbing the black apron of a passing waiter. His wife and his mother both looked uncomfortable, and both turned their attention to the two children, trying to act as if nothing was wrong.

The older man looked at Hunter and smiled apologetically. "Stress," he said. "He has a stressful job." He looked toward Alora, who stood waiting in the lobby for Hunter, and regarded her for a moment with a puzzled frown. "She left him, years ago. I guess he's a little bitter about it."

"I won't make trouble unless he does," said Hunter. He took one last look at the man in the leather jacket, nodded to the older man, and walked away.

"Thanks very much, Tom. I owe you," said Hunter into the phone in Alora's hotel room, then turned to Alora. She had been pacing between the window and the bed, rubbing her hands together with a soft swishing sound. As Hunter dropped the phone in its cradle, she stood still and inhaled deeply. "He says they've had a cancellation and he's had them save the room for you. Not much of a view from that room, he says, but I'm sure you'll feel more at ease."

"Thank God!" She exhaled and managed a smile. "If I'd had to stay here and risk running into Mike every time I left my room, I probably would've left Whistler on the next bus." She shook her head and shivered, as if she'd tasted something foul.

"How long before you're ready to go?" Hunter asked. "I'll go get my car."

"No!" She grabbed for his arm as he turned toward the door. She seemed embarrassed, and hurried to add, "I'll just be a minute. I'm not scared, really. At least, I shouldn't be. I can't imagine he'd try anything with his mom and dad here, not to mention his wife and kids. Poor woman. Did you see her?"

Hunter smiled sadly, nodding.

"And I sure feel much safer with you around." She pulled a suitcase from out of the closet and opened it on the bed. "You're staying at that hotel too, aren't you?"

"No. I'm actually sleeping in Tom's spare room. He just lives a few miles away. Tom's an old friend of mine from the RCMP, retired like me but he got hired on as head of security for the Chateau Grande Montagne here." Hunter smiled. Thomas Halsey and he had worked together on a number of cases. They'd spent more than a few evenings, along with Hunter's best friend Ken, buying each other drinks and talking shop — shop and life and the pain of life — until after midnight, losing track of time until one of them looked at his watch and they all realized they were in trouble with their wives. Tom was the lucky one. He still had his wife. Or his wife still had him. "He loves to ski. Working at a Whistler hotel is his dream job."

"And you're a trucker," she said. She was taking items from the closet and folding them to fit into the suitcase, but paused to face him. "Is that your dream job? Why aren't you working at a fancy hotel in a nice resort?"

He shrugged. "I'm not the fancy hotel type," he said with a wry smile. He had walked out on his dream job five years ago, never really thinking of what he was going to do after that, what his life was going to be like after leaving the RCMP. After his resignation, Hunter had the urge to go for a long solitary drive. He shared a table with a driver at a truck stop restaurant where he'd stopped for coffee. The driver was giving up life on the road and selling his truck. You have to like being alone, he'd told Hunter. The rest was history. "And I guess I'm restless. Just the thought of staying in one place all day makes me feel caged up. Driving from place to place, a change of scene and weather from day to day, it suits me just fine."

"Did you split up with your wife before or after your career change?" She threw the question over her shoulder as she disappeared into the bathroom.

Hunter winced. One personal question always led to another and he didn't like to talk about himself. "Before," he said. To forestall more discussion of his own past, he turned the tables. "So tell me about you and Mike."

She came back into the room carrying a soft-sided case with zebra stripes and a small white hair dryer. "I was young and horny, he was charming and sexy, the usual story." She tucked the dryer into her suitcase and zipped up the zebra case, dropping it into a large leather satchel. "It was all roses and champagne until we got married, then it was like he figured he'd bought himself a woman and had the receipt to prove it. He didn't want me seeing my friends or even my family, gave me the third degree every time I walked in the door: who did I see, what did I do, why was I eight minutes late. He hit me once — just once, I'm proud to say — and I had the good sense to know that if I stayed, it wouldn't be the last time." She zipped up her suitcase and then surveyed the room, looking for items she might have missed. "I walked out on him, left in the middle of the day while he was at work, with the help of a good friend. I took my dishes and books and every scrap of clothing out of there." She picked up her satchel and Hunter grabbed her suitcase. "Was he pissed!"

"Has he threatened you?"

She waved her free hand in front of her face. "I've lost count. The first time he found me, I was at work. I was a teacher, for God's sake, in front of a class of twelve-year-olds. Didn't faze him a bit. Came up to my desk and grabbed me by the hair like a caveman. One of the kids ran to get the principal, the principal called security, and I got a restraining order, but I also got the boot from my job. Too risky for the kids, they said." They walked out into the hall, the door closing behind them with a soft click.

"I'm sorry ..." he started to say but she waved him off.

"I didn't like teaching anyway. I do like law."

Hunter pushed the down button and they watched the little light above the elevator start to move. "He's like a recurring nightmare," Alora continued. "I was glad to hear he'd married. With another woman in his life I thought he'd lose his obsession with me, but it doesn't look that way. He found me last summer, I guess you figured that out. I had to change my phone number. Thank God he at least respected the new restraining order and hasn't bothered me at work. I guess he's mellowed, at least a little." The elevator opened, a small Asian couple moved their wheelie bags to make room for them, and they stepped inside. Alora frowned. "Does a restraining order from Los Angeles have any effect here in Canada?" she asked.

"Don't worry," said Hunter. He picked up both the suitcase and the satchel as the elevator doors slid open. "I'll make sure he doesn't bother you again." He wasn't sure he could do that, but he would certainly try. First he had to get her settled into the Chateau Grande Montagne. Then he would get Tom Halsey to make sure her room number wasn't released to anyone making inquiries about her. He would do a little unofficial investigating about Mike and the reason why he was here, see if he could establish some kind of schedule for the man, so he could make sure Alora didn't run into him anywhere. Tom had said he'd do what he could to help, and that he knew the head of security for the Coast Peaks Hotel. An introduction from Tom would make things easier.

"I can bring the car around while you check out," said Hunter. He nodded toward the lobby doors. The outside lights illuminated specks of snow swirling against the night sky. Alora looked around the lobby, then peered in the direction of the restaurant. From the lobby, only the restaurant's reception area and part of the mahogany bar could be seen. There was no sign of Mike. Hunter could tell she was nervous, although he was sure she was safe here in the lobby. "Or if you don't mind the snow…"

"I don't mind the snow," she said. "After all, that's why I'm here. No snow in L.A., remember?"

He nodded. "Okay," he said. He looked at her boots, then showed her his own. "You'll have to hold me upright, anyway. These boots aren't made for walkin' at Whistler, that's for sure."

Hunter strolled over to the restaurant entrance while Alora took care of business at the hotel desk. He could see the table where Alora's ex and his family sat, all busy with the food in front of them. As if he could feel Hunter's eyes on him, Mike glanced toward the door. His father followed his glance and they both stared at Hunter, who smiled slightly and nodded, then turned his gaze toward the watching woman at the corner table. She was still there, and she, too, had her eyes on Hunter, but quickly lowered them to her book. Who was she watching? he wondered. And why?

CHAPTER

TWO

Meredith Travis watched her target leave the restaurant with his family. It was eight o'clock, and she could tell that the kids needed putting to bed. Both of them had been rubbing their eyes and pouting, whining a little and fighting with each other. The two women had them by the hands, gently pulling them out into the lobby ahead of the men. Meredith was sure that her target habitually abused his wife, emotionally if not physically. Although she smiled and laughed and appeared to carry her share of the dinner conversation competently, she had a sad, resigned air about her, no challenge in her facial expressions, as if she had been defeated in battle, a prisoner of war. No surprise. If her target had been stupid enough to antagonize a man as powerful as her client, he was stupid enough to mistreat women. Meredith sympathized with her. She hoped that what she had been hired to do would ultimately help the poor woman.

It had been a long day of travel. For some reason, she'd been unable to sleep on the morning's flight as she'd intended to, so Meredith was already tired, but she knew she couldn't retire to her room. Not now, and not until midnight or maybe later. She would have to keep watch for her target in case he left his room, see what he was doing, who he was talking to, drinking with, spending any time at all with. In the space of a few days, she would get to know him better than anyone else knew him in the present, even, she liked to think, his wife or his parents. For their own peace of mind, his family needed to see more good in him than bad, but she had no such weakness. She put her powers of observation, research skills, and psychology degree to work in concert to accomplish her assigned task and satisfy her client. This was her bread and butter, but it was also her passion, her art. She knew she was good at it, one of the best. She would not only have a complete picture of his current behavior, she would be able to predict his future behavior. She wished it was something that she could write about, or film, or somehow get recognition for, but to keep doing her job she had to remain discreet.

Meredith didn't wait for the server to bring her bill, but tucked the book she'd used as a prop into a capacious bag she pulled from under her chair, gathered up her coat and went to the restaurant reception desk where she could keep uninterrupted watch on the lobby in case the target didn't take the elevator with his family. Based on the confrontation she'd witnessed between her target and the man in the sheepskin jacket, she knew he was a dominant, aggressive male. Not the kind to tuck himself in with his wife and kids early in the evening. He'd also knocked back several mixed drinks during dinner. The conference he was attending wasn't due to start until Monday, but like some others she'd seen arriving, he had opted to come early and spend the weekend enjoying the resort. She gathered he was a skier, and was looking forward to shadowing him on the slopes. That would be challenging. If she had any luck, he would be a good skier. Meredith loved to ski. Another thing she was good at.

"Should we charge this to your room, Miss ...?" asked the server.

"Clark. Stella Clark," she said, shaking her head. She held out an American twenty, along with a five. "You take American dollars?"

"Of course."

"Keep the change," she said. The change was an average size tip, not too little, not too large. The less everyone noticed her, the better. She usually liked to pick an occupation that gave her an excuse for poking around: photojournalist was the one she liked the best. Travel writer would work well for Whistler, or sports magazine writer. Even a women's magazine might like an article on life at the resort.

However, she needed to stay close to her target, which meant a cover that allowed her to attend the conference he was here for.

She was registered at the conference as Stella Clark, Senior Purchasing Agent for a brand new company called Tamblyn-Brown Manufacturing, headquartered in North Carolina. She'd begun work on her cover story as soon as the client's retainer check had cleared. The world of purchasing agents and managers, or supply professionals, was relatively large, but she didn't want to take any chances of sitting beside anyone who might blow her cover by recognizing it as either a real or a fake company, or a real or fake address. A startup company that was still seeking a building site was the best option, and a certain air of secrecy would be understood. She picked a relatively common product: decorative light fixtures. She wasn't looking forward to sitting through hours of seminars and speeches, but she was looking forward to acting the part. She settled into an armchair with a view of the hotel and parking elevators, as well as the hotel exit, pulled a copy of Purchasing magazine out of her bag, and tucked the bag out of sight under the chair.

Less than fifteen minutes after the target and his family had left the restaurant, Meredith watched him exit the elevator, cell phone to his ear. He hailed a bellman. "How far is it to the Grand Mountain? Can I walk?"

"You mean the Chateau Grand Montagne?"

"Yeah, whatever."

When the bellman told him it was about a twenty minute walk, he glanced out at the swirling snow and said, "Get me a cab, would you." Into the phone he said, "I'll be there as soon as I can," and flipped it shut.

Meredith made her way toward the restaurant entrance, putting two chatting couples between herself and the target. She watched from there until his cab pulled away, then walked as casually as she could over to the bellman and asked for a cab for herself. She pulled on her coat, dark side out, and slipped into the shadows to wait for the cab to arrive. By the time the cab pulled up, she had her hair tucked into a black fleece beret and was wearing oversized glasses with dark frames. The cab had to wait briefly for a car to unload in front of the hotel, so Meredith sank into the back seat and took advantage of the hotel lights to study her reflection in a compact and apply some red lipstick. Her Bohemian look. Plain Jane to bored cosmopolitan in under a minute.

It took only minutes to reach the other hotel, passing lighted chalets and dark stands of tall evergreens, all glimpsed between a swirling veil of weightless white dots. She didn't waste any time getting inside the hotel, but as she feared, the target had already left the lobby. The lounge was her first stop, and she lucked out. He was sitting with two men near a large four-sided fireplace, and the server had just set down a double whiskey, then a small decanter of water, in front of him. One of his companions, a dark-haired man in a navy cable-knit sweater, was drinking beer, a Stella Artois. The other man had a dark complexion and neatly combed grey hair. He wore a beige cardigan with buttons that gaped across his belly. Whatever he was drinking was mixed with Coke.

The lounge was spacious and high-ceilinged, with subdued lighting and a glossy black Steinway grand in the corner opposite an immense bar of polished granite with a black iron foot rail. A female pianist wearing a green satin blouse was playing a jazz piece that Meredith didn't recognize. Meredith spotted an empty chair by the darkened window; close enough for her to hear the conversation, but behind the target so she wouldn't be noticed. Perfect. She breezed past the target's table with her face turned away, toward the bar, but before she had time to sit down, the target turned in her direction and shouted, "Hey!"

Meredith didn't miss a beat. There was no reason for him to recognize her, so she glanced at him with a mixture of curiosity and annoyance, then followed his gaze to a table in the shadows just behind her. A man sat there opposite a blonde wearing designer jeans and a short leather jacket the color of butter that probably cost as much as a flight on the Concord. A bottle of wine, the neck wrapped in a white napkin, chilled in a bucket on their table and there was half a glass in front of each of them. She couldn't see the blonde's face, but the man was good looking, even by Meredith's standards, with an air of "just off the slopes": tousled hair, a five o'clock shadow and a ski sweater that showed off his broad shoulders. He didn't look happy to see Mike Irwin.

"Brent, you son of a bitch!" yelled her target, a hostile tone to what for some might be considered a jovial greeting.

Meredith turned her face toward the window, but watched the couple behind her out of the corner of her eye. The blond twisted toward the voice for just an instant, just long enough for Meredith to see that she was about half the age of her companion, her face very pretty and tastefully made up. Then she, too, turned her head toward the window, raising a hand to the side of her face as if to keep from being recognized. The man called Brent set his jaw but didn't acknowledge Irwin.

"Don't ignore me, you prick." Irwin threw back his chair and stood up, glaring at Brent. His companions looked at one another, obviously uncomfortable, and Irwin seemed suddenly aware of their presence. He took a deep breath and lowered his voice. "I'll catch you later," he said, then with a malignant smirk, "after your Viagra wears off."

The man with the hiball laughed coarsely and raised his glass. "Good one, Mike. He's with Phoenix in Riverside, isn't he? Carruthers. Hand tools?"

"Used to be," said Irwin. "Got his ass booted out of there for screwing the boss's daughter. Looks like he hasn't learned his lesson."

"He and Mike worked together there," added the man in the navy sweater. "Isn't that right, Mike?"

"Fuck him," said Irwin. He picked up his whiskey and drained the glass, then looked over to where the server stood at the bar, but the server was facing the bartender. Irwin watched him for a moment, his hand half raised to beckon him over, but the server didn't turn around. "I'll go get us another round," he said, pushing his chair back.

Meredith could hear the couple behind her whispering. "Go now," the man was saying, urgency in his voice. "I'll see you back at the hotel." The young blonde swept past Meredith leaving a faint wake of floral perfume and moved swiftly and soundlessly across the lounge, but Irwin intercepted her on his way back from the bar, stepping quickly to stand in her way.

"Too late, sweetheart. I know who you are." She brushed past him and he called out to her back, "... and I know who your daddy is. In fact, I'll be talking to him on Monday." He laughed, as he sat back down at the table. "Carruthers is fucked," he said. "Second job in a row he's started banging the boss's daughter. What was he thinking?" He turned around and tossed the same line over his shoulder at the man seated behind Meredith. "What were you thinking, Brent? You're fucked."

The man in the navy sweater hoisted his glass in the direction of Brent Carruthers. "What's your secret, pal? My boss's daughter looks right through me every time she stops by the plant." He gave an awkward laugh and lowered his voice so Meredith could barely hear. "Hot young chick like that, might be worth it, don't you think?"

"No woman is worth losing your job over," said Irwin, dismissing his companion with a shake of his head.

Meredith heard Carruthers pull the bottle out of the ice bucket and refill his glass. She permitted herself a faint smile as she studied the menu. Carruthers was obviously a bigger man than her target, not rising to the bait. For some reason, she thought of the expression, "Don't get mad, get even," and she wondered what Carruthers could do for payback if Irwin followed through with his threat.

Irwin's table had settled into sports talk. She couldn't afford to tune it out, but it took an effort of concentration to follow what they were saying. She caught herself staring out the window and thinking about her plans for the next day when she heard Irwin raise his voice, "Well, well, well. Can't get enough of me, can you, monkey?"

She glanced toward him and saw the couple from the restaurant at Coast Peaks Hotel standing just inside the entrance, the woman searching her companion's face. The man in the sheepskin jacket and cowboy boots nodded and guided her past the long bar to a table against the wall on the far side of the room, far from Irwin's table.

Irwin's eyes followed them. The man pulled out the chair facing the wall for his companion to sit down, and then slid into the seat across from her, with his back to the wall. While she shrugged off her jacket, he sat stone faced, his eyes fixed on Meredith's target.

Meredith shivered involuntarily. His stare was intense and somehow threatening. Irwin must have felt it, too, for she noticed he had looked away, but seemed agitated. Meredith looked back toward the far table and felt a little shock go through her. The man in the sheepskin jacket was now looking right at her. He nodded once with a crooked smile.

He'd recognized her. Damn.

"I can't believe he's here, of all the places in Whistler he could have gone to meet his cronies." She snorted softly with a wry smile. "Just my luck, I guess. Great vacation."

"He can't hurt you here," Hunter said, picking up the little leather folder that stood open in the center of the table. "You can take away his power over you by not letting him scare you. Right here, right now, you're safe."

Alora closed her eyes and took a deep breath, then her shoulders relaxed and she settled back into her chair. "You're right. I can't let him spoil my evening."

"What'll you have?" Hunter checked out the drink menu, flipping through several pages of wines and cognacs. "Still want that dirty martini?" He thought that carrying on as if everything was normal would take her mind off of her ex-husband and allow her to ignore him. It seemed, though, that she needed to talk about it.

She played with a round drink coaster on the table in front of her, spinning it on its edge. "I managed to stay under Mike's radar until I was caught on the KTLA noon news being interviewed about the 'Iceman' case." Hunter nodded. She'd been the lawyer representing a woman truck driver last July, at Hunter's request. The woman and her husband had been arrested and charged with murder after a frozen corpse had fallen out the back door of their refrigerated trailer. "I hadn't seen him for so long before that, I'd begun to hope that he'd moved on, lost his obsession with me, you know? Maybe even left California. Yeah, I could sure use a dirty martini." She nodded emphatically. "Maybe two."

The pianist returned from a break, started a soft rendition of 'Moon River'. They both paused to watch her shoulders sway dreamily behind the gleaming black instrument before Alora continued. "He called me at home that night, must've wangled my home number from the temp receptionist at my law firm." She shook her head. "He can be very persuasive. Charming when he wants to be. Typical sociopath, right? You used to be a Mountie. You must know."

He nodded. The server came by the table and they placed their order. Beer for him again, the dirty martini for her. "Most of these guys are cowards, that's why they prey on women. Makes him feel like more of a man." He glanced at Mike, who was talking to his colleagues. "You're safe here," he repeated. Hunter opened his arms to encompass the lounge: a safe, civilized place, a grand piano playing an old Pat Boone song, cheerful fires in the two big fireplaces, dozens of witnesses. The server arrived and set down their drinks.

"I don't understand why he can't leave me alone."

"Like most bullies, he's encouraged by your fear. Ever encountered an aggressive dog? Most of them will chase you if you run, but there's a good chance they'll back away if you walk toward them."

She cocked her head to one side. "What would happen if I went on the offensive?"

"It's possible that would take the wind out of his sails."

She took a healthy sip of her martini and a smile played across her face. "You know, I do feel safe here, with you. What better time to turn and face that mean dog?"

"Hold on, now. Some mean dogs *will* bite."

"Not here, he won't," she said. "Not with you and everyone else in this room." She stood up, nodded vigorously at Hunter, then turned and strode across the room. She stood directly behind her ex-husband, placed her hands on his shoulders, and said something to his companions. The two men both laughed, while her ex-husband stared straight ahead, a thoughtful, almost confused look on his face. She took hold of his upper arm and pulled gently, motioning toward Hunter with her head. Hunter read her lips. "C'mon," she said. "Come join us."

Hunter smiled. She did seem to be having fun with this. Her ex-husband looked hesitant, but must have decided it was unreasonable for him to refuse. He picked up his drink and followed her back to their table. Hunter pulled a chair from the neighboring table and offered it to Mike, along with his hand. Mike hesitated, then put down his drink and gave Hunter's hand a quick shake.

"We kind of got off on the wrong foot back there," said Hunter. "How about we start over. I'm Hunter Rayne, from Vancouver." When Mike didn't immediately respond, he added, "And you are...?"

"Mike. Mike Irwin." He picked up his drink and took a mouthful, then studied his half empty glass. "You buying?" he said to Alora, ignoring Hunter.

Alora looked at Hunter, as if to ask 'What next?' Hunter winked at her. He knew this guy wasn't going to be an easy nut to crack, but he'd seen worse. Hunter's ex-wife had once called him 'a master manipulator'. He knew it wasn't supposed to be a compliment, but he took pride in the skill and put it to good use during his time as a member of the RCMP.

"So. Mike," said Hunter, leaning forward with his chin on his hand, eyes on Mike's face. "What brings you to Whistler, chief?"

Mike was obviously not in the mood for small talk. "Look," he said, turning to face Hunter. "I don't know what your game is, buddy, but ..." He paused, looked from Hunter to Alora and back again. They both waited for him to continue. He seemed to be holding his breath, trying to make up his mind about something. Hunter half expected him to get up and walk away. "Conference," he said finally, leaning back in his chair and taking a deep breath. "Purchasing conference. How about you?"

Hunter was pleased that Mike had decided to cooperate. "Skiing, mostly." He smiled in Alora's direction. "I told Alora when I met her in L.A. last summer that if she ever came to Vancouver, I'd show her around. I didn't exactly mean Whistler, but I was due for a break. I'm kind of rusty on the slopes, not to mention out of shape. She'll probably ski rings around me tomorrow. Right, Alora?"

Alora laughed. "Not the way my muscles feel tonight. I'm lucky I can still walk."

"How about you, Mike? Do you ski?"

"Yeah. Used to ski a lot, not so much since I started a family." Mike Irwin was chewing on the end of his swizzle stick and barely opened his mouth as he spoke. He was staring at Alora's breasts, or at the amber pendant that lay between them.

"Wait'll your kids get a little older," Hunter said, cheerfully. He was hoping that Alora would start to lead the conversation; it would help to change the dynamics between her and her ex. "Once they're hooked, they'll be dragging you off to the ski hill every weekend. Where do you ski? Big Bear?" He glanced at Alora. Her hand had closed over the amber pendant, and she was looking from one face to the other, as if she were following a debate.

"Yeah ..." Mike Irwin started breathing heavily through his nose, looking from side to side, obviously uncomfortable.

Before Mike had a chance to speak, Hunter turned to Alora. "Do you ski there, Alora?" he said, trying to draw her in. Their eyes met, and he nodded encouragement.

"Used to," she said. "I haven't had much time lately. We used to go together, when we first started dating, didn't we, Mike?"

Mike nodded.

She started to laugh, her hand over her lips. "Hey, remember when you hit the moguls your first time on that black diamond run and did a major face plant? Ouch! Your nose was bloody and I had to hike back up to help you. We both snowplowed all the way to the bottom." Alora continued to giggle and Mike spun his empty glass on the polished table top, working his jaw. "You looked like a train wreck for the rest of the weekend, remember?"

24

Hunter heard the swizzle stick snap as Mike drew a deep breath and lifted his shoulders.

"Ice bitch," said Mike with a snarl. He raised his voice and Hunter saw the bartender glance in their direction. "You think you're hot stuff? Well, you're not." He turned to Hunter. "If you think she's a good fuck, your standards are pretty low, pal."

Hunter set his jaw and was about to stand up when Alora spoke up again.

"Ever think it might be because you're such a ham fisted lover? You're a caveman, Mike. I pity your poor wife."

Mike picked up the glass to hurl it in Alora's direction, but Hunter was on him in the blink of an eye and grabbed his wrist, squeezing until Mike dropped the glass on the table. It landed with a thunk and rolled across the table where it hit Alora's martini glass, knocking it over and sending gin and olives into Alora's lap. She leapt to her feet, knocking over her chair. Mike also stood, tried to take a swing at Hunter with his free hand but Hunter grabbed that arm and in an instant had swung Mike around with the arm twisted behind his back. Mike swore loudly and repeatedly, and tried to kick backwards. Hunter planted a solid kick behind Mike's other knee and Mike dropped to his knees like a rock.

"Cool it, chief," said Hunter, just loud enough to be heard. "You don't want to get thrown out of here, do you?" He saw Thomas Halsey walking calmly but quickly toward them. "Too late. Here comes hotel security."

Hunter tried to help Mike to his feet, but Mike shook his arm off and pulled himself up off the floor by hanging onto the chair. His face was red and his jacket crooked. Alora had picked up her chair and was mopping up the spilled martini with a napkin. Mike pulled his jacket on straight, glaring at Hunter and Alora in turn. "Like I said earlier, cowboy. You better watch your back."

"What's going on here?" asked Thomas Halsey in a low voice. "Hunter?"

"Hi, Tom," said Hunter to Halsey. "Sorry about this. A little misunderstanding. Mike here was about to apologize to the lady for some off color remarks he made." He turned to Mike. "Isn't that right, Mike?"

"Fuck you."

"I beg your pardon, Mike." Hunter stepped toward him, staring him down. Mike averted his eyes. "That wasn't exactly the kind of apology I had in mind."

"Fuck off." Mike turned to leave but Hunter grabbed him by the arm and spun him around.

"Apologize to the lady, Mike," said Hunter, holding fast to Mike's bicep and starting to squeeze. Mike raised his other arm but Thomas grabbed it from behind and forced it down.

"It's okay, Hunter," said Alora. She moved closer to him, placed a hand along his arm. "It's okay."

"No, it's not okay." Hunter knew at the back of his mind that this could make things worse for Alora. Mike would be angry and want to take it out on her if and when a future opportunity presented itself. However, he couldn't let Mike walk away from this the winner. His pride wouldn't let him, and he knew Mike would be angry regardless. "Be a man, Mike. Apologize."

"I'm sorry …" said Mike. Hunter and Thomas both released his arms and Mike shrugged, pulled his jacket sleeves down, then straightened his back, turned, and started heading away from the table. Then he turned and threw a snarl back over his shoulder, "I'm sorry that I didn't hit you, bitch."

Hunter took a step toward him but Thomas grabbed his arm and held him back. He felt Alora's arm go around his waist, her body tuck itself under his other arm. "Yo, chief!" Hunter raised his voice so Mike could hear him. "You so much as get close to her and I'll make sure you never hurt her again, you hear me?" Mike dismissed him with a backwards wave and walked out of the lounge, spitting into a potted plant as he passed.

"Damn," said Hunter. "That turned out badly." He turned toward Alora and she pressed against him. His arms went around her and, almost as a reflex, his lips caressed her temple. He whispered against her hair, "Sorry. That shouldn't have happened." Then to Thomas, "Sorry, Tom. Guess I've lost my touch."

"Can't win 'em all, Hunter." Thomas turned and signaled the waiter for another martini. "Have a seat. And have another round on the house. I'll go see our friend out and make sure he doesn't come back again tonight."

Hunter gave Alora a gentle squeeze, then released her, stepping back. Alora smiled and took a deep breath. "Thanks. Both of you." She laid a hand on Hunter's arm.

He could feel the coolness of it through the cotton fabric of his sleeve, and resisted the urge to pull her close again. He hadn't been with another woman since Chris, and it was hard to get used to the thought of being intimate with someone he didn't know all that well. That had never been his way. He liked to think it was because he had too much respect for women, but it had occurred to him that perhaps it was almost the opposite, that he was afraid to lose respect for himself. Old fashioned? Straight laced? Maybe it was time for him to change. He avoided her eyes and took his seat.

"No need to apologize, Hunter. Mike's the bad guy in all this. If he weren't such a jerk, he'd still be sitting here and we'd all be having a civilized conversation."

And if she hadn't provoked his anger, Mike might have continued to play along, Hunter thought to himself. He rested his chin on his fist and stared glumly at Thomas's retreating back. "I've just managed to promote him from a jerk to an angry jerk with a score to settle." He smiled wanly at Alora. "And that *is* my fault. I'm sorry."

The waiter set down a fresh martini and Alora raised her glass. "But I feel better, thank you. I feel somehow empowered by what just happened. I yanked his chain, instead of him yanking mine, and that makes me feel stronger."

"You may feel stronger, but that doesn't make him harmless, I'm afraid."

"Of course not," she said. "But I think what just happened helped change his perception of me, and more importantly, my perception of myself." She took a long sip, then let out a deep breath.

"Right now, I don't feel like I'm running scared. I can be on the attack, if I need to be."

"Let's hope your paths don't cross again. There are thousands of people here, two big mountains with dozens of ski runs, lots of restaurants and bars. There's no reason to expect to see him again."

"Even if I do, with all those thousands of people here, what could happen?" she said. She was smiling, but he thought not with as much courage as she pretended to possess.

"Whatever you do tomorrow," said Hunter as he picked up his beer, "don't let him catch you alone."

CHAPTER

THREE

Kelly couldn't sleep. The clock beside the bed said 11:37. It wasn't so much that she was anxious for Mike to come back to the hotel room. In fact, she'd be more relaxed if she knew he wasn't coming back, and she planned to feign sleep as soon as she heard him at the door. She slid out from under the covers and crossed the room to where the kids slept on the pull-out couch, then perched on the arm of the couch and watched their quiet breathing. She could feel the textured fabric of the upholstery through her flimsy nightie.

Corenna was on her back, one arm thrown above her head, the other tucked under the blanket. Jordan was on his side, his mouth crookedly open, one arm at right angles to his body with the hand hanging limply off the edge of the mattress. She could hear his breathing, not quite a snore. Her heart ached for him. Jordan had never asked out loud, but his eyes often searched her face for an answer: *Why doesn't Daddy love me? What have I done wrong?* She wished she had the courage to leave Mike, take the kids far away where he'd never find them. "You've done nothing wrong, my sweet, sensitive little man," she whispered.

Kelly sighed softly, and went to the window. The curtain was open, the world outside bright with snow, flakes softening the edges of roofs and roads. She could make out the dark shapes of trees between the buildings. A car wound its way up the road, its headlights illuminating cones of dancing snow. The room was silent except for Jordan's breathing and the faint noise of a fan. *And what about me?* she asked herself. *I've done nothing wrong either.*

She thought back to the woman she was before Mike entered her life. She was strong then. Young, strong and alive. She'd been a good student, graduated college with honors, was on the threshold of a career in journalism. Mike was ten years older, handsome, charming, and the son of her late father's best friend. Being with him made her feel safe, like she had felt with her father. Mike wanted to marry her and start a family, he was forceful and persuasive, and she let herself be swept away, willingly abandoning her own plans for his. It was wonderful at first. She felt like a princess. She wasn't sure exactly when the sense of being looked after was replaced by the sense of being controlled, but it was during the year after Jordan was born. From fairy tale to horror story in only two years.

Little by little, her husband had chipped away at her self esteem until she now pictured herself a wraith, a pale phantom of her former self. She knew the woman she'd seen in the restaurant today was Mike's ex-wife, Alora. Early in her marriage to Mike, Kelly had been jealous of Alora and dreaded the thought of ever running into her. Ironic, wasn't it, that when she finally saw Alora today for the first time, she was jealous of the woman, not because of Mike, but because she'd had the courage to leave the bastard.

Her father would be outraged, she knew, if he were still alive. That hurt, too. She was letting her father down by allowing Mike to treat her this way. He would have helped her out of this. Not for the first time, Kelly vowed to make some drastic changes in her life. The only question was, how? Mike had always been a good provider. She and the kids had a comfortable lifestyle, there was no denying that. How would she be able to support herself and the children if… The thought stopped dead. She knew Mike would never let her keep the children, and she shuddered to imagine the possibility of living apart from Jordan and Corenna, and what Jordan's life would be like without his mother.

Kelly watched another pair of headlights sweep up the road toward the hotel, and decided it was time to crawl back into bed.

Meredith's room in the Coast Peaks Hotel had to be one of the worst. It was small, on the second floor, with a view of the parking lot and right above the dumpsters outside the main kitchen. However, at last minute and with her budget, it was all they had available. She couldn't complain about the quality of the room itself, great Jacuzzi tub and tasty décor, bed like a cloud. All she really needed was a bed and a bathroom. Her job was the 24/7 type, no time for entertainment or relaxation beyond what she could grab while her target was locked safely (she hoped) in his hotel room.

Beyond the parking lot lights, it was still dark outside when Meredith stepped out into the hall, closed her room door behind her and headed for the elevator. It was only six a.m. and the lifts wouldn't start until eight thirty, but Meredith didn't want to risk losing her target again, especially today. Last night he had stormed out of the piano lounge with hotel security on his heels and she wasn't able to make a fast enough exit to catch him. The bellhop couldn't tell her where his cab was headed, or even if he caught one of the cabs parked in front of the hotel, but when her own cab headed toward the village there was no sign of a solitary figure hiking through the swirling snow.

She had asked the cabbie if he'd heard where the last fare was taken, but he said no, they weren't likely to radio in to dispatch enroute unless they were heading out of town. She toyed with the idea of checking out some of the bars in the village, even went so far as to ask the cabbie where would be a good place to get a drink. Too many choices. He could be anywhere. She decided her best bet was to return to the Coast Peaks and check out the two bars there. No luck. She had camped out in the lobby until after midnight before she decided to get some sleep and hope for better luck in the morning. Back in her hotel room, kicking off her wet boots, she couldn't resist a warm soak in the Jacuzzi but forced herself to leap out when she started nodding off. She usually didn't need help waking up, but had turned up the volume on the radio alarm clock, just in case.

There'd been no sign of her target yet this morning in the lobby or restaurant, so Meredith grabbed a table near the entrance of the brightly lit coffee shop adjacent to the restaurant and ordered a coffee, a juice, and a Denver on toast. The table had a peek-a-boo view of the elevators. She gathered that Irwin was planning to ski today, so she wore her ski pants and a wool sweater, hung her jacket over the chair back behind her. She'd brought her own skis and boots — she would have no time to get fitted for rentals if she were trying to keep up with her target — and she'd asked the concierge to make sure her equipment was ready by the door.

Meredith took a sip of her coffee. The cup was white and heavy, the coffee black and strong, just the way she liked it. A good start to her day.

It was still snowing; sharp white flakes stung his face, so Mike kept his scarf hooked over his nose like a bank robber in an old western. He settled himself into the seat of the chairlift, paying little attention to the skier who had boarded after him. It was still early, the crowds light, so there were only the two of them on the Harmony quad chair up to the lower peak of Whistler Mountain, both sitting to the outside of the bench to balance the chair.

Mike's mouth was dry, and he felt lightheaded. He knew he'd had too much to drink, starting on the flight from L.A. and ending by himself in that nightclub in the Village. The crowd there had been too young for him, the music loud and unfamiliar, so he had just sat and drank and watched three skinny girls with pierced lips and noses gyrate on the dance floor until he took a cab back to the hotel. He pulled down his scarf and spat off to the right, then took off one of his gloves and searched in his jacket pocket for the little bottle of Johnny Walker he'd taken from the hotel mini-bar. It felt good to be dangling thirty feet above the slope, heading into a white blur of falling snow, hearing only the hum of the moving cable and the tiny pok-pok-pok of frozen flakes on his jacket. The snow had started falling faster.

He glanced over at the skier next to him, an androgynous form in padded ski pants and a bulky black jacket, with a plain red scarf tucked in at the throat like an ascot. Whoever it was had turned his face away, not that it mattered, because he was wearing a full mask. Mike drank half the scotch, screwed the little top back on and tucked it back in his pocket. He'd save the rest for a short rest at a viewpoint somewhere on the downhill run, if the snow thinned enough for a decent view. He had time for one more leisurely run before his morning rendezvous. He looked forward to boasting about his morning solo run from the peak of Whistler when he met the guys for a drink later. He bet he was the best skier at the conference.

He thought about his wife. Kelly had pretended to be asleep when he got back to the hotel last night, and again this morning when his alarm sounded and he got out of bed. He could tell by her breathing that she wasn't really sleeping. She was avoiding him, and Jordan did the same. He really was hard on them both sometimes, he admitted. It was just that he found their lack of backbone irritating, and he couldn't help reacting to it, simply trying to get a rise out of them, goad them into standing up for themselves. He decided to make an extra effort to be nice to them for the rest of the trip, maybe take them shopping for something in Whistler Village later today. At least during the conference he wouldn't see much of them, nor of his parents. Life was easier that way.

And what about Alora? And that loser cowboy she was with? Fuck him. Not worth Mike's time. He pictured Alora, that heavy amber pendant hanging down between her breasts, and he smiled. Cat and mouse. Let the mouse scurry away for a bit, it made the game more fun. He could track down Alora again when they were back in L.A., if he wanted to.

They must be over half way to the top, thought Mike, peering into the white curtain ahead, barely able to make out the chair ahead. The tips of his skis bounced as the chair swayed passing a tower, and Mike was aware that the skier beside him had moved toward him and stretched his arm along the back of the chair, almost touching Mike's shoulder. *Fuckin' faggot*, he thought to himself, and was about to say something when the skier pointed urgently at something off to Mike's left. Mike turned to look, but he didn't see a thing.

The lift attendant had gotten a radio call from one of his counterparts at the top of the chairlift. "Hey, Parsons! Some guy fell asleep in chair seven. I was busy and didn't see him in time to stop the lift, so he's on his way back down to you. We gonna let him ride back up without going to the back of the line? Your call."

Parsons decided to ask the guy when the chair reached the bottom. Maybe he was riding down intentionally. Maybe he was sick, or got an important phone call on the way up. More likely, he'd chickened out and decided to stick to the shorter runs at the bottom half of the mountain. He was helping a foursome of cute ski bunnies get in position for the chair when the number seven came around again.

"What the hell?" He yelled, "Stop the lift!" The guy in the chair was not sleeping, but obviously in no condition to get off. His eyes were open but unseeing, the rest of his body limp but held upright by a red scarf wrapped around his chest and tied to the back of the chair. One of the four girls, the shortest one with a hot pink ski jacket and matching toque, began to scream.

"Call the medics," said Parsons after he and another attendant had wrestled the man's body off the chair laid the still form on the platform. He examined the glove on his right hand, the one that had cradled the man's head. It glistened, wet with blood. "And the police," he added. "Shit!" He pictured the hundred or so skiers hanging in the falling snow and freezing air between chair seven and the top tower.

Would the police consider chair seven to be a crime scene? Would they make him leave it here at the bottom? That would leave all the skiers stranded on the lift for how long? He shook his head, and decided to keep the chairs empty, but restart the lift so those already on board could get off up top. He glanced at the four young girls, who stood silently hugging each other as far from the man's body as they could get.

The other attendant returned from the hut and said in a low voice, "They're on their way. Shouldn't we be doing CPR?"

Parsons pulled him close and whispered in his ear. "Won't help, but no need to spook the clients. Let's pretend he's just hurt, okay?"

"Seems there was an accident," Parsons said to the girls, gesturing toward his partner, who was patting the prone figure and telling him he was going to be okay. "The guy's hurt, but we've got the paramedics on the way. Sorry, but we'll have to close this lift until we get it checked out. I'm afraid you'll have to head back down the mountain to one of the other lifts."

He shepherded them back toward the lineup and raised his voice to inform the rest of the skiers waiting in line. "Harmony's closed! Until further notice, Harmony's closed!" This wasn't going to be a good day.

It had been after two a.m. by the time Hunter followed Tom Halsey back to his chalet in Alpine Meadows on the outskirts of Whistler and fell asleep on one of the guest beds in Tom's basement. He had escorted Alora to her room in the Chateau Grand Montagne around eleven. She had asked him in for a nightcap, but he declined her invitation, saying they were both probably tired after the stresses of the evening. She had put her arms around his neck and pulled him close for a kiss, and he returned it, instinct drawing him into a tighter embrace, his hands exploring the curves of her back. He felt a stirring in his groin and had to remind himself to back away.

"It's been a long day," he said, running the back of his fingers gently down her cheek. "I'll see you tomorrow."

He turned to look before he rounded the corner to the elevator, and she still stood at the open door, watching him, unsmiling. He could still taste her lipstick as he found an armchair in the lobby. It would have been easy to give in, he thought, forget the consequences.

What consequences? He didn't know, and perhaps that was the problem. He killed time in the lobby reading abandoned newspapers and magazines until Tom was ready to leave. He slept like a stone, awaking to natural light and a digital clock that read 9:24. He called Alora's room and there was no answer, so he had a shower, shaved and dressed before following the smell of coffee to Tom's kitchen.

Tom was arranging sausages in a fry pan on the stove. "Help yourself," he said, nodding toward the coffee pot. "My wife is in Vegas with her sister for a few days, so you'll have to put up with my cooking. How did you sleep?"

"I was dead to the world as soon as my head hit the pillow. It's so quiet down there, I didn't even hear you get up." Hunter poured himself a mug of coffee, dressed it up with cream and sugar, set the dirty spoon in the sink, and pulled out a chair for himself at the kitchen table. The table had a nice view of snow covered trees and the peaked roof of a neighboring chalet.

"What's your girlfriend up to this morning?" asked Tom, poking at the sausages with a fork. They were just starting to sizzle.

"Don't know," said Hunter. He blew across the surface of his coffee and took a cautious sip. "She's not a girlfriend, chief," he added. "Acquaintance is more like it."

Tom turned from the stove, his eyebrows raised. "Are you crazy? That's not what I saw last night," he said.

Hunter shrugged. "I met her in L.A. last summer and we went out for dinner. Once. That's it. She called me up a few weeks ago and asked me if I'd like to come skiing while she was here on vacation. It sounded like a good idea at the time."

"And it's not a good idea now?" He laughed, and added, "I guess not, or you wouldn't have been sleeping at my place."

"I'm not sure I want to complicate my life like that." And he wasn't sure how to put it into words, but he *was* sure that he didn't want to explain his feelings to Tom. Being alone was easy, and safe. No demands, no fights, no guilt. He didn't want to give up the emotional simplicity of his life. Being with Alora was like staring at a fire: it was fascinating to watch and it enticed him to draw closer to its warmth, but he knew the flames would burn, and couldn't imagine walking into it. His old scars still hadn't healed.

"We planned to go skiing together today. I'm supposed to call her to set it up, but she didn't answer." It occurred to him that he'd left his cell phone beside his bed in the basement. "I should try again," he said, pushing back his chair and getting to his feet, then decided against it. "After breakfast." He sat back down and picked up his coffee.

Hunter met up with Alora just outside the flags marking the entrance to the quad chairlift that would take them over a thousand feet up Whistler mountain, giving them a chance to warm up and try out the conditions on a shorter run before going higher. It was a few minutes before noon, and the snow had let up, just a sprinkling of small flakes meandered through the chilly air. Alora wore a pink and black jacket with black ski pants, and a pink and black toque, considerably more stylish than Hunter's plain navy ski jacket and pants.

She lifted her goggles to her forehead. "You and blue," she said. "Blue truck, blue jeans, blue ski jacket," she moved closer to him and looked into his face, "blue eyes." She smiled and laid a gloved hand on his arm.

"Blue me," he said, smiling back and patting her hand. "Black toque, though." He pulled a black wool toque out of his pocket and snugged it down over his ears, then turned toward the lift lineup. "We should get in line. Ready?"

She nodded and they pushed off toward the lineup, Hunter hanging back to let Alora take the lead. It felt good to be on skis again, but from just the short distance he'd gone so far, he could feel tightness in the muscles of his thighs. He pulled up beside her at the back of the line. "It's a lot busier than it was yesterday," she said as the line inched forward.

The woman in front turned around and said, "The Harmony chair's closed, so nobody can ski the Little Peak. Some kind of accident there this morning."

Hunter nodded his thanks.

The woman was middle-aged, wearing a yellow ski jacket and matching toque. "Not that I was planning to ski there anyway," she said. "I just graduated from the bunny hills." As if to illustrate the point, one of her skis slipped and she began to lose her balance. Her companion laughed and grabbed her arm to steady her as the line moved forward.

"No sign of your ex this morning?" Hunter asked Alora.

She looked down at the tips of her skis and shook her head. "I'd prefer not to think about him. One evening of Mike is more than enough."

They skied down the first run, and decided to go higher the second time. The first run, she was faster than Hunter and had to stop and wait for him to catch up once or twice. He soon got his ski legs back and kept up with her easily on the second run. He even passed her once, and pulled off to a familiar view point, waving her in to join him.

This was what he loved about the sport. The boundless mountain vistas and the silence of snow. They stood side by side, leaning on their ski poles and soaking in the beauty of it. When he turned to look at her, he half expected to see his ex-wife Christine, they had stood at this exact spot together so many times in the past. He tried to picture himself in a relationship with the woman now standing beside him. Scenes flashed through his mind: long intimate dinners and good wine, making love, waking up together, maybe she liked to golf, or travel, or ... He tried to mesh those romantic fantasies with the reality that was his life. On the road for weeks at a time, barely enough money to cover his living expenses and still contribute toward his daughters' education. He could barely afford new clothes, let alone pay his share of nice dinners, golf games and the type of lifestyle an attractive young lawyer would expect. He couldn't let her pay, and he didn't need another blow to his pride.

"Nothing else matters when you're speeding down the slope, does it?" said Alora.

Hunter nodded. In the moment, life was as it should be. They stood in silence for a few more minutes, then he motioned for Alora to start down ahead of him. She waited for a trio of snowboarders to slide past, then pushed off and they were moving again.

One more run and Hunter's legs had reached their limit for the day. "Do you want a lift back to your hotel?" he asked, and she said yes.

They carried their skis through a sprinkling of snow to where he'd parked his Pontiac, the conversation safely confined to skiing and snow conditions. Hunter had no roof rack, so their skis poked out the rear window for the short drive.

Hunter pulled up in front of the Chateau Grande Montagne and turned off the ignition before getting out to unload Alora's skis. "Want to come in for a drink?" she asked.

He was about to say, "Sure, why not?" when Thomas Halsey stepped out of the front door of the hotel and motioned him over. He nodded to Tom and excused himself to Alora.

"What's up?"

Tom took his arm and turned him away from Alora. "Just wanted to give you a head's up," he said. "That guy you had the dust up with last night? Mike Irwin?"

Hunter nodded.

"Somebody executed him with a single shot to the cerebellum on the Harmony Quad this morning."

Hunter sucked in his breath. A dozen questions came to mind, but he said nothing.

"When you were in the force, did you ever come across Shane Blackwell? How about Colin Pike?" asked Tom. Hunter shook his head.

"They're the investigating officers and they've already been by here asking questions. Seems one of the deceased's associates — at the conference, I assume — told them about the little altercation last night. You're now on their list."

"Their list?"

"You and your girlfriend are both 'persons of interest', and I have no choice but to call Shane and let him know you're here." He smiled wryly, and half shrugged.

"Of course," said Hunter. He glanced over at Alora. The bellhop had taken her skis to the ski check and she stood just inside the door of the hotel, watching him and Tom. "Tell them we'll be in the lounge," he said, and added, "thanks, Tom."

Alora was waiting for Hunter in the lounge after he'd parked his car. He had hoped the police wouldn't arrive before he did, and was relieved to see she was still alone. She was seated at a table by the window, looking out at the snow-draped evergreens, her hands in her lap. There were two black napkins on the table, waiting for drinks. Hunter pulled his chair closer to the table and sat down.

There was no easy way to say it, so he didn't put it off. He took a deep breath, then said, "I just heard from Tom Halsey that your ex-husband is dead."

She leaned back with a puzzled frown, as if he'd just told her the moon was purple. "What do you mean?"

"Your ex-husband was killed this morning."

The color drained out of her face. "You're joking." She leaned forward, bracing herself against the table with the heels of her hands. When he shook his head, she said, "What? How? A skiing accident?"

"Murder," he said. "The police should be here to talk to us any minute."

"Talk to *us*? Why?"

"Someone told them about the incident here last night. All part of a police investigation, questioning anyone who might have had a motive ..."

"A motive! Am I a suspect?" Her eyes widened; she pulled her hands off the table and placed them back in her lap. "Are you?"

Hunter smiled. "Everyone's a suspect this early in the game. At least, unless there's a video tape of the crime, they should be. I guess

I should have said the police want to talk to us because we saw Mike last night. They're looking for information on everything he did and everyone he saw since arriving in Whistler."

Just then two men arrived at the lounge entrance and paused. Tom Halsey came up beside them and nodded in Hunter's direction, then all three men approached the table.

"Hunter Rayne?" The one speaking was a barrel-chested man about Hunter's age, his dark hair shot with gray, and had a bass voice. He wore snow boots and a long black winter jacket, but the way he carried himself was red serge. He stuck out his hand. "Hunter Rayne? Tom tells me you were a member at one time. I'm Staff Sergeant Shane Blackwell." He motioned toward the tall and slender younger man beside him. "And this is Sergeant Colin Pike. You're Alora Magee?" he said, turning toward her.

Hunter stood and shook his hand, then extended his hand to the younger man, who bowed his head slightly and smiled softly, as if apologizing for his height. Hunter liked him immediately.

"I'd like to speak with you both, separately," continued Staff Sergeant Blackwell, "regarding your reported contact with Mr. Michael Irwin yesterday evening. Mr. Irwin was found dead under suspicious circumstances earlier today. Mr. Halsey has offered the use of his office. You first, please, Ms. Magee."

Alora glanced at Hunter, who nodded slightly, then she stood and allowed the detective and Tom Halsey to escort her out of the lounge.

Sergeant Colin Pike folded himself into the chair across the table from Hunter. "You look like you've had a day on the slopes," he said.

Hunter could feel the windburn on his face, and could imagine how his hair looked after spending a few hours compressed by a wool toque. "First time in a long time," he said. "My legs feel like rubber."

"Have you skied Whistler much?"

Hunter shrugged. "A few times over the years. Are you a skier?" he asked.

The sergeant flashed a grin that verged on a laugh. "I'm fresh from Winnipeg," he said. "Stoney Mountain is 100 vertical feet." He leaned forward, elbows on the table. "How well did you know Mike Irwin?"

"Just met him yesterday," said Hunter.

"I understand you had a confrontation with him last night."

"Yes."

"Want to tell me about it?"

Hunter thought briefly that at this point, anyone with something to hide would be wise to contact a lawyer, but it was second nature for him to trust and cooperate with the police. "He was rude and verbally abusive toward the woman I was with," Hunter nodded in the direction that Alora had gone with Colin's partner, "his ex-wife. I indicated to him that wasn't acceptable behavior." It was easy to slip back into the stilted language of police reports.

"So you didn't like him."

"He wasn't a likeable man."

"In general, or just for you?"

"The man was a bully. And a stalker. He'd evidently been stalking Alora for years. Who else have you talked to?"

"You know I can't answer that."

"Okay, then maybe I can give you a lead. Mike Irwin was being watched." Hunter described the woman he'd seen at both the Coast Peaks restaurant and the lounge they were in. "I don't know why she was watching him, or even her name, but I think you should talk to her before she leaves Whistler."

The young sergeant had taken down notes as Hunter talked, but now clicked his pen closed and put it back in his pocket. "You want us to find a woman in Whistler — right away — without a name or photograph? How do you propose we do that?"

Hunter smiled crookedly. "You may already be too late."

CHAPTER
FOUR

Alora watched Hunter walk away with Staff Sergeant Blackwell. The taller, younger cop named Pike pulled out a chair for her and motioned for her to sit, almost bowing. "I'll keep you company until they're done," he said in a mellifluous voice.

"I need the ladies room," she said. She felt an urgent need to pee.

"This way," he said, and began to escort her toward the restrooms.

"I can find it myself," she said.

"No problem." He smiled, but continued to follow her. "I'll just wait for you in the hallway here."

She finished in the stall and washed her hands at the sink before looking at her reflection in the mirror. Her eyes were puffy from lack of sleep. She had replayed the scene with Mike over and over in her mind, then Hunter's brief embrace. He'd behaved like a white knight, they'd exchanged a few seconds of tenderness, and then he'd grown aloof again. Pulled back. Just like in L.A. If he wasn't interested in her, why did he accept the invitation to join her this weekend?

All that didn't seem so important now. Mike was dead. She let the cold water run and splashed her face, then combed her wet fingers through her hair. It was a little frightening that the police didn't want her out of their sight. Did they really consider her a suspect? What about Hunter? She patted her face dry with a couple of tissues and applied some fresh lipstick. *Cowgirl up*, she told herself.

Back at the table, the waiter took her order for a Spanish coffee. Sergeant Pike asked for a hot tea. She didn't want to be here, and had to fight a restless urge to get up and run, with no destination in mind. She absently rubbed the tips of her fingers along the table until she realized he was watching her — for signs of nervousness, she guessed.

"This is very upsetting to me," she said. "My ex-husband was a bastard, but we were very close at one time. As a defense lawyer, I've met a number of bereaved spouses but when it happens to someone you know, murder is a frightening thing."

"I imagine you're relieved, on some level. I understand he was stalking you."

"Yeah. I'll be able to sleep better now, and not be continually looking over my shoulder when I'm out in public." She sighed. "I don't know why he was so obsessed with me. He had a new wife, two cute kids."

"How did you spend this morning?"

"I went over my whole day with your partner, there," she protested. "I *am* a lawyer. I know I don't have to talk to you. I have nothing to hide, but I don't like feeling that I'm under suspicion."

"Of course. We're just looking for background at this point. You must know the drill. I'm just trying to fill in the blanks for myself, if you don't mind."

So polite, she thought. Disarmingly so. "I was rattled last night after seeing him here in Whistler. It was a total shock. So I didn't sleep well, and dreaded running into him again, so I decided to just stay in bed until I heard from Hunter." She had dozed off, woken up, dozed off again, she told him. "I guess it was around 10:30 before he called."

The waiter set down their order, first her Spanish coffee, then his tea.

"Did you order room service this morning? Did you bring in your paper?"

"You mean, can anyone vouch for the fact that I was in my room?"

The young cop just smiled.

"No. Look. I am just not capable of killing anyone. I never even expected Mike to be here, so how could I have planned something like this? It's just a coincidence that we were here at the same time. I hope you've been talking to his colleagues or whatever you call them at the conference. Mike was an all around asshole, so I am sure he's pissed off more than one of his coworkers, or competitors, or even his bosses. I hope you're checking out that angle. It's not always a relative, you know."

"Of course, we're looking at all the possible angles," he said, taking a cautious sip of his hot tea. "Tell me more about last night."

Meredith sat on the bed in her room, watching the TV news. She'd been back in the lobby of the Coast Peaks Hotel with a magazine in her hands, watching people come and go, when two men arrived and approached the front desk. They spoke in low voices and held up badges for the desk clerk, so she took them for plain clothes police. The desk clerk called the manager, a slightly overweight dark-haired man in a navy pinstriped suit, who led them over to the concierge desk. The concierge pointed them toward the restaurant.

A short time later, Mike Irwin's family emerged from the restaurant. The father had his arm around the mother, who had covered her mouth with a tissue and appeared to be crying. They walked a few steps, then stopped as he embraced her, his hand rubbing her back. Behind them was Irwin's wife. She held the boy by the hand, and carried the little girl. The woman's face was expressionless, and the little girl was sucking her thumb. The little boy was looking up at her, and Meredith heard him ask, "What happened, Mommy? Why is Grandma crying?"

The manager ushered the adults into the hallway leading to the hotel's administration office, while a female desk clerk took the children by the hand and led them to a couch in the lobby. Meredith heard her say, "Mommy is going to be busy for a few minutes. Let's sit down here and we'll find you something to play with. Do you like to color?" The little girl nodded, her face serious.

"Why do those men want to talk to Mommy?" asked the boy.

"Just some business," said the clerk. "Mommy will tell you about it later."

A short time later, the two women returned to the lobby, then headed to the elevators with the children, while Mike Irwin's father left with the police. At that point, Meredith rose and walked quickly toward the elevators to stand behind the little family.

The older woman was saying, "... best for the children, don't you think?"

Irwin's wife nodded, then bent down to the kids. "We'll go play in our room with Grandma until Grand-da gets back. Won't that be fun?"

Meredith got into the elevator with them. The older woman closed her eyes and took deep breaths, while Irwin's wife muttered, "It so hard to believe," and sighed, shaking her head. Neither woman even looked in Meredith's direction.

Meredith cleared her throat. "I couldn't help noticing," she began, and smiled sympathetically at Irwin's wife. "Bad news?"

Irwin's wife compressed her lips, closed her eyes and nodded.

"I'm so sorry," said Meredith, as the elevator door opened and the sad little troupe stepped outside.

Once in her room, Meredith turned on the television and searched for local news. A red banner with white lettering appeared above the news anchor's head. BREAKING NEWS it read, and at the side of the screen appeared a photograph of a chairlift as the news anchor began speaking.

In Whistler today, chairlift attendants were shocked to discover that one of the passengers riding on the Harmony Express chairlift was dead. Our Whistler correspondent, Yoshika Sullivan, is live on the scene.

An attractive Asian woman in a white jacket with a fur lined hood spoke into the black ball of a microphone.

We're live at the base of the Harmony Express chairlift on Whistler Mountain. Behind me is where the body of a man was removed from one of the quad chairs earlier today. Police are not releasing the details, nor the name of the dead man, but homicide detectives have been called in so it is believed that foul play is suspected. The chairlift was shut down after all other passengers on the lift had been able to disembark. At present there is no estimate on when the lift will re-open.

Meredith switched off the TV and stood at the window, watching the snow. She knew that the dead man they referred to was Mike Irwin. She would now have to decide whether to stay or leave the conference. The decision would have been easier if she wasn't sure that the man in the sheepskin jacket had noticed her watching Irwin. Whether or not her job here was over, she couldn't risk exhibiting suspicious behavior, like checking out of her hotel room before her scheduled stay was over.

She picked up the telephone receiver and held it to her cheek, considering how to word her call. Then she dialed her client. Whatever the decision, it was her job to keep the client informed.

Hunter had spent an hour sitting with Alora after the two RCMP investigators left. His own informal interview by Sergeant Pike had been followed by a more intensive, recorded one by Staff Sergeant Blackwell, while Sergeant Pike sat and talked with Alora. Hunter knew that the two officers would compare notes later for inconsistencies in both their stories. He'd been on the other side of the table often enough to know that homicide detectives were not infallible, and that there was a very real risk that he himself would be considered a prime suspect based on last night's confrontation with the victim. In spite of the fact that he had been a guest in Tom Halsey's home, he knew Tom couldn't unreservedly vouch for his presence there until after they'd met in the kitchen at around ten o'clock.

He had no idea what kind of evidence they had found so far. The police weren't sharing anything with him. They told him that Tom Halsey had given them permission to search his house, and then asked Hunter for permission to search his car. "Absolutely,' he said. They had requested that both he and Alora not leave Whistler without notifying them.

"I have to leave tomorrow by mid-afternoon," he'd told Staff Sergeant Blackwell. "I drive a truck, long haul, for a living. I'm scheduled to pick up a loaded trailer Sunday night."

"Loaded to go where?" asked the detective.

"Northern California," he'd said.

"Not gonna happen."

"I can't afford to stay here." Hunter supposed Tom Halsey would let him stay a few days longer, but he couldn't afford not to work. He had payments to make on his Freightliner tractor, rent to pay on his basement suite in North Vancouver, and he was still paying his share of expenses for his two teenage daughters.

"I can't afford to let you leave," countered the detective. "Look. You know how it is. I don't want to arrest you, but I will if I have to. Then you'll be in custody until at least Monday morning."

Hunter sighed and nodded. "Okay, chief," he'd said.

Alora had gone to her room to rest, and the police had driven Hunter back to Tom's chalet in his own car, which they planned to search after searching the house. Not allowed into his room, he parked himself in Tom's kitchen and made a call to his boss's cell.

"Watson!" barked his dispatcher. Elspeth Watson was a freight broker with a small stable of independent owner operators, Hunter included. The drivers owned their own tractors, as the big trucks used for hauling trailers are called, and paid their own expenses. Watson Transportation found loads for them and negotiated a fair rate from the companies whose goods needed transporting. She collected money from the customers and paid the drivers the going rate for their services, less whatever the difference was between the driver's share and the fee she was able to negotiate with the customer. She had to hustle to find good paying loads and keep her drivers working. There wasn't a big margin in trucking, but El was good at her job and managed to make a modest living for herself and her drivers.

"Hello, El," said Hunter. "I've run into a situation here. How critical is the delivery on that load to Redding?"

"Very," she said. "I told you that, Hunter. The customer's plant is going down without those parts. I told you they needed them by Monday at ten p.m. at the very latest so they can install them before the Tuesday morning shift. Even leaving Sunday night was stretching things, and I would've given the load to Samuels if you hadn't promised to make the deadline."

"Right." Hunter paused to think.

"So what's the problem? Don't tell me you're in love." Even though El had never met Alora, she'd known of her since the previous summer when Hunter had recruited Alora to be the defense lawyer in Los Angeles for one of El's drivers.

Elspeth Watson routinely said things to him that he would never accept from others. He considered her more of a friend than a boss, but he never underestimated her power over his livelihood. He pictured her, old stained blue jeans, steel-toe sneakers and an oversize navy polo shirt, sitting at her computer with her little dog, Peterbilt, in her lap. She was a big woman with a big voice and, as tough as she might come across, an even bigger heart.

"I'm a murder suspect," he said.

There were fifteen seconds of silence at the other end of the line, followed by, "Come again?"

"I'm a murder suspect, El. Alora's husband showed up here in Whistler, and this morning he was found dead."

When El responded, it was almost a whisper. "You?"

"Of course not!"

"Alora?"

Hunter realized he couldn't answer her question. "I don't think so," he said.

"Then who?"

49

"If I knew don't you think I'd tell the police?"

"Then find out. You need to be free to pick up that load tomorrow night."

Hunter laughed. "Might take me longer than that, El. I'll line up a substitute driver for my rig."

"Who?"

"Don't worry."

"Not Sorenson."

"Why not Sorenson?"

"Why him?"

"He's the only driver I know hard up enough to drive up here to pick up my keys. I should've left a set with you at the yard."

He heard El sigh. "Yeah. Okay. Why not?"

Kelly sat in one of the two armchairs positioned in front of the gas fireplace in the hotel room, and Mike's father, John Irwin, was in the other. Mike's mother, Beth, sat at the end of the bed, watching the two children play. Corenna was turning the pages of a cloth book and pretending to read, while Jordan was coloring cartoon characters, being very careful to keep his crayon within the lines.

Kelly sighed deeply. She wished they could just leave this place, but the police had asked them to stay for a few days. "We may need your help with our investigations," the Mountie had said. Kelly felt an almost unbearable yearning to be home, but when she pictured the house she had shared with Mike in Pasadena, she realized she had no desire to return to it. Her mind searched its rooms, and every room held derision and criticism from her late husband. She knew she should pretend to care who had killed Mike, especially for the sake of his parents. "I feel like I'm in a bad dream," she said, staring into the fire.

She felt her father-in-law's eyes on her, but he didn't speak. Beth did. "You know you're like a daughter to us, Kelly," she said. "You and the children can stay with us until you get your bearings. We'd love to have you, all three of you."

50

"Yes," said John. "It would be a comfort to us, after losing Mike, to have you and the children nearby. Your father was my best friend, and we promised each other we'd watch out for each other's family if anything happened to one of us."

Kelly nodded. "I remember Dad saying that," she said. "I thought he'd be happy to know that I'd married your son…" She didn't finish the thought aloud, but was aware of a glance that passed between Beth and John. "I'm sure he…," her voice faltered, and she held her breath, her hand over her mouth, stifling a sob. "I'm sure he was."

"Corenna and Jordan," she continued, looking at John, "are a little bit of both of you, you and Dad. I'm sure Dad is happy about that."

Jordan looked up from his coloring book. "My dad?" he asked.

She shook her head. "Your Grampa Lucas," she told him. "You never met your Grampa Lucas, but he was my father. He died before you were born. He died before I married your Daddy."

"Didn't he like my dad?"

Kelly looked at her father-in-law, who spoke up before she could answer. "Of course he did, Jordan. He knew your dad when he was just a little boy, like you."

"My dad wasn't like me," he said, still coloring carefully, "he told me that. He said I was a sissy boy, and he didn't like sissy boys."

"No, Jordan! Your daddy loved you," said Beth, reaching out to stroke his hair.

Jordan smiled sadly. "I love you, Grandma," he said, and turned his attention to choosing a new crayon.

Kelly's heart constricted. She wished she could have shielded Jordan from his father's hurtful remarks; she loved that little boy more than anyone could know.

"What do you say, Kelly? Will you and the kids stay with us in Seattle, at least for a little while?" John Irwin got up and put his hands on her shoulders. "It would be good for all of us."

"Yes," said Kelly. "Yes, of course." Images of a new life in Seattle flashed through her mind. A warmth started in her belly and spread to her entire body, and it had nothing to do with the fireplace in front of her. It was comfort, comfort mingled with happiness and hope and love, a feeling she hadn't experienced for years. *I'm happy that Mike is dead*, she said to herself, not daring to look away from the fire.

"Good!" John patted her shoulder, then stepped over to the bed and embraced his wife. "If you and the kids want to stay here, I think I'll go to Kelly's room and see if the police are finished there. If they are, I'll lie down for awhile, if that's okay," he said, kissing her on the cheek. When she moved to stand, he said, "You can stay here with Kelly and the kids."

After he left, Kelly moved to sit beside Beth on the bed. Corenna had tired of her book, and was playing with toys on the floor at their feet.

"Is Grand-da okay?" Kelly used the name that Jordan called his grandfather. "He looks pale." She'd been wondering about his health since she first saw him at Sea-Tac airport. She was shocked at how thin he looked, almost like a shrunken version of the vigorous military man he'd been just two years before.

Beth shrugged. "He's seventy-two. Age does that. I don't have the energy I used to have either." She squeezed Kelly's hand. "I could use a nap myself."

"Do," said Kelly. She pulled her mother-in-law close and hugged her. "Go nap with Grand-da, if you want. We'll be fine. I'll put the kids down here in your room. It's been a rough day for all of us."

When Beth stepped back and nodded, tears ran freely down her cheeks, and suddenly Kelly couldn't hold back tears of her own. "I'm so sorry, Mom," she said. "I'm so sorry that you've lost your son."

Hunter considered what El had said. If he had to stick around here in Whistler, he might as well do what he could to find out who had killed Mike Irwin, if he could do it without making things worse for himself by antagonizing the investigating officers. He decided that the first person he'd like to contact was the watching woman, if she was still around. It stood to reason that she would be at the same hotel as the Irwin family, so Hunter headed over there as soon as the police concluded there was nothing of interest in his car.

He parked his Pontiac in the underground lot, wincing at the hourly rate as he pulled a ticket from the automatic dispenser, and found his way up a cold stairwell to the hotel lobby. He scanned a hotel directory on the wall that listed events taking place in the hotel conference rooms. He knew that Mike Irwin had been in Whistler to attend a purchasing conference of some sort, and on the board was "The Coast Peaks Hotel welcomes the Purchasing Professionals of America to Whistler", but there was nothing listed on the directory for Saturday evening. It made sense that the conference attendees would be spending the weekend enjoying the resort and start the business end of things on Monday, so he went to the reception desk to inquire. The clerk informed him that there was a welcome reception planned for Sunday night, but that a section of tables had been reserved tonight in the restaurant for those who had arrived early. The reservations were for seven o'clock, she said.

Hunter looked at his watch, and decided to sit in the lobby for the next hour and watch for anyone he knew to be connected to Mike Irwin, preferably the watching woman. He found a leather couch with a view of the entrances from both the elevators and the main doors, and sat down. The warmth of the hotel soon forced him to remove his sheepskin jacket and drape it over the arm of the couch. He'd been there for about ten minutes when he noticed one of the men who had been sitting at Mike's table in the Chateau Grande Montagne enter the hotel lobby from the direction of the elevators. The man wore a knit shirt with a collar under a heavy green sweater with a V neck. He was clean shaven and his dark hair looked still damp from a shower.

He reached the man at the entrance to the lounge and asked if he could speak to him privately for a few minutes. "I understand you know Mike Irwin," he began. "My name is Hunter Rayne. You may have noticed me in the Chateau Grande Montagne last night."

The man nodded. "Yeah. You're the guy who got him kicked out. He was..." he started to say, then his eyes widened and he took a step back.

Hunter smiled wryly. He imagined it had suddenly occurred to the man that Hunter had killed Mike. "You've heard what happened to him, then. And, no, I didn't kill him, nor did I see him at all after he left the bar last night. I am, however, investigating his death, and would like to know more about him, starting with who he knew at the conference."

The man searched Hunter's face, but didn't respond.

"Where did you know Mike from? Did you work together?"

"I already talked to the police. Who are you?"

"I'm a retired RCMP homicide investigator. From time to time, I help the RCMP with their investigations," said Hunter, hoping that would be enough. "How is it that officers Pike and Blackwell knew to contact you?"

The man hesitated.

"I'm not a reporter, if that's what's worrying you," said Hunter. "Anything you say is just between you and me, and you can feel free not to answer any question that seems out of line." Hunter had been told often enough that he still looked and talked like a cop. He hoped that would carry some weight. "I don't have a badge to show you, because I'm no longer officially a detective. I can, however, give you the names and numbers of my RCMP colleagues."

The man chewed on his upper lip, then said, "Mike's phone. They found my number in Mike's phone. He called me last night to arrange to meet."

"And you are ...?" Hunter held out his hand.

The man returned his handshake. "Todd Milton," he said, glancing toward the bar. "I've known Mike for years."

"You look thirsty," said Hunter. "How about if I buy you a drink?"

"I ... uh." The man hesitated, then said, "Okay."

They settled on two polished oak stools at the bar and the man ordered a Stella Artois while Hunter ordered a draft beer. Todd told

Hunter that he and Mike had first worked together at the same company almost fifteen years ago, along with the other man who'd been at their table Friday night, and that the three of them kept in touch doing business together, booked a game of golf once in a while, and met up at conferences like this one. The bartender placed a black square of folded napkin in front of each of them, followed by a sleeve of amber ale for Hunter and a Stella for Todd.

"What was Mike Irwin's current position," asked Hunter. "Who did he work for, or was he his own boss?"

"He was the purchasing manager — sorry, the supply chain manager — at a company called Blue Hills Industries in Sylmar."

"Blue Hills? What kind of a business would that be?"

"They manufacture specialty aluminum products, including aerospace components, and have some DND and aerospace contracts."

Hunter raised his eyebrows. "Military?"

Todd shrugged. "Military, yes. If you're thinking top secret, not necessarily. Not likely any cloak and dagger stuff, like international espionage. Although there *is* a lot of money involved in that kind of contract, so secrecy is a big thing in businesses like that. Big business is cutthroat, you know?"

"Are you in the same industry?"

He shrugged. "I know what I'm talking about, if that's what you're asking."

"Was Mike doing well there?"

"As far as I know. He certainly seemed to be doing well." He lifted the Stella to his lips, then paused and added, "He bought a boat last year. A thirty two foot cruiser, probably set him back a good hundred grand. He said his goal was to move to Newport Beach."

"Does that kind of money make sense for the job he's in?"

"Could be. There's always bonuses for meeting deadlines, coming in under budget, that kind of thing. Some of those contracts are probably worth tens of millions."

"Can you think of any reason why someone would want Mike Irwin dead?"

Todd took several gulps from his beer before he replied. "Mike could be a real asshole, especially when he was drinking. That was his ex-wife you were with, wasn't it? I know they had a bad split so I'll bet she was happy to see him gone."

"Anybody else?"

"You saw Brent Carruthers at that other bar last night?"

Hunter shook his head, placing his glass back in the center of the napkin, on the wet circle of condensation. "Who is Brent Carruthers?"

"You must have missed it. Brent used to work at the same company as Mike, down in Riverside. Phoenix Fabrication, about five years ago. I think Mike was always jealous of Brent, 'cause he was younger, good looking and smart, managed to get promoted real fast." He took another swallow of beer. "Anyway, Brent started banging the boss's daughter on the sly — she worked in the accounts payable department during the summers and had to have been ten years younger than Brent. Heck! She was just a college sophomore. So Mike reported it to the boss and Brent got canned."

"Did Brent know it was Mike?"

"Mike boasted about it. You know, to some other guys in the field. It's a small world in business, sometimes, and I have no doubt it got back to Brent." He waved at the bartender. "Hey, can we get some nuts or pretzels or something?"

Hunter took a sip of his beer, but Todd didn't continue so he said, "You said Brent was in the bar at the Grande Montagne last night. What happened?"

"Like I said to the police yesterday, he was with a young woman — a very attractive young woman. Mike said it was another boss's daughter, at wherever Brent is working now. Right in L.A., I think. Mike didn't threaten him outright, but he pretty much implied that he was going to rat on him to his boss again."

"And Brent. What did he do?"

"Nothing. The young lady left, but Brent just sat there, pretty much ignored Mike. It wasn't long after that when you came in, and … you know. Brent paid for his drink and left soon after Mike did, if

I remember right. I don't expect you would've have noticed him." He drained his beer and turned around in his chair, looking out at the room.

"Listen. I got some friends here now."

"Thanks, Todd. I appreciate you taking the time to talk to me. If you think of anything else that might be significant, maybe you could call." Hunter reached behind him where his jacket hung on the back of the bar stool to search his jacket pockets for the card Sergeant Pike had given him, and handed it to the man. "Call Sergeant Pike, okay?"

The man glanced at the card, seeming surprised. "Oh. The RCMP guy. Right." He tucked the card in his wallet, nodded to Hunter, and left to join his friends.

Hunter slid his beer back and forth on the granite surface of the bar, thinking about how to find this Brent Carruthers fellow, then pulled out his wallet and signaled the bartender for the check.

He still had to find the watching woman.

CHAPTER
FIVE

After another hour and a half sitting in the lobby, Hunter was considering the wisdom of staying where he was when he saw John Irwin, Mike's father, walk from the elevators toward the bar. The man's gait was slow, but his back was straight and his shoulders squared. Hunter took a deep breath and headed to intercept him.

"Excuse me," he said. He knew it might not be easy to get the man to talk to him.

"Yes? Oh, it's you. Alora's friend." There was no animosity in his voice; it was flat and weary. "Under normal circumstances, I might be apologizing for my son's behavior last night, but these aren't normal circumstances." He took a deep breath and let it out again. "My son is dead," he said simply. John Irwin's face was drawn, with dark crescents below his eyes.

"I know. I'm very sorry for your loss, Mr. Irwin." Hunter waited for a reaction, but there was only a blank stare, as if the brain behind the eyes was too distracted to process what they were looking at. "Can I speak with you? I'd be happy to buy you a drink, if you have the time."

"A drink? Yes, I'd like a drink. That's why I came down." He ran his hand absently over the grey bristle on his chin. "I just had to get out of the hotel room for a while." He headed toward the bar and

Hunter followed at his elbow. "My wife took a sleeping pill and she's finally resting. The mother always takes it the hardest, you know?"

Hunter introduced himself, once again implying that he was helping the RCMP with their investigations, and the older man nodded, saying, "When I saw you last night, I thought then that you looked like a military man, or a policeman at the very least. Please, call me John."

The bar was filling up with the after dinner crowd, but they were able to find a quiet table near the wall. Hunter adjusted his chair so he still had a view of the bar's entrance along with a corner of the lobby. A tiny halogen fixture hung above the table, giving off a muted amber light. John slumped back in his chair with his eyes closed and heaved a sigh, then as if calling on a reserve of energy from within, straightened up and looked Hunter in the eye. "Do you have any idea who killed my son?" he asked. "Do the police?"

"They have their suspicions." Hunter suppressed a smile. *And I'm one of them.*

A tall young woman dressed all in black came to take their order. A double scotch for John, a bottle of Labatt's Blue for Hunter.

"They have their suspicions, do they?" said John. "Do you?"

"I know it wasn't me," said Hunter.

"That's always a good place to start."

"Do you know why anyone would want to hurt your son?"

John snorted softly. "Yes. My son could be abrasive." He paused. "More than that. My son was not a kind man. He didn't seem to care who he hurt. I can imagine someone would want to hurt him back. But for someone to feel strongly enough to decide to end his life?" He shook his head. "My poor, dear wife. I wish I could spare her the pain."

The drinks arrived, and John took a hearty slug of straight scotch. "What about you? Any theories?"

Hunter shrugged. His cell phone started to ring, so he reached into his pocket and killed the sound. "It appears that your son had made some enemies in business."

"I'm not surprised. But I'm afraid I don't know anything about his work." He tilted his glass of scotch, staring into it, as if studying its color. "... and little enough about his home life. We were never really close. The military life takes its toll on families, keeping them apart."

Hunter couldn't help thinking about his own family, how his wife had accused him of not being there for his daughters for highlights in their young lives: school plays and soccer games, birthdays and broken hearts. "It's my job," he would say to her. "You knew it when we first got married, that being a police officer is more than a nine to five commitment."

Once she had replied, "Screw your job excuse! I'm tired of hearing it. The worst part is that you don't even seem to care!" It seemed the more she hurt, the more she needed to hurt him back, and the harder it became for him to get close to her.

He took several long swallows of beer before speaking. John seemed unbothered by the break in conversation, both men lost in thoughts of the indelible past.

"I hear you," he said to John. "You think you can make it up to them when they get older, but before you know it, the years go by and they get busy with their own lives, their friends, their jobs ... you can try to catch up, but you never do."

"That's right. And then suddenly time's up. Here, let me get the next round." John signaled the young woman, pointing to Hunter's half empty glass, then continued. "I had a real good friend, almost like a brother. We were in the same Marine battalion early in the Vietnam war, saw a lot of men die ..." His voice faded, his eyes drifted as if he were lost in horrific remembrance. "Most of them started out as scared, skinny kids, but that war made men out of them in a hurry." He paused, his face grim. "So, Scott, my best buddy, we went through some hellish things together in Nam. Back home, we both lived in L.A. County so we'd keep in touch — times like this," he gestured at the drinks on the table, "talking things out, things we'd seen, adapting to life back in the States, our wives, our kids."

Not so different from me and Ken, thought Hunter.

"My wife's a strong woman. We had three children. Do you have kids, Hunter?"

"Yes. Two daughters in their late teens."

"So you know how it feels." He shook his head. "They can break the heart of the toughest marine without even trying."

Another silence followed, then John spoke again. "Our oldest son fought in Iraq — good kid — came home wounded, married a nice girl and they live in her home state of Texas. We try to visit them once a year, seems they're too busy with their lives to come out west. Our only daughter died of a brain tumor when she was only nine."

"I'm sorry." Hunter couldn't imagine losing Lesley or Jan at that age, or at all. He wondered if the good kid's choice to live in Texas was a heartbreak as well.

"Like I said, Beth's a strong woman. She coped. Mike — well, you met Mike. But I was telling you about my friend Scott. He had one child, a daughter. His wife wasn't a strong woman, and she had some pretty heavy demons that she couldn't shake loose of. She killed herself when Kelly was barely in her teens, so Scott had to be both mother and father to that little girl. He made me promise to take care of her if anything happened to him."

Hunter thanked the server for his beer, suggested another scotch for John. John shook his head, and said he'd switch to beer himself, asking about the local beers but deciding on a Budweiser. Hunter waited for John to continue.

"Scott passed away when Kelly was still in college. She was a bright girl, had a good head on her shoulders. We always kept in touch with her, invited her for Thanksgiving and Christmas, looking out for her, almost like a daughter. Our Mike went through Cal Berkeley on a football scholarship. He was popular, attractive, liked to party — then got a good job in his field in Southern California. We were happy when he settled down with a smart, attractive woman like Alora. She was a school teacher then; Beth thought that boded well for grandchildren. After she left him — Beth never understood that, still blames Alora for it — I guess his ego took a hit. Next time he saw Kelly — Thanksgiving, I think — well, I guess she was young, pretty, I want to say wholesome but that doesn't quite capture it — and we figured it was just what the doctor ordered, for both of them." He sighed.

"Kelly's his wife?"

John nodded. "Sorry, I lost my train of thought again. I meant to say that Scott died unexpectedly — he had a heart attack, they figure, and his car hit the pillar of an overpass at freeway speed — and suddenly there was no time left for him to tell his daughter anything he might've left unsaid. You know what I mean? Sometimes there's no second chances."

They both fell silent as the server delivered John's beer.

"I had a friend like that, too," said Hunter. He felt an unusual kinship with John, as if they'd known each other years ago, and had most of a lifetime in common. "His name was Ken Marsh, and we went through basic training at the RCMP depot in Regina together, then got posted together to a detachment in the Yukon before connecting again in the Vancouver area." He thought about all the times he'd sat with Ken, just like this, talking things out. Ken and his wife Helen had a son. They had named the boy Adam Hunter Marsh. Where were they now? he wondered. "His wife is a strong and beautiful woman. He was the one with the demons."

"Was?"

"Accidentally shot himself cleaning his gun," Hunter said with an ironic smile.

"Of course." He nodded. "The family needed his pension."

They talked for almost an hour, through another round of drinks. Hunter related Ken's downward spiral, his depression and how his drinking kept getting worse. "I tried to get him to look at things in a diff—"

Hunter caught sight of a familiar figure walking past the entrance in the direction of the elevators. "I'm sorry, John." He stood up abruptly and grabbed a twenty dollar bill out of his jeans pocket. "There's someone I need to talk to." He held out the twenty but John waved it away. Hunter grabbed his jacket and bolted for the lobby.

There was no time for a "see you later".

Hunter reached the elevators just as the doors began to close on the furthest one. He sprinted the last five yards and put his arm between the doors, just in time. The doors opened and the watching woman took a step backward, her eyes wide with surprise, then said, "Shit."

"We need to talk."

"You talk," she said. She looked up at the digital display above the elevator doors. "You've got about fifteen seconds."

Hunter pulled his cell phone out of his shirt pocket, began to punch the numbers. "Nine. One…"

"Stop!"

"Your room or the lobby?"

She glared at him, but held up a room key. The elevator stopped, and he took her by the elbow as they stepped out. She was dressed for walking outdoors, insulated pants and snow boots and a long quilted coat. Her nose and cheeks were red and her hair still gave off a faint scent of mountain air. She was almost as tall as he was, probably very fit, no doubt was trained in martial arts, and he had to admit to himself that she could possibly take him in a fight. He couldn't afford to let that happen. When they got to her room, he made sure to get his foot inside before she got the door open wide enough to enter.

"What do you want?" Keeping her coat on, she sat down on the bed, her hand resting on the night table beside the telephone. "Or should I tell hotel security you forced your way into my room?"

Hunter tossed his jacket on the floor and held his hands out, palms up. "All I want is information," he said. "What was your interest in Mike Irwin?"

"Who's he?" Her voice was clipped, her jaw set firmly.

"Quit playing games. I can have the police here before you finish packing your toothbrush." He pulled his cell phone out again and added, "I don't think you want the local police involved if you can help it."

She frowned. "Who the hell are you?"

"How about if you answer a couple of questions for me first. Who are you, and what was your interest in Mike Irwin?"

The woman was silent for awhile, staring down at the floor. Hunter, standing between her and the door with his arms crossed over his chest, gave her time to think.

"I'm a licensed private investigator," she said finally, "and I know enough not to talk to complete strangers about myself and my work. So answer my question. Who the hell are you and why should I tell you anything?"

Hunter took a deep breath, considering the best tack to take with this woman. Telling the truth was his first choice, whenever possible, and he couldn't come up with a better option. "My name is Hunter Rayne, I'm a former member of the Royal Canadian Mounted Police, and through a series of coincidences, I've become a suspect in Mike Irwin's murder. I have a vested interest in finding out who might have wanted him dead." He smiled. "I figure that if you were hired to kill him, you would have been on your way out of Whistler before the police reached his body."

One corner of her mouth curled up, but she said nothing. Hunter wondered if that was exactly what she wanted him to think. Female assassins weren't unknown.

"But I do believe that you know something about the man that could help me out. I'd like to know why you were hired to investigate him, but first, what's your name? Can I assume you're from L.A.? "

The woman shrugged out of her coat. She was wearing a pale green turtleneck sweater that hugged her body, and Hunter realized he'd been right about the kind of shape she was in. She had broad shoulders, well defined biceps and lean curves from neck to waist. She squared her shoulders and threw back her head, as if defying him not to look at her breasts, appraising him in turn from beneath half closed eyelids. Hunter didn't break eye contact.

"My name is Stella Clark, and yes, I'm from L.A. Want to see some ID?"

"What can you tell me about Mike Irwin?"

64

"You're talking about the man you had the fight with last night? Just off the top of my head, from what I observed last night, I'd say he's a man with narcissistic personality disorder, bordering on sociopathic. If he can't attain what he believes he's entitled to by working for it, he'll find another way to get it, even if it means engaging in illegal or immoral activity. He lacks empathy, can be cruel, but is not necessarily prone to excessive violence, since he's not much of a fighter." She shrugged, a cold smile playing on her lips. "Sorry. I guess I should have used the past tense. Does that help?"

"And your client's interest in him?"

"Who said my client was interested in him?" She tilted her head, looking him up and down. "Who's the woman?"

"Uh-unh." His turn to smile.

"Okay, don't tell me. Let me guess." Her expression turned almost coy. "You and he were fighting over his ex."

He didn't change his expression.

"Ex what doesn't really matter," she continued. "Girlfriend, wife — aha! The ex-wife. I'll bet it's her."

Hunter hid a smile. Without openly admitting it, she had just revealed that she was aware that Mike had an ex-wife and he would bet that she was also aware of the restraining order against him.

"My turn," he said. "Your client. I doubt that it was anyone wanting information about Mike's personal life. So ... my guess would be either his employer or a prospective employer." He tapped his lips with a forefinger. "Wait a minute ... a prospective employer would be more likely to check references, talk to former employers, clients, co-workers. That wouldn't take any kind of clandestine spy, now would it?"

The woman pressed her lips together, then lifted her chin and said, "Spy?"

"Would you prefer undercover operative?"

She laughed. "That sounds much more respectable."

"So," Hunter continued, "that would mean his current employer suspected him of something and wanted it confirmed. Am I right?"

She smiled and looked at the floor.

"DND and aerospace contracts worth millions of dollars," he continued. "That would certainly make Blue Hills Industries a target for industrial espionage, wouldn't it? Did Blue Hills executives suspect Mike Irwin of selling secrets?"

"All you'll get from me is my name, rank and I don't even have a serial number."

Hunter scooped up his jacket from the floor and turned toward the door. His hand on the door handle, he turned and smiled at her.

"What's your real name, Stella?"

He didn't wait for an answer. He knew it wouldn't come.

Hunter ransomed his car from the underground lot. It was getting close to 10:30 and he wasn't ready to return to Tom's empty chalet for the night, so he decided to return to the Chateau Grande Montagne to see if Alora was still up. He didn't see her in the lounge, and the restaurant was almost deserted, so he pulled out his cell phone.

There was a message. He had forgotten that he'd missed a call.

It was from Chris, his ex-wife. "I left a message on your home phone, but haven't heard back so I assume you're on the road again. That means you also didn't get a message from Helen. Helen Marsh. She's been trying to reach you, and I guess it's urgent. It's about her son, Adam. I said I'd try to get hold of you and give you her number."

Hunter's gut dropped. He hadn't spoken to Helen for years, but that didn't mean she didn't cross his mind. Often. Chris had left Helen's number, but it was a 403 number, which meant she was still in Alberta, which would make it an hour later. He decided to retrieve the messages from his home phone first.

It was the same silken voice he remembered, but there was no mistaking the anxiousness in its timbre.

"Hunter. It's Helen Marsh. Are you there?" There was a pause, as if she were waiting for him to pick up the phone. "I know it's been a long time, and I wouldn't be bothering you but Adam, my son…

Ken's son. He's gone missing. It's not like him, Hunter. The police here in Calgary… they think he's just a runaway. He's never done anything like this before. Please, can you help? Call me just as soon as you get this." She left her number.

Hunter stood for a moment, staring at his cell phone. Calgary was over six hundred miles away. What could he do from here?

Hunter found a quiet table in the lounge, with his back to the wall. He listened again to Helen's message and noted her number down on the back of an old business card he found tucked behind the drivers license in his wallet. As the phone rang, he turned over the card. It was the one Alora had given him in L.A., with the name and number of her law firm.

"Adam? Is that you?" It was Helen's voice.

Hunter cleared his throat. "Helen. It's Hunter."

"Oh, thank God! I'm beside myself, Hunter! Adam's gone missing." Her voice broke. "I'm sorry. It's been a long time. I'm so happy to hear your voice. I heard about you and Chris. I'm sorry," she said again.

Hunter caught himself on the verge of apologizing back to her about the death of her husband, his best friend. He'd done it over and over already, and it was old news now. There was no sense bringing it up. "I'll do what I can to help find Adam. Tell me about it."

"He's been gone since Wednesday, hasn't called, didn't say goodbye."

"Where was he on Wednesday? Was he at school?"

"Yes. I was at work, as usual. I do the books for a small restaurant chain. Ever since he turned twelve, either he goes to hang out with a friend after school or lets himself in at the townhouse until I get home from work."

"You and he live alone?" Hunter was almost afraid to ask, but he needed to know.

"Yes, of course. Adam's been my whole life since Ken… you know… he's generally a good kid, but…" She paused.

"But?"

"Of course, Ken's death — Adam's been moody sometimes. Last fall he became friends with an older boy who failed a grade. His name's Nathan LeBlanc. Adam started to change."

Hunter had heard the same story repeatedly when he was on the force; good kids, bad crowd. He could almost guess the rest, but asked, "In what way?"

"He started being less respectful. He got his nose pierced, and a skull tattoo on his… My God, Hunter, he's only fifteen! He's too young to know what this could lead to. I can't let his life go off the rails!"

"Did you have an argument?" He spoke gently, trying hard not to let it sound accusatory.

"Not you, too!"

"Helen, I have to know everything. What did you argue about?"

He heard her take a deep breath. "I'm sorry. Of course you do." She paused, then said, "Nathan told Adam he was quitting school. He said he was sick of the cold winters in Calgary and had friends who lived in Vancouver. He told Adam he should come, too." Another pause. "I grounded Adam on Tuesday night. I think he went with Nathan."

"Have you talked to Nathan's parents?"

"He lives with his grandmother, and yes. Nathan's gone, too. I think Adam went with him to Vancouver. That's why I called you."

"Can you find out the names of the boy's friends in Vancouver, where they live?"

"His grandmother doesn't know."

Hunter knew she would want him to go to Vancouver right away, and didn't want to have to tell her that was impossible. "I'll need photographs…" he began, and looked up to see Alora walking toward him with a big smile on her face. She wore skinny jeans and a plaid shirt with the top buttons undone, no coat or boots, so she must have come down from her hotel room.

"There you are!" she said as she approached the table. "Buy me a drink, handsome?"

Helen was just asking about where she could fax the photographs and stopped short, "Who's that?"

Hunter held his hand up at Alora. "A friend," he said into the phone.

"A girlfriend? Of course. I — I'm sorry. I should have thought. You can't just drop everything for me."

"It's okay, Helen. Of course I'll help in any way I can. It's just that I'm not at home right now and it could be a day or two…"

"Yes. Yes, I see." Her voice was more subdued. "I was thinking maybe I should go to Vancouver myself, anyway."

"No. Don't. I don't think that's a good idea." He was sure she wouldn't even know where to start looking, and could put herself at risk. "You have to stay home where he can call you if he needs to, or in case he comes back."

Alora had stood beside the table for a moment, looking confused, and now shrugged and started walking backwards, putting some distance between them. Hunter beckoned her to return.

He gave Helen his boss's fax number and asked her to send photos of both Adam and Nathan, along with any other information she could get hold of, to Elspeth Watson at Watson Transportation. "I'll call you as soon as I receive them," he said.

"Thank you, Hunter. God, it's good to hear your voice!" and she hung up.

"Did I interrupt something?" Alora seated herself across from Hunter just as a young man in a white shirt and black slacks arrived at the table to take their drinks order. She wondered who this Helen was, but asking outright would sound too much like a jealous girlfriend question.

Hunter closed his phone and put it in his jacket pocket, then took his jacket off and hung it on the back of his chair. "An old friend," he said, "needs help finding a runaway teenager. Her son."

"As if you need something else to worry about at the moment. Who is she?"

"Just a friend." He looked her straight in the eye as he said it, and she took it as a warning to drop the subject. She couldn't help thinking that 'a friend' was exactly what he'd said to his other 'friend' on the telephone about her. His expression softened, and he said, "How are you doing? Did the police search your hotel room?"

"That they did. They rummaged through all my luggage and left things strewn over the bed. It makes me feel violated, at least my privacy. I hope that Mounties keep their hands clean." She said it with a wry face, but had felt embarrassed about strangers pawing through her underwear, not to mention the negligee she had purchased especially for the trip. She was beginning to wonder if she would even wear it. Hunter had been running hot and cold — make that lukewarm and cold — and she had no idea how he really felt about her.

"No gun?"

She detected the hint of a smile on his lips. "Not in my room. How about yours?"

His smile widened and he shook his head.

"I felt so creeped out by the search that I called the Coast Peaks to see if they still had my room. They did manage to find one for me, so I'm moving back there tomorrow."

Just then the server arrived and set down their drinks, beer for him, red wine for her. They picked up their drinks and clinked glasses across the table. She was considering whether or not to say some variation of "to us" when he beat her to the toast.

"Here's to a quick solution to Mike's murder so we can get back to our own lives," he said.

She put her glass down without taking a sip. "What's that supposed to mean?"

"Just what I said. I'm not comfortable with being a murder suspect, are you?"

"But getting back to our own lives? Honestly, Hunter. Has anyone ever told you that you can be an insensitive jerk?" She lifted her chin up and looked away, then sighed heavily and picked up her wine. Now she did have an idea of how he really felt about her — or how little.

Hunter had hung his head. "Yes. My ex-wife used to say it all the time. I guess I have a way with words. A bad way." He smiled at her and shrugged apologetically. "I really didn't mean it like that."

Alora couldn't help but think it was a Freudian slip. What the hell was the matter with her? Here she was practically throwing herself at a truck driver. She rolled the stem of her wineglass between her thumb and forefinger, turning it around and around on the smooth tabletop.

"I'm sorry," he added.

"Sure." She took a sip of wine. It was a Napa Valley merlot, and its rich warmth immediately brightened her mood. Mike was dead. She could stop hiding and go ahead with being an attractive young L.A. lawyer. Her future held infinite possibilities, a promise of freedom she hadn't experienced since before Mike. "Did your Mountie friends tell you anything about Mike's murder? They were definitely not open to answering any of my questions. I don't even know how he was killed. Was it a gun?"

"They're not sharing anything with me, either, but I believe that was what they were searching for."

"Like we'd be stupid enough to bring the murder weapon back to our rooms."

He looked up sharply, his eyes narrowed, a hint of a smile. "What would you have done with it?"

"Okay. Whoever did it had to have skis on, right? I don't know whether he…"

"Or she…"

"Or she," Alora paused, tilting her head, "could have jumped from the lift right after the murder or risked riding right to the top and just skied like stink out of there before anyone could get a good look at him. Or her."

Hunter had leaned back in his chair and was watching her closely. When she hesitated, he said, "Go on." She couldn't help wondering if he really thought she had done it.

"How deep is the snow here?" she asked.

"Could be six, ten feet, maybe more."

"How many tree wells between the top of that lift and the Village?"

"So you'd toss the gun into a tree well when no one was looking."

"Wouldn't you?"

He nodded. "Makes sense."

She drained her glass and waited. He seemed lost in thought. Was he preoccupied with his other 'friend'?

"I'm going to need a lift back to the Coast Peaks tomorrow," she said.

"What time?"

"Some time before checkout time here, obviously. Right after breakfast maybe?"

"Right." He spoke absently, as if his attention was somewhere in the darkness beyond the plate glass window. Her less-than-subtle hint that they spend the night together had either gone right over his head, or was being pointedly ignored.

When he said nothing further, she got to her feet. "I'm done. Good night."

He looked a little taken aback, but didn't say anything, didn't reach for her hand, no protest of any kind.

"That's right," she said, unable to keep the irritation out of her voice. Why was he just sitting there, not speaking? "You and me? Just not gonna happen. I'm fine with that."

He pushed his chair back.

"No. Sit down. Finish your beer. You're paying for it." She pulled a ten dollar bill out of her wallet and threw it on the table. Going dutch expressed just how she felt. She leaned toward him, her hand on his shoulder, knowing that he couldn't help but notice the top of her breasts in the V of her shirt. "You must be tired after your busy day. I can find my own room."

"Alora, hang on. I —"

But she waved him off. "Besides, I don't have to worry about Mike any more…" She pulled her room key out of the back pocket of her jeans as she walked away, her hand sliding slowly up the curve of her butt. Let him see what he was missing. "…now do I?"

CHAPTER
SIX

Hunter woke to an empty house. Tom had the day off, and had told Hunter that he was leaving early for Vancouver to run some errands, then pick up his wife at YVR. Hunter stood at the kitchen window while the coffee maker did its job. The sun wasn't up yet, but the fallen snow already reflected the pale light of dawn to reveal the army of snow-draped fir trees surrounding Tom's chalet. Smoke rose from a neighbor's chimney. He poured himself a coffee before calling Elspeth Watson, his dispatcher. Even though it was 7:30 on a Sunday morning, he knew she would be at the office.

"Watson!"

"Mornin', El."

"Hunter! Can you come back to work yet? Did they catch the guy?" El seldom wasted time on pleasantries. Work was a game she loved to play, and Hunter was used to her single-minded devotion to it.

"I've lined up Sorenson to do the run for me. He's meeting me at the White Spot in Squamish at eleven. But, tell me, did you get some photographs on your fax machine?"

"Yeah. Just came through. What the hell are they? I would have figured them for a wrong number but my name was on the cover page." He could hear her flipping through papers.

"It's a missing kid. His mother in Calgary thinks he might be in Vancouver, and I was hoping you could make a bunch of copies. I'll need a couple, and if you've got anyone doing deliveries downtown…"

"I get it. Sure. I'll hand a few out. Needle in a haystack, but I guess it's worth a shot."

"I'm going to call Sorry right now and get him to swing by the warehouse for the pictures on his way here."

"If you can drive to Squamish, why not …"

"I can't clear my name by sitting in the cab of my truck, for starters. And they don't want me to leave the country yet, El."

"You sure Sorenson can do the job without screwing up?"

Dan Sorenson and El had hit it off like hail on pavement. Hunter knew that Sorry often gave the impression that he was a big goof, but he wasn't a stupid man. "Don't worry, El. Redding isn't far from where he used to live. He knows his way around northern California."

"You don't think there's a chance you'll solve the case and be freed up by tonight?"

Hunter laughed. "I'm flattered that you would even consider that possible."

"You're the man, Hunter! Call me later." And she was gone.

Hunter sighed and redialed her number.

"Watson!"

"I need another favor, El." He asked her to see what she could dig up on Blue Hills Industries, to see if she could connect with any of her fellow truck dispatchers or drivers to find out if there was something known about the company's operations that could shed light on Mike's possible enemies. Given Mike's position as supply chain manager, what he did could very well be reflected on the company's loading dock. Might as well find out all he could about the man.

"You bet," said El. "I'm on it!"

Hunter smiled as he hung up the phone. El had tried to help out with his investigations in the past, sometimes doing more harm than good. He hoped this time would pay off.

Meredith Travis threw back the bed covers but made no move to get out of bed, reviewing the events of the past twenty-four hours in her mind. After the man who called himself Hunter Rayne had left her room last night, she had seriously considered walking out the door and driving away from Whistler. In her business, she couldn't afford publicity, and the media was already all over what they had dubbed 'The Chairlift Killer'. Rayne had connected her to Mike Irwin, but what reason would the police have to do so? He had threatened to inform the police, but would he?

Still undecided about whether to leave, she had known when she heard the confident knock on her door less than half an hour after Rayne left that it was too late. He had passed on her room number to the police. She hadn't wanted to give the tall young cop any more information than she had given Rayne, but he insisted on seeing her official ID, and using a fake ID didn't seem to be a good idea where the police and a homicide investigation were concerned. He advised her that he would need to verify her investigator's license with the State of California and suggested it would be in her best interests not to leave Whistler, at least until he had done so. To reinforce his 'cooperate or else' stance, he pointed out that she was legally required to notify the Registrar of Security Services in British Columbia before coming here on a job. Now running away was no longer an option.

Her client had made it clear that she had better not allow his name to be connected with the murder of Mike Irwin. Her reputation depended on keeping her clients happy and her career depended on keeping her license. She couldn't allow either herself or her client to become an object of suspicion. She considered her options for almost an hour after the cop had left her room, then cleared her mind with meditation before turning in for the night, confident that the answer would come to her in the morning.

Now she continued lying in bed, staring at the ceiling, until a new plan had started to take shape. She inhaled deeply, and let out her breath slowly with a big smile.

"I'm always up for a new challenge," she said aloud, as her feet hit the floor.

Ten minutes later, Meredith was dressed in sweats and heading for the hotel's workout room. Her focus may have shifted, but she was still on the job.

Hunter wished he still had the same access to information that he'd had as a detective. It could prove a challenge to find and interview Brent Carruthers, the man who might have had a motive to shut Mike Irwin up for good. Obviously the man had been in the bar that night, but Hunter hadn't had any reason to notice him, although he did recall a dark-haired man sitting behind 'Stella', alone at a table with two wine glasses.

He found a space in an outdoor lot behind the Coast Peaks Hotel. He couldn't help searching for Alora Magee as he crossed the hotel lobby to the reception desk. There were four parties in front of him, and only two clerks, so he stood behind an elderly couple and turned around to look for Alora again. He wondered if she had already checked back in.

He wasn't sure how he felt about her departure from the lounge last night. Had she just been tired and showing the effects of stress, or had he really done something to make her totally lose interest in him? If so, was he relieved that she no longer represented a threat to the simplicity of his life, or did he care about her enough to pursue her, to prove to her and to himself that he was ready for and capable of a healthy relationship with a woman? He wondered if he could make things up to her by taking her out for dinner, or if he would be doing her a favor by staying away.

When it was his turn at the front desk, he leaned toward the clerk and spoke in a low voice. The clerk was a well-groomed woman with a businesslike demeanor, her dark hair pulled into a tidy bun. "I'm trying to locate a friend of a friend who's in Whistler for that purchasing conference. Would you be able to tell me whether you have a Brent Carruthers registered? I know he's in town, but my friend didn't know which hotel he'd be at."

The woman typed something into a computer keyboard. He was fascinated by how quickly she could type in spite of long fingernails; they shone with a burgundy polish that looked still wet. "Yes, he's here," she said. "I'm afraid I can't give out his room number, but I could take a message for him. Did you want to leave your cell phone number, perhaps?"

Hunter looked at his watch. It was still only a little before nine o'clock, and with any luck Carruthers would still be in his room. "Could you please call his room for me? I'd like to get this out of the way as soon as possible."

After a quick call, the clerk informed Hunter that Carruthers was on his way down, so Hunter crossed the lobby to stand close to the elevators. One elevator opened and two middle aged men stepped out, paying no attention to Hunter as they passed him without interrupting their conversation. The doors of the next elevator opened to reveal a tall, tanned man with a youthful bearing. He could have been the man from the lounge. He looked directly at Hunter and raised his eyebrows.

Hunter stepped toward him. "Brent Carruthers?"

"That'd be me. How can I help you?"

Hunter extended his hand. "Hunter Rayne. I believe you may already have spoken to RCMP officers Blackwell or Pike about Mike Irwin."

The man frowned and nodded as they shook hands. "Tragic," he said. "Shocking."

"I'm assisting with the investigation, and I wondered if you could spare me a few minutes of your time. I'm trying to find out as much as I can about Mike Irwin, and what might have lead to his death."

"I don't see how I can be of much help."

"Coffee?"

"Sorry, I'm meeting someone. I don't have much time." Carruthers glanced over toward the restaurant.

"Could we just sit down for a moment? I'll be brief." Hunter knew he'd have a better chance if the man was off his feet, and his attention off the restaurant.

Carruthers hesitated, then allowed Hunter to usher him to one of a pair of chairs in the lobby. He perched on the edge of the chair, looking uncomfortable.

Hunter leaned forward, his elbows on his knees. "I understand Mike Irwin threatened you in the lounge here Friday night. What was that about?"

Carruthers rolled his eyes and shook his head. "Jesus Christ! It was about nothing. I was having a drink with a colleague, and that..." He inhaled deeply. "Irwin was joking around. Whoever said it was a threat was smoking something." His eyes widened and he raised a forefinger. "You. You're the guy who had the fight with Irwin." He got to his feet. "What the hell are you trying to pull? If anyone had a reason to kill Irwin, my money would be on you."

Hunter stood, too. "Hold on there, chief."

"The hell I will." Carruthers started to walk away, then turned to face Hunter. "If you want to ask me any more questions, do it through my lawyer."

Hunter's eyes followed the man into the restaurant. He wasn't happy with himself. He hadn't finessed that interview well at all. He was sure, however, that Carruthers was not only uncomfortable answering questions about Mike Irwin, he was also lying. Mike hadn't been joking, and Carruthers had been angry about whatever he had said.

Hunter picked up a newspaper from one of the tables in the lobby, made his way to the restaurant and asked to be seated at a vacant table not far from where Carruthers had joined a young woman. She looked like a model — blonde, perfect skin, a cream-colored sweater that begged to be stroked — and Hunter knew she must be the 'colleague' Carruthers had referred to. Carruthers scowled at him as he approached. Hunter smiled and nodded, said a cheery "Good morning, Brent," and seated himself with his back to the couple.

"Who's that?" he heard the young woman ask.

He couldn't make out Carruthers' response, but the fact that Carruthers had lowered his voice, and that subsequently the young woman did, too, told Hunter enough for now. It might be that they had something to hide.

Hunter ordered coffee and toast, mentally calculating how much drinks and meals had already cost him since he'd arrived in Whistler. Another couple of days, and he'd be in overdraft. He unfolded the paper and scanned the front page. 'Chairlift Murder Victim from California' was continued on page two, but had little additional information beyond the discovery of the body.

"There you are," said a woman's voice. "Mind if I join you?"

Hunter looked up to see the watching woman approaching his table. "Stella?"

She shook her head. "No. It's Meredith. Meredith Travis." She smiled as she opened a menu. "I believe you and I have a common interest."

Alora Magee moved forward a few ski lengths in the lineup to the Emerald quad chairlift. She adjusted her goggles with a gloved finger, ski pole dangling from her hand. The sun was out, but it was cold. She had begun to regret her conversation with Hunter the night before. It wasn't often that she encountered a man she felt attracted to, and she'd enjoyed the excitement of getting to know him. Wasn't the mystery and uncertainty the spice of a new relationship in the first place? Wasn't it possible that his aloofness was a result of old fashioned values, and not an indication that he didn't find her attractive? She remembered the kiss they'd shared, and felt a tingle down her spine. He had a power in him, an intensity. You could see it in his eyes, and she had felt it when he held her, however brief their embrace had been.

"You a single?" Again, louder. "Are you a single? Ma'am?"

Alora looked up to see the lift attendant motioning her forward.

"Room for a single here," he said. "Hurry!"

The two foursomes of skiers in front of her made room for her to get by, and she was positioned in front of the chair just in time to be scooped up and lifted off the platform. She could feel the cold bench even through her ski pants as she wriggled over slightly to the right, enjoying the slight bounce and swing of the chair. Her pole clicked against her neighbor's ski. "Sorry," she said, looking over at the woman beside her.

The woman glanced at her, saying, "It's okay," then leaned closer, staring intently. She lifted up her goggles and said, "Do you know who I am?"

"Oh! You're Mike's..." Alora was stunned. With all of the people boarding lifts at Whistler on a Sunday, she was sitting next to Mike's widow. She didn't know what to say, but wanted somehow to express her sympathy, and more than her sympathy, her sense of kinship with the woman. "I'm so sorry for your loss," she said, then reached over and laid her hand on the woman's arm. "I truly am sorry."

"I'm Kelly," the woman said. "Your name's Alora, isn't it?"

Alora nodded. She peered at the two skiers on the other side of Kelly. Young boys, German flag emblems on their toques. They rode in silence for a minute. A group of young snowboarders on the chair ahead broke into the chorus of Queen's 'We are the Champions'. No time for losers. It occurred to Alora that it was an appropriate anthem for her and Kelly today.

Kelly spoke again. "I— uh— Beth, Mike's mother, doesn't understand why you left him." She smiled sadly. "But I do."

"I'm so sad for your children. How are they taking it?"

Kelly sighed. "They're so young. We told them that Daddy went to Heaven. Corenna — that's the two year old — she keeps asking when he'll be back. Jordan's five. He put his little arms around my neck and said, I'll look after you now, Mommy. I won't make you cry, he said." She wiped a tear away with a gloved knuckle. "He's my little man."

Alora squeezed her arm, and they fell silent. The chair approached a tower, with a louder hum and a soft clunk, then the noise receded and they were gliding through the cold, clear air. The two teenage boys sitting to Kelly's left stared straight ahead, their skis bobbing gently to unheard rhythms. Alora saw wires leading from under their toques into their collars.

"What will you do now?"

"I guess I'll have to go back home and settle things. There's the house, three cars, all of Mike's things. Beth volunteered to take the kids, but I don't know. I'd like to sell everything as soon as possible and move to Seattle, start fresh in a new city."

"Don't you have family?"

Kelly shook her head, staring up toward the highest peak. "Only Beth and John, and my kids."

They watched in silence as three snowboarders expertly carved their way across the wide slope beneath the moving chairs.

"Do you think it's wrong of me to be skiing today?" Kelly didn't look at Alora as she spoke.

Alora shook her head. "No. I understand. I can't imagine sitting in a hotel trying to deal with... something like that." And then, "If you want to talk about it, please, go ahead. I imagine talking could help you make sense of how you feel."

"Funny you should put it that way, to make sense of how I feel. That's the trouble, isn't it? You of all people can understand me." She paused as another tower hummed past. "I never thought, even deep inside, that I hated him, and early on for sure I thought I loved him. I *did* love him. I'm sorry that he was the way he was, but as hard as I try, I can't be sorry that he's gone. And that makes me feel guilty. I should be sorry. I should be grieving for my husband."

"I don't think I hated him either, so much as I hated what he did to me. He made my life ugly and unpleasant. He made me less of a human being, somehow. He should have been a kinder man." Alora tapped the tip of her ski gently with a pole. "He had it all: a beautiful wife, two beautiful children, a good career. " She suddenly realized that she was only assuming that Mike was abusive to Kelly. "Did he hit you?"

Kelly's shoulders slumped and she sighed. "He never hit me, exactly. He would grab me by the arms, or sometimes by the front of my sweater, and push me up against a wall, and yell into my face," she shook her head and screwed up her face as if she'd tasted something bitter. "Sometimes his spit hit me in the eye. Or he would push me so I stumbled, or throw me back into a chair, or on to the bed. And he would push things into my face — dirty laundry, or a smelly dishcloth, or..." She paused, pressing the back of a hand to her mouth. "It wasn't the physical so much. He made me feel stupid and incompetent and... in front of the kids. He took away my confidence, and my freedom, and my friends, for God's sake! He wouldn't let me see my friends!"

Alora slipped the ski pole off of her left hand and moved it to her right, then put her arm around the younger woman and hugged her. "I know. I know. You're free now. It'll be okay. We're both free now." Kelly turned to face her and Alora gave her a reassuring smile. "It's okay to feel that way. It's okay to be happy that he's gone."

"Yeah?"

"Yeah."

Kelly hugged her back, and gave a little laugh. The laugh grew, a small step away from hysteria, and Alora tried but couldn't keep herself from joining in. The two women stopped abruptly and looked at each other in shocked silence for a few brief seconds, then started to laugh again. Alora felt giddy with a sense of freedom, and would bet that Kelly felt the same.

"It's only right that you came skiing. Look. Look." Alora waved her arm first in one direction, then in the other. "What better symbol of freedom than the view from a mountain? The clean snow, the mountain air, the vast distance you can see from here. The sky's the limit, honey. You're free to be who you really are. We both are."

They were still smiling when the chair reached the top.

The Sea to Sky highway between Whistler and Squamish had been plowed since yesterday's heavy snowfall, and Hunter made good time. The waitress, a cheerful older woman with a stubby pony tail, was just warming up his coffee from a fresh pot when Dan Sorenson burst through the double doors, stamped the snow off his boots, and strode up to the booth.

"What's the special?" he asked the waitress. Even when he was using his inside voice, Sorry sounded like a boom box. He looked taller than his six foot three, had a massive chest above a slight paunch, and even when not riding his old Harley, he dressed like the biker he was. He slid onto the bench across from Hunter. "What're you having?"

Hunter shook his head in wonder. They hadn't seen each other for months, and all Sorry could talk about was lunch. The waitress told them there was no special. Hunter ordered a bowl of clam chowder and a toasted shrimp sandwich. Sorry ordered the chowder with a Triple-O burger, fries and a Caesar salad.

"Oh, and a milkshake. Chocolate," he added as the waitress turned to go. "One bill. You're buying, aren't you, Hunter?" Sorry shrugged out of his jacket, pulled a large envelope, folded in four, out of the inside pocket. "Here's some stuff from the fat broad," he said.

"Elspeth. Her name's Elspeth, and she'll be signing your paycheck," said Hunter, extracting two sheets of paper from the folded envelope and trying to smooth them out on the table. There were three photographs on the top page, two on the other.

"But don't she remind you of the Fat Broad in the comic strip? Hey. Who's the kid?"

Hunter didn't answer. He was studying what was probably a school portrait, in the black and white quality typical of a fax, of Adam Marsh. Ken's son. Helen's son. He hadn't seen Adam since the boy was eight — maybe nine — round-cheeked, always grinning and full of energy. Until Ken's funeral. At the cemetery the boy had taken a cue from his mother and stood quietly, somber — stoic even. He felt a heaviness in his chest as he pictured Helen, sadly dignified, dry eyed, acknowledging the condolences of Mounties in red serge, himself included. "I'm sorry," he'd said, holding her hand a little longer than the others did.

"Thank you," she'd said, and a look passed between them. They shared a secret.

The boy whose head and shoulders appeared in the photograph had grown mature enough to exhibit his father's mouth and jaw, his father's nose, and his mother's eyes. In a second photo on the page, the boy stood holding a bicycle with fat tires. He wore the rebel uniform of a nineties teenager. Limp oversized shirt, unkempt hair, the look on his face was impatient, a little annoyed, as if he were saying, "Hurry up, Mom, I'm late." A third photo was of two boys — Adam and a taller, dark-haired boy — and the hand-written note across the photo identified the second boy as Nathan LeBlanc. Nathan's sleeves were rolled up to reveal heavy tattoos. Adam, if not smiling, at least looked pleasantly at the camera, but the other boy's face displayed a dark scowl. They both looked so young to Hunter, and he couldn't help reflecting how much more worldly teenage boys had become since his own youth. What happened to playing scrub softball and going bowling and watching TV westerns in your spare time?

"Who were your heroes growing up?" he asked Sorry. His own heroes were the Lone Ranger and Roy Rogers. Becoming a Mountie seemed like a modern alternative to a crusading cowboy.

"What makes you think I've grown up?" Sorry threw back his head and laughed at his own joke. His hair was so blond it was almost white, and it fell in unruly waves almost to his shoulders. He sported a blond moustache but no beard. El had once referred to him as the Biking Viking.

"No. Seriously. When you were fourteen or fifteen, who were your role models?"

The biker's face grew thoughtful. In a surprisingly soft voice, he said, "Fourteen? I only had one role model." His fingers grabbed a packet of sugar from a little ceramic dish on the table. "My dad. You know. The guy who knew how to throw a football, catch a trout, use a shotgun, all that stuff I used to think was important."

Hunter watched Sorry's face closely. His eyes were on the sugar packet but his thoughts seemed far away.

"Are you a lot like him?"

Sorry looked up. "Not a bit." He shook the sugar packet and ripped the corner off, held it over Hunter's coffee cup. "More sugar?"

Hunter shook his head and covered the cup with his hand.

"Nope. Last time I said more than two words to my dad, he told me I was a waste of skin. Had to be over twenty years ago."

Hunter raised his eyebrows. "Is your dad still alive?"

"As far as I know. I talked to my mom at Christmas, and she didn't say he'd died or nothin'." He tipped his head back and poured the contents of the sugar packet into his mouth, then made a face as he swallowed it.

"You had a fight?"

Sorry shrugged. "When I left high school. I wasn't a kid anymore. I wanted to explore the world. He wanted me to work in the family business. A hardware store. Can you imagine me spending my life in a small town hardware store?"

"So you left town on your bike."

"Nope. I had an old woody. The bike came later, after I moved north." The waitress returned with Sorry's milkshake and he took a long sip before continuing. "I've dropped in to visit my mom at least every few years, and I've hardly said fuck-all to my old man."

"His choice or yours?"

"He pretends to be busy at that damn hardware store all day, and I just visit with my mom at their place, never stay for dinner. That's not like me, is it?" He snorted and stroked his moustache. "I guess we're more alike than I thought."

"Make the first move, then."

"What if he doesn't want to see me? I'm a waste of skin, remember?"

"Come on. Twenty years is a long time to get hung up on one single remark. If your dad dies before one of you does something to mend the rift, you'll regret it. You're a father now yourself. You love your kids. You don't just switch off how you feel about your own child."

They fell silent as the waitress set down their meals. Hunter tucked the papers back into the envelope.

"Besides, didn't you ever say something to Mo or the kids that you didn't really mean because you were hurt or angry? Or maybe just tired and frustrated?"

"I guess. But you know me. I've got a big mouth and nobody takes me seriously anyway." He picked up his burger, pulled out a piece of lettuce that was hanging loose, and opened wide to take a bite, then paused. "You're right. You're always right. How can you live with yourself?"

Hunter was busy with his clam chowder and felt no need to answer anyway. He couldn't help reflecting that he usually didn't take his own good advice. Although they hadn't fought, he hadn't spoken more than a few words to his own father in the past year. His parents had moved to Hawaii, something his father had insisted on in return for agreeing to move back to the Canadian prairies so Hunter's mother could be close to her parents in their declining years. He had spent the seven years prior to his retirement as a railway executive in Winnipeg, Manitoba. Hunter only kept in touch by telephone on special occasions, and his mother usually did most of the talking.

"So what's happening with this murder thing?" Sorry asked between bites. "Are you really a suspect? Did you do it?"

"Of course not! But yes, I could be considered a suspect. I had a ... sort of a fight in public with the victim the night before he was killed."

"How did he die?"

"The police won't discuss it with me, but they let slip to the friend I'm staying with — he's also ex-RCMP — that he'd been shot in the back of the head, right at the top of the spine. Instant death, no hope of survival."

"Sounds like an execution. A professional hit?"

"Could be. I'm trying to get the lowdown on his business dealings. It makes sense that that's the most likely scenario where a professional killer would become involved."

"I saw a show on TV the other day where the wife hired some guy to kill her husband for the insurance. She thought so, anyway. Turns out she was trying to hire an undercover cop." He laughed loud enough to turn heads.

Hunter shrugged. "The wife wouldn't be my first choice, but it is a possibility. That's one thing I learned about working homicides. Always keep an open mind. Tunnel vision on the part of the police has put a lot of innocent people in jail, and even one is too many."

Sorry looked up from his Caesar salad. "Especially if it's you."

After they finished their lunch and Hunter handed Sorry the keys to his Freightliner, along with a hand-drawn map of where he was to pick up the trailer to take to California and an admonition not to smoke in the truck, it was after twelve o'clock. Hunter headed back up the highway to Whistler to meet with Meredith Travis, the woman who had originally introduced herself as Stella, but he wasn't sure whether it would get him any closer to the truth about what happened to Mike Irwin.

She had approached him about joining forces to investigate Mike Irwin's death. Hunter wasn't sure how to take it. She could just be trying to divert suspicion away from herself or her client, but then again, wasn't he doing exactly the same thing to get himself off the suspect list? He had told her that he would consider her suggestion, and meet with her when he got back from Squamish with his decision.

He was trying to determine if there was a down side to working with her, and weigh it against what she could bring to the investigation that he couldn't. She had pointed out that she was in a position to talk to others at the conference without arousing suspicion, since she was ostensibly one of them. He would certainly like to know what she could pick up about Brent Carruthers and the young woman he'd been having breakfast with, the one Mike Irwin had threatened to expose. And maybe Meredith could find out just how serious a threat it was, given that Carruthers was openly spending time with the woman in the hotel. It couldn't be totally clandestine if they weren't trying to hide their relationship, although they had arrived for breakfast separately.

What was her motivation for cooperating with Hunter? To plant information was the first possibility that occurred to him. Misinformation. If not, what did she think he could do that she couldn't? Perhaps she saw an advantage in his RCMP background and his connection with the investigating officers because of it. Perhaps it was his relationship with Alora.

What relationship? He hadn't seen Alora since she'd effectively kissed him off the night before, but Meredith Travis didn't know that.

Hunter had decided to play along with her and see where it led.

He parked the Pontiac in a free lot and made his way along cleared paths through Whistler Village to the arranged meeting place, the lobby of a small hotel not far from the Coast Peaks. The icy cold of the concrete and cobblestones penetrated the thin soles of his cowboy boots and he paused in the entrance to stamp his feet, more to encourage circulation to his frozen toes than to shed the clumps of snow clinging to his heels.

Meredith was seated on a sofa near the front of the lobby, and stood when he approached. He had seen two versions of her on Friday night, and a third version Saturday evening. Sunday's version appealed to him the most. She wore jeans and a leather bomber jacket with a fur lined hood, a combination that showed off the slender curve of her hips. Lace-up snow boots hugged her calves, almost to the knee. No noticeable makeup, just a fresh healthy glow and glossy lips.

"Want to grab a coffee?" she asked.

He shook his head, then changed his mind. A hot drink would be good. "Maybe a hot chocolate or something. Is there a cheap spot...?"

She nodded and motioned him to follow before he could finish his sentence. He was relieved to see that it was a casual, cafeteria-style location frequented by skiers fresh off the slopes. The downside was that the only empty chairs were at a window counter near the outside entrance, with cold skiers regularly passing by accompanied by an invisible cloak of cold air. Dozens of spirited conversations clashed in the room, almost guaranteeing that their own quiet words would go no farther than their own ears. Hunter picked up a hot tea for her and a hot chocolate for himself. It still cost him the better part of a ten dollar bill, almost sixty miles worth of diesel for his Freightliner at 1997 prices.

"Well?" she said as he settled himself onto a wooden stool to her left.

"You make a good point," he said, stirring some sugar into his mug. "You're already perfectly set up to investigate his industry ties."

"Not only that," she said. "I already have some background on the guy."

"What's in it for you?" He looked at her sideways as he took a cautious sip of hot chocolate.

She waited for a laughing trio of snowboarders to pass before replying. "Credibility. I'm an outsider. I was, for all intents and purposes, stalking the victim prior to his death. I am here under an assumed name. You think the cops will be eager to believe any self-serving information I can provide them with?" She raised her eyebrows as if to say, "Well, do you?"

He shrugged.

"I saw you with the security boss at the GM that night," she said. "You're tight with him. He's tight with the cops. You vouch for me, and I'll give you information you can use."

"How can I be sure you're not setting me up?"

"Meaning?"

"I'm the dupe feeding misinformation to the police?"

She smiled at the window. "The being sure part is up to you. You want some references? Maybe a polygraph?"

It was Hunter's turn to smile. Risk versus reward. He would have to take a chance on her or find another way to get inside information.

"Got any questions for me?" she asked. "Go on. Give me a try." She winked at him as she raised the mug of tea to her lips.

"Were you following him yesterday morning?"

"No such luck." She smiled ruefully. "He left the hotel before I was ready to tail him. Try another question."

"Brent Carruthers," he said. "That stud Irwin threatened to expose to his boss. You were there that night. What's the story?"

She looked sideways at him. "It just so happens that I ran into his little blonde friend in the hot tub yesterday afternoon. It's a great way to relax after a day's skiing. We struck up a conversation, as women tend to do, about the men in our lives. I told her I had a hush-hush relationship with a wealthy married man in Florida. She informed me that she had come to join her fiancé here while he was out of town and it was great to be able to spend time together. She said they had to be more discreet when they were back in L.A., because her fiancé worked for her dad's company and they weren't ready to tell her father about their relationship.

"I asked her why it would matter. She said her boyfriend was an older man, twice divorced, and had a bit of a reputation, but that he was a changed man since he met her."

"According to him?"

"Precisely." She smiled and nodded. "He'd given her an engagement ring — she showed it to me, a moderately priced diamond — but they didn't want her dad to find out about their relationship until the time was right."

"Did she happen to mention how they met?"

"I happened to ask her just that."

"And?"

"A fundraiser art auction. Her father's pet charity. She was there with her father and mother. It seems that Brent — she actually called him 'my Brent' — was passionate about Rwandan refugees as well." She sipped her tea. "She and Brent were admiring the same piece of art, and he complimented her on her good taste."

"Did he buy it for her?"

She made a face at him. "Of course not. Brent's not quite in their league, financially. Her words. That's why her father isn't likely to approve, until he gets to know Brent better, of course. He's such a talented and compassionate human being, after all."

Hunter smiled. He liked her. She was sharp as a tack and had a good sense of humor. He leaned toward her and held out his hand.

She smiled back as she shook his hand. "Okay, partner. Tit for tat. Who's the woman?"

"When did you start investigating Mike?"

She frowned, but didn't object. "About six weeks ago."

"What did you find out about his ex-wife?"

"Her maiden name was Alora McGuire. They were married only briefly. She took out a restraining order against him when they split up some years ago, and reapplied for one just last summer under her new name of Alora Magee. I just didn't get around to finding her photo."

"You already know more about her than I do."

"So she *is* Alora Magee."

He nodded.

"Did she know Irwin was going to be here?"

"She says not."

"She says not," repeated Meredith with a series of small nods. "I expect she was pretty tired of the bastard. She thought she was free of him, started this great new career, and suddenly he turns up again — like dog shit on a shoe."

Hunter leaned back and crossed his arms, looking up at her from under his brows. "I expect she was."

Meredith Travis was looking at him sideways again. "So, Mr. Chivalry Personified." She paused, a half smile playing on her lips. Before he could protest, she added, "Don't forget, I saw you in action coming to her defense when he started using foul language. Twice!" She held up two fingers, then turned her hand around and pointed one finger at his chest.

"So-o-o, partner. Still think it's me who's setting you up?"

CHAPTER
SEVEN

Sundays were usually quiet business-wise at Watson Transportation, but they had a charm of their own. Elspeth Watson habitually started the day out with a couple of Egg McMuffins from McDonald's, accompanied by hash browns and a large coffee, while her little black half-Spitz, Peterbilt, ate his breakfast. He'd always look up at her as he crunched a mouthful of kibble, his curled tail wiggling as if he were saying "Thanks for the grub, Mom." She turned on the local country music station, JR-FM, so it played quietly in the office and louder in the warehouse. If there were no pressing phone calls to and from drivers and it wasn't raining too hard, she would usually take little Pete for a wander outside in the truck yard before settling down to paperwork. Sundays were great for catching up on filing and bookkeeping, since there weren't many interruptions.

The drivers kidded her about her devotion to work, and her answer was always the same. "It ain't work if you're having fun." And she *was* having fun. She loved the sight and sound of big diesel rigs, loved the banter with the drivers, and loved the rush when she secured a new load. She thrived on the stress of handling calls from customers when deliveries were late, and the challenge of working out schedules so she could get the trucks there on time. The whole trucking business was a game she loved to play, more than she'd enjoyed the tedium of sitting in a truck as a driver. The drivers were the chess pieces, the dispatcher was the player. Her office wasn't fancy and the warehouse had seen better days, but it was her domain.

El knew a lot of the drivers figured her for a butch dyke, but she had no interest in women. She worked in a man's world and it would have been stupid to dress in girly clothes, wear makeup or have some fussy hair style. Besides, she was a big boned gal, just a couple of inches shy of six feet and close to three hundred pounds, a comfortable mix of muscle and fat as far as she was concerned. She could lift heavy boxes and climb over skids when she had to. With her job and her size it would be silly to dress up. Even when she'd started out as a driver, she liked being 'one of the guys', joking with the drivers and the boys in the warehouse. Life was good.

Hunter Rayne had been one of her drivers for a few years now, and she considered him a friend. She bossed him around like she did all of the drivers — she had to; it was the only way to keep their respect and no dispatcher could afford to let a driver call the shots — but she had a lot of respect for the guy. He seemed to possess an inner strength and an outer confidence that few people in her world had, probably from being a cop for so many years. When he asked for her help getting information, she was tickled pink and eager to get started.

"Blue Hills Industries," she muttered to herself. She fired up her computer and started a search through her database of customers, green characters scrolling on a black screen. "Bantam ... Barnhart ... Bentall ... Blackwater ... Bluebird ... ah-ha! ... Blue Hills." She moved the cursor to highlight the probill number beside the name and brought up the particulars of the shipment. It had been about a year and a half ago, and was a collect shipment consigned to one of her regular customers in Abbotsford. She could tell by the truck number that it had been handled by a U.S. based driver that didn't do much work for her. She didn't expect to get much information from him, but the customer could be a different story.

And the customs broker, she realized. The consignee's broker was Hastings & Toop, and she had a good friend there by the name of Marilyn Jenkins, or MJ. Sunday was not a good day to call a customs broker, and neither was Monday morning. Monday mornings were crazy for El as well, so she resigned herself to following up with MJ on Monday afternoon. MJ was always up for a rum and coke after work, and El would do her best to free up her own schedule to make it happen.

She kept on clearing up paperwork until her stomach reminded her it was long past lunch time. She had some tinned soup for emergencies, but decided to stave off her hunger with a handful of roasted nuts and a mug of instant cocoa. Just one driver to get out on the road and she could call it quits for this Sunday and go grab a proper meal. She swallowed the last few mouthfuls of cocoa in a hurry as Peterbilt started dancing around her chair, a sure sign that he needed to do his 'business'. El shrugged on her jacket and began humming along with Toby Keith and "Dream Walkin'" as she accompanied Pete out behind the warehouse.

The little guy had tucked his butt under him and was just laying a couple of neat turds in a patch of weeds beside the chain link fence when she heard a car with a hole in its muffler round the corner into the yard. It only took a couple of seconds for El to recognize the battered yellow Volvo that belonged to Dan Sorenson.

"About fuckin' time!" she hollered as Sorry pulled up beside The Blue Knight, Hunter's workhorse of a 1991 tandem axle Freightliner. It was a no frills truck with a basic sleeper, but Hunter kept its 350 Cummins in good running order. She always thought it suited him. Modest on the outside, powerful on the inside.

"Don't park your fuckin' jalopy where the trucks park! Four wheelers over there!" She pulled a hand out of the warmth of her jacket pocket and pointed to the area designated for driver parking. "Oh! I'm sorry. I didn't see your wife. Hello, Simone."

Simone smiled and gave her a cheerful little wave. "Hello, El. So nice to see you again. How's little Pete?" She stepped out of the passenger side of the Volvo and walked around the back of the car, then crouched so she could scratch the little dog's ears. Simone was a slender and graceful woman with a musical French Canadian accent and a gentle nature, and it always amazed El that such a beautiful girl seemed so happy to be Sorry's wife. The back door opened and two young children scrambled out to join her.

"Oh, shit!" El covered her mouth with her hands. "Your kids, too. Me and my big mouth." Sorry was now standing beside her, and she punched his shoulder. "You shoulda said something, you big lug."

"If you would just shut the heck up for five seconds and let me speak, woman!" boomed Sorry. "Sasha. Bruno. Say hello to the big lady."

The two kids looked up briefly from petting Peterbilt and said in unison "Hello, big lady." One was a little girl about seven years old, the other a little boy of about five. They were both as blonde as Sorry.

"Her name is Miss Watson," Sorry said.

"Hello, Miss Watson," they chimed together again.

"You prick," El said under her breath to Sorry. "Hi, Sasha. Bruno. You can call me El."

"Back in the car," Simone said to the two kids. "Vite! Dans la voiture. Il fait froid." Then to Sorry. "Get your bag, mon coco. We should let you go to work."

"Hang on. Come for a kiss, kids." Sorry squatted and held his arms wide, and the two children tumbled into his hug. He planted a noisy kiss on each child's cheek. "You be good for Mom, now. I'll see you in a few days." He grabbed a big duffle back out of the trunk of the Volvo and dropped it on the ground, then wrapped his arms around his wife. "Bye, Mo. I'll call." They exchanged a tender kiss.

Looking away, El scooped up Peterbilt and gave him a hug.

"Love you guys," Sorry said, throwing a series of big kisses at his wife and kids as Simone backed the Volvo into a turn. "Bye."

"You know where to pick up the trailer?" El immediately got down to business. Sorry was the kind of guy who needed a firm hand. "You need a map of Redding?"

"Yes, boss lady. No, boss lady." He pulled some keys out of his pocket and unlocked the Freightliner's door, climbed up to the cab and tossed his duffle bag over the seat.

"Fire it up, buddy." El put Pete back on the ground and turned toward the office. She yelled back at Sorry over her shoulder, "Let the engine warm up while you come in for your paperwork." She could hardly wait for him to leave the yard. Somewhere in New Westminster was a pepperoni, mushroom and green pepper pizza with her name on it, and she knew just where to find it.

After Meredith Travis left the restaurant, Hunter felt a need to speak to one of the investigating officers about the case, although he wasn't sure it would help. He pulled Shane Blackwell's card out of his wallet and punched in the number but it went straight to voicemail. He left his number, and zipping up his sheepskin jacket, headed back outside. A wind had come up, so he pulled his collar up over his neck and plunged his hands deep in his pockets. By the time he reached his car, his toes and ears were so cold they hurt.

He'd had enough of sitting around in Whistler hotels and restaurants, and it was too cold to sit in his car, so he headed back to Tom Halsey's chalet, letting himself in with the key Tom had given him. Tom would be back in Whistler around dinner time, he knew, bringing his wife back with him. Hunter had expected to be back on the road before Tom's wife got home, and wasn't feeling real comfortable about extending his stay. He couldn't afford a hotel, and going back home to his basement suite in North Vancouver was an unattractive option, given it would involve several hours of travel daily on the Sea to Sky highway in winter conditions if he wanted to continue looking for answers in Whistler.

He turned on the gas fireplace in the living room and pulled a chair up close to it before he tried Shane Blackwell again, and this time the burly staff sergeant answered on the first ring.

Hunter identified himself and said, "I realize this is a little unorthodox, but I'd appreciate the opportunity to go over some of the circumstances surrounding the last days of Mike Irwin's life. Obviously, I'd like to be taken off the suspect list as soon as possible, but I'm also developing a personal interest in finding his killer. I would hate to see the wrong person accused." This morning he would have wanted to see Alora ruled out as a suspect as well, although Meredith Travis had given him pause. What were the chances he could have been set up? Was it possible that Alora had learned of Mike's planned conference before she'd called to invite him to Whistler?

The detective on the other end of the line cleared his throat. "Hunh. Can you be at the station in fifteen minutes?"

"I'm on my way."

Hunter switched the fireplace back off and, his jacket still on anyway, was on the road in less than a minute. It was a ten minute drive to the RCMP detachment on Blackcomb Way. Fortunately there was parking just outside and Hunter was at the reception counter pretty much on time. He wasn't waiting long before Staff Sergeant Shane Blackwell had him shown into an interview room. Hunter sat at one side of a small nondescript table, and Blackwell pulled up a chair with his back to the door. Hunter turned his chair so his back was to the wall.

"Okay, shoot," said the detective, leaning back in his chair.

Hunter leaned forward, his elbows on his knees. "I'd like to help," he said. "I know it sounds unorthodox — maybe downright unacceptable — but I'd like to help find Mike Irwin's killer."

The big man snorted, then began to laugh. "What makes you think I'd invite a suspect to help in a murder investigation?"

Hunter nodded. "I know," he said. "Look. I spent a lot of years in your position, and I have no doubt that my reaction to the idea would have been the same as yours. All I can ask is that you imagine yourself in my position."

Blackwell opened his mouth, but Hunter held up a hand.

"Think about it. A few years down the road, you're retired from the force, you unexpectedly find that you and a friend of yours are suspects in a murder investigation. You're not under arrest, but you're under a cloud of suspicion and have been told you can't resume your normal life until you've been cleared. You know, of course, that you're innocent. Do you think, with your training and experience, you'd be able to sit back and twiddle your thumbs until the police had the right man — or woman — in custody?"

Blackwell tilted his head, his eyes focused on a point somewhere beyond the corner of the ceiling, his thumb idly stroking the edge of his jaw. Finally he sighed.

"Wait here," he said, and left the room.

Hunter sat back and looked around the room. He knew he was on camera, quite possibly being watched at the moment. Although he felt restless enough to pace up and down the small floor, he just stuck his hands in his jacket pockets and began to tap his feet.

Almost twenty minutes later, the detective opened the door of the room and motioned for Hunter to follow him. Soon Hunter was seated in a more spacious room with a big metal desk and matching credenza. A window behind the desk showed that the daylight was beginning to fade. Blackwell moved to sit on the other side of the desk, while Sergeant Colin Pike stood and extended his hand to Hunter before taking a chair to Hunter's right.

The two detectives exchanged glances, then Blackwell pursed his lips and cleared his throat before speaking. "This is completely off the record," he began, looking straight at Hunter. "You understand?"

"Yes."

"Colin," he nodded at the tall young officer, "has made some phone calls. He checked with your former commanding officer, as well as several members that he was aware you'd been in contact with since your resignation, including Staff Sergeant Al Kowalski of the Burnaby detachment. Colin?"

The young man started speaking with a serious look on his face, but a twinkle in his eye. Hunter reflected again what a likeable man Colin was. "They speak very highly of you. They said that in addition to being a very skilled detective during your years on the force, you always had the utmost respect for the law. They were quite convinced that you would never take vigilante action, and that you most certainly were innocent of the murder of Mike Irwin. Al Kowalski's comment was that if you had killed the man, he had no doubt that you would have promptly shown up at the detachment to turn yourself in."

Hunter caught the senior detective rolling his eyes. He wondered if they found it amusing, and whether he was some kind of fool for taking justice so seriously. He'd once been called a 'goody two shoes' for his refusal to break the rules, and as much as he hated to let the remark bother him, it did.

Pike continued. "Kowalski said you had assisted him in the past, and even helped an outside agency — L.A., wasn't it? — solve a case. He recommended we let you in on the investigation on a limited basis, and to label you as an informant in the official reports. Does that work for you?"

Hunter said yes.

"Before we let you have any information," said Blackwell, "we'd like you to share with us first."

"He did give us the information on Meredith Travis," said Pike.

"That's a start. Go ahead, Rayne. Give us what you've got so far."

Hunter rubbed his jaw, taking a moment to consider what to say. "Keep in mind, detectives, that I'm like a blind man who's been asked to describe an elephant. I don't have any facts surrounding the man's death."

"Understood."

"Okay. I've seen the man in action myself, and so far I've spoken with four people who have a longer history with him than I do. From my own encounters with the man, I can confirm that he was a bully and a mean drunk. To say he had an abrasive manner would be an understatement. He was rude and antagonistic. I have no doubt that he rubbed a lot of people the wrong way.

"I first heard of him from his ex-wife, Alora Magee. I met Ms. Magee last summer in Los Angeles when we were involved in the case you mentioned earlier. She was the lawyer for one of the suspects arrested for murder. At one point, Ms. Magee stopped answering her home telephone and then had her number changed. Although she didn't say anything about it at the time, it was because Mike Irwin had just managed to get her home number from the law

100

firm she was working at, and began making harassing phone calls. I should say, resumed making harassing phone calls.

"I'm sure you've already received this information from Ms. Magee yourself, but she left him and filed for divorce after he became physically abusive. Prior to that he was controlling and emotionally abusive. He subsequently attacked her in front of a classroom of kids when she worked as a teacher, and she was forced to take out a restraining order against him. She took out another one this past summer."

Hunter noticed that Pike had moved his chair closer to the desk and was furiously taking notes in a spiral-bound notebook.

"I also spoke to a man by the name of Todd Milton, who has known Mike Irwin both socially and professionally for a number of years." Hunter outlined the information he'd received from Todd, including Mike's employment history and his recent encounter with Brent Carruthers.

The senior detective nodded. "We spoke to Milton as well."

"Mike's father, John, didn't have much to say that would be of use in the investigation. He and his wife live in Seattle, and they haven't had much contact with their son in recent years." Hunter remembered what John Irwin had said, that sometimes there's no second chance to make it up to loved ones. If the police had now ruled Hunter out as a suspect, shouldn't he leave Whistler and go look for young Adam Marsh in Vancouver before it was too late? He imagined Helen sitting at home in Calgary, waiting helplessly by the telephone for a call from Adam or himself, relying on Hunter to do the leg work, while he remained in Whistler trying to investigate the death of a stranger instead of doing something that could save the life of his best friend's son.

"Go on," prompted Blackwell.

"Brent Carruthers was not prepared to talk to me about it. Can I assume that you've spoken to him? Did he cooperate?"

"What else have you got to tell us?"

Hunter sighed. "Meredith Travis." He paused, considering how much to share with the police. "You have more leverage than I do.

She knows a lot about Mike Irwin because she's been investigating him for the past month. Unfortunately, due to client confidentiality, she isn't willing to share everything she's learned about his business dealings. Obviously, there was something worth hiring a private investigator for, and I doubt that Meredith comes cheap.

"From my blind man's perspective, I would say that this was a premeditated killing, precipitated by the arrival of a good opportunity. I am only guessing at the manner of death. I have had no opportunity to question witnesses at the crime scene or examine the location." He gestured at each detective in turn. "You have. What can you tell me?" With that, he leaned back in his chair and crossed his arms over his chest.

The two detectives exchanged glances, then Blackwell said, "Can we get you a coffee? Colin and I are just going out to pick up some for ourselves."

"Sure." Hunter decided that if the RCMP detectives weren't forthcoming, but agreed to officially rule him out as a suspect, he would leave for Vancouver as soon as he cleared his belongings out of Tom Halsey's chalet. No. He owed it to Alora to tell her he was leaving. Meredith, too. The question would be whether he should try to talk to Alora in person, or just call her on the phone.

Twilight seeped into the room as he waited for Pike and Blackwell to return. He looked at his watch. Sorry should be picking up the load in Port Kells within the next hour or so, and hitting the border with it by about six o'clock. A newspaper lay on the corner of the desk, so Hunter picked it up, then got up to switch on the ceiling lights. Just then the door opened, and the two detectives came in, Pike handing Hunter a mug of coffee. The navy blue mug had the RCMP crest on the side, *Maintiens Le Droit* wrapped around the head of a buffalo at its center. Maintain the law. Hunter had one just like it at home.

Blackwell closed the window blinds before sitting down. "You're on. Given your background as a homicide detective, we'd be foolish not to take advantage of your help."

The younger detective had opened a file folder on the desk in front of him, then started flipping through the pages of his notebook.

"Right now," Blackwell continued, "Colin will go over what we've got so far, including the preliminary report from the medical examiner, and tomorrow morning at first light ... ," he took a sip of his coffee, then put down his mug and almost smiled, pointing first at Hunter and then at himself. "Tomorrow, we ski."

Hunter thought about what he'd just learned about Mike Irwin's death as he sat trying to keep from shivering on the cold vinyl seat of his old Pontiac. He had turned the heat on full blast to defrost the windshield, but would have to wait for the engine to warm up before there was any significant change in the temperature inside the car.

Based on initial examination of the body, Mike Irwin had been shot at close range with what appeared to have been a relatively small bore but lethal gun. The entrance wound was close to the base of the skull, and the bullet would have instantly destroyed the brain stem, shutting down heart beat, respiration and consciousness in the blink of an eye. It was quick and it was clean. Mike Irwin had been executed.

That raised the possibility that the murder was a professional hit, but how did the killer engineer boarding the chairlift alone with his victim? Or had Mike Irwin known the killer? Is it possible that there was more than one person on the quad chair with Mike that morning? One of the first things Hunter wanted to find out was if Mike Irwin had gone skiing by himself, or if he had made arrangements to meet someone that morning. According to the detectives, the victim's wife didn't know what his plans were, other than that he intended to spend the day skiing. She had assumed that he was skiing with someone from the conference, but had no idea who that would be.

Hunter had asked a lot of questions of Blackwell and Pike that they couldn't, or wouldn't, yet answer. Where was Irwin's wife throughout the morning? What was the exact time that Mike left the hotel? Were there surveillance cameras at any of the locations Mike might have met up with his killer? Did the attendant at the bottom of the chairlift remember Mike getting on the lift, and who was on the chair with him? Did the attendant at the top of the chairlift see who else left the chair when it circled the top support without Mike getting off? Had anyone skied the possible routes the killer could have taken? Was it possible to locate and interview the skiers who were in the chair directly behind Mike and his killer?

Mike Irwin still had his cell phone and wallet inside his jacket when his body was searched. Hunter wondered why the killer hadn't taken his victim's ID to delay identification of the body. The probable answer was that the killer didn't intend to run so didn't need the extra time to get away, or else was confident that he or she wouldn't be connected with the victim.

There was also a remote possibility that the killer had secured Mike Irwin to the chair and then jumped from the chairlift before it reached the top. It had been snowing fairly heavily at the time, and if the killer timed it right, he or she might have been able to drop from the chair into a snowdrift while it was difficult for the occupants of the following chair to see. It would have been riskier — more noticeable — to drop a lifeless body from the chair. If it hadn't been snowing so hard, would the killer still have made his move that day? It confirmed to Hunter that even if the murder had been premeditated, the execution of the plan had still been dependent on the right set of circumstances.

Chair number seven had been dusted by the crime scene unit on the off chance that there would be some usable prints. There were none. Not surprising, given all of the gloved hands that had made contact with every available surface on the chair, and the fact that it was continually exposed to the elements. The only useful evidence bagged from the scene was the red scarf, which was a plain acrylic scarf five feet in length with no labels or identifying marks. It didn't look new.

Motive. Who might have wanted Mike Irwin dead? Love and money. The man had been abusive to both his wife and his ex-wife.

No doubt there was life insurance. Could there also have been another woman? Or was his wife having an affair? He was being investigated by Meredith Travis for something apparently related to his employment. Was he involved in something illegal or unethical related to huge defense contracts? Industrial espionage? How about Brent Carruthers? Who was Brent's girlfriend? Was Brent just one of several enemies Mike had made?

The Pontiac had warmed up enough to defrost the windshield, so Hunter activated the wipers to clear the melted frost, turned on the car's lights and backed out of the parking stall. Blackwell and Pike had separated to conduct a few more interviews before their day was done, and Hunter had told them he was going to look for Alora Magee. He didn't feel comfortable with the way their last evening had ended, and wanted to find her to apologize. At least, that was one reason. He couldn't help thinking about the private investigator's suggestion that Alora had set him up.

He parked underground at the Coast Peaks Hotel and took the elevator to the lobby. It was almost seven o'clock and he decided to check the coffee shop, lounge and restaurant for Alora before he tried to call her. Judging by her parting words last night, there was a good chance she wouldn't even pick up his calls, and he reasoned it would be harder for her to brush him off in person.

He saw a familiar figure sitting in the lounge, her back to the entrance. The leather jacket on the back of the chair confirmed that it was Alora, but she wasn't alone. Hunter was momentarily stunned when he realized who her companion was. It was Kelly Irwin, Mike Irwin's wife. There were no drinks on the table, so he assumed the two women had just arrived.

Before he could move, Kelly glanced toward the entrance and saw him standing there, and must have said something because Alora turned around and looked straight at him. Just as quickly, she turned away. Hunter sensed that she wasn't happy to see him. This wasn't going to be easy, and for a brief second he considered moving on. He took a deep breath and walked directly to their table.

"I've just come from a meeting with Staff Sergeant Blackwell," he began, not giving Alora an opportunity to rebuff a casual greeting. "I'm afraid it's not good news."

Kelly wasn't sure what to think about the arrival of the man she had previously assumed to be Alora's boyfriend. She didn't think he had any reason to recognize her, but he turned to her and said, "My condolences on the loss of your husband."

She whispered a 'thank you' and averted her eyes. He must wonder what she was doing here in a bar the day after her husband's death, but he didn't ask. After she and Alora had met on the chairlift, they skied together for almost two hours. That, too, seemed wrong for a grieving widow, but she would have gone crazy sitting in the hotel. Mike's mother, Beth, had urged her to go skiing, saying it would be good therapy for her and John to spend time with Mike's two children, and good therapy for Kelly to be outdoors.

"There's nothing like facing a mountain to make your troubles seem small," John had said. "Go."

When she got back to the Coast Peaks Hotel, feeling pleasantly tired from the cold air and exercise, the kids were napping and their grandparents were spending some quiet time in front of the fire. Kelly had showered and changed, then the five of them had gone downstairs for an early dinner. Kelly told John and Beth that she had met an old college girlfriend on the mountain, and that she'd been invited to join her for a drink later, but had declined. Beth would have been upset to know she was spending time with Alora. "You've probably had enough of the kids, Mom," she said, giving them an easy out.

"Nonsense," said Beth, always the strong and cheerful grandmother. "You go ahead. We'll get Jordan and Correna ready for bed, and stay in your suite until you get back. It'll do us all good." Beth had turned to Correna and tousled her hair. "Wouldn't that be fun, Sweetie? How about you, Jordan? Want to watch a video with Grandma and Grand-da?"

"It does nobody any good to sit around together moping about Mike," said John. He put down his fork and Kelly realized that none of them had eaten much dinner. She guessed that a death in the family had that affect on the appetite. "We'll have lots of evenings in Seattle to remember the good times. It'll be good for you to visit with old friends right now."

Back in the room after dinner, she felt like a school girl when she called Alora up, saying, "Mike's parents say I can come."

Alora was waiting in the lobby for her, and gave her a big hug when she arrived. "I feel like your big sister," she said with a grin. "I guess it's because we have an abusive family relationship in common, although it was a husband instead of parents."

"He wasn't all bad," Kelly found herself saying. Tender moments with Mike came unbidden to mind — him calling her 'my beautiful princess' on their honeymoon, how reverently he held his newborn children — and she began to regret coming.

"I know. I'm sorry." Alora's face grew serious, and she hugged her again, gently, and led her toward the lounge. "Let's talk about it."

And now this man had arrived. For some reason, she hadn't yet spoken to anyone except the police about who could have killed Mike — the topic seemed to be taboo around Beth — and she had told the detective that she had no idea who it could be. In her mind the killer was a nameless, faceless man in black, like something out of a crime thriller movie — but it occurred to her that the man pulling up a chair and sitting down at their table, the man who had been with Alora on Friday night, was a suspect, and she had a surreal feeling that she was now a part of that movie.

"The RCMP will want to speak with you again, Mrs. Irwin," he said. He had a nice voice, deep and somehow soothing, like a doctor with a good bedside manner.

"My name is Kelly." She spoke almost involuntarily, with a sudden insight that she didn't like being called Mrs. Irwin. She tried to bring back the tender feelings for Mike, but Alora distracted her by speaking.

"Why are you here?" Alora asked the man, but instead of answering, he extended his hand to Kelly.

"My name is Hunter Rayne," he said. "I'm a former homicide detective with the Royal Canadian Mounted Police, and became involved in the investigation of your husband's murder due to my relationship with Alora." He nodded toward Alora, then turned and spoke to her. "I apologize for intruding here. I know I wasn't invited to sit down, but I felt it was important that I bring you up to date."

Kelly could see Alora's jaw muscles working, as if she were trying to control her anger. She guessed the two of them had some kind of argument. Perhaps he wasn't her boyfriend after all. He was handsome in a rugged sort of way, but his face was stern, as if he were still with the police and on the job. Just then the young man who had taken their order arrived at the table and set down two glasses of white wine. They had both ordered an unfamiliar wine from British Columbia, although there were good California wines available by the glass.

"What can I get you?" he asked the uninvited guest, who shook his head and said he was fine, thank you.

"The detectives are now going through the process of ruling out anyone who could be considered a potential suspect in Mike's death. At this point, there is evidently no one who can vouch for the whereabouts of either of you between eight o'clock and ten o'clock on Saturday morning."

"You know where I was," said Alora, picking up her wine and setting it back down. "I was in my hotel room at the Chateau Grand Montagne waiting for your call."

Kelly could hear the tension in Alora's voice.

"Where were you?" Alora glared at Hunter.

"I won't go into details, but I think you should know that I am *not* a suspect," he said. "You don't know me, Mrs. ... Kelly, but I do have an extensive background with the RCMP. I don't know how much Alora has told you, but she and I haven't known each other long. We were just getting to know each other, but it appears that Alora has had enough of me already." He smiled a sad sort of smile, but didn't seem upset. "I'm sorry about that," he added, turning to Alora.

Alora started fiddling with one of her earrings and looked away.

"How about you, Kelly? Who were you with Saturday morning?"

Kelly took a sip of wine. It was a pleasant pinot gris from a local winery with a French name. Mike always ordered red wine for them both, so it was a treat to order white. She wasn't sure she should be speaking to this man who wasn't really a detective, but Alora, too, looked like she was waiting for Kelly's answer.

"I... I was with my two children in the hotel room." The kids were already up and playing when Mike left the room. Kelly had pretended to be asleep, but had opened one eye just enough to watch him leave. He'd picked up Correna and given her a big smooch, then patted Jordan on the head, holding a finger up to his lips and whispering, 'Let Mommy sleep in, okay?' She doubted that he was being kind. More likely he was in a hurry and didn't want to waste time telling her where he was going, or maybe he didn't want her to know.

"Did you order room service? What did you do for breakfast?"

Kelly wondered what her mother-in-law had told the police. "I wasn't hungry. I usually just have coffee in the morning, and there was a coffee maker in the room." Of course, the kids had to eat. "Beth and John — Mike's mother and father — wanted to take the kids out to McDonald's for breakfast. She picked the kids up at..." Kelly paused, trying to remember. "I don't remember what time, exactly. You'd have to talk to Beth."

"So you waited for them in the hotel room?"

Kelly couldn't believe anyone would seriously think she could have killed her husband. Would it be better for her to lie about leaving the hotel, or tell the truth? If they actually started to investigate her movements, it would be better if she told the truth, she decided. There could be video surveillance in the hotel. Perhaps someone remembered seeing her leave. "I went for a walk," she said, her hands clasped in front of her on the table, as if she were praying. "It's been a long time since I had a chance to go for a walk in falling snow. A quiet walk by myself is always a treat. If you were a mother of small children, you'd understand." She lifted her chin and tried to smile.

"How long were you gone?"

"Let her alone, Hunter." Alora reached across the table and covered Kelly's hands with her own. "Listen, Kelly. You don't have to answer anyone's questions, especially his. He's not a cop. If you want, I'll be your lawyer. Just say the word."

Of course. Mike's ex-wife was a lawyer. Why not? "Yes. Yes, I would like that. Thank you."

Hunter took a deep breath and let it out slowly. Kelly expected him to argue, maybe ask a different question, but he just said, "Okay. Alora is absolutely right." He turned to Alora. "I'd like to buy you a drink later, if you'd be willing. I'm sorry I upset you yesterday, and I'd like a chance to talk about it."

There was a moment of uncomfortable silence. Kelly looked from one to the other, feeling like a voyeur.

Alora frowned and opened her mouth to speak, but Hunter held up a hand to stop her. "Think about it," he said. "You've got my cell number. Just give me a call." He stood up and returned the chair to a nearby table, then gave a nod to each of them in turn. "Thank you for your time. Sorry for the intrusion."

And he was gone.

CHAPTER
EIGHT

In spite of a twenty minute lineup in the truck lane, Dan Sorenson cleared the border without any difficulty. Simone had packed some sandwiches for him, but he'd eaten most of them while inching forward in the lineup. He drank two bottles of Coke and finished off his last sandwich between the border and Seattle, so he had to make a pee stop in a rest area somewhere south of Olympia. It was quiet except for the sound of traffic on the I-5 and he was tempted to stop for a nap, but the thought of getting both Big Mother Trucker and Hunter mad at him made him fire up the engine. He yawned and stroked his moustache as he waited for another eighteen wheeler to go past before he could pull out into the access road.

Sorry wasn't normally averse to speeding — what biker was? — but El had warned him about the fuckin' fifty-five mile an hour speed limit for trucks. You could usually go sixty without getting pulled over. He had to be at the customer's dock by six a.m. on Tuesday, and Redding was almost thirteen hours of driving time away. According to the hours of service regulations, he could only work for fourteen hours straight, or actually drive the truck for eleven hours, before laying up for a full ten hours. El had written it all down, so he couldn't plead ignorance. He'd picked the trailer up just before six o'clock, so between then and Monday at six p.m. he could only drive eleven hours, then he needed a rest of at least ten consecutive hours before he could drive again. Fuckin' stupid, but that was the law.

The night was black and wet, not so much a rain as a steady drizzle that left the asphalt slick and glossy, so there wasn't much to see except the lines on the highway and the lights of the other vehicles. Sorry yawned again and cranked up the radio. He'd lost his favorite Vancouver station, JR-FM, around Bellingham and had to scan the stations now and then to find decent music. Rock, country — it didn't matter as long as it had a beat and some wicked guitar licks. He felt around in the duffel bag beside him for his pack of smokes and lit one up. If he kept the window rolled down when he smoked, Hunter would never know.

Hunter's Freightliner, The Blue Knight as El called it, wasn't a bad truck, but Sorry had driven better. It didn't have the bells and whistles some trucks had — only a bunk, no microwave or TV — plus at six years old it was already past its prime. The rig was a bit like Hunter himself: no frills, hard working, a decent friend but not someone to party with. Still, it had a reliable 350 horsepower Cummins engine and ten near new tires. And he was getting paid to drive this big puppy south, out of the rain. Not a bad deal.

He was hungry again soon after he got back on the highway, and famished by the time he pulled into the Rebel Truck Stop near Kelso to fuel up and get something to eat. He jumped down from the cab, jacket in hand, and double checked that the doors were locked, then headed straight for the can. He threw his leather jacket on the sink counter, and sashayed up to the urinal, in a hurry to get to a table and order food.

The door opened and somebody walked in, so he twisted his neck to get a look. You always gotta watch your back. It was two pimply kids, and one of them was eyeing his jacket. The kid was wearing a dirty jeans jacket that was two sizes too big for him and was bareheaded, with strings of brown hair falling in his eyes. The other one had a puffy black jacket with sleeves too short for his skinny arms. He wore a Cleveland Indians cap that had seen better days. They both looked wet and cold, and carried grimy canvas duffle bags.

"HEY!" Sorry's voice came from deep in his chest and made both boys jump. He jiggled the drips off his dink and tucked it back in before turning around. "Don't even think about it."

The boys looked at each other, and they backed out of his way as he zipped up his jeans and walked over to the sink. It had been nice and toasty in the truck, so he was just wearing a plain black tee shirt. He sniffed his fingers and checked the state of his hands — they were smeared with road dirt from touching the truck — so he figured he should wash up before eating. Soaping his hands he made sure to show off the cobra tattoo that wound up his right forearm and the Harley tattoo on his left bicep. The boys were respectfully quiet and had dropped the duffle bags and stuck their red hands under running water.

"Where you boys from?" They didn't look like the kids in the pictures he'd brought Hunter, but it wouldn't hurt to ask. When they didn't answer right away, he said, "Hey! I asked you a question. You with the hat. Where you from?"

It was the one in the jeans jacket who answered. "Minnesota."

"Yeah. Fuckin' Minnesota," said the other one.

"Where in Minnesota?" If they were lying, this could take them a while.

"Thief River Falls." They spoke in unison, without looking at each other.

"Why're you all wet?"

"Guy dropped us off in the middle of nowhere. We been walkin' for hours."

"Yeah. We're fuckin' cold."

"Hitchin'?" There were no paper towels, just one of those damn blower things, so Sorry dried his hands on his jeans.

They both nodded. "We're meeting somebody in California."

Sorry looked them up and down, stroking his moustache. "California's a big state. I hope you got a city picked out."

The one with the cap smiled, showing crooked front teeth. The other one thrust his hands under the blower and it started up. Sorry figured he was still trying to warm them up. The kids looked too young to be out in the world by themselves.

"How old are you? You run away?"

"Eighteen."

"Nineteen."

Sorry laughed. "Good try. Fifteen's more like it. You run away?" he asked again.

They just shrugged. Sorry thought about his boy, Bruno. Bruno was just a little tyke, and he couldn't imagine Bruno growing up, let alone growing up and running away.

"You boys got money?"

The boys looked at each other, then the one in the jeans jacket shook his head. "We... uh... spent it already."

Sorry shook his head. "Shit." He picked up his jeans jacket. "Look at you. Skinny as a fuckin' stick." He patted his own massive chest, "You could fit the both of you in one of me. You boys clean yourselves up a bit and then come find me." He motioned out the door toward the restaurant with his chin. "I'll buy you a couple burgers." He didn't have a lot of spending money himself, but he figured he could spare a few bucks.

Sorry didn't get many more words out of the boys until after they had wolfed down their burgers. Kids that age eat like gorillas. He could tell their hunger was far from satisfied, but he couldn't afford to give them more. He ordered a coffee to top off his steak and spaghetti, then broke down and ordered hot chocolate for the boys. He found out that the kid with the jeans jacket was Peter, and the one with the Indians cap was Conner. The town they were from, Thief River Falls, was small and fuckin' cold in the winter. Peter called it a hick town.

"You going south?" asked Conner.

"Go home," said Sorry.

"What?"

"I said, GO HOME. You kids made a mistake. Admit it. Wait till you can afford a car. And gas. Call your folks and ask them to send you a bus ticket home."

Both boys looked down at the table. Conner played with his fork, stabbing at a piece of tomato that he'd pulled out of his burger.

"Eat that," said Sorry.

"I don't like tomatoes."

"So what? You're fuckin' starving. EAT IT!"

The kid put it in his mouth, made a stupid face as he chewed it, an even stupider face as he swallowed it. "My dad will kill me if I go home," he said.

"Really?" Sorry directed the question at his buddy, Peter.

Peter shook his head. "I don't think Mr. Lipfert believes in punishing his children. He's a psychologist."

"Fu-uck," said Sorry, shaking his head. "So that's his problem. How about *your* dad?"

"I don't have one. He died when I was three."

"Then borrow his dad."

They looked at each other as if he were crazy.

"Listen. I'm serious. You kids should go home. Or your mothers will never know what happened to you until some guy walking his dog comes across your skulls in twenty years or something."

Sorry looked at his watch. He'd already been here longer than he intended. "I gotta go. Good luck to you guys. But take my advice." He leaned down and spoke right into Conner's face. "Go HOME." He reached in his jeans pocket and pulled out a handful of change, then realized it was all Canadian money, so he stuffed it back inside and peeled an American ten off his small stash. "Here," he said, throwing it on the table. "Spend it on a phone call. Call his dad," he jerked his chin toward Conner as he stood up, "and get him to send you two bus tickets."

The one named Peter closed his hand around the bill, and the two kids looked at each other for a few seconds. "Thanks," they said in unison.

Sorry shrugged into his jacket and walked away. But he wasn't thinking about the two boys from Thief River Falls, Minnesota, nor the two runaways from Calgary that Hunter was looking for, and he wasn't even thinking about his little son, Bruno. He was thinking about a man named Henrik Edvard Sorenson, owner of Hank's Hardware in Yreka, California, and wondering whether, some twenty five years ago, Hank would have sent his runaway son Daniel a bus ticket home.

Hunter didn't expect to hear from Alora for a while, if ever. He considered seeking out Mike Irwin's parents to see if they would consent to talk to him and confirm Kelly's story, but he was reluctant to interrupt the couple in the midst of watching a movie with their grandchildren, a small respite from thinking about their son's murder. He liked Mike's father John, and regretted having to cut their conversation short the way he had.

With the business side of Mike's life being investigated by Meredith Travis, Hunter pulled the envelope Sorry had brought him out of his jacket pocket and took a closer look at the faxed photos of Adam Marsh and his friend, Nathan. He had an old friend with a law office in the Gastown neighborhood of Vancouver. It wasn't uncommon for homeless youth to gravitate to the downtown neighborhoods and Gastown was one such neighborhood. It was an area popular with tourists and safer than the east side of downtown. Hunter decided to fax a copy of the photos Helen Marsh had provided to his friend, Joe Solomon, and ask him to pass it on to contacts in the neighborhood. Hunter brought up Legal Joe's number on his cell phone and made the call.

Legal Joe was a full blooded member of the Tsilhqot'in First Nations, from whose name the region of British Columbia's interior known as the Chilcotin was derived. They were a people known for their hunting skills, and Hunter hoped Joe was no exception. As he waited for Joe to answer, Hunter turned to the second page of photographs. Again, there was a photo of Adam and Nathan together, this time holding electric guitars and smiling at the camera, but the photo that immediately grabbed Hunter's attention and wouldn't let it go was of Adam and his mother. They were both dressed in shorts and tee shirts, smiling and squinting slightly into the sun, and she had her arm over his shoulder. They were in the foreground, standing in what appeared to be a parking lot, and in the far background was a massive dinosaur that dwarfed the cars and trucks parked near its base.

Helen hadn't changed. Perhaps there were a few more lines in her face, and her cheeks were a little fuller, but it didn't matter. The grey shadings of the two dimensions captured in the photograph were transformed into three dimensional color in his imagination. He saw the honey highlights in her hair and the rose blush on her tanned cheeks in the summer sun, the blue of her eyes bright with unshed tears that pooled above the lower lids. His finger traced the outline of her neck and shoulder.

"Hello? Who's calling? Hello?"

Hunter blinked and gave his head a quick shake. ``Joe? It's Hunter."

"Hey! Good to hear from you! What's up, Kemosabe?" Hunter had never been sure if Joe called everyone Kemosabe, or reserved the name just for him. Ironic that he felt more like the Lone Ranger since he'd left the RCMP than he'd ever done before.

"I might need a lawyer, Joe. The RCMP suspect me of a murder."

"You're kidding, right?"

"Only partly. I definitely was a suspect up until today. Maybe I still am, but I've been told that I'm in the clear." He filled Joe in on the story surrounding Mike Irwin's murder, then said, "That's not actually why I called. I need a favor."

"Are we talking unbillable hours?"

Hunter laughed. If there was any lawyer who thought less about billable hours than Joe Solomon, he had yet to meet one. Working from a small office not far from Vancouver's downtown east side, Joe was a champion of the city's down and out First Nations people, or as Joe facetiously called them 'us injuns', who were unlucky enough to find themselves on the wrong side of the law. "You betcham. What would you need money for anyway?"

"Gambling and women."

"Is that all? You've sworn off drugs and drink? I'm calling about Helen Marsh." Joe had also been a friend of Ken's and had helped Helen out with legal issues connected to Ken's estate after his death. "Her son Adam has run away from Calgary. She thinks he was headed for Vancouver."

"You got photos?"

Hunter smiled. Joe was already on it. With his network of contacts, from clients to friends to business associates, including hot dog vendors and social workers, he had as good a chance as anyone to get a lead on the boy. "What's your fax number? You'll have some as soon as I can find a fax machine."

Alora did call. Hunter had faxed the photos to Joe Solomon from the hotel office and made a few more calls from the lobby — one to his landlord in North Vancouver, just to let him know where he was, and a couple to old friends who worked in the city of Vancouver — then had faxed photos of the runaways off to them as well. He was waiting for the elevator to the underground parking when his cell phone rang.

"Still want to buy me that drink?" She was sitting at the same table in the lounge, she said. Kelly had gone back to her kids.

"I'll be there in five minutes," he told her. He felt that he owed her an apology, but he still wasn't sure why. There was a small gift and sundries shop off the lobby where they sold books and magazine, toiletries, aspirin and cold remedies, plus souvenir items. Hunter just wanted something small: a rose? a box of chocolates? a 'whatever I've done I'm sorry' sort of token. He settled on a package of maple syrup fudge.

"I brought you a sweet souvenir," he said. He smiled and handed her the fudge before sitting down. "I apologize for upsetting you the other night."

She sighed. "Fudge. Thank you." She shook her head. "Men can be so clueless sometimes." Then, "No. No. Forget I said that." She reached across the table and placed her hand over his. "I'm sorry. I guess seeing Mike — everything with Mike — has been such a downer, I kind of lost sight of what I was doing here."

Hunter smiled, without enthusiasm, not sure any more of what to say to this woman. It had seemed so easy and casual at first, and then being with her turned into the same bewildering minefield he had to tiptoe through with his ex-wife Christine, where at any second something he did or said could be turned against him somehow. But Alora was right. The appearance of a stalker and then being interrogated about his murder wasn't exactly conducive to the success of a new relationship. He turned his hand over and gave hers a gentle squeeze.

"Can I buy you that drink?" That had to be a safe topic.

She gave a slow, exaggerated nod. "I definitely think I could handle another glass of wine."

Hunter looked around the lounge. It was dim except for soft pools of light at each table. Many of the tables were still occupied, and most of the conversations were subdued, but occasionally loud laughter erupted from a large table near the back. Hunter caught the eye of a server and beckoned him to the table.

"How long are you planning to stay now?" Alora asked after the young man in black left with their order. Her fingers played with the stem of her almost empty wine glass.

"A day or two, at least," he said. "I'm really hoping the RCMP can put a lid on this case by the time I leave, so I'm doing what I can to help them. Any new insights on your part?"

"You mean from Kelly," she said. "She's hurting. Funny, isn't it? Mike's death has to be the best thing that's happened to her lately, and she was feeling her first taste of freedom today, but she got all weepy about the bastard after a single glass of wine."

"She's your client now?"

Alora shrugged. "We didn't discuss any lawyer-client arrangement after you left. Besides, there's nothing I can tell you about her that relates to Mike's murder. She's a nice girl, smart, attractive, and she managed to fall for the same abusive creep I did. Suddenly, now that he's gone, she decides that he wasn't all bad. Of course, he wasn't all bad. Just bad to be married to." She took a sip of wine. "No, for her, not even that. He made lots of money, she had a nice house and the family had lots of toys, he was gone at work much of the time so it was just her and the kids — a good thing in his case — but the bad thing is that she lost all her self-respect and who knows how their poor little boy would have ended up. She said the poor kid couldn't do anything right, from Mike's perspective. He'll be much better off with a single mother, I have no doubt."

"Speaking of boys with single mothers..." Hunter thought it was time to change the subject and was going to bring up the runaways, but Alora carried on as if he hadn't spoken.

"I wonder if Mike was jealous of his son. I wonder if it was another part of the dominant male thing. Any male was a threat, even his own five year old kid. What do you think?"

"I don't know. I thought the dominant male's priority was to ensure the survival of his own genes. Then again, in some species the alpha male kills any infants that are too weak to contribute to the tribe. Maybe..."

"The child wasn't up to Mike's standards?" said Alora. "I could see that. Kelly said he's a bit of a momma's boy. Mike would feel that reflected poorly on the macho image he had of himself. Or was the boy a wimp because his father destroyed his self esteem? Didn't Freud say that a person's character is largely set by his environment in the first few years of life?"

Hunter tried to imagine how he would feel about a son. He had two daughters, both now in college. He couldn't imagine not being proud of them, but then, they had turned out well. As far as he knew, they were both generally happy and well adjusted. He and Chris had done *something* right together. But what about Ken's son, Adam? A runaway at fourteen. Was how his father treated him in early childhood responsible for that behavior? Or was it the loss of his father before he reached his teens? He couldn't imagine that Helen

120

had been anything but an excellent mother. She would have been loving, but firm. Or did he not know Helen as well as he thought he did?

Alora again interrupted his train of thought. "Do you think that maybe Mike wasn't really the boy's father?"

Hunter paused with his beer glass halfway to his lips. "Why do you say that?" His mind ran through a possible scenario: the child's biological father wanting to protect him, feeling a need to eliminate Mike. No evidence of that, but then, no one had been looking for it.

"You saw as much of the child as I did. Did he look like Mike?"

"No, definitely not. But my daughters don't look like me either."

"You probably just don't see it. Have you got a picture?" She held out a hand, as if she expected him to pull a picture out of his pocket.

Alora seemed as happy as he was to move away from the topic of Mike and his family. He had no pictures to show her, but did his best to describe Janice and Lesley, his two daughters. Jan was the oldest, and studying Marketing at BCIT. Lesley had recently graduated from high school and had surprised him by choosing to study Criminology at Simon Fraser University. Her goal was to join the RCMP. Both girls managed to work part-time, but Hunter contributed what he could to keep them in school. He knew he didn't see them as often as he should, but he was on the road much of the time with an uncertain schedule that didn't allow him to plan much ahead, and they had busy schedules that usually didn't mesh with his last minute calls.

They managed to talk their way pleasantly through a second drink, then Hunter escorted Alora back to her room. They kissed in the hallway. This time it was the kind of kiss that could lead to something more, but Hunter felt himself hit a wall. It should have been easy to ignore the angel on his shoulder that told him he wasn't ready for the next step, but its voice was insistent enough to make him lift his hands from Alora's soft curves and place them on her shoulders. "I have an early morning," he said. His voice was husky and he had to clear his throat. "I have to meet detective Blackwell at the Whistler RCMP detachment, skis in hand, before dawn so we can be up the mountain before the Harmony chairlift officially opens. I'll call you."

Alora seemed to accept his departure without taking offence. No more minefields.

As the door of her room closed after a final kiss and Hunter started toward the elevator, he recognized the angel on his shoulder. Maybe she'd been on his shoulder all this time, but it wasn't until today that she had found her voice. It was a sweet and evocative voice from his distant past.

It was the voice of Helen Marsh.

Sorry arrived in Yreka before sunrise, although the sky brightened enough for him to see the familiar scrub-dotted brown hills along the I-5. It was almost exactly eleven hours of driving time. "Here of all places," he said aloud. "What the hell is going on?" He hadn't given his father much thought in years. Then yesterday morning, the conversation about Hunter's runaways, followed by running into the two scrawny kids at the truck stop in Yoncalla; his father had been on his mind and here he was driving down South Main Street past Hank's Hardware, stuck in town for ten full hours before he could take this puppy back out on the highway to finish his trip. "Weird shit."

He had contemplated stopping at the rest stop at Hornbrook or in the parking lot at the Super 8 just off the highway in Yreka, but it didn't make much sense to spend the next ten hours twiddling his thumbs in a parking lot when he could hang out at his mom and dad's, get some home-cooked meals and catch a nap in a cozy house instead of the narrow bunk behind him. Besides, it was going to get cold in the truck unless he kept the engine running, judging by the frost on cars that had been parked along the street overnight.

In spite of the early hour, there were lights on and movement inside the old hardware store. It was a plain old post-war box of a building, single story, but with a coat of dark green paint that Sorry hadn't seen before. The ubiquitous OPEN sign in orange neon

122

glowed in the front window, and the cast-iron bicycle rack still stood between the window and the door. It used to be the only place in town to buy bike parts and inner tubes. Sorry's friends would often ride their bikes over and hang out while he stocked shelves for his father during the summer.

On an impulse, Sorry pulled the Blue Knight over to the curb and sat with his emergency flashers on. He could see the front door of the store reflected in the passenger side mirror, and an early bird customer in a feed-store cap walking out with a small sack of something, maybe nails. The customer stared at Sorry's rig for a few seconds, then turned around and went back inside. A moment later, he emerged again, accompanied by a man in a red jacket. Sorry smiled. His dad always wore something red when he was working in the store, so the customers could spot him easy if they had a question. He remembered working winter weekend mornings in his early teens, how cold it would be until the old furnace had taken the chill off the big open room, and that his dad had an old L.A. Angel's jacket he liked to wear. Looks like he still had it.

A moment later, Sorry was peering down at an older version of a man he'd seen almost every day of his life for over seventeen years. The blonde hair had turned white, the hairline receded, the strong, straight cheeks were crumpling like a paper sack. His mouth seemed larger, his lips less well defined.

"Hey, driver! You got a delivery near here? Can't just park that thing on the street, you know." The voice was older in a way Sorry couldn't quite explain: a little deeper, a little rougher, but still strong enough to penetrate the closed window, and not unkind. He realized his father couldn't really see him from below the passenger side window, probably from lights reflecting off the glass.

Sorry opened the driver's door and got down out of the cab. When he cleared the front bumper of the Freightliner, he said, "Hallo, Pappa." He held out his hand for a handshake, although he half expected his father to spit in his face.

It must have taken the old man a few seconds to get his head around what was happening, then he reached for Sorry's outstretched hand and clasped it firmly in both of his own. His hands were warm and strong and just held on. Sorry realized with amazement that his father's eyes had filled with tears, and even more amazing, that his own eyes began to sting. His father seemed smaller than he remembered him, although he was a big man by most standards, just a couple of inches shorter than Sorry but not as broad in the chest.

"Daniel," his father said. "Daniel." Then softer, almost to himself, "My son, Daniel."

Sorry was afraid to speak, afraid he wouldn't be able to control his voice. He looked away, toward the store, where the customer still stood clutching his bag of nails. Sorry nodded a hello in the man's direction and cleared his throat, once, then once again.

"Who's minding the store?" he finally said.

"I have to get back. Come have a coffee, Daniel. There's a fresh pot." His father still held tight to Sorry's hand.

Sorry jerked his head in the direction of the Blue Knight, intending to use it as an excuse.

"Leave your truck. Just leave the flashers on. At this time of day, I'm the only one who would complain."

His father walked around the front of the Freightliner, nodding his head and smiling, while Sorry grabbed his jacket and wallet out of the truck, then locked the doors. They walked together toward the store, and the old man grinned at the customer as they passed. "This is my son, Daniel," he said. "He lives up north." The customer smiled and shook Sorry's hand before walking away.

The old man brought two mugs of coffee from a pot at the back of the store, and they sat on stools behind the counter sipping and talking while two or three customers wandered into the store, working men seeking out items they would need for the morning's job. Sorry told his father he was only in town for ten hours before he had to be back on the road.

"You'll go spend time with your mother," said the old man. "She works part-time at the old folks home, but Monday is one of her days off." He was hailed by a customer in the plumbing section, and excused himself to go help out.

Sorry stroked his moustache as he watched his father walk away. He'd taken off the Angels jacket, and wore a red cotton sweat shirt above a pair of worn khaki pants. He still had a firm stride, but there was a small hitch in his gait. He remembered his mother saying a few years back that the family doctor had warned them the old man would need a hip replacement one day. He wondered when the old man was planning to retire — he must be pushing seventy — or if he had someone to spell him off in the store, but he was afraid to bring it up. A small shiver ran up his spine when he remembered his father's set jaw and blazing eyes the last time they'd spoken about it. "Maybe I shouldn't have come," he muttered to himself. He didn't want his father to think, even for a second, that he would consider moving back to Yreka and taking over the store.

As if he'd been reading Sorry's mind, after the old man rang the plumbing purchases through the till, he sat back down on the stool, picked up his coffee, and said, "I've been trying to sell the store."

"And?"

"No luck. The real business goes to the Lowes in Medford or the Home Depot in Phoenix. Nobody wants to buy a small town family business anymore." He swept his right arm toward the back of the store. "Old building. A pile of obsolete inventory. Not an easy sell."

Sorry looked around at the mismatched shelving units with narrow aisles between them, the uneven floors covered with faded lino tiles, and the old light fixtures hanging from the low ceilings, with a sense of familiarity in spite of the years that had passed since the last time he'd been inside the store. "What are you going to do?"

"Sell the land. Being here on Main is worth something, at least." The old man took a sip of coffee, then winced and shook his head. "Nothing lasts forever. Not even Hank's Hardware."

His father's wounded smile was such a downer, Sorry had to bite his lip to keep from saying something. He wasn't sure what that would have been, but he hadn't stopped in his old home town to be put through some kind of emotional wringer. Just then another customer showed up at the till, and Sorry sighed with relief. He had to get out of here, fast.

When the customer left, he said, "How's the road out to the barn?" Sorry's parents had a small acreage up Greenhorn Road with a kitchen garden, chickens and, last he saw, a Jersey cow and a couple of horses.

"I'd park next door at the Lovetts' place, if I were you. Remember Ernie Lovett? He was a couple years behind you in school. He and his wife live there in a double wide and he parks his eighteen wheeler out in front of their machine shed when he's in town."

Sorry nodded. "Sounds good. Mr. and Mrs. Lovett still there?"

"The old Mrs. died about ten years ago, but George married again. The new wife had to put him in the home."

"She won't know me."

The old man snorted. "She's friends with your mother. Alice will know who you are, you can bet on it."

Sorry walked out of Hank's Hardware into a cool grey morning. Maybe it would be the last time, he thought. They would probably tear the old place down, but he couldn't summon any real emotion. It was still just a lousy little hardware store in a lousy little northern California town. The thought of staying here made him feel so claustrophobic he wanted to scream and run. It would be like a prison, he reflected as he climbed back into the truck, wondering why he should feel that way when a few thousand other souls were content to call it home.

He thought about how life had continued on here in his home town without him, and had the weird feeling that in spite of being away, he was still a part of the town, a piece of him stuck solidly in its history, his picture in dozens of high school yearbooks, his name still coming up over tea or coffee or cans of Budweiser. Hank and Susan's boy. Too heavy to play baseball, but was a pretty good fullback on the high school football team. Ran off and joined a biker gang. Lives up north, in Canada.

The kid that got away.

CHAPTER
NINE

Hunter grabbed a coffee and breakfast sandwich on his way to the detachment to meet Staff Sergeant Shane Blackwell. It was still dark, with just a hint of grey dawn in the eastern sky. His thigh muscles were a little stiff from his skiing on Saturday, but he knew that once he got out there, he'd forget about it. Murder investigations had always had that effect on him. He'd get so caught up in his work, he'd forget to eat, forget to sleep, forget that his wife and kids were waiting for him. That thought brought him up short. Was there something he should remember today? All he could come up with was that he was supposed to call Meredith Travis later, to see if she'd learned anything at the conference.

Shane was in his office, working at the computer, when Hunter arrived.

"A whole shitload of emails overnight," he said. "Got to go through them in case there's something important, but most of them are crap. CYA stuff."

"CYA?"

"Cover Your Ass. Nobody wants to be told they forgot to pass on important information to somebody who could use it. You never know what's important or who's somebody, so everybody gets everything." He typed furiously for a few minutes. "Almost done. Help yourself to coffee."

Hunter declined. One coffee was enough before a long chairlift ride in frigid temperatures.

To reach the Harmony chairlift, they had to take the gondola to the Roundhouse and ski back down. They rode up in the gondola with Whistler staff, both of them silent, listening to the mostly young people around them talk among themselves. One young man was speculating on how the dude who'd murdered the guy on the Harmony chair had managed to get away.

"He had to of jumped, dude. There was lots of soft powder. Who's going to remember seeing some dude planted on the slope? He just would of had to time it right."

His buddy came back with, "Get real, dude. Too risky. He must've timed it right at the top, hit the snow and pushed off before anybody caught a good look."

"I could do it, dude. I could jump. Ride the Harmony with me next day off and I'll show you."

Shane and Hunter exchanged looks.

"Bullshit, dude," said the buddy.

There were lots of whispers they couldn't catch, along with frequent glances at the stern unfamiliar faces of Hunter and Shane. Hunter wasn't sure if it was just because they weren't regulars on the pre-opening lift, or if it was because they looked like cops.

Shane was a good skier in spite of his size and weight, and Hunter had to work to keep up with him on the way to the Harmony base. It was an amazing feeling, skiing down just after sunrise. The mountain was massive and quiet and very, very cold, and they were two small almost hairless beings, just a few inches of man-made insulation away from freezing to death. It was humbling and exhilarating at the same time. They could see fresh tracks. Someone — several someones — had been down the run ahead of them.

Shane had arranged for the same lift attendants who were there on Saturday to be present this morning. The attendants who'd been at the top of the lift that day were waiting for them at the base as well. They'd been interviewed on Saturday by the local officers, but Shane wanted to conduct a more in-depth interview personally on site. He and the first liftee went into the hut, leaving Hunter and the others outside.

Besides Hunter, there were four young men and one young woman left outside, all wearing jackets and toques with the Whistler-Blackcomb logo. The woman and one of the men sat on one of the quad chairs, now stationary, and sipped out of steaming thermal mugs. Hunter could smell the coffee as he approached, and he wished he had one. He inhaled deeply and asked if there was a coffee maker in the hut.

"Kettle and instant, if you can drink that stuff," said one of them, making a face. "Powdered cream, and no sugar left."

"I'll wait then," said Hunter with a smile. "Seems like a great job for a skier, being on the mountain every day. What's it like?" he asked.

The answers were more reserved than he expected. "It's okay." "Good. It's a good job, if you like to be outside." "Yeah. I like it."

"Which of you were up top Saturday?"

A young man with a blond pony tail hanging below the back of his black toque raised his gloved hand. He had a reddish beard and moustache. "Me and her," he said, pointing to the woman, who had her feet planted on the platform trying to stop her companion from making the chair swing back and forth.

She was tall with nose and cheeks already rosy from the cold. She stopped in mid-sip and looked up when mentioned. "Did you want to talk to me?" She had an accent, Australian maybe.

"Just wondering who first noticed that the victim hadn't gotten off the chair. Or what happened that the lift wasn't stopped when he didn't get off? Isn't there some kind of auto shut off?"

The two of them looked at each other, then the young man nodded to the girl. "You talk," he said.

"No safety gate on the lift, not here. As for not noticing sooner…" She gave a small shrug. "Shit happens," she said. "A couple of boarders got tangled up just below the dismount area. I was trying to help them get up and out of the way, and Brad was being accosted by a pair of cougars. Right Brad?" She grinned up at the bearded liftee.

He shook his head and rolled his eyes. "*Clients,*" he enunciated forcefully. "They were mature female *clients*, Megan." Then to Hunter, "It just happened that we were both preoccupied. Besides, it's not all that unusual for someone to just go up and down a lift for the ride. It's not usually a guy with skis on in snow season, but it happens. And no, we didn't really notice the other guy dismount. Just another skier, nothing special about him to notice, I guess."

"But someone was on that chair with the victim? And you think it was a male."

Brad rubbed his neck. "Just an assumption, I think. I've tried to remember for sure, but I can't really. Maybe someone got off and maybe it was a male, or that's what's stuck in my subconscious. I'm not a hundred percent sure — not even fifty percent. You remember?"

Megan shook her head. "When I heard you yell at the guy, I looked first at you, then at the lift, and by the time I looked around, I wouldn't have been able to tell who had just gotten off." Then to Hunter, "Sometimes there's a few clusters of people at the top. You know, a few boarders waiting for their mates, people chatting about whether to go down Harmony Ridge or the Saddle or whatever. Then they head off in ones and twos. Hard to know who just arrived and who was straightening their gear before pushing off."

"We both tried hard to remember, but there's up to four people getting off every six seconds or so." He shrugged. "Wish we could be more help."

"You yelled at the guy?"

"I yelled at the guy on the lift. Something like, 'Hey! You okay? Need help getting off?' But by then it was already too late for him to get off. Nothing to do but let him ride back down."

Hunter wondered what the killer had planned to do if he and the victim were noticed. Unless the killer had jumped off the lift somewhere en route, he — or she — had to have been pretty confident he could ski out of there fast enough to avoid being caught.

130

Or maybe he reasoned that no one at the top would think to follow him. Why would they even connect the skier who didn't get off with the one who did?

He turned away and looked up the line of chairs hanging still and silent from the cable every forty feet or so, diminishing in size up the mountain until the last ones were mere black dashes in the white distance. Maybe the killer hadn't taken such a risk after all. But something was now clear. It had to have been someone familiar enough with Whistler Mountain to know his way around the slopes.

And someone who knew the chairlift had no safety gate at the top.

Meredith was happy with her choice of outfit for the opening day of the conference. The conference package they had sent to her had suggested attire be 'business casual', which was comfortable enough and gave her a chance to adopt a suitably businesslike persona. She wore grey slacks, black patent low heeled pumps, a tailored blue linen blouse and a royal blue blazer. Her earrings were small silver hoops. She had considered carrying her laptop, but opted for a zippered binder of black leather. She had taken care with her makeup. She held a half full cup of coffee, but had no intention of drinking. She didn't want her lip gloss to lose its shine. People, especially men, were much more likely to respond to attractive members of the species.

She hovered near the table that held urns of coffee and hot water, chatting off and on with arriving conference attendees, peering at their name badges to see if she could identify anyone from Blue Hills Industries or their two main competitors, Cameron-Watts or Hildebrandt Metals. Her main interest, however, was Brent Carruthers, but she'd take what she could get during the opening presentation. Her goal was to get some kind of off-the-cuff reaction to Mike Irwin, something that wouldn't be possible for a police interrogator. She tucked a strand of hair behind her ear and smiled at a nervous-looking young man dressed in a suit that was too big for him. He looked almost shocked but returned her smile, then started to blush before ducking his head and hurrying past. She couldn't read his name tag but took him for a rookie in the industry.

In spite of what she'd told Rayne, she wasn't terribly worried that the police would find any evidence to connect her with Mike Irwin's murder, so she wasn't just pursuing this to help clear herself as a suspect. In fact, she was still on her client's payroll. Irwin's death didn't entirely solve the problem. What Irwin had already done could still have expensive consequences for her client, so there were secret connections to uncover and potential threats to neutralize. But Rayne could come in handy as a second pair of ears and eyes, and perhaps to keep her apprised of what the RCMP were discovering in their investigations.

Meredith recognized one of the men who had been with Irwin that night in the Chateau Grande Montagne lounge, the one who had been drinking the Stella Artois. He was wearing a dark green sweater over a knit shirt. He looked average: average height, average build, middle age, his face was too fleshy to be handsome, with round cheeks and a double chin that made his eyes and nose look too small. He approached the table, put a briefcase down on the floor beside his foot, and picked up a cup and saucer from the table. He was filling the cup with coffee from the urn when Meredith stood beside him and accidentally on purpose knocked over his briefcase.

"Oh! I'm sorry. Is that yours?" She gave him a glossy smile, tried to look a little shy to make herself more approachable.

He put down his cup and bent to pick up his briefcase, placing it next to his other foot before turning to take a good look at her. "It's okay," he said. "Almost need three hands in a place like this." He reached to pick up his cup again.

She read his name tag. "Nice to meet you, Todd Milton from Cameron-Watts Aerospace in Irvine." Bingo! She held out her hand, trying not to seem too excited. Not only was this guy with Mike Irwin on Friday night, he was also working for Blue Hills' biggest competitor.

"Make that four hands," he said with a grin, giving her hand a firm shake and peering at her own name tag. "Stella! One of my favorite names. What does Tamblyn-Brown do?"

"Retail light fixtures. They have a factory in New Jersey, and are now looking for a California location — and I'm new to the job, as well." She gave him her best dewy-eyed stare, finally releasing his hand. "I'd love to know more about what Cameron-Watts does. Aerospace sounds way more impressive than home lighting."

"Have you found a seat yet?" he asked. His small eyes looked shocked and eager at the same time. Meredith was sure he wasn't used to having attractive women come on to him. "Let's sit together and I can give you some tips, if you're just starting out."

They made their way, carrying white cups balanced on saucers, to two chairs a few rows from the back of the large room. She tucked her binder under her chair, then smiled at him as she wiggled her hips to inch herself backwards on the vinyl seat.

"So, tell me about working in aerospace," she said. "Is there money to be made?"

He nodded, lips pressed together as if he had a secret, then said, "Not so much just from your regular paycheck, maybe. But there are bonuses."

"Bonuses?" She looked up at him from under her lashes. "What kind of bonuses?"

He didn't answer right away. He seemed to be assessing her, then changed the subject. "So tell me about your experience, so far. Just graduated? First job?"

"I'm flattered," she said, batting her eye lashes. "I'm older than you think. I have a Masters degree in Business Administration, and spent over six years gaining experience on the marketing side of things. The company I worked for had quality control issues, and I worked closely with the factory to rectify the problem by finding better suppliers for the components. It worked, and I liked it, so I changed direction. How about you?"

He nodded, his double chin undulating like a squeezed water balloon. "Good move on your part," he said, "if it's big money you're after."

"Really? I thought marketing had a lot of potential."

"Depends ..."

Just then the microphone came alive with a burst of feedback as they regulated the volume, and then one of the conference organizers began to speak.

Meredith leaned over and spoke softly into Todd Milton's ear, brushing his cheek with her cupped hand. "I hope you'll tell me more later," she said.

"Absolutely," he said, then reached over and tentatively patted her knee. "Stella."

Meredith looked away briefly, clenching her jaw, then turned back toward him with a flirty grin. "Great," she mouthed.

But to herself she said, *You're hooked now, buddy. I'm going to play you like a trout.*

Back at the top of the Harmony Chair, Hunter and detective Shane Blackwell were about to start a second run down Whistler Mountain. They had pored over the map and discussed the options with the two most experienced lift attendants. Hunter thought it would be like looking for a needle in a haystack, but you never knew, they might get lucky, or it might turn out to be easier than he expected.

"Could be dangerous," the lift attendant named Parsons had warned. "You'd better stay together because skiers have accidentally fallen into those tree wells and not been able to get back out. You fall in head first, and you'll suffocate pretty quick. Like drowning in snow."

Whoever had killed Mike Irwin and planned to escape on skis — or a snowboard; not likely but there was no way of knowing — had probably discarded the murder weapon on their way off the mountain. It was also possible that they had thrown the weapon from the chairlift, but that would have involved a greater risk of being noticed, or of missing the intended target. Yes, it could have sunk into deep powder, but reaching a tree well across the wide vertical gap in the mountain vegetation beneath the chairlift would be more difficult. Parsons had suggested the route which would afford the greatest opportunity to ditch the weapon out of sight of the chairlift, and away from the busiest ski runs. Hunter took the left side and Shane took the right side, each of them looking for indentations in the snow that would indicate a single skier had veered close to a tree well, then back closer to the fall line for a quick run down the mountain.

"Harmony Ridge," Parsons had said. "There are several routes through the trees to choose from, especially if he was a good skier. Or better yet, Harmony to Burnt Stew Trail. Lots of trees down that route. Easy to ski out of sight for a few minutes. Then somebody could ski on down to the Village, or confuse things by taking the Harmony or Emerald Express back up the hill, or … hell, if somebody was trying to be tricky, it's a total maze of lifts and trails, you know." The lift attendant shook his head and said, "Good luck" as if he didn't hold out much hope for their success.

Now that they were back on the slope, Hunter didn't hold out much hope either. They skied down slowly, skis tracing parallel lines through the surface of the slope, one on each side of the run. Every now and then one of them would holler, "Whoa!" as they peeled in closer to a tree well, or followed a ski track off the main slope behind some snow covered firs. Hunter found a promising recent track behind a tree, peered into the tree well from as close as he dared, and was rewarded with the sight of a small pocket of yellow snow.

A few hundred yards further on he heard Shane yell, and followed the sound behind a large tree on the other side of the slope to see Shane's skis and poles stuck upright in the snow. Shane was nowhere to be seen, but tracks showed that he had waded through deep snow toward the tree well of a big fir. A few of the closest branches were bare of snow.

"Hunter. Here!"

"Oh, shit." Hunter inched his way over the snow, keeping his ski tips snowplowed in, until peering between branches, he could see Shane in the deep hole that surrounded the trunk of the tree. He took a firm hold of his right ski pole and extended it into the hole. The detective managed to grab it, and Hunter sidestepped away, a few inches at a time, until Shane was able to climb out of the hole on his hands and knees. He stood and took a step, sinking up to his thigh in the soft snow.

"Find anything?"

"Zilch. Pass me my skis, would you? This is a fuckin' useless exercise."

"We should've brought a rope," said Hunter.

"How many trees on this slope, anyway?"

Hunter laughed. "Who said he was even headed down this slope? There are a dozen ways he could have gone. There must be a million trees." He couldn't help thinking of how Alora had been the first one to mention throwing the weapon into the tree well. "Or she," he added. "Plus they could've just spiked the gun into the soft snow anywhere off the groomed runs and we'd never see a trace of it."

Shane nodded. "We can't even be sure the killer ditched the gun on the mountain. Maybe he threw it in a restaurant dumpster in Whistler. Maybe he threw it into the Cheakamus River on his way back to Vancouver, or off a cliff along the Sea to Sky highway into the ocean." Shane lost his balance trying to fasten his boot onto the second ski, and fell on his butt. "Fuck!" he said, reaching for help from Hunter's ski pole again. He pulled too hard and Hunter's skis slid out behind him, pitching him forward into the snow.

For a moment they looked at each other in silence, then both burst out laughing. Two homicide detectives — one current and one former — floundering in soft snow, barely able to stay upright. They both managed to struggle to their feet, their skis perpendicular to the slope, and considered the situation.

"You know," Shane said, turning to point at the tree well behind him with a ski pole, "the gun could very well be under the snow in there. I would have absolutely no way of finding it without a metal detector and a shovel and too much time."

"The tree well I checked out was the site of a piss stop. How many more of those will we find? You can't get too close to them, because the snow under the branches is full of air pockets. It just collapses and sucks you right in." He rubbed his cheek with his glove. His face was starting to get numb from the cold. "You're the boss, chief. Do we carry on?"

Shane looked up toward where they had been, and down to where they were heading. His nose was red, but his forehead glistened with sweat in spite of the temperature. The lifts had started running, and it wouldn't be long before the slope was alive with skiers and snowboarders. He took a deep breath, sighed, and said, "We're here. Might as well keep an eye out for promising signs until we reach the bottom." He started turning his skis, preparing to push off. "But let's stick closer together."

As his skis started sliding down the slope, he threw back over his shoulder, "I don't want to end up in one of those hell holes face first."

The little farm on Greenhorn Road looked much the same as it had last time Sorry had pulled into the driveway, except the trees had grown. He'd been on his Harley that time, as he had several times before that. This time, he was on foot. He had managed to back The Blue Knight into the neighbor's driveway and park it in a wide gravel space in front of the farm's machine shed, as his father had suggested. He could see his mom's white and yellow Chevy pickup parked beside the same old horse trailer. The paint was dull and pocked here and there with rust. Both of them had seen better days.

Sorry climbed the front steps and banged hard on the front door. No answer, so he turned away from the door and yelled, "Mom!" at the top of his lungs, then "Mor!" Neither he nor his mother spoke Norwegian, except for a few common words they'd picked up from Hank's parents. Mor was one of them.

"Danny?" he heard her call from behind the barn. Of course she was with one of her 'pets', as her husband referred to all of the farm animals, from a two pound chicken to a twelve hundred pound horse. As he walked toward the sound, he heard the clink of a chain on a metal gate, and a few seconds later she emerged from the other side of the barn, lugging a bucket. She looked a lot younger than her sixty-three years in spite of her gumboots and a bleach-stained hip-length jacket that must have been one of Hank's. She was still fit and strong and hardly overweight. She placed the bucket on the ground and reached up to give him a hug. She was only five foot three to his six foot two. He hugged her back until she pushed against his chest so she could look him in the eye.

"You should've called."

Close up, he noticed that the skin above her eyes seemed to sag, and there were pouches under her eyes and lines around her mouth he didn't remember seeing before. "Last minute thing, Mom. I'm doing a delivery to Redding, got a ten hour layover."

Her expression said, "Huh?"

"Trucking regulations. There's my truck." He pointed over at the eighteen wheeler, visible through the naked aspens that lined the neighbor's field. "I drove for eleven hours, I've got to stop for ten." He gave her another quick hug. Her jacket smelled a little bit like horse manure. "Got anything to eat?"

"Don't be an ass. We don't hear boo from you for a couple of years, then you show up without calling and expect me to drop everything to feed you?"

She made him help her finish up the chores, pushing a wheelbarrow full of manure from the barn to a pile out back and filling up water buckets for the horses and cows. Since his last visit, she'd added a couple of yearling Herefords. "What are their names?" he asked. "Sirloin and Brisket?"

She rolled her eyes at him as she said an emphatic, "No."

Twenty minutes later he was sitting in the familiar kitchen waiting for the kettle to boil. For some reason his mother's kitchen always smelled slightly of dill. His mother was heating up a pot of homemade soup, and putting together a cheese and salami sandwich. She had changed from jeans and boots to sweats and slippers, and she made him leave his own boots in the mudroom. He rubbed his stocking feet together under the table.

"Place looks good," he said. It hadn't changed much since his last visit. The floor was some kind of linoleum that looked like red sandstone tiles, and they had installed oak cabinets and ordered a solid oak table from a local woodworker somewhere around 1986. He remembered the year, because his mom told him she was thinking about coming for the '86 Expo in Vancouver but that they couldn't afford it because they'd renovated the kitchen.

"Only if you don't look too close," his mother said. She held up her right hand for him to see, and he realized that her finger joints were swollen. "Arthritis," she said matter-of-factly. "Scrubbing and polishing was never my favorite thing, and now it even hurts."

"Dad said he was trying to sell the store."

She turned from stirring the soup, obviously surprised. "You've seen him?"

He nodded.

"And... ?"

Sorry shrugged. "He seemed kind of bummed about selling the store. Otherwise, it went okay. He didn't spit in my eye or nothin'. I think he was even happy to see me."

"Of course he was. I don't know why you always put the blame on him for you two not getting along. You're the one who stays away for years at a time." She put the lid on the soup pot, walked to the table, and sat down. "I'm worried about him, Danny."

Sorry's gut dropped. Even if he and his old man had behaved as if they hated each other for years, somehow at the back of his mind he figured his old man would be around long enough for that to change. "Why? Is he sick?"

"No," she said, absently drawing little circles on the table top with a finger. "Not physically sick. Not yet, anyway."

"What do you mean, not yet?"

"You know your father. That hardware store has been his whole life. I'm just worried that when he sells it, he'll be one of those men who retires and then dies a couple of months later."

"That's crazy talk, Mom." Sorry didn't want to say it, but he thought maybe she was right. "Doesn't he want to retire?"

She worked her mouth a bit, as if she was thinking hard. "He says he's too old to work that hard. He says he wants to take it easy, but it doesn't feel like a good thing when he says it. It feels to me more like he's giving in to his age." She sighed and shook her head. "More like he's just giving up. I can't see him doing volunteer work or taking a part time job working for somebody else. Hank's Hardware has been part of who he is since before you were born, Danny."

The kettle whistled and she got up to make coffee in the same old Bodum Sorry remembered from years ago.

Sorry sat without speaking, playing shuffleboard from one hand to the other with the empty coffee mug in front of him, then stroking his moustache as he thought about what his mother had said. What the hell *would* his father do with his time?

"Besides, it'll drive me crazy to have him around here every day. There's only so much he can do here. It's not a big farm, and he's never been interested in the animals." She poured him a coffee. It looked weaker than the Tim Horton's he'd grown used to.

"He needs a hobby. You got cream and sugar?"

"He doesn't really have one. You can't call yard work and home maintenance a hobby. More like a chore." She brought a carton of cream from the fridge and a sugar bowl from the counter. "A real hobby's something that makes you feel more alive."

"Like my bike," said Sorry, reflecting on how great it felt to have the machine power up to full throttle underneath him, how free and happy he felt ripping up the open road with the wind whistling past his ears. He even got pleasure from polishing every inch of it now and then on a winter evening when the weather was too shitty to ride.

"Like my horses," she said, sitting down with her own coffee. "I wish your dad liked to ride, but with that hip of his, I don't think that's even remotely possible."

"Maybe you guys could travel. You could come up to see me and Mo and the kids."

She snorted softly, as if it was a bad joke. "We'll see. Tell me about your truck. It's a pretty nice looking rig."

Sorry remembered how happy his father had seemed about the truck, that he obviously hadn't noticed that the name on the door was J.H. Rayne. He had meant to explain that the truck wasn't his, that he was just hired to drive it, but then he figured it wouldn't hurt for the old man to think otherwise. He was probably just glad that his son hadn't roared into town on a Harley like he'd done in the past, always in summer, always in a muscle shirt that showed off his Black Cobra tattoo. If the old man was bummed out about getting old and selling the store, maybe it wasn't such a bad thing for him to think his son was doing something respectable.

"It ain't paid for yet," he told his mom. "You don't make a ton of money haulin' freight these days."

She smiled. "It looks nice. You must take good care of it." She was back at the stove, and lifted the lid off the soup, letting steam and a wonderful aroma loose into the room.

Sorry inhaled deeply. "Mom, you make the best chicken soup in the world."

"It's turkey," she said.

Ten minutes later, he was ready for a long nap.

CHAPTER
TEN

Meredith was pretty happy with her morning, in spite of sitting through three conference presentations aimed at purchasing professionals and supply chain managers. You never knew when information about the purchasing field might come in handy in her line of work. Between presentations, she'd spent most of the time pretending to hang on every word Todd Milton said about how to be a successful purchasing manager in the aerospace industry. Sadly, it involved a lot of engineering knowledge that she didn't possess, she'd told him. She found it terribly exciting, though. Did he have any stories to tell about top secret aerospace plans, or maybe industrial espionage?

Unfortunately, he didn't know anything about espionage, he said. He did say there was so much money floating around, especially from government contracts, it was easy to coax some of it your way, if you knew how things worked. Bonuses for getting orders delivered faster, for example. Bonuses for getting a better price on components. Even bonuses from your suppliers for giving them lucrative contracts. "Bonuses?" she'd asked, and he smiled slyly and winked.

They sat together during lunch, placing her binder and his briefcase on adjoining chairs while they went to the buffet table. She dished herself two kinds of salad, a whole wheat roll and some cold cuts while he piled his plate with a portion of almost everything on the table. When they were settled at their table, she asked him if he knew 'the poor guy who was killed on the chairlift'. At first he didn't answer.

"He was supposed to be at the conference, wasn't he?" She looked sideways at Todd while raising a forkful of romaine lettuce to her lips.

Todd was chewing something and just nodded.

"I'll bet it's making people think twice about sitting on a chairlift with someone they don't know."

"I doubt that it was a random murder," he said.

"How would you know? I mean — did you know something about the guy?" She leaned closer and touched his arm.

"Yes." He took a few swallows from his water glass, and Meredith got the impression that he was stalling. She left her fingers touching his arm and gave him her full attention.

"Let's just say, Stella, that I knew his reputation."

"Don't tease me, Todd. I've never been so close to a real murder before, and it's kind of exciting. Tell me more," she said, giving his shoulder a playful poke. Interesting, she thought, that he wouldn't admit to having drinks with Irwin the night before he was killed, although it was in a public place and already known to the police. Why would he hide it from her? Did he somehow know who she was, and who she was working for?

He lowered his voice, and leaned in close to her. "Rumor has it he was on the take."

"Okay." She waited for him to elaborate.

"Let's just say, he wasn't as loyal to his company as they would have liked."

He was confirming what she already knew. "Industrial espionage?"

He shook his head and put a forkful of roast potato into his mouth.

"Then what?"

He seemed to be considering how to put it. "Or yes, but maybe not in the way you think. It's not about selling designs or manufacturing secrets. More like purchasing espionage, you might say. Do you know how valuable it would be to a company to know what their competitors were bidding on a contract before they submitted their own bid?"

Meredith smiled and turned her attention back to her salad. Her client had been right. "And something like that could get him killed? Are the stakes really that high?"

"I didn't say that," he said, putting a hand up, as if to say 'whoa'. "He could have made some enemies, is all I'm saying. Plus the guy was a jerk on a personal level, and he tended to piss people off."

"It sounds like you knew him fairly well, then." She pretended to be busy with her salad, so it would seem more offhand than it really was.

Todd pushed a roasted carrot around his plate before spearing a piece of beef with his fork. "I've seen him in action a time or two," he said, looking off in another direction until he had chewed and swallowed. "I'm sure the Mounties will find his killer. Don't they always get their man?"

Meredith was convinced that Todd Milton was somehow part of the puzzle she had been hired to solve, but it was time to back off on the subject. The question remained, however, could Todd Milton be a viable suspect in Mike Irwin's murder? She washed down her lunch with a drink of Perrier before turning to her companion with an ingenuous smile.

"So tell me, Todd … do you ski?"

Hunter still wanted to talk to Mike Irwin's wife, but he knew it wasn't going to be comfortable for her, and perhaps she wouldn't even consent to see him. Not only had she seen her husband confront Hunter in the restaurant at the Coast Peaks soon after their arrival in Whistler, she had now also been talking to Alora. Girl talk. No doubt he had come up in their conversation, and he had no idea what Alora would have said about him after he left their table. After all, she had been upset with him at the time.

He considered calling Kelly Irwin at the hotel, but decided it would be just too easy for her to say no over the phone. He was going to need almost impossible luck to find her alone.

Hunter glanced at his watch as he entered the Coast Peaks Hotel lobby. Noon was still fifteen minutes away, and it would be a reasonable time to expect a family with small children to be finishing up lunch. He remembered doing that with Chris and the girls when they were small. Little kids tended to wake up early and get hungry for lunch early. 'Let's go early before the rush,' was a standard phrase. Chris was always self-conscious if the girls started making too much noise and disturbing the other patrons. As a matter of fact, so was he.

He had changed out of his ski clothes after arriving back at the RCMP detachment with Shane Blackwell, donning his usual jeans and boots and sheepskin jacket. They had both been frustrated with the results — or lack of them — from the morning's ski adventure. Shane's first fall in the snow was followed by several more during their inspections of suspicious tree wells, and his mood had turned blacker with each one. They had found nothing of value, and by the end they were convinced that only a miracle would turn up the murder weapon on the eight thousand some odd acres of Whistler and Blackcomb mountains. When they got back to the detachment, the reception desk told Shane that he had an important call to return, so he had gone directly into his office, closing the door before Hunter could ask him what his next move would be. Hunter shrugged and left.

His hunch about finding what was left of the Irwin family in the restaurant for an early lunch paid off. He sat down at a small table near the entrance and ordered coffee and a sandwich. When John Irwin got up to visit the men's room, Hunter followed him.

"Hello," he said. John had walked up to a urinal and Hunter felt he couldn't just stand and watch, so he bellied up to the adjacent urinal and unzipped his fly. "We meet again."

The man glanced over briefly. "Hello. Hunter, wasn't it? Why do I get the feeling you don't really need to be here?" He motioned at the urinal with his chin. "You trying to catch me with my pants down?"

Hunter laughed. "I just wanted to catch you alone. I enjoyed our talk Saturday night, and I wanted to apologize for leaving so abruptly." He debated telling John about his morning with Staff Sergeant Blackwell, but decided against it. Now that he was essentially being included in the investigation — although Shane's mood when they parted made him question how long that would last — he would be betraying the trust of the detectives if he revealed new information without their consent.

They finished at the urinals and moved to the sinks as Hunter continued. "I can understand if you don't want me speaking to your wife. As Mike's mother, I'm sure she's taking it harder than anyone else, so I won't even ask. Do you think Mike's wife would agree to talk to me? I spoke to her briefly the other night, but I've got more questions."

"She might. I don't really know."

"Any chance you can put in a good word for me?" Hunter opened the door for the older man, and they walked back toward the restaurant.

"You're sitting here?" John asked, as Hunter stopped beside his table near the entrance. When Hunter confirmed it, he added, "The kids are just about finished. I'll ask Kelly to wait in the booth for you. It's a little more private."

Hunter thanked him and prepared to sit down, but John remained standing by the table, an absent look on his face. Finally he nodded with a tight smile. "Kelly seems to be having a bad day. Go easy on her," he said. "You know, I wouldn't mind meeting you again for a drink. We can talk some more. Can you come by again tonight?"

Hunter hesitated, sitting down and straightening his chair to buy time. He had no specific plans, but he didn't want to commit in case something else came up. Something with the RCMP, or maybe something with Alora. He looked up at John's face again and changed his mind.

"I'd like that," he said. "Meet you in the lounge at eight?"

The older man put a hand on Hunter's shoulder. "That'd be fine," he said, and walked away.

Five minutes later, John saluted as he left the restaurant behind his wife and the two children. Kelly remained seated at the booth, and Hunter immediately got up to join her, signaling his intention to his server as they passed each other.

"May I sit down?"

She nodded, not meeting his eyes. His immediate impression was that she was uncomfortable about talking to him. With the natural light coming in through the restaurant window, he could see her more clearly today than he had in the lounge the night before. She didn't look all that much older than his own daughter, Janice, but the strain of the past two days had obviously taken its toll. There were dark circles under eyes that darted everywhere: from her hands, to the window, to the adjacent tables, landing for a brief second on Hunter, then gone again. Her hands were in constant motion as well, touching her fork, her cup, a napkin, then each other. Hunter felt he had to calm her down, for the sake of her sanity if nothing else.

"Thank you for agreeing to talk to me. I know your lawyer told you not to, but please be assured I'm not trying to accuse you of anything. I just want to get as much information as possible about your husband." When she said nothing, he continued. "Are you okay with answering a few questions?"

She nodded again, then said, "I have nothing to hide."

He was about to speak when she said, "Look. I'm sorry about yesterday. It was nothing personal, refusing to talk to you. And it wasn't even what Alora said about being my lawyer. It's just that I want this whole thing to go away. I want to stop having to think about it; about Mike, about death, about his mother hurting so much, about what I'm going to do next." She put her hands over her face and shook her head vigorously, as if trying to shake all of the unpleasant thoughts right out of it. "Have you ever just wanted to stop the world and take a break from life? I feel like my head's going to explode, or I'm going to go totally crazy."

Hunter bowed his head and sighed. He knew exactly what she was talking about. He had been going through the same thing after Ken's death — piled on top of his divorce from Chris — when he resigned from the RCMP. That's when the solitude of long haul trucking suddenly seemed so attractive. Better, he thought, than turning to the oblivion of alcohol, not that a few drinks now and then didn't help to blunt the pain.

"How about a glass of wine?" he asked her. "That might help take the edge off. It sometimes works for me."

She seemed surprised.

"I'll keep you company," he added, waving the server to the table. "A sauvignon blanc good for you?" and she agreed.

"I get so tired of holding it together for the kids and Mike's parents. That's why I spent time with Alora yesterday. I didn't have to pretend with her, you know?"

He smiled sympathetically.

"I don't want you to get the impression that I wished Mike any harm, but the fact is, he made me miserably unhappy. I was so worried about how he treated our son, Jordan. Jordan is only five, but he's my little man." She smiled, her eyes closed. "He's sensitive and kind, and Mike hated that. He wanted Jordan to be more like him. A tough guy. A jock." She looked up abruptly. ``Do you have a son?"

Hunter shook his head. "Two daughters," he said. "They're in their late teens, not that much younger than you." *And God forbid they should ever go through what you've been through*, he added to himself.

"I'm almost thirty, but I feel like I'm forty," she said.

"Forty's not so bad."

"Mike would've been forty next year."

The wine arrived, and Kelly picked up hers immediately, took a good sip, and put the glass down with a sigh. She rubbed her cheek, then her elbow, then started massaging her other hand. "Beth offered me one of her pills — some kind of sedative — but I said no. I was

148

looking forward to another one of these," she nodded at the wine glass, then picked it up for another sip.

"You'll feel better soon," he told her. "Time really does heal. I promise." He remembered what John Irwin had said about her father. "Of course, you already know that. You lost your dad, too. Life isn't fair, I'm afraid."

"You can't compare them!" She seemed to be startled at the vehemence of her response. "I mean, my dad's death was an accident. Oh my God. I still truly, truly miss my dad." She grabbed a napkin and dabbed at the corner of her eye.

"Did Mike ever talk to you about his work?" Hunter was anxious to get the conversation on a less emotional plane. He always felt uncomfortable watching a woman cry. Either he felt helpless, like now, or if he felt manipulated, it made him angry.

Kelly seemed to be trying to pull herself together. She took another sip of wine and he could almost see her start to relax as she considered the question. "Yes. He would have a scotch or two and start to talk about his 'scores', as he called them. And about the 'losers' — also his word — that he had outsmarted at work."

"Do you remember him referring to anyone specific? Any specific names or situations you can recall?" Hunter realized that his own glass was still full, while she had less than half of her wine left. He took two large swallows; he didn't want her to start feeling self-conscious.

She rubbed her forehead. "I'm sorry. Names pretty much went in one ear and out the other for me. I didn't enjoy listening to him, but I didn't want to make him mad so I pretended to be interested." She told Hunter that she only half-believed Mike's stories of his 'scores', taking most of them for drunken boasting. "He obviously was doing well, though, because he kept on buying things. Expensive things and I mean really expensive. He bought a boat. No, a yacht. He called it a yacht." She related how he had made such a big deal of buying the boat, how much it had cost, and where he wanted to keep it. That weekend, he had her bundle up the kids and he had driven them through L.A. on a Saturday — almost an hour and a half each way —

and taken them for a tour. The new boat was parked at the seller's marina in Huntington Beach. "Correna was running a fever that day and wouldn't stop crying. Jordan wasn't suitably excited — I think he was feeling intimidated — so Mike started giving him a hard time. I was preoccupied with Correna and he accused me of not appreciating all the things he did for me. The drive home was hell." She drained the last of her wine. "I never saw the 'yacht' again."

"Did you ever get the impression that Mike was doing anything..." Hunter paused, not sure how to express it without offending her. "Let's say, not quite above board?"

She tilted her head. "Funny you should say that." The wine was working its magic and she was now visibly more relaxed. "I almost got the impression that the guy who was showing us the boat was some kind of Mexican mobster. I tried to figure out how it would work, selling a boat as part of a money laundering scheme or something, but I'm just not sophisticated that way." She laughed. "A degree in journalism didn't prepare me for investigating criminals."

"You're a journalist? Good for you."

"No. I wanted to be a journalist. I studied journalism. That doesn't make me a journalist."

"Sure it does. You're just a journalist who doesn't have a job. Yet."

That made her smile.

He found her more than willing to answer questions for the time it took for both of them to polish off another glass of wine. From her descriptions of sudden financial windfalls and Mike's contemptuous attitude toward his bosses, Hunter was convinced that someone Mike had dealings with through his work, possibly someone who felt Mike represented a threat, or someone he had double-crossed, had a motive for murder. Fear or revenge. If the stakes were high enough, both could be powerful motivators, as powerful as jealousy and greed.

He finally broached the subject of her whereabouts the morning of Mike's death, and her answers were vague. She left the hotel, she walked in the falling snow, she returned to the hotel. She wasn't certain about times and places, saying she didn't know street names but could maybe retrace her steps, and then she looked at her watch and said, "I've got to get back to the kids. Beth and John are going to need a break."

The interview was over.

Elspeth Watson had been clock-watching since ten o'clock, which was highly unusual for her. Normally, time went by quickly because hers was a busy job. Phone calls from shippers, phone calls from receivers, phone and radio calls from drivers; it wasn't uncommon for her to have three or four lines going at the same time. Then there was Wally, her main warehouse guy, popping in and out of the warehouse for instructions, drivers leaning on the front counter wanting to chew the fat while their trucks were being loaded or unloaded, and Peterbilt skittering around looking for an errant piece of kibble or needing to go outside for a pee.

Today, however, she watched the clock because she was anxious to help Hunter out with his investigation, and couldn't wait for the pace to slow down so she could make a few phone calls. The most important one was to her friend, Marilyn Jenkins, aka MJ, at Hastings & Toop Customs Brokers.

"MJ! You had lunch yet? Wanna meet me at Edna's?"

"What the ... you never take a lunch break on Mondays, girl. You sick or something?"

Ten minutes later, they were seated across from each other at a small table against the wall in Edna's Kitchen. 'Edna' was actually a Chinese couple who called themselves Susan and Walter. Walter did most of the cooking and Susan yelled out the orders from tableside in Chinese, which usually didn't sound anything like 'soup and sandwich special' or 'deluxe burger with fries'. It was the only place to eat in the immediate area, so it was usually busy, but you never had to wait long for a table. Their coffee was weak and the chairs were small and hard, so diners didn't linger. The chairs were especially uncomfortable for diners as large and heavy as El and MJ, so El got right to the point.

"I need a favor. I need you to get in touch with some of your pals across the border and see if you can dig up anything on a company called Blue Hills Industries in Sylmar, California."

MJ looked at her as if she'd just suggested going to the gym.

"I'm serious. You cleared a shipment from them two years ago for Northstar in Abbotsford. You must know *something* about them."

"Get real, El. I can't even remember the name, let alone anything about them."

"What about you look in your files."

"No. Our files from year before last are all in boxes at the back of our warehouse. Besides, there won't be anything but an invoice in our files. What's that supposed to tell you? What do you need to know about them for anyway?"

Susan showed up with the coffee pot, ready to pour. El waved it away and asked for a Coke. "What's the soup du jour?"

"Today special chicken noo-doh wif egg samitch."

"What comes first?" asked MJ. "The chicken or the egg?"

"Come together. You want?" Susan was short and skinny and always seemed to be in a rush. She wore a blue dress and white apron like an old fashioned waitress, and big white Reeboks.

They both agreed to the special, after which Susan yelled something unintelligible at Walter, then hurried to the next table.

"I need to know if there's anything — you know — peculiar about the company." El was starting to feel a little irritated.

"Peculiar? Peculiar in what way?"

Elspeth huffed. She realized that she didn't have a good fix on what she was supposed to be looking for. She tapped a spoon on the empty coffee cup in front of her to help herself think, and before she knew it, Susan had breezed past the table and whisked the cup away.

"Well?"

"Okay. Look." El lowered her voice. "You hear about that guy who got killed on the chairlift at Whistler?"

MJ leaned closer, nodding.

"He worked for Blue Hills Industries. I can't divulge too much, but I'm helping with the investigation." She looked around the restaurant, as if there might be industrial spies listening in instead of hungry warehouse workers and data-entry clerks grabbing a quick lunch. "We need to know if something going on there could have been a motive for the guy's murder."

MJ scrunched up one side of her face. "Who was the guy? A shipper?"

"Purchasing manager, more or less."

Susan rushed up to the table with two white plates, each containing a sandwich on white bread and a small bowl of steaming soup. The service at Edna's Kitchen was fast, no doubt about it.

"Jeez, El." MJ examined her soup spoon, then gave it a good wipe with her napkin before starting on her soup. "What could I possibly find out? What could *you* possibly find out?"

El took a couple of spoonfuls of soup. She suspected Walter's only role had been to open a big tin and heat it up, but it tasted fine. "New accounts, lost accounts, something that happened recently. How hard would it be to find out who does their documents?"

MJ took a bite of her sandwich, chewed and swallowed before she spoke. "Don't forget, El. Canada is small potatoes to most American companies, and you can't get information on the company's domestic shipments from a customs broker."

El knew she was right. Even with her U.S. broker contacts, MJ wasn't going to be much help.

"Can't you just call and ask them?"

El almost spat out a mouthful of soup. "Are you kidding? Who the hell would talk to a total stranger about their business, especially where something like aerospace contracts is concerned? Even a shipper would know better than that."

"Just a thought." MJ sounded a little hurt.

"Unless ..." El said. She put down her spoon and tapped her lips with a forefinger.

"What?" MJ asked, but didn't look up from her soup. There was nothing left of her sandwich but a few small crumbs.

"Drivers. Drivers talk to drivers." El took a bite of her egg sandwich but couldn't wait to chew and swallow before adding, "And they generally don't work for the shipper. They work for the trucking company. No company loyalty to the shipper. See where I'm goin'?"

MJ nodded.

"I get a driver to hang out and watch a truck leave the plant, follow the driver to a coffee shop or rest stop, start up a friendly conversation ..."

"Do drivers like to gossip ... e-e-eh?" MJ's eyes lit up.

"Do drivers like to gossip! You ever knew any drivers who seemed to like sharing, uh, juicy bits of information with you?"

They both started to laugh — both big women had big laughs — until several others in Edna's Kitchen turned to look at them. Susan bustled over.

"You need somefing? You want pay now?"

"What's for dessert?" asked MJ.

"Dessert? We never have dessert here," said El. She put the last of her sandwich in her mouth.

"You want apple pie?" said Susan, looking from one to the other as she picked up their dirty dishes, but not waiting for an answer. "I bring two apple pie."

El happily picked up the tab.

Hunter answered his cell phone on the first ring. He was in the lobby of the Coast Peaks Hotel again, waiting for a break in the conference proceedings so he could buttonhole someone to talk to about Mike Irwin, and he was starting to feel impatient. It was frustrating not to have the investigative tools that he used to have when he was a legitimate detective with the RCMP.

"Any news?" It was Helen Marsh.

Hunter felt a twinge of guilt that he hadn't spared a moment of his day to think about her runaway son, he'd become so focused on the murder investigation. *Just like the old days.* "Not yet," he said. "I've got several feelers out, and there are posters with his picture being distributed downtown." Hunter hoped that was true.

"You still can't leave Whistler?"

"I'll have to stay here another day or two," he lied. He was starting to feel pretty confident that the RCMP had crossed him off their list of suspects, but he now felt like part of the investigative team and he knew he couldn't walk away from it. He'd always been that way. Once he started working a murder, there was a strong magnetic pull that didn't let up until the case was solved, or went cold. He hated to let a case drop before it was solved, and he still carried details of cold cases more than a decade old around in his brain, pending a new lead.

He heard her suck in a breath, and knew she couldn't rest until she had news of her son. His feelings of guilt multiplied.

"I'm going crazy, just sitting at home."

"You'll feel worse on the streets of Vancouver, wondering if he's calling — or even coming home to — your empty house."

He heard a soft groan on the other end of the line, and remembered what Kelly had said about stopping the world and taking a break from life. Helen needed that break right now.

"Listen," he said. "I'll make a few phone calls right now and call you back. Go make yourself a cup of coffee — or tea, maybe, something that might make you feel better — and just relax for an hour or so, knowing that there are people in Vancouver working on finding Adam for you."

"But they aren't his mother, Hunter. It's not as important to them."

"Adam *is* important to them, Helen. To them, and to me."

"Oh, God, Hunter. How could he do this to me? Why doesn't he call? I'm so afraid that something terrible has happened to him."

"Listen to me, Helen. It's okay not to think about him for an hour or two. Give yourself permission to take a break. Watch your favorite soap opera or take a bath or read a good book. It won't change where Adam is or what he's doing to worry yourself sick about him. Take care of yourself for *his* sake. Understand?"

She agreed, and Hunter flipped his cell phone closed. He looked around the lobby, but there was no exodus of conference attendees from any of the hallways, or a hubbub from the mezzanine floor at the top of a wide staircase. His cell phone beeped, a low battery warning.

Hunter swore under his breath. Either he'd have to go sit in his car to recharge the phone battery, or take a run back to Tom Halsey's and pick up the spare battery from where he'd left it in his room, parked in the charger. He patted his jeans pockets for change before realizing that his best option was to use his credit card and make the calls from the lobby pay phone.

Legal Joe had no news for him. "I'll make a round of the shelters tonight, hand out some photos to the social workers," he said. "It's wet and cold and unless they've got friends with a decent roof to stay under, that's probably where they'll be." Hunter told him he hoped that he was right. "You're going to owe me after this, pal. Big time."

"I know, Joe. You've got my cell number on the photos you're handing out?"

"Of course. I can't ask them to call long distance to Helen in Calgary — just won't happen — and my office line just goes to voicemail after hours, I turn my cell off during the day, and no way I want people calling my wife at home. Besides, you're the main man on this, Kemosabe."

Another reason to charge up his cell phone, and soon. He took a look at it and discovered that, its battery now virtually spent, it had turned itself off.

His next call was to El at the Watson Transportation office. He took the liberty of using her 800 number from the pay phone.

"Watson!"

"El, it's Hunter. I need some good news about the runaways. Anything from your contacts downtown?" A few seconds of silence gave Hunter a sinking feeling. "Did you forget?"

"No, no, I didn't forget. I haven't sent any drivers downtown today, but I faxed copies to some of the brokers I know downtown. They spend time on the sidewalks. Well, maybe not so much this time of year."

"That doesn't sound too hopeful."

"Wouldn't the cops do a better job?"

"Yes, if they wanted to. Adam's mother tried to file a missing person's report but the local police put her off. I'll suggest she try again."

"Don't you have friends in the VPD? Couldn't you pull some strings?"

"You overestimate me, El." He wished he could tear himself loose of Whistler to work on finding the boy himself, but he still felt there was a stronger urgency to solving Mike Irwin's murder than to finding Adam Marsh.

Maybe he was wrong.

El felt she had let Hunter down by not doing more to find the kid, but Monday morning was one of the busiest times of her week. At least she'd taken time out to meet with MJ about that other thing he'd asked her.

"Hey, Hunter. You're still looking for information on that Blue Hills Industries right?" Another phone line started to ring, but she ignored it.

"You've got something for me?"

He sounded eager, and she didn't want to disappoint him again. "Not yet, but I've got a plan."

"A plan?"

"The next best thing to having inside information on a company's accounts is to pump the drivers who handle freight in and out of their warehouse, wouldn't you say? Hang on." She put him on hold, told the other caller to hold on a minute, and punched his line again. "You still there?"

"You know these drivers?"

"At Blue Hills? Well ... no ... but I could get one of my guys to snoop around there some, follow a truck, talk to other drivers at the local truck stops or whatever."

"Forget it, El. That's a long shot, and what are the chances you'd have a driver with free time to snoop around in Southern California? Besides, none of your drivers will know what questions to ask or how to ask them, and they could end up getting into trouble. We're talking about something worth killing over, remember?"

She sighed. A driver walked in the front door, waving a bill of lading. "Gotta go," she said. "Talk to you later, Hunter."

In the same tone of voice a mother would use to warn a naughty kid, Hunter was saying, "El. Did you hear me?" just as she hung up the phone.

Meredith felt she'd gotten enough out of Todd Milton for the day, and told him a warm "Good bye, see you later," as she excused herself from the table after lunch. He had a possible motive for Irwin's murder and apparently he did ski, but just how well remained to be seen.

Next on her list was Brent Carruthers, if she could find him. She kept an eye out for his handsome face, or the blonde hair of his young fiancée, as she made her way from one workshop or seminar to another, standing by the entrance as if waiting for someone, or poring over her handouts as if trying to choose the best speaker to listen to for the next hour and a half.

Just as she was getting ready to give up and go to plan B, which was to find the second man — the grey haired man with a pot belly that she'd seen at Irwin's table in the GM lounge on Friday night — she spotted Carruthers leaving the men's room off the lobby. But he wasn't heading for a workshop. With a furtive look around him, he opened the fire door and ducked into the stairwell beside the elevators. Oh, crap! She knew from experience that those stairs went both up and down, so he could be heading either to the underground parking or to an upper floor.

She walked across the lobby as quickly as she could without attracting attention, and stepped inside the stairwell, taking care to close the door softly behind her as she listened for the sound of footsteps above or below. She thought she heard the thud of a fire door closing from up above, and it sounded no more than two flights away. Grabbing the handrail, she raced up the stairs two at a time, wishing she had sneakers on instead of patent leather pumps, but glad that the venue hadn't called for stilettos.

When she reached the third floor, she quietly pulled the door open just enough to peer into the hallway. Nothing. To the left and right the central hallway intersected at right angles with perpendicular hallways. She entered the hallway and listened. She caught a faint sound from the hallway to her right before she heard the elevator doors open to her left, and saw an Asian man and woman step out and walk left, trailing two travel bags on rollers behind them. She took a chance on the hallway to her right.

Expecting to catch little more than a closing door, Meredith let her stride carry her into the hallway. About four rooms down, Brent Carruthers and his blonde fiancée were engaged in a little doorway foreplay. Before Meredith could duck back behind the wall, he raised his eyes, and by the way his head lifted she knew he'd seen her.

Sneaking off now would look too suspicious, so she opted to walk on down the hall, hoping that they would be inside their room before she reached the door. No such luck. By this time, they were both watching her walk toward them.

"Oh, hi!" She gave the blonde a friendly wave. "Good to see you again, Tracy." She pulled a piece of paper out of her pocket, preparing to refer to it, as if looking for information.

"Stella, right? I'd like you to meet my fiancé, Brent." The blonde turned to Carruthers. "Stella and I met in the hotel hot tub yesterday, honey. She's here for the conference, too."

Carruthers nodded, frowning. "Nice to meet you, Stella."

She was impressed. He was as attractive close up as he was from a distance, and she had an unwanted visceral reaction to his sexuality. No wonder the boss's daughter fell for him.

He turned and started to guide Tracy inside, but she stood firm and addressed Meredith. "Are you on this floor? Didn't you get off the elevator before me?"

Meredith waved her piece of paper. "No. I was supposed to meet someone." She unfolded the piece of paper and glanced at it before rolling her eyes and stuffing it back in her pocket. "Darn. I misread the number. I *am* on the wrong floor."

"Hey, listen. Are you taking any time off from the conference? I need someone to ski with while Brent's tied up in meetings. Any chance you'd be free tomorrow?"

Meredith wished she had time to consider more carefully, but her immediate reaction was to say, "I didn't see anything particularly appealing on the agenda for tomorrow morning, and I'd love to go for a couple of runs." She thought she might already have enough information to make her client happy, but tunnel vision could be as dangerous for a private investigator as it was for the cops — or more correctly, for the poor sucker at the end of the cops' tunnel. Until she had something more conclusive about Todd Milton, it couldn't hurt to have an 'in' with Carruthers, and maybe with Tracy's father as well.

"Meet you in the lobby at eight-thirty?"

Meredith took the elevator back down. By now, the grey-haired man was no doubt locked in the middle of a row of chairs listening to a seminar on logistics or negotiating skills. She checked out the audiences as best she could, and thought she saw the back of his head in the 'Warehouse and Inventory Management Software' audience. She would come back before the scheduled break to accidently run into him as left the room. That gave her roughly an hour and a half of free time.

She wondered if Hunter Rayne had found out anything new worth listening to. Just as she decided it was time to give him a call, she caught sight of him stepping into the elevator that led to the underground parking.

She found herself in the stairwell again, this time heading down. By the time she reached the door to the parking area, cold from the concrete stairs had penetrated the soles of her shoes. She caught up with him just as he was backing an old Pontiac out of a parking stall. He braked at the sight of her and rolled down his window.

"What's up?" he asked, his breath a brief mist in the cold air.

"Where are you going?"

160

His jaw muscles bunched, but he answered pleasantly enough. "I just have to run back to the chalet for a few minutes. What are you doing?"

She didn't answer, just walked around to the passenger side and pulled on the handle. He reached across the passenger seat to open the door and she slid in.

"Crank up the heat, would you?" She was dressed for inside the hotel, no coat, no gloves. "You're coming right back, I hope." It was too late. The car was already on its way up the exit ramp.

CHAPTER
ELEVEN

Hunter dropped Meredith off back at the entrance to the Coast Peaks Hotel, and decided a visit to the RCMP detachment was in order. He hoped that Staff Sergeant Blackwell was in a better frame of mind, or that perhaps he could connect with the younger detective, Colin Pike, for an update on the case. The information he'd just received from Meredith could be the lead they needed to take the investigation to another level.

He stamped the snow off his boots while holding the front door open for a middle aged couple. The woman was so busy talking, and the man so busy listening, that they totally ignored Hunter's polite gesture. "I can't believe they won't even fingerprint the car. That camera was worth over two hundred dollars, and I want it back," she was saying.

He had just taken a seat in the waiting area and was about to check for messages on his cell phone when Sergeant Pike showed up at the counter and motioned him to follow. Shane Blackwell was seated behind a desk, and nodded a curt greeting.

"I was just filling Colin in on our morning's adventure. I would love to get my hands on that gun, but trying to find it in a mountain full of snow would be a waste of manpower. I don't even think we'll find it after the snow melts — barring incredible luck — given the territory we'd have to cover." He rubbed his jaw. "The conference will be over in two days, if the perpetrator hasn't left Whistler already. Anything new your end?"

"Our PI from California has shared a little information from her investigation that might be a good lead," Hunter began. Colin's eyebrows went up. "You've interviewed Todd Milton, a friend and former co-worker of the victim's?" He waited for a nod. "He may have been involved in some kind of scheme with Mike Irwin, possibly something to do with bribes or kick-backs — fairly substantial ones. Six figures, from the sounds of it."

"He actually told her about it?" asked the older detective.

"She said she posed as a newcomer to the business, and kind of came on to him. He fell for it, and wanted to play the big shot, so he told her about some of the unofficial perks of a purchasing position that involved negotiating large aerospace contracts. Mike Irwin's name came up, but Milton stopped short of implicating himself."

"Espionage?" The two detectives exchanged glances.

"Of a sort. It didn't involve handing over engineering or technical secrets, but it did involve revealing secrets related to competitive bids and supply contracts." Hunter sat back, letting the information sink in, waiting for one of the detectives to respond.

Shane leaned forward. "So the PI thought this Milton character might have killed our vic? Is that it?"

"What he told her speaks to motive," said Hunter, "but not necessarily his."

"So if this is a lead, where do you figure it's leading?"

"If Todd Milton has a Whistler ski pass, he's worth looking at more closely. If he was involved with Mike Irwin in something shady, and Mike Irwin was murdered, you'd think that Milton himself could be at risk. Or, unless he knew who killed Irwin, he would consider himself at risk. Did you get that impression from him?" Colin shook his head. "Neither did I."

"I doubt that a ski pass would confirm anything," said Shane. "According to the lift attendant, they barely look at lift passes on Harmony. Anybody who's already been up the first set of lifts on the mountain is assumed to have a valid pass. Besides, the murderer could have paid cash for a day pass or even stolen one. It's like an expensive bus ticket."

"True. But there's no arguing that the murderer had to know how to ski — or snowboard. He or she had to come back down that mountain. According to Meredith, Todd told her he used to ski some as a teenager, but he hasn't skied since he arrived here. Did you ever ask him for an alibi?"

"SOP," said Shane. "He said he had too much to drink the night before and slept in. We didn't check to confirm, because we had no real reason to suspect he was involved."

Hunter ventured a question. "Have you been able to find any worthwhile information on Irwin's job or the company he worked for? Or on Irwin himself, for that matter?"

Shane shifted in his chair, looked over at Colin and nodded.

Colin cleared his throat. "Except for the restraining orders by his first wife and a handful of speeding tickets, there's nothing in his record. We haven't been able to find out much about the company beyond what's listed in the usual business databases. No sign of pending bankruptcy or any kind of fraudulent practices that would raise a red flag. It's a solid, well-established company."

"Did you speak to Irwin's boss?"

Again the two detectives exchanged glances. This time Shane spoke. "Colin tells me he isn't returning our calls. He left a message with his secretary that he has no reason to believe that Irwin's job had anything to do with a motive for murder, and that Irwin has a history as an outstanding executive for the company."

Hunter frowned. "Either he's lying, or I'm way off base in thinking that Meredith Travis is working for Blue Hills Industries. Any way of finding that out?"

"She hasn't shared that information with you?"

Hunter shook his head. "She's a private investigator." He emphasized the word 'private'. "Who she works for and why is a matter of strict confidentiality, she says."

"Ditto," said Shane. "I doubt that we could subpoena the company's bank records to find out if there were any checks issued in her name — or the name of her PI firm — especially since we don't have any evidence that the top brass at Blue Hills was involved in the murder."

"Now what? Do you think you can put pressure on Todd Milton, see whether he'll talk?"

"We can try, but if he has any sense, he'll just lawyer up. Looks like the PI is our best hope for finding information we can work with."

Colin cleared his throat again. "No, Shane."

"No what?"

"The PI isn't talking to us, remember? But so far she *is* talking to our friend, here." He gestured toward Hunter. "So it looks like our best hope right now is *him*."

Meredith was back in time to watch the audience drift out of the conference room in ones and twos and groups of chatting men and women. Half of them had a cell phone to their ear by the time they passed through the doorway. She glanced at each in turn, and finally caught sight of the grey head she'd first seen Friday night in the lounge of the Chateau Grand Montagne.

"Ha!" She couldn't help but say it aloud, although she wasn't yet sure of the significance of what she was seeing.

The grey-haired man was on crutches, with a cast on his lower right leg.

Hunter checked his cell phone messages in the warmth of the detachment reception area, before heading out to his sub-zero car. The first message was nothing but background noise that consisted of unintelligible voices coming and going as if the caller had been in some public space, and a hang up. Wrong number? Some street person calling about Adam Marsh? Who was it that didn't want to leave a message The second message was from Alora.

"I need to know what's happening, Hunter. I'm leaving tomorrow, remember? Let's have dinner together. Call me right away, okay?"

Hunter flipped his phone shut and took a deep breath. He was meeting John Irwin at eight o'clock at the Coast Peaks, and he had no idea how long that would take. He could try for an early dinner with Alora — say five-thirty — so they had time for a leisurely meal, and he could still be on time to meet John, or he could try to set up a late dinner with her. Judging from the last time he'd sat down with John, he wouldn't be at her hotel until nine-thirty or even later. Either way, he had a feeling Alora wasn't going to be happy. He decided there was no point in putting off the call.

"Mike's dad? For God's sake, why?" was her reaction.

"He asked me. We kind of hit it off the other night, and I believe he just needs to talk to someone other than family."

There were a few seconds of silence.

"Look, I'm sorry. If you don't want to have dinner early or late, I could get hold of John and try to reschedule."

"Don't bother. It's the thought that counts."

"What's that supposed to mean?" He asked, but wasn't sure he wanted to hear the answer.

"Did I say 'thought'? I actually meant thoughtless. I don't know why I'm even talking to you again. I should have kissed you off for good the other night. Have a nice life." And she was gone.

Hunter sat back, his shoulders slumped, holding his cell phone and thinking about Alora Magee. He had a choice here. He could make it all her fault — an overly-sensitive bitch and good riddance to her — or he could accept the blame for screwing up yet another potential relationship. He pocketed the cell phone without deciding either way. Yes, it had been a mistake to schedule a meeting with John Irwin on Alora's last night in Whistler. He just hadn't remembered that Alora was flying home tomorrow. And he *had* offered to reschedule.

166

He sighed. He realized that was the point. He hadn't cared enough to keep track of how much time they had left before she went home. "Women care more," he said quietly to himself, but not quietly enough. The female officer behind the reception desk looked up and smiled.

"Sounds like an epiphany. Congratulations, sir," she said.

Hunter shrugged and gave her half a smile. Then he stood up, fastened his jacket, and braced himself for the cold.

The man with the grey hair was standing beside the self-serve bar trying to juggle a plate of hors d'oeuvres, a bar drink, and a pair of crutches. Meredith approached him from behind with a cheery, "You look a little overloaded. Need another hand?"

"Oh, thank you," he said, looking relieved. "I thought I could manage, but it's harder than I thought. I'd like to find a spot to sit down." He nodded over toward the tables that were set up for the conference reception and dinner. The room was large, and there were about twenty-five tables with white tablecloths, each table set for ten. There was a raised dais on the far side of the room, set up with a few chairs, a lectern and microphone, and near each of the two entrances on the near side were self-serve bars, both with a lineup. Many of the tables had chairs tipped up against them as a sign that the seats were taken.

"Do you know where you're sitting?" she asked, taking the drink and plate of hors d'oeuvres off his hands.

"I'm looking for someone I know." He was scanning the room, hitching the crutches into his armpits in preparation for takeoff.

She peered at his nametag. The company name was Cordero and Associates, and the name above it was Dave Cordero.

"You're lucky you know someone," she said. "I'm new to the industry and don't see anyone I've worked with here." She gave him one of her most engaging smiles, and was happy to see him do a double-take, but he didn't return the smile. Instead, a dark hint of suspicion crossed his face; it bordered on menace, and she realized he wasn't as innocuous as he'd looked when she'd seen him with Irwin that first night. He started moving toward a table on the left side of the room.

"Skiing accident?" she asked, shouldering past a man in the bar lineup to keep up with Cordero.

He seemed to ignore her question, or didn't hear it. He reached an empty table. There were two chairs tipped up, and no personal items on the table's surface. "This will have to do for now," he said, transferring his right crutch to his left hand so he could pull out a chair. "Thank you very much."

"I'd like to join you, if you don't mind," she said, pulling out a chair for herself before he could answer. She couldn't tell if he was annoyed, but again he didn't return her smile.

"Of course." He was occupied with stowing his crutches out of the way, on the floor beside his chair.

She wondered if she had missed the crutches on Friday night. Perhaps the cast on his leg pre-dated Mike Irwin's murder. "Skiing accident?" she asked again.

He shook his head. "Soccer."

"Broken?"

"Bad sprain. I stepped in a hole." He picked up his drink and took a sip.

"A hole in a soccer field?"

"It's a poor neighborhood, a barrio in Santa Ana. I coach some kids there." He looked her straight in the eye as he said this, as if defying her to find fault.

She held his gaze and smiled. "Much more impressive than a skiing accident." She stood up and put her binder on her chair. "I'm going to get myself a drink and some appetizers. Can I bring you anything?"

As she stood in the bar lineup, Meredith wondered if Cordero was being honest. She couldn't afford to take anything at face value, or anybody's word for it. Did the man really injure himself on a soccer field in Southern California, or did he jump from a chairlift on Whistler Mountain? Or did he injure himself at all?

By the time she got back to the table, there were two men occupying the reserved seats, and another man sitting to Cordero's right. Meredith didn't recognize any of them, but Cordero had been speaking to the man beside him as she approached. She set down her plate of hors d'oeuvres and glass of red wine, then settled herself at the table. Cordero and his companion had fallen silent.

"So tell me," Meredith said, "Dave, just what does Cordero and Associates do?"

He looked at her with half-lowered lids, his lips turned up slightly on one side. "What do we do? *We*," he accented the 'we' and paused for a few seconds, "are a consultant."

"And just who do *we* consult for?" she asked, tilting her head with a playful smile.

"Anyone who will pay us."

She frowned. "No, seriously. I'm trying to learn all I can about the industry. What type of consulting do you do?"

"Supply-contract negotiations."

"Do you help the supplier or the buyer?"

"It depends."

She raised her eyebrows, waiting for him to elaborate. He took another sip of his drink. There wasn't much left. "Do you want another drink?" she asked.

"That would be nice of you."

"Depends on...?" she prompted.

"Whoever is prepared to pay the most."

"You must be good at what you do."

"I am," he said, then added, "Very good. The best."

She pursed her lips and nodded. *So am I, Dave. So am I.*

While his car warmed up, Hunter pulled a worn vinyl folder containing business cards out of his glove box and found the number for the Vancouver Police Department. It had been a while — over five years, in fact — since he'd had any dealings with the VPD on an official level, and he had no favors to call in, so he just asked for the

Missing Persons Unit. The officer who answered the phone was hesitant about taking information from a third party, and recommended that the boy's mother make the report. He did, however, suggest that Hunter try calling the Community Policing Center in downtown Vancouver.

"They've got eyes on the street. If the subject is, in fact, in that area, you might get lucky."

Hunter thanked him, and called the downtown CPC. He identified himself as a retired RCMP sergeant helping out a friend and described the situation.

"Hang on a minute," said the female officer on the other end of the line, "that rings a bell." She was away from the phone for almost two minutes, and Hunter was finally feeling warm air blowing around his knees when she came back on. "A local lawyer dropped off a photo here just yesterday. We've posted the photo, and our guys are on the lookout for the two boys. Is this phone number yours?"

Hunter thanked her, and called Helen's number.

"Hunter," Helen sounded breathless, "what have you heard?"

"You've got many eyes and ears working for you in Vancouver now, Helen. Joe Solomon is making the rounds of the shelters tonight, and the downtown Community Police have copies of Adam's photos and are on the lookout. Go ahead and call the VPD Missing Persons Unit and make your report with them, in case the boys are somewhere other than in the downtown area." He gave her the number.

"But no one's seen Adam yet?"

Hunter thought about the hang up on his voicemail. His hesitation seemed to give her hope.

"Has someone called?" she asked.

"I don't know," he said. "I had a dead battery for a while this afternoon."

"You don't know? Do you think someone did call?"

"Someone hung up without leaving a message."

"Do you know what number?"

"No."

170

"Oh, God. I hate not knowing where he is. Call me right away if you hear anything, anything at all. Right away. Okay?"

He agreed, and she said, "We better not tie up your line. 'Bye. And Hunter ..."

"Yes?"

"Thank you. I don't know what I'd do without you to turn to."

He flipped the phone shut and sat there staring at the steering wheel, letting the Pontiac's heater do its job, images of Helen from his past playing in his mind. He and Helen had a complicated past and now there was an uncomfortable present, but he couldn't see a future. He didn't know why not, and wasn't ready to ask himself why.

In the semi-darkness, the room didn't look familiar. At first, Sorry couldn't remember where he was and had a sinking feeling that he'd fallen off the wagon and done something he'd regret, if he ever remembered what it was. It had been a long time since that had happened. He still smoked weed and popped the occasional pill, but the thought of Mo and the kids kept him from going back to booze. Most of the time.

He was stretched out on a sofa covered in a rough, brown fabric, and there was some kind of lumpy cushion under his head. He raised himself on his elbows and looked around. Was that a sewing machine on that table? On the wall above it there was a painting — or a print — of an Indian on a spotted horse. Of course. He was back in Yreka, he'd been driving all night, stopped for a ten hour break, and had to be in Redding by nine o'clock. It was already getting dark? Fuck! He rolled off the sofa and thudded to the window to pull back the heavy curtains. From the look of the twilight sky, the sun had already set.

He opened the door and heard his mother's voice, and although he couldn't make out the words, he could tell it was a one-sided conversation. She must be on the phone.

Uh-oh. He was supposed to report in to Big Mother Trucker so she would know he was on schedule. She'd been pissed off that he had no cell phone, so he'd promised to call.

"Mor!" he roared, heading for the kitchen. He could smell frying onions and maybe potatoes, an aroma that made his mouth water. "What's for dinner?"

She whirled around and glared at him, then put a finger to her lips before turning away and speaking into the receiver. "I'm so sorry to hear that, Meg. What's he going to do now?"

Sorry shrugged and went to wash up. By the time he returned to the kitchen, his mother was busy at the stove.

"What time do you have to leave?" she asked. "Your father gets home at six thirty. It would be nice to have dinner together."

"Sure, but I've got to be on the road by seven," he said as he unhooked the receiver from the wall phone.

El seemed satisfied with his progress, but she told him to hold on a minute while she finished another call. He stretched the phone cord as far as it would reach to get close to the stove and peer over his mother's shoulder. "Smells good, Ma. Whatcha cookin'?"

"Meatloaf with onion gravy," she said.

He said "Yum" and licked his lips just as El came back on the line.

"What?" She sounded shocked.

"You wanted me to hold on, remember?"

"Right."

Just then his mother called out, "Something to drink, sweetie?" and he called back, "Just milk."

"Huh? Where the hell are you anyway?"

"I'm at my mom and dad's. In Yreka."

"Who'd have guessed you had parents," said El. Then, "Listen. After you drop the trailer in Redding, I want you to deadhead to Sylmar."

"Sylmar? That's practically L.A. Why? You got another load for me?"

"Uh. I'm workin' on it."

"Then what the fuck …"

"I'm the dispatcher, you shithead. You just drive."

"You gonna tell me where in Sylmar?"

"Pull in at the Pilot in Castaic. Call me from there tomorrow morning and I'll tell you what you need to know. Got that?"

He knew she was about to hang up, so he yelled, "Wait, El! Does Hunter know?"

A pause. "Of course he knows. Look, this is important, Sorenson — don't fuck up."

His father arrived home just before six-thirty, and Sorry's mother told him by the time he'd washed up, dinner would be on the table. He left the room grumbling.

Sorry had already bellied up to the table and sat holding his knife and fork. When his father came back, it felt like he might need the knife to cut through the tension in the room. Bless his mother. She came up behind old Hank and hugged his neck, then planted a kiss on his cheek and asked him how his day had been.

Hank patted her arm, nodded and with something close to a smile said, "Pretty good, Momma. Made some money. Saw some old friends." He didn't look at Sorry when he said that. "What's the big rush for dinner? You know I like to unwind a little first, watch my news."

She gestured toward Sorry with her chin. "Danny's got to be back on the road in half an hour. Right, Dan?"

Sorry glanced at the clock above the stove. "Twenty minutes," he said.

His father took a long, hard look at Sorry, then turned to his wife with a face as expressionless as a chunk of lava rock. "Feed him, then. I'm going to watch the six-thirty news." With that, the old man pushed back his chair and left the room.

His mother set down a plate with a generous portion of meatloaf, and Sorry ate in silence until his plate was almost empty. After one taste he was able to push his father from his mind. Meatloaf and mashed potatoes with onion gravy was the food of the gods. His mother continued to putter in the kitchen, washing some dishes, putting things away, pouring him another glass of milk and herself a glass of red wine. "You make the best meatloaf in the world, Mor," he said, picking up the milk. The sound of the television came from the living room, and he rolled his eyes in that direction. "I hope I haven't ruined your dinner."

"He's hurt," she said, sitting down next to him. "You come to town once in a hundred years, then eat and run like we aren't important, and he has no say in the matter."

"Maybe if he wasn't such a cranky old bastard he might get more visitors."

"We're not talking about *visitors*, Danny." Her voice was low and patient. "*You*. You're his only son." She put her hand on his arm as if to draw his attention, but he couldn't look her in the eye.

"Gotta go, Ma," he said, getting up from the table.

Ten minutes later he was guiding The Blue Knight and its heavy trailer out of the neighbor's driveway. He looked back through the trees toward his parents' place. His mother was at the front door, waving.

He thought he saw his father's face at the living room window, just for a few seconds, but he wasn't sure.

Hunter was early, and there was no sign of John Irwin in the lounge at the Coast Peaks Hotel. He took the opportunity to do a little poking around in the hopes of seeing someone he could talk to about Mike Irwin. The conference was obviously in full swing, judging by the men and women wandering across the lobby or standing in groups of three or four, all wearing matching blue name tags on black cords around their necks.

Most of the people with nametags seemed to be gravitating toward one of the main conference rooms, and Hunter followed a man carrying a laptop case in that direction. The room was large and the floor space between two self-serve bars was crowded with people holding glasses of beer and wine, standing and chatting in groups. He made his way inside and began scanning the tables for familiar faces, but a thin woman wearing a yellow name tag stepped in front of him.

"Excuse me, sir. I don't see your name tag. Are you registered for the conference?"

"No, I …"

"I'm sorry, sir. This dinner is for conference attendees only. Is there something else I can help you with?" She smiled without opening her lips, lifting one arm as if to usher him back out the door. The name on her yellow tag was Sandra Gough. She waved him on with her other hand, like a traffic cop.

He bent and spoke in her ear, soft and low. "I don't want dinner, Miss Gough. I'm here to find a killer." He regretted giving in to the impulse as soon as he said it.

Her smile disappeared. "I really don't think this is a good time…"

Hunter caught sight of Meredith Travis walking away from one of the bars, carrying two drinks. She wore a name tag and looked every inch a registered attendee. "You're right," he told the woman. "This is not a good time." He watched Meredith put down one of the drinks in front of a grey-haired man and take a seat beside him. He would catch up with her later. He walked past Miss Gough and out the door, resisting the urge to glare at her.

By the time Hunter got back to the lounge, John Irwin was seated at the same table they had shared Saturday evening, the day of Mike's murder. The older man looked freshly shaved and wore a burgundy polo shirt with a golf course logo on the chest, but his face was pale and he didn't smile when Hunter pulled out the chair across from him.

"You a golfer?" asked Hunter. When John looked confused, Hunter added, "The crossed clubs on your shirt. Are you a member?"

John nodded, then shook his head. "A friend of mine's a member of Broadmoor. I used to golf once or twice a week."

"Does that mean you don't anymore?"

The older man smiled. "Not in the rain or snow."

"Of course. I try to get out with my landlord when I'm in town, but we're fair-weather golfers, too."

They made small talk until they'd been served. Hunter raised his glass, but didn't make a toast.

Quietly, John said, "Non Sibi Sed Patriae."

"Sorry?"

"Huh? Oh. Latin leftover from my army days. Just feeling down about my son." He sighed, then raised his beer to his lips and took several swallows.

Hunter did the same. When John remained silent, he asked "How's your wife doing?" as gently as he could. He wondered if the older man had changed his mind about wanting to talk.

"She's a strong woman. It amazes me sometimes how the physically weaker sex can show such emotional strength." He paused. "She calls me her rock, but she's mine. She's my rock."

Hunter couldn't help but reflect on the fact that he had no woman in his life to be his rock, or to be a rock to. Unless he could count El Watson. But no. El was no rock. His landlord, Gord Young, was the closest thing he had to a rock. The retired medical doctor always seemed to understand him, listened without judging, dispensed sensible advice. The old man never turned the conversation around to himself, the way some people did.

"You're lucky — both of you — to have each other." Maybe it was a stupid thing to say. Their son had just been murdered and he was calling them lucky, but he had felt a need to respond in some way. Again, he waited for John to pick up the conversation.

"You've talked to the police?"

Hunter nodded. "And you?"

"Following up some leads, is all they'll tell me." He put down his glass and reached behind him to pull a sweater off the back of his chair. He draped the sweater over his shoulders. "I know if I put it on, I'll end up being too hot, but it's a bit cool in here. A ski bar doesn't cater to patrons in golf shirts." He nodded toward Hunter's arm where it lay on the table, his fingers curled around the beer glass. He wore a long-sleeved flannel shirt that looked like a Scottish tartan.

"What can *you* tell me?" asked John.

Hunter inhaled and exhaled as he considered how much to say. He didn't want to betray the confidence of the RCMP detectives, but he felt sympathy for John Irwin and wanted to give him something.

"Not a lot more. They're looking for information on your son's associates and his employer, maybe some kind of shady business deal.

Perhaps your son knew too much. As far as I can tell, that's the direction the investigation is taking." He looked the older man in the eye. "Do you think they're on the right track?"

John returned Hunter's stare for several seconds, then looked away and nodded, almost absently. "Sounds like a good bet," he said. Suddenly he clenched his fists on the table top so tight his knuckles turned white. "I hate this. I hate what happened, and I hate feeling so helpless." His fists relaxed. "I wish I could put a bullet in the bastard who killed my son, but I can't do that to my wife."

Hunter understood. Sometimes the satisfaction of revenge can be obliterated by its consequences.

"Sometimes I think it would be better if I didn't know what the detectives find out, but I can't ignore the results of their investigation." He leaned forward. "Listen. I know you probably have to go back to work, but are you going to stay on top of this? Are you going to stay in touch with the police?"

"I'm only involved peripherally because myself and Alora were — maybe still are — considered suspects. I can't see the detectives keeping me in the loop, but as the father of the victim, I'm sure the RCMP will keep you informed." He shook his head, frowning. "Aren't you comfortable talking to them directly?"

John sighed. "Yes. Of course."

"But?"

John drained the last of his beer and looked around for the server. Hunter shrugged, then raised his own glass and drank while he waited for John to speak again. John signaled the server for another round, then gave Hunter a wry smile.

"I told you that I lost my best friend," he said. "It was a few years ago. You did, too, you said." He waited for Hunter to affirm. "Men like us — you and me — we don't make friends easily. Good friends, I mean, the kind you can ... I don't know ... 'bare your soul' sounds so touchy-feely, but that's kind of what I mean." He snorted softly. "Like a brother, I was going to say, but some brothers aren't good friends, are they?"

"I understand," said Hunter.

"Well, I think you and I could be friends like that, if there was time."

"If there was time?"

The older man shrugged. "You're going back to work. Me? I'm going home. To Seattle. With my wife, and my daughter-in-law, and my grandchildren. We need to go home. Being here in Whistler... well, Whistler is now all about Mike's murder. There's no joy here. We need to go home."

The server arrived with two bottles of beer, and both men nodded their thanks. In silence, they each filled their glasses.

"I think you're right," said Hunter. "We could be good friends." He raised his glass and John raised his; they clinked them lightly together and drank.

"We're leaving tomorrow." John reached behind him and brought out a pocket-sized notebook which he opened on the table in front of him, then produced an expensive-looking ballpoint pen and began to write. When he was finished, he tore off the page and handed it to Hunter. "My address and phone number," he said, then pushed the notebook and pen across the table. "Please."

Hunter wrote down his own address and phone numbers, both cell and landline, then closed the notebook and passed it back to John. He folded up the page John had given him and tucked it into his wallet. "What time do you go?" he asked.

"We'll pack up the van and leave after breakfast. Are you and Alora staying on?"

"Alora is flying back to California tomorrow. I don't expect to see her again."

John raised his eyebrows.

Hunter shrugged. "We didn't know each other well. I guess we never will."

There didn't seem to be much left to say, so they finished their drinks in comfortable silence, the way friends sometimes do. John signed the bar tab, and both men stood up to leave.

"Call me. If you hear anything from the RCMP, even if they say they've already talked to me, please call me. Now you *have* to stay involved in the case."

Hunter smiled. "Yes. Yes, I do."

They walked side by side as far as the elevators, then faced each other. Hunter held out his hand and they shook hands; John laid a hand on Hunter's shoulder as they did so. His eyes searched Hunter's face, as if looking for something more.

"Of course I'll stay involved," said Hunter with a sad smile. "The case is critical to a friend."

CHAPTER
TWELVE

It was after ten o'clock when the after-dinner speeches were done and groups of people began to drift toward the elevators and bars. Meredith said goodnight to Cordero, and found his parting words disturbing. "Keep your nose clean, sweetheart," he said. It wasn't the words so much, as the lack of a smile when he said it.

She couldn't resist her own parting shot. "See you on the slopes, Dave," with a nod to his cast and crutches as she overtook and passed him on the way to the door. The smile she gave him was, she thought, warm and friendly, but her feelings toward him were anything but.

She had sat beside him all during cocktails, dinner and dessert, followed by a round of liqueurs and the interminable speeches. The keynote speaker was a man who must have been a cheerleader during college, and his 'rah rah' energy level during his presentation on 'Demand and Supply Chain Integration' was distracting. It was hardly a fitting topic for a motivational speech. Meanwhile, Cordero spoke so low to the man seated next to him that Meredith couldn't make out more than a few words, and at first he made no attempt to disguise his lack of interest in talking to her.

"How long have you been coaching soccer, Dave?"

"Long enough."

"So, do you live in Santa Ana, Dave?"

"No."

"Where is it that you live?"

"South of Los Angeles."

"Do you have a card, Dave?"

"No. I ran out."

The woman who took the seat to Meredith's left began to tell her all about the company she worked for in Phoenix, and Meredith listened politely, tried to ask all the right questions and make appropriate comments, just loudly enough so that Cordero would hear, drop his suspicions (if that was indeed the problem) and perhaps start to warm up to her. There was wine at the table, and after a glass or two, Cordero did begin to make a little small talk, just minutes before the speeches were to start.

Meredith had started to become annoyed that the woman from Phoenix was insinuating herself into her conversation with Cordero when the woman gave Meredith a gift. "Did you hear about the man who was killed on the chairlift?" she asked, addressing both Meredith and Cordero.

Meredith was about to reply when Cordero beat her to it. "I knew him," he said.

"Did you really?" The woman from Phoenix was wide-eyed. "Was he a friend of yours?"

Meredith leaned back in her chair and let the two of them talk.

"A business acquaintance," said Cordero. He made a face as if he'd tasted something sour. "He was not a man I would have wanted to be friends with."

"Oh, my. Why is that, Mr. Cordero?"

"Where I come from, a handshake is as good as a contract drawn up by a lawyer. It seems he did not feel the same."

"Oh, dear. Did you do business with him then?"

Cordero seemed to be considering whether or not to reply when the chorus of "I Believe I Can Fly" erupted through the speakers, and three men mounted the dais to start the after-dinner speeches.

Cordero more or less dismissed the woman from Phoenix with a wave of his hand and turned away.

Meredith tried to reintroduce the topic between speeches, but Cordero just said, "The man is dead. Not a pleasant topic for the table," with a suspicious frown in her direction, and shut down. As far as she knew, there was no reason for him to be suspicious of her. There had to be another reason for his reluctance to talk.

She was tired and frustrated — not a good frame of mind for a private eye — and decided a short workout and a Jacuzzi were in order, but first she wanted to touch base with her new 'partner'. She waited until the room door clicked shut behind her before pulling out her cell phone.

"Can you talk?"

"Yes," he answered. "What have you got?"

"Remember that innocuous looking fellow at Irwin's table the other night?"

"The one with the grey hair, drinking beer?"

"That's him. Did you notice he was on crutches?" She thought it was possible that Hunter had seen the crutches on the floor beside the man's chair from where he sat. "Did you see the cast on his leg?"

"What? You're kidding."

"He says he sprained his ankle coaching kids' soccer back in California. He's got a beer gut and doesn't look like a skier, but then he doesn't look like a soccer player either." Meredith kicked off her pumps and began pacing from the window to the bed and back on the carpet. It felt good to set her toes free after a long day in dress shoes.

"So you're thinking he could have hurt himself jumping from the chairlift? I can have the RCMP check with the local hospital."

"Or it's a cover."

"Also possible. What's your intuition tell you?" he asked.

She pulled back the curtain and looked out the window. It was snowing again. "That he's not as harmless as he looked the other night."

"Tell me more."

"I managed to sit beside him at dinner. He's a freelance consultant on purchasing contract negotiations. The way I read it, he's a mercenary bully of some sort." She tucked the phone under her chin and took off her jacket as she spoke. "Or maybe he's an intermediary who promises to keep his client's identity secret until the deal is made. Sound plausible?"

"Not my field, but it might make sense."

"And listen to this. He didn't like Irwin. He implied that Irwin reneged on a deal they'd made." She stepped out of her slacks and tossed them on the bed.

"Good work, Stella. Sounds like he's worth a closer look. What's his name?"

She smiled at his use of her alias, almost as if it were a pet name. "Cordero. His name's Dave Cordero."

"Sounds Latino."

"Yeah. So what?" She sat on the bed.

"Mexican?"

"He teaches soccer to kids in a barrio. Why? What's the significance."

"Maybe nothing."

"Tit for tat, remember?"

"Mike Irwin's wife said he bought a boat from a guy who reminded her of Mexican mafia."

"South of L.A., by chance?"

"Huntington Beach."

"Get the cops to follow up, okay? I'll talk to you tomorrow."

Meredith finished undressing and pulled on her workout clothes. She loved it when pieces of a puzzle started falling into place. She was humming as she headed for the elevator, and broke into a smile when she realized what it was.

It was the chorus to "I Believe I Can Fly."

Hunter could hear Tom Halsey and his wife still talking in their kitchen as he sat on his bed in the basement guest room. He briefly debated calling Alora one more time. This time his motivation wasn't to salvage their relationship — if it had ever existed — or to apologize. After the seed Meredith had planted in his mind, he had begun to wonder if finding him insensitive was the reason Alora wanted to stop seeing him, or if it was the other way around. Perhaps her need to stop seeing him was the reason she accused him of being insensitive. He knew that if he were truly looking for Mike Irwin's killer, he couldn't afford to cross Alora Magee off the list.

And she was flying back to L.A. tomorrow, unless he or the RCMP did something to stop her.

His cell phone beeped, indicating a message, so he punched in some numbers to retrieve it. As he waited for the message to play, he suddenly realized how tired he was. It was more than physical. Much more. He was tired of trying to understand Alora, let alone to please her, tired of playing games with the detectives, tired of the weight of the Irwins' grief, tired of people in general. He thought about how uncomplicated life was sitting in his big Freightliner for hours at a time, seeing people from the height of his driver's seat, at a distance as he passed them in their cars, on the sidewalks, in their homes, on the other side of shatterproof glass. As much as he had once loved his job as a detective, he had left the RCMP and taken to the road because this same emotional exhaustion had started to affect his work. He knew he was not yet healed.

The voice on the recording jarred him out of his reflection.

"Who the fuck are you? What gives you the right to hand out pictures of us all over the fuckin' city? Whoever you are, leave us the fuck alone."

"Glad I caught you." Hunter had shaken off his weariness and was back in detective mode. "Just something you might want to start the ball rolling on before you pack it in for the night."

"Hunh." Staff Sergeant Shane Blackwell didn't sound too happy to hear from him.

184

"Alora Magee, Mike Irwin's ex, is booked on a flight out of YVR tomorrow."

"Meaning?"

"Have you been able to corroborate her alibi for Saturday morning?"

He heard Shane sigh. "What's this all about? You think your girlfriend's guilty?" His tone implied he didn't take Hunter seriously.

"Not exactly. I just don't feel she can be ruled out, unless you know something I don't."

"Go on."

"She has motive. And she's been trying really hard to distance herself from me the last couple of days."

"Could be another reason for that, dude."

"Entirely possible, chief. But it's got me wondering if I was just part of her cover for being here. One minute she's in my arms, the next minute she doesn't even want to talk to me."

"Means nothing, Hunter. She's a woman." He sighed again. "Okay. You might have a point, but we've got nothing to detain her on. She has every right to leave Whistler."

"Can you take a closer look? Canvass hotel employees, ticket sales, lift operators, anyone who might remember seeing her on Saturday morning?"

"We'll never get that done before she leaves. We'll still know where to find her, and since the victim was an American citizen, I'm sure we won't have any trouble getting the FBI involved if we do find something incriminating." He paused. "Hell hath no fury, eh?"

Hunter clenched his jaw. He wasn't angry at Alora for pulling the plug, he was relieved, but he wasn't prepared to discuss it with Shane. He said nothing.

"You've spent time with her. You think she's capable?" Shane asked.

"I hope not."

"That's not much of an answer."

"I can't help thinking about all of the naïve friends, relatives and neighbors I've interviewed who were convinced that Joe Blow couldn't have killed his wife. To be honest, chief, I just don't know."

Hunter made arrangements to meet with Shane again the following morning, then dialed the Vancouver Police Missing Persons Unit.

"I got a call from a boy reported missing by his mother in Calgary. The message is on my cell. Any chance of tracing the call?"

The response was, "Not as easy as it sounds, I'm afraid. You know for sure it's him? We get cranks calling in all the time." Hunter wasn't surprised.

His next step was to call Helen, see if he could play the voicemail for her so she could ID the voice. He hoped it wasn't Adam. He hated to think that Ken and Helen's son would speak that way, or would care so little about his mother that he wouldn't realize it was her trying to find him. He checked his watch but he knew it didn't matter what time it was. He had to make the call. He didn't think he could play the message for her on his own phone, so he went upstairs to the kitchen.

"What's up?" asked Tom. "I thought you were turning in for the night." His wife was wiping down the kitchen counter.

"I might have a lead on that missing kid. I'd like to play the voicemail for his mother, if you don't mind me using your phone."

Tom's wife had rinsed out and put away the dish cloth. "I'll get out of your way," she said. "Good night, Hunter."

"There's no need ..."

"Didn't get much sleep in Vegas," she said with a grin. "I'm beat. See you in the morning."

"I'll be along in a minute, hon," Tom said to the closing door, then to Hunter, "You can't stay out of it, can you? You're still a cop, Hunter. Why the hell are you driving a truck?"

Hunter shook his head. "It's only been four days and I'm looking forward to getting back on the road already. It's peaceful out there, Tom. It gives me the time and space I need."

186

"Why do you need time and space on the job? I get mine out there." He gestured toward the window, in the direction of Blackcomb Mountain. The window was a black mirror, reflecting the two ex-cops standing in the kitchen, looking beyond their reflections at a world they couldn't see.

Hunter just smiled, and Tom punched his shoulder lightly as he walked past. "Good night, detective," he said, and left the kitchen.

Helen answered on the second ring.

"You've heard something?"

"Just a voicemail, Helen. I'm going to play it for you. I want you to tell me if you recognize the voice." She said nothing while his cell phone beeped for each button he pushed to bring up the message. He held its speaker up against the mouthpiece of Tom's home phone. He could hear Helen's voice even before he returned the receiver to his ear.

"Nathan. That was Nathan, I'm sure of it. They're there, Hunter. I have to come."

"Wait, Helen. Wait until I've found the boy."

"I'll drive. I'll come get him and bring him home."

"Listen to me." She kept on talking about her plan to leave first thing in the morning so he had to raise his voice. "Helen. Listen to me. It's not an easy drive at this time of year. Give me a few more days."

"But I can't just sit here ..."

"Better there than behind a snow plow in the Rockies."

"But I can drive him home."

"I'll drive him home. Stay in Calgary and wait for us, okay? Give me a few more days. I'll find him and I'll bring him home."

After he hung up the phone, Hunter sat at Tom Halsey's kitchen table for over half an hour thinking about what he'd just done. "Why did I say that?" he whispered, shaking his head. Yes, he wanted to find Helen's son and see him safely home. He wanted to help the Whistler RCMP detectives find Mike Irwin's killer. He wanted Alora Magee to be innocent. But each and all of those things he wanted, he couldn't begin to reconcile with what he truly wanted most.

He remembered what Mike Irwin's widow had said. *Have you ever just wanted to stop the world and take a break from life?* Hunter wanted to be back in The Blue Knight, cruising south on the I-5, listening to the hum of the engine and watching the world go by from the driver's seat, where the most complicated thing about his life was shifting gears.

By the time he'd unhooked the trailer and pulled away from the factory in Redding, Sorry was hungry enough to eat a horse. He passed a Burger King on his way back to the highway, but it was across the median on the other side of the street, so he carried on down the I-5 to the TA truck stop at exit 673. He found a table in a corner of the 24-hour restaurant so he could sit with his back to the wall. He didn't expect to run into anyone with a score to settle here in California, but he still liked to keep an eye on the door. He ordered steak and eggs.

Sorry stirred some cream and sugar into his coffee as he watched an old trucker in a Budweiser ball cap come through the entrance. The guy wore army green pants and shirt, like a uniform of some kind, and had a ring of keys hanging from his belt. It looked like the keys were heavy enough to pull the pants down over his skinny butt. He was a little bent over, like his back was giving him trouble, but he grinned and waved at the waitress on his way to a table. Sorry was reminded of his dad. It seemed his dad was cheerful and friendly to almost everybody in the world except his son.

Am I a wayward son? he asked himself. He refused to take over his dad's hardware store and turned his back on the small town where he'd grown up. Was that so unforgiveable? He tried to picture Bruno grown up, to see if he would feel the same way. What if he started a business and taught the kid everything about it and then the kid flipped him off and left town. It was no good. Not only could he not picture Bruno flipping him off, he couldn't even picture little Bruno grown up. It occurred to him that his own father had long ago stopped thinking of Sorry as his little boy.

"He's hurt," his mom had said. *That makes two of us*, thought Sorry, watching the old trucker chat with the waitress as she took his order. He, too, sat facing the door. What if his old man did die soon after retirement, like his mom was worried about. "Bruno should meet his dad's old man," he decided aloud, just at his steak and eggs arrived.

"What's that, sugar?" said the waitress. She was about as old and skinny as the trucker, and he could tell by the way she talked that she didn't have her own teeth.

"Did you get along with your dad?" he asked her, reaching for the salt.

"He died in the war," she said. "Iwo Jima."

"Sorry 'bout that."

She laughed a smoker's laugh. "Ain't nobody given their condolences about my dad for over forty years." She turned away and coughed a couple of times, then said, "I'm over it. Why'd you ask?"

Sorry's mouth was already full, so he didn't reply, just shrugged and the waitress moved on. He pictured his dad's face — and his mom's — when they saw Sasha and little Bruno for the first time. He stopped chewing and almost teared up just thinking about it. Now that he had his own son, it was easier to understand where his dad was coming from. The more he thought about it, the more important it seemed for him to make it up to his old man before Hank croaked. He would drive down with Mo and the kids this spring. Done deal.

The steak and eggs dinner was good, and he washed it down with a glass of milk, then sat back and patted his belly. A nap would go good, or he could drive another nine hours and make it to Castaic by morning, like El wanted. Yeah. He needed the money, and if he was late to pick up the load in Sylmar, assuming El really had one for him, he'd piss off Hunter as well as the fat broad. He'd grab another coffee to go and hit the road.

Sorry paid his bill and stepped outside, lighting up a cigarette as soon as he was settled in the cab of The Blue Knight. Blowing out a lungful of smoke toward the four inch gap between the top of the window and the door frame, he decided that as long as he kept the window cracked open, Hunter would never know.

Alora's shuttle to YVR was scheduled to leave at ten o'clock, so she was all packed and ready to leave by eight, with plenty of time for breakfast in the restaurant downstairs. The hostess was leading her to a table for one when she heard her name called. It was Kelly Irwin, with her two children, at a table she had just walked past.

"I'm glad I got a chance to see you," Kelly said. "We're leaving today."

"So am I."

"Mike's dad has just gone to meet one last time with the police."

Alora nodded, wondering if she should have let the police know she was leaving. Surely if they still considered her a suspect, they would have been in touch again. She smiled at the two small faces looking up at her. There wasn't much she felt she could say to Kelly in front of them, but she thought she should acknowledge them. "Hi, kids. Are you happy to be going home?" She smiled at each of them in turn.

The little girl nodded, a tight little smile on her face. The boy first looked toward his mother, then said, "We're not going home to California. We're going to Seattle because our dad got killed."

Alora felt as if her smile had frozen on her face.

"That's right, Jordan," said Kelly, then to Alora, "I've got your card. I'll be in touch." She glanced over Alora's shoulder, then said, "You'd better go."

Before Alora had a chance to understand what Kelly meant, Beth Irwin was beside her. The older woman gripped her arm, as if she were scolding a child.

"Why are you here? As if we're not in enough pain, you're here to gloat about it, aren't you?"

Alora took a step backwards, stunned, and Beth let go. The older woman's face was contorted with a combination of grief and anger.

She looked smaller than Alora remembered her, somehow shrunken and disheveled, in spite of the tasteful sweater and slacks she wore.

"I hope you're happy now," she continued, her voice bitter. "I have nothing more to say to you. Please leave us."

The hostess, who had been two tables ahead holding a menu, stared at Alora with her eyes wide. Alora swallowed hard, raised her head high and walked on toward the hostess. It didn't matter. She wouldn't see any of the Irwins again. Not even Kelly, she decided.

She chose the chair facing away from the door so she wouldn't have to know if Beth or the children were staring at her, but still she felt uncomfortable. She studied the menu, not sure if she felt like eating, and ordered coffee with a light breakfast.

Yes, I am happy now, she said to herself. *I am going home.*

She thought about the ugly weekend she had just endured. The scenes with Mike on Friday night, the awkwardness with that truck driver — an aborted 'relationship' better forgotten — the interviews with the police detectives, and now this encounter with Beth Irwin. The only bright spot was meeting Kelly on the chairlift, and knowing they were both better off. The only bright spot besides Mike's death, she corrected herself.

And the skiing. The skiing had been fun. She had to admit that spending time with Hunter Rayne wasn't a total loss, but it was better if she never saw him again either. She wanted to make a clean break from anything and everything that had any connection to Mike Irwin.

"You wanted coffee?" A young server with the red cheeks of a frequent skier stood before her holding a stainless steel carafe.

"God, yes," she said, holding up her cup. When the server had gone, she raised the cup to the window, as if she were proposing a toast to her own transparent reflection.

To the first day of the rest of my life.

Meredith watched Mike Irwin's father arrive at the entrance of the restaurant and make his way to the table where his wife and daughter-in-law sat with the kids. The older Irwin woman still looked upset from her encounter with Alora Magee, and although she couldn't hear what was being said, Meredith could tell from the gestures that she was pointing out Alora's presence to her husband. He just nodded with a pained smile as he took his seat.

Meredith turned her attention back to Alora Magee. The woman had seemed a bit rattled when she first sat down, but had begun to look more relaxed. She was reading one of the hotel's complimentary Vancouver newspapers as she ate her breakfast. So was Meredith. The Chairlift Killer was still in the news, but relegated to an inside page.

> *Whistler RCMP would like to hear from anyone who was on the Harmony Express chairlift between 8:00 and 9:00 on the morning of Saturday, February 8, who might have seen Mike Irwin (see photo) or noticed any unusual activity on the chairlift at about that time.*

She was glad she'd opted to pass on the morning seminar and accepted the invitation from Carruthers' boss's daughter to join her on the slopes. She'd been on the phone to her client at seven o'clock, as previously arranged, and had reported what was pertinent to her assignment. The client told her to stay on until the end of the conference, as planned, and had asked her, "Are you still a suspect in Irwin's murder?"

Meredith replied that she didn't think so.

When the server came by with the coffee carafe, Alora Magee checked her watch, then turned her head far enough to catch a glimpse of the Irwins' table. The fact that they were still there was probably the reason she let the server refill her coffee cup, then went back to her paper.

Meredith left enough cash on the table to cover her bill and a tip, picked up her ski jacket, then walked over to Alora's table.

"I've seen you at the conference, haven't I?" she said, sliding onto the bench across the table from Alora. "I decided to pass on this morning's topics, too. There's only so much a girl's brain can absorb, don't you think?" She followed up with a light laugh and a perky smile. "I'm going to ski a couple of runs this morning, so no conference badge. I'm Stella." She thrust her hand across the table.

Alora reacted with a confused frown, then gave Meredith a smile that bordered on condescending. "No, I'm not here for the conference. I'm leaving Whistler on the airport shuttle this morning."

Meredith withdrew her hand. "Heading home? Where are you from?" Meredith kept her voice light and friendly.

"Southern California. L.A. And you?" Alora's lips barely moved, as if speaking to Meredith was painful for her.

"Oh, my gosh! Did you know the guy from L.A. who was killed on the chairlift?" Meredith pointed to the newspaper, implying that she'd read about it there. "Wasn't that just awful? It freaked me right out. He was a guest here, did you know that? He was registered for the conference I'm at. I'm kind of nervous about going on the chairlifts here, at least until they find the guy who did it, weren't you?"

"Don't worry. I'm sure it wasn't a random murder."

"Really? How do you know that? Did you know him?"

Alora Magee's face got hard, her lips pressed together in a thin line. "Look," she said. "I don't know you, and I don't want to discuss something that neither of us have any business speculating about. I don't like to be rude…"

"Oh, I'm sorry. I didn't mean to upset you."

"I'm not upset."

"Yes, I've upset you. I can tell. I'm just trying to be friendly." Meredith looked down at her lap and in a subdued voice said, "All these stuffy older men — I know what they want when they make conversation with me — away from their wives and having a few drinks — I just wanted to talk to somebody — you know. I'm here by myself and…"

"Okay, okay. I'm sorry. It's not that I don't like you, I just don't have much time."

"What time is your bus?"

"I still have to go upstairs and finish packing." Alora pushed her plate away and started gathering up her things.

Meredith changed her tone. "The chairlift guy. Did you know him?"

Alora stopped dead, her eyes narrowed, and in an icy voice she said, "Who *are* you?"

"Like I said..."

"Are you a reporter?"

"No. I just..."

Alora straightened up and her eyes widened. "Oh my god. You're working for the police, aren't you?"

Meredith looked away and kept her mouth shut. She remained seated as Alora picked up her purse and left the table, then she watched as Alora swept past the Irwins' table without looking in their direction, threw some money down on the cashier's desk and hurried out into the lobby.

Meredith smiled to herself. That little discussion may not have advanced her investigation — or that of the local police — but sometimes a girl just likes to have a little fun.

CHAPTER
THIRTEEN

It was one of those mornings in the mountains that takes your breath away. The trees that lined the side streets were coated with snow like a layer of fresh whipped cream, and to the east rose the regal white peaks of Blackcomb and Whistler mountains against a sky as bright and blue as summertime. Hunter rolled `down his window and inhaled lungfuls of the cold mountain air. He arrived at the Whistler RCMP detachment just before nine o'clock for his meeting with Staff Sergeant Shane Blackwell. Shane was just dismissing Sergeant Colin Pike, who smiled and clapped Hunter on the shoulder as he left the room. "Off to the salt mines," he said cheerfully.

Hunter sat down without being invited. "Anything new?"

"Just talked to the victim's father again."

"And?"

"And nothing. Can't help the guy. Says he has no theories, but of course he wants to know who killed his son. Wish I knew enough to say."

Shane tossed a copy of the morning's paper across the desk, folded open to an inside page. "Seen this?"

Hunter picked it up and read a brief article on the Chairlift Killer case, ending with a request from police for witnesses to come forward. "Something useful turn up?"

"Colin is heading off to interview three of the callers. We've had eight calls so far, and are expecting more. From past experience, I know that over ninety percent of the calls will be duds, but a few could very well pay off. Anything from your end?"

"A lead from our lovely PI. Did you interview a David Cordero, one of Mike Irwin's contacts from the conference? Meredith and I both saw him sitting at the table with the victim on Friday night in the GM."

Shane leafed through a file on his desk, and shook his head as he flipped the pages back down. "What about him?"

"He's worth taking a look at. Evidently he had some kind of grudge against the victim, and may have had a deal with him go sour earlier this year."

Shane picked up a pen and made some notes. "C-O-R-D-E-R-O?"

"As far as I know, that's how it's spelled. And get this — Cordero has a cast on his leg. Maybe your guys can check to see if he arrived with it on, or if he visited a clinic while he was here."

Shane's eyebrows went up.

"He may have made a deal with Irwin involving the sale of a yacht in Huntington Beach. I don't know that for sure, but Kelly Irwin said the man who sold her husband the yacht looked like some kind of Mexican Godfather, and Cordero fits the description. He claims to have hurt himself coaching kids' soccer in a barrio. Meredith said there's something threatening about him."

Shane scratched a few more lines, then threw down his pen. "Why is it that every time you come in here, you point us toward another suspect? Don't you think it's about time you start helping us narrow the field?"

Sorry shook himself awake and rolled down his window to get a better look at the commotion on the loading dock at Blue Hills Industries in Sylmar. El had sent him there after his breakfast break at the truck stop in Castaic. He wasn't sure what the Fat Broad was thinking, getting him to do some kind of weird stake-out to collect information for Hunter.

196

"Remember, if anybody asks, you're officially off-duty," she'd said. "You're just hanging out until I find you a load home. Just see what kind of scuttlebutt you can pick up from any drivers you see leaving the plant."

"What-butt?" He held the phone at arm's length and scowled at it before adding, "What the fuck are you saying, woman?"

"Scuttlebutt, you pinhead. Rumors, gossip, whatever juicy tidbits the drivers want to drop on you about Blue Hills Industries or the people who work there."

"And why would they want to talk to me?"

"Because you're friendly and charming and a good listener, you asshole. Don't you want to keep Hunter out of jail?"

"Does Hunter know about this?"

"Duh-uh," she had replied, whatever that meant.

The Blue Hills plant was a large, sprawling building on San Fernando Road, with a manicured front lawn, leafy trees and lots of plate glass on the office end, and a big parking lot in front of a substantial warehouse on the other. The entire complex was surrounded by a chain link fence with three strands of barbed wire along the top. There was an automated black-barred gate at the entry to the parking lot. He was able to pull in on the street just past the gate, shaded by a leafy tree, with a decent view of the yard and the four closed doors of the loading dock if he looked back out of his passenger side window.

When he arrived, the lot was full of parked cars, but there was little activity on the warehouse side. There were two unmarked forty foot trailers backed up against closed doors on the loading dock, but no sign of a tractor or driver. He'd smoked a cigarette leaning up against the front fender, ground the butt into the asphalt with his heel, then climbed into the passenger seat of the cab where he promptly fell asleep.

Awake now, he saw two tractors in the yard; a red Kenworth sat idling directly in front of a black Freightliner. The Freightliner was backed up to one of the trailers. The doors of the loading dock were up, and he could hear two male voices in a heated back-and-forth, but the only syllable he could make out clearly was 'fuck'. Then a wiry little black dude stormed out of the warehouse door carrying a yellow paper cup, which he tossed through the open window of the black tractor. Judging by the way it flew, the cup was at least half full.

The guy climbed into the red Kenworth and slammed his door much harder than necessary, then gunned the engine before shifting into gear and peeling around the lot, narrowly missing a shiny blue Beemer taking a corner. Sorry wondered if the guy was mad enough to take out the gate, but he skidded to a stop short of it and leaned on his horn until an armed security guard jogged over, yelled at the driver to chill out, and stuck a card in a slot to open the gate.

"Cool!" Sorry hiked himself over to the driver's seat and fired up The Blue Knight so he could follow the Kenworth. The driver had to be pissed off enough at someone to spill some dirt. As the Kenworth tractor roared past him, he caught sight of the name on the red door in black letters. *Jerome Jefferson, Pomona, CA.* He had to boot it to keep the guy in his sights as he raced through a residential neighborhood — lost sight of him when he made the right turn on Encinitas off Bledsoe — until they reached the I-5 North. Sorry wasn't surprised when the Kenworth took the exit for the 210 East in the direction of Pomona.

He didn't pay any attention to the speedometer until he saw the flashing lights in his rearview mirror. "Oh, shit." He slowed the truck down to 55 and watched with some relief as the California Highway Patrol passed The Blue Knight and caught up with old Jerome ahead. Unfortunately, a second CHP car came up from behind and as soon as the shoulder allowed, both trucks were pulled over on the side of the highway, each with two cops in a cop car behind it. "Fuck."

"Hands where I can see them!" A big round-faced cop with his right hand on his holster motioned Sorry out of the truck and gave him a little shove, indicating he should move around the front of the truck. When they were on the shoulder side, the cop had Sorry lean up against the fender with his hands on the hood of the truck so he could frisk him. When the cop felt the knife sheathed in Sorry's boot, he drew his gun and called his partner to come and remove the knife.

198

Sorry sighed, and lifted one hand off the hood to gesture, which resulted in the feel of a cold steel barrel behind his right kidney. "You ever walked through a truck stop parking lot at two a.m., officer? Trust me, it ain't no picnic. Can't carry a gun, so a guy's got to have some means of protection. What are you doing with that? C'mon. It was a gift from my late brother. It's got great sentimental value to me."

"Shut up. Where's your ID?"

Sorry was about to pull his wallet out of his back pocket, but a nudge to the kidney reminded him to keep his hands on the hood. "Wallet. Back pocket," he said. "Hey! I didn't say you could feel me up."

"Shut up." The cop handed the wallet off to his buddy, a younger cop with biceps trying to burst through his shirtsleeves, who walked away with it.

"Hey! Where you goin' with my wallet? I'm a law abiding citizen. From Canada, no less. You guys should show some respect."

The cop had holstered his gun. "It's a felony to carry a concealed weapon. There's nothing law abiding about that. Plus you were going 85 miles an hour."

"Sorry 'bout that. It was that guy's fault." He thrust his jaw in the direction of the red Kenworth. "Can I turn around now?"

"No. Shut up."

"Look. I told you I'm from Canada. How was I supposed to know about the knife thing?"

"Bet you can't carry a concealed weapon in Canada either, buddy."

"If I walk around with a knife on my belt, my wife gets embarrassed."

"Hey, don't you Canadians know the meaning of the word 'Shut up'?"

"That's two words, officer. Where's my wallet?"

"Where's your wife?"

"Home. In British Columbia, Canada. With our two kids. Why do you want to know?"

"She won't be embarrassed if you wear the knife on your belt here in California then, will she?"

Sorry sighed and shrugged at the same time. He saw the cop's partner rummaging around in the glove box of Hunter's truck. "Can I turn around now, officer? I feel like a tool standing here like this."

"Jeez-us!" said the cop. "Don't you ever shut up?"

"When I'm asleep." Sorry ventured to take his hands down and turn around, just in time to see the cop roll his eyes. "Look, I'm a nice guy. But a long-haul trucker has to be able to protect himself, you know?"

"This isn't your truck," said the second cop, looking down at them from the passenger side window. He waved some papers in one hand, flipped open Sorry's wallet in his other. "It's registered to a Hunter Rayne, North Vancouver, BC. Canada."

"Is that your wife?" asked the round faced cop.

"What? He's a buddy of mine, an ex-cop. Hunter is a man's name, you... uh... officer."

"Yeah? What about Hunter Tylo, that actress on The Bold and the Beautiful?" said the younger cop with the biceps, opening the passenger door of the truck and handing down Sorry's wallet before climbing down.

"You guys watch that soap, too?" said Sorry. "I forgot about her. Dr. Taylor Hayes. She's quite a babe, isn't she?" He heard the engine of the Kenworth start up. "Shit! I'm followin' that guy. Get your buddies to stop him, would ya?"

The round-faced cop stepped back and with a wave of his arm, indicated that Sorry could get back in the truck. "You're lucky we're in a good mood. Don't let us catch you speeding again."

"Hey, thanks guys. See you next time, eh?" Sorry shot back over his shoulder as he scrambled into the Blue Knight and over to the driver's seat. As he fired up the engine and eased back onto the highway he could still see the red Kenworth about a quarter mile ahead, so he put his foot down and moved to the passing lane. It wasn't until they'd taken the exit at Pomona that he remembered the cops hadn't given him back his knife.

"It's been forty-eight hours and we haven't got a solid suspect yet. Forensic evidence doesn't point to anyone so far. This case ain't gonna be a slam dunk." Shane told Hunter that, barring the appearance of an eyewitness or a voluntary confession, there was a lot more leg work and background research to be done before they had any chance of solving Mike Irwin's murder. "We're bringing in Todd Milton for a second interview, and we'll talk to this Cordero guy as well. Go on home," he said. "Just keep in touch."

"What about 'Stella'?" Hunter asked. "The conference is over tonight, and I believe she's scheduled to fly back tomorrow morning."

"You feel we need to talk to her face-to-face?" asked Shane.

Hunter shrugged. A good cop could get as much information from a person's face and demeanor as he could from the words they spoke. In fact, he would've liked to speak directly with Cordero and Carruthers himself. After years of interviewing 'persons of interest', he'd learned to trust his instincts about which of them had something to hide. But he wasn't the investigating officer and, like it or not, he was going to have to leave the job to Shane Blackwell and his team. In spite of his desire to get back out on the highway, it wasn't going to be easy for him to let go of this investigation.

Hunter drove back to Tom Halsey's chalet. Tom hadn't yet left for work, and Hunter was surprised to find him just coming out of the basement room where Hunter had been staying.

"Oh, there you are," said Tom. "I was wondering if you'd left yet."

"Did you want to talk to me?"

"Well, I... Petra... my wife... " Tom had a pained expression on his face.

"She wants me out of here, right?"

Tom sighed. "It's just that she's already invited a friend of hers from our old neighborhood to come up for a few days, starting tomorrow. She'd like a little time to clean up, and..." He put his hand on Hunter's shoulder. "I told her I'd talk to you. I don't mean to rush you, if you still need a place to stay, maybe…"

"No problem." Hunter brushed past him to dislodge Tom's hand, then pivoted to face him. "I'll pack up right now. You going to be upstairs for a while? I'll talk to you before I go." He watched Tom walk away. On the stairs, Tom turned to look at him and Hunter smiled, not without difficulty.

Hunter looked around the room. He'd known Tom for years, but that didn't mean they were good friends. Had Tom been going through his things? He tried to remember exactly where everything was when he'd left that morning. Had his ski clothes been moved? If so, why? Was Tom working for the RCMP, or was it something else?

Hunter packed all his belongings into his duffle bag, double checking the cramped bathroom and shower for items he might have left behind. When he was sure he had everything except his skis and boots, which were in the Halsey's garage, he climbed the stairs and left his bag beside the back door. He'd decided that he was being too suspicious about Tom. Suspicion was a career habit that was hard to break.

Tom offered him a coffee. "So what's happening?" he asked, his back to Hunter as he fiddled with the coffee maker. "I see the police are publicly looking for witnesses to the chairlift murder."

"Right. They've already had several calls."

"You've talked to them again?"

Hunter nodded. "Haven't you?"

"Of course," said Tom. "Are you going home to North Van?"

"Yes. For now." Hunter thought about his promise to Helen to bring her son home. He might soon be on the highway to Calgary.

The two of them sat in uncomfortable silence for a few minutes, each with a section of the Vancouver Province newspaper on the table in front of them, until gurgles from the coffee maker signaled the brewing was complete.

"What's your take on the murder, chief?" Hunter asked as he stirred milk and sugar into his coffee.

"I don't know. Why would I know?"

"You must have heard something. Aren't you in tight with the detachment here?"

"Yeah, we talk sometimes. Mostly cases of theft, sometimes drunk and disorderly, only to do with my hotel, though." Tom put the milk back in the fridge and paused, holding the fridge door open. "Want some banana bread?"

"Some of the conference goers are staying at your hotel, right?"

"So?"

"They must be talking about the murder. Overheard any theories?"

Tom pulled out a loaf wrapped in aluminum foil and set it on the counter. "Only one," he said.

Hunter took a cautious sip of coffee. It was already cool enough to drink. "What's that?"

Tom smiled wryly, holding up a knife he'd pulled out of a knife block on the counter. "Seems there's a rumor going around that the Chairlift Killer is you."

"So what did he say?" asked El. Sorry didn't have his own cell phone and she'd been on pins and needles waiting for him to call. Now he was at a pay phone in a noisy McDonald's just off the San Bernardino freeway.

She heard him yell, "Don't touch that!" then he said, "Hang on" and all she heard was background babble for twenty seconds. "Chick just about threw out my Big Mac," he said, coming back on the line. "You can't leave your stuff on a table here or they throw it away."

"What did the guy say? Just tell me what happened and you can get back to your lunch."

"First he jumped out of his rig ready to fight me. This little black dude weighs — what? maybe a hundred and forty pounds soaking wet — and he wants to take me on."

"Why?"

"Duh. 'Cause I was following him, right back to his neighborhood. Guess he thought I was planning to beat him up for what he did to that other joker's truck." A pause, then Sorry's voice turned blurry.

El couldn't make out what he was saying so she interrupted him. "Have you got your mouth full, you asshole?"

She heard a gulp, and then, "So I was saying. I followed him to this lot beside a little park, and the guy comes out of his truck with blood in his eye and a tire iron in his hands. Me, I got nothin' to fight back with. Probably a good thing I didn't have my knife or it could've got ugly. 'What you want?' he says. I tell him I just want to talk about what happened back there at Blue Hills. 'The hell you do,' he says and takes a swing at my head. I grab the tire iron before it hits me and lift it as high as I can to get it away from him, but damned if he doesn't hang on, and next thing you know I got this little black dude swingin' around me like I got a fuckin' cat by the tail, you know?"

"Holy ..."

"Dude finally lets go and goes staggerin' off into the curb and trips and falls on the grass. Good thing he let go when he did, or he coulda stuck his head through the windshield of a silver Toyota."

"Got it. Let's move on. Did he tell you anything about Blue Hills? What did the guy say?" Wally walked into the office from the warehouse but she waved him away before he could open his mouth.

She heard Sorry sigh. "He was promised a good paying load outa there and turned down another job to take it, then when he gets there this other guy's scooped it. Jerome needs all the cash he can get right now, because his parents have spent all their retirement savings on hospital bills to keep his old man from dying of cancer, but he's gonna die anyway — any day now the doctor says — and then his mom is gonna have to move in with Jerome and his family."

"Boo hoo. Look, I don't need his life story. What did he say about the other guy?"

"Says he dresses like the Maytag repairman, but he thinks he's some kind of gang-banger. The guy in the warehouse knew that Jerome had been promised the load but the fucker didn't back him up, he says. Probably scared shitless."

"Got a name? The guy's name or who he drives for or whatever?"

"I told you. Jerome Jefferson. He's an owner-operator."

"Not him, shithead. The gang-banger."

Another sigh. "He said but I can't remember exactly. Something like Juan Valdez."

"What? That's the coffee guy with the donkey."

"Oh, yeah." He was mumbling again, no doubt with his mouth full of Big Mac.

"Think." El waited through a series of swallowing and smacking sounds and was about to lose her cool when Sorry started to speak again.

"Wait. It's coming to me. Juan Var... no, José Ves... José Vasquez. Does that sound right? Vasquez?"

"How should I know?"

"I think that's it. José Vasquez."

"And was there a company name?"

"C'mon, El. I wasn't close enough to read the name on the truck, and Dude there didn't tell me."

"Did you ask him?"

Silence.

"Go back and ask him, Sorenson." She heard another sigh, but this time it verged on a growl, so she decided it was time to change her tack. "Please, Sorry. I can't go back to Hunter with useless information. Can you imagine how many José Vasquezes there are in the state of California? There must be thousands. We need more than just the driver's name. Please?"

"Gimme a break. How am I supposed to find Dude again? He left the parking lot right when I did."

"Is there a phone book at the payphone?"

"Well, yeah."

"So look him up."

Another sigh.

"And, Sorry..."

"Yeah?"

"Don't forget to call me back."

"Found him, Hunter. Him and his friend." It was Joe Solomon.

Hunter was on the Sea to Sky highway, just outside of Squamish. "You've got them with you?" he asked. He was following a big green bus that was belching black smoke.

"No, but I just heard from a buddy who has seen the two of them hanging around at a pizza joint near the Waterfront Skytrain station. He says he thinks they're the same two kids he saw panhandling in the area a couple days ago."

"How long ago did your buddy see them?" Hunter could see the red and white of a Petro Canada station up ahead and decided to pull in for gas.

"Last night, just before he caught the Skytrain home."

"What time was that?"

"Probably six thirty, sevenish. He works late most nights, but he usually tries to get home for dinner."

"They could be almost anywhere now." Hunter pulled into the Petro Canada lot and came to a stop beside a self-serve pump. "I'm on my way to Vancouver, Joe. I'm going to stop at home, maybe grab some lunch and make a few phone calls. Then I'll be in touch to see if you've heard anything else before I leave."

"Leave for downtown?"

"Yes. Might as well give it a shot."

"You could be lucky. I noticed that someone's been pulling down my posters from here in Gastown to Granville Mall. If it's them — and I can't see why anyone else would — they've probably been hanging out in the area." Joe said, "See ya later," and hung up.

Hunter used his credit card to fuel up, and he couldn't help wondering when he'd be back on the road earning the money to pay it off. He wondered if Sorry was still in northern California with his truck, and hoped that El had found a paying load to bring The Blue Knight back to BC. If so, he wondered if she could find him a load for Alberta or points east so he could take the kid back home without losing another day of work. That was one of the calls he'd make from home.

He finished fuelling up and was just getting back in the car when he saw one of the airport shuttle busses lumber past on the highway en route to YVR. Alora Magee might be on that bus, he thought. He wasn't surprised to feel a great sense of relief. She was an attractive, intelligent woman, but the past few days had taught him a lesson. He should have gone with his first instincts and declined her invitation to meet up at Whistler.

He accelerated his Pontiac out onto the highway behind a string of SUVs sporting ski racks and settled in for the drive from Squamish to North Van. Reflecting on his own rather old-fashioned attitude toward sex, he wondered how it felt to be a Brent Carruthers, a man who felt entitled to seduce a woman — or a series of women — half his age. Even in the freewheeling sixties, Hunter had stayed monogamous. He'd had just two steady girlfriends before he met Christine up in the Yukon Territory and asked her to marry him well over twenty years ago.

Ken and he were both at the Whitehorse detachment at the time. Ken was more of a ladies' man, and used to kid Hunter about being so serious when it came to women. 'Lighten up. Have a little fun, man. She's a babe and she likes you; go for it.' Hunter used to try to figure it out. Was it out of respect for women, or respect for himself? Had it been his mother's lectures on being a gentleman, his father's advice? The influence of early TV shows like Father Knows Best and Roy Rogers? Or was it the almost monastic lifestyle of the years he spent mastering jujitsu? Who or what was it that made him uncomfortable about sex outside of a committed relationship? He didn't want to revisit that topic now in his early fifties. He was who he was, and he could see no reason to try to change.

South of Squamish there was very little snow, less and less as he approached the Lower Mainland. The view of the Howe Sound fjord was spectacular from several stretches of the Sea to Sky highway on a clear, sunny day. Hunter stopped the car at one of the viewpoints and got out to drink in the sight of the shifting waters of the Sound, the darkly forested mountains top-dusted with white, and the brilliant blue sky. He stretched and took deep breaths of the cold air, and his old sensei's admonition to be fully aware in the moment came back to him. In the moment. Was that where a man could most vividly appreciate his existence? On a sudden impulse, he executed the first moves of his kata, something he hadn't done for many years. It had always served him as a moving meditation, helping to ground him during challenging days on the force. Now his moves were sloppy from lack of practice. He took one more deep breath and got back in the car.

As he resumed driving, Hunter was teased by a sense of peace that had been absent for a long time and now seemed just out of his reach. He missed practicing martial arts. He thought about the jujitsu philosophy of yielding to the opponent's force instead of trying to use your own force against it and wondered if that philosophy had bled into the way he handled — or didn't handle — relationships. Was he always waiting for the other's move, preparing to turn it back against them? It certainly influenced the way he approached investigations. Once he zeroed in on the perpetrator, he would try to present the suspect with an opening to reveal himself rather than accuse him — or her — directly.

It had been a long time since he thought about the concept of fudoshin, but he considered it now. During his martial arts training he had worked hard on attaining that 'immovable mind', a sense of composure no matter what he was faced with. Outwardly, that ability to remain unperturbed had not deserted him, even after Ken's death. If he could still convey that image of self-control to others, why had he felt unable to do his job, or even to remain with the RCMP? Maybe once again he was yielding to his opponent's force, and his opponent was fate. He shook his head. He was tired of trying to figure himself out, so he looked out across the Sound to bring himself back into the moment.

"I *will* find Adam Marsh," he said aloud, "and I *will* find the one who took Mike Irwin's life."

CHAPTER
FOURTEEN

Meredith met Brent Carruthers' fiancée, Tracy, in the lobby as previously arranged and they took a skiers' shuttle from the hotel to the base of the Gondola. They made small talk on the shuttle, but both the shuttle and the Gondola were too crowded and noisy for intimate conversation. Meredith — Stella to her companion — was intent on finding out more about Brent Carruthers, and hoped that Tracy could shed some light on his relationship with Mike Irwin. The lovers must have discussed the death of the man who had threatened them with exposure the night before his murder, if she could just get Tracy to open up.

It was a beautiful morning to be on the mountain. Tracy and 'Stella' were both knockouts even insulated in ski wear, judging by the looks they were getting from both male and female skiers and snowboarders loitering near the Roundhouse. The building where several mid-mountain restaurants and bars were located was a popular meeting place, especially on a sunny day when skiers could grab a coffee or hot chocolate and sit outside. The two women chose to ski down the Pony Trail as an easy warm-up, then took the Red chair back up to the Roundhouse. Sitting on the chair was Meredith's first opportunity to get personal. "Your Brent is a total hunk, you lucky girl. How long before you get married?"

Tracy smiled, but it seemed a little forced. "Don't know," she said with a shrug. "Since my parents don't know about him yet."

"You mentioned that the other night. You don't think your parents will approve. It must drive you crazy having to keep it secret."

Tracy shrugged again. "I know my parents are going to like him, once they get over the age difference, but he's worried that my father will think he's dating the boss's daughter just to get ahead in Dad's company."

Meredith suspected just that, and wondered why Carruthers would make a habit of seducing the boss's daughter if that wasn't his motivation. Some form of payback? "Well, if your dad knows you two are serious about planning a future together, why wouldn't he want to help your fiancé's career?"

Tracy sighed. "Yeah, but Brent wants to make it on his own merits. And now there's something else."

"Yeah?"

"He's planning to leave Dad's company. He's applying for a new position — more responsibility, better pay — at a different firm and he thinks he's a shoo-in for it."

"A competitor?"

Tracy pressed her lips together and ran her finger across them.

"Aw, c'mon. I may be in purchasing but I'm not even in the same industry. You can tell me." She had researched Tracy's dad and the company he managed, and she was already aware that some of their product was purchased by the same aerospace companies that did business with Blue Hills Industries. Was it possible...?

They were approaching the top, so Tracy just smiled and turned her attention to getting off the chair. Once off, the two of them skied off to the side, out of the way of new arrivals, and huddled over a copy of the map to figure out where to go next.

Meredith suggested they take a run on the side opposite the Pony Trail, which meant skiing down G.S. to the Harmony Express chair. "We'll still have time to take the lift back up to the Little Peak and do a nice run down Harmony Ridge before I have to head back to the hotel."

The run was great. Perfectly groomed snow, not too crowded, the day so clear you could see a thousand miles. Meredith let Tracy take the lead and was delighted to find that her young companion was a good skier and did the run fast enough to keep it challenging. They did a high five and laughed when they reached the bottom of the run. It wasn't until they were almost at the Harmony Express loading area that 'Stella' pointed out to Tracy that this was the lift where the so-called Chairlift Murder had taken place. Tracy was silent until the chair was past the first tower, then she said, "Brent knew the guy."

"The guy who was killed?"

Tracy nodded. "They used to work together." They both watched as a snowboarder picked himself up from a face plant on the slope below and to their right, then Tracy looked over at 'Stella' and added, "He was a real prick."

When she didn't continue right away, Meredith prompted her with a "You knew him?"

"Not personally, but from what I saw of him, it's no wonder somebody wanted to kill him."

Meredith asked why, but Tracy said, "It's pretty ironic. The prick wanted to get Brent fired — he got him fired once before — but now Brent will probably end up getting the asshole's job."

Meredith suppressed a smile. "Does Brent have any idea who might have killed the guy?"

Tracy appeared to be considering the question. "I can't say."

"You don't know, or you won't say?" Meredith asked with a mischievous smile. She was confident that Tracy wouldn't suspect her own fiancé.

"He has a theory. Just that: a theory."

"I hope it's not related to the job," said Meredith. "You wouldn't want that sexy fiancé of yours taking chances with his life."

"Brent wouldn't be that stupid."

"Meaning?"

"The guy pissed off the wrong people, didn't he?" That was all Tracy would say.

Meredith mulled it over on the long series of runs down to the base, the two of them skiing sometimes side-by-side, sometimes one or the other taking the lead. Meredith had already known that Carruthers had issues with Mike Irwin, but she still didn't know whether the issues were purely personal, or if money was involved. If Carruthers knew — or thought he knew — why Irwin was killed, did he also think he knew who had killed him? Just how much did Carruthers really know, and how much of what he said to Tracy was just meant to impress her? She also wondered if Tracy was about to lose her fiancé to his next boss's daughter, whoever Carruthers' *real* boss turned out to be.

She said goodbye to Tracy at the base of the Gondola and headed back to the Coast Peaks on the shuttle bus. The windows were steamed up from the warm breath of passengers, and the floor was wet from snow stomped off dozens of ski boots. She was scheduled to report back to her client again in the morning, and wondered if an earlier call was warranted. No, she decided. Not yet. Tracy had planned to grab a quick lunch then spend the afternoon shopping in the trendy boutiques of Whistler Village.

It was time for Meredith to take a run at Brent Carruthers.

As he passed Horseshoe Bay in West Vancouver, Hunter debated driving down into the little village by the water for something to eat. The slice of banana bread he'd accepted from Tom Halsey hadn't held him for more than the first hour on the road. Normally he would enjoy sitting down for a plate of fish and chips, watching the ferries for the islands off the coast depart and washing down his meal with a pint of ale. Normally, however, he would be in the company of his landlord, Gord Young, a retired medical doctor, and sometimes Gord's older brother, John, and not in a hurry to get somewhere. Sitting there alone and rushing through a meal didn't have the same appeal.

He hit the tail end of the line of cars that had just disembarked off the big ferry from Nanaimo on Vancouver Island. There was a knot of traffic headed in the direction of Vancouver but it spread out quickly as he drove east. He tried to remember what his refrigerator held, and thought there was a block of cheddar in the door and a loaf of bread in the freezer. That and a can of soup or beans would have to do for lunch.

He pulled into the driveway of a modest house on the lower flanks of Grouse Mountain in North Vancouver. He lived in a downstairs suite, while the two Young brothers — retired and in their mid-seventies — lived upstairs. At this time of year, they were both in residence, but during warmer months, John Young lived at his property on Shuswap Lake not far from Eagle Bay. Hunter carried his duffle bag down a damp and narrow cement walkway that ran along the east side of the house. It was crowded by the neighbor's tall cedar hedge and ran downhill toward the ground level entry to the basement. Just as he put his key in the lock, he heard a tap-tap-tap on an upstairs window, so he stepped back and looked up to see Gord Young waving to him. Gord motioned him to come upstairs, and held up a steaming mug of something. Hunter hoped it was an invitation to lunch, and signaled back 'five minutes' with an open hand.

Hunter stepped over a few envelopes and flyers that lay under the mail slot, dropped his duffle bag near the door to his bedroom and went over to his desk. He pushed the play button on his answering machine, then slid open the curtain and looked out the window beside his desk. He had a peek-a-boo view of the waters of Burrard Inlet beyond the wet grassy lawn of the back yard. In the middle of the yard, a skeletal apple tree with a moss-encrusted trunk stretched its bony fingers toward the sky, dwarfed by two immense cedars at the base of the lot.

As expected, there were messages from Helen Marsh about Adam, and from his ex-wife Chris about Helen. There was also a message from his youngest daughter, Lesley, saying "Got a question for you. Call me when you can." He pulled his cell phone from his jacket pocket and set it up on its charger, then shrugged off his jacket and headed for the stairs. As soon as he opened the door that separated his suite from the stairway leading to the main floor, his nostrils were flooded with the hearty scent of onions and beef. He rounded a wall into the kitchen and saw Gord scraping a spoon around the sides of a large pressure cooker on the stove. "Please don't tell me there's nothing left in the pot."

The old man knocked the contents of the serving spoon into a bowl on the counter and said, "There's nothing left in the pot." He set the spoon on the counter and picked up the bowl. "This is for you," he said. He wore a pair of baggy blue jeans and a well-worn white and grey sweatshirt commemorating Rick Hansen's 'Man in Motion' tour of 1985. In spite of his age, he still had a full head of brown hair, with just a touch of grey at the temples. He always looked tanned, probably because he was out on a local golf course whenever the weather allowed.

"Gord's Goulash," said his brother from behind his own bowl at the kitchen table. He held up a piece of beef on his fork and recited to it.

> *"Some hae meat and canna eat,*
> *And some wad eat that want it,*
> *But we hae meat and we can eat,*
> *And sae the Lord be thankit."*

"Robbie Burns?" said Hunter, accepting the bowl from Gord and carrying it to the table.

"Aye, laddie." John dunked a chunk of French bread in his bowl and said nothing more. His thinning hair was white, and he was perpetually pale because he avoided the sun, even when he was out at the lake.

"How was Whistler?" asked Gord, joining them at the table. "Want a beer with that?"

Hunter noticed neither of the older men had a beer, so he declined. Gord saw him glance at the coffee pot, and was about to stand when Hunter motioned him to stay seated. "I'll get it in a minute," he said. "Whistler was... interesting."

He gave his landlord the Coles Notes version of the weekend. Gord's mouth fell open as he listened, then he swallowed audibly and adjusted his bifocals. "A murder suspect. You. That's hard to believe." He picked up his coffee mug and added, "You set them straight, didn't you?"

John stopped eating and looked at Hunter thoughtfully. "The wintry whistler wind," he said.

"What?"

"John D. MacDonald might have called it 'The Wintry Whistler Wind'," said John.

"No, John. MacDonald used colors in his titles. It would probably be 'The White Whistler Weekend'," said Gord. "Besides, Travis McGee lived in Florida."

John just shrugged and went back to his stew.

"And the girl?" Gord asked Hunter.

Hunter's mouth was full, but he smiled ruefully and shook his head.

Gord nodded slowly. "Just as well."

Hunter thought for not the first time that his landlord seemed to be the only one who understood him. Those three simple words made him feel more at peace about what had happened with Alora. "Where's the cat?" he asked, looking around his chair.

"Sleeping on the heat register. You're safe."

"Gord's Siamese is a fearsome cat: she's called the Hidden Claw,
For she's the master criminal who flaunts our every law.
She's the bafflement of Gord himself, and Hunter Rayne's despair:
For just when he thinks he's safe from her, the Siamese is there!"

Looking out the window at the sky, John finished reciting his parody of the T.S. Eliot poem, then stood up to take his empty bowl to the sink. "Good afternoon, gentlemen. I think I'll go read," he said, and left the kitchen.

"Why did you say 'Just as well'?" Hunter asked Gord.

Hunter's landlord had left the table, and came back with a cup of coffee for Hunter, followed by a carton of whole milk and a sugar bowl. He sat back down and took a careful sip out of his own refilled coffee mug before replying.

"I wouldn't go changing my life right now, if I were you." The retired doctor looked, and sounded, stern. "In my opinion you are exactly who you are supposed to be."

Elspeth was fed up. The jolly biker just wasn't cut out to be a private eye. He was supposed to get the name of that gang-banger trucker who had muscled in on poor old Jerome's load out of Blue Hills Industries. She realized that it might not be important, but then again, it could be the piece of the puzzle that allowed Hunter to solve the case. She'd screwed up trying to help Hunter out in the past, and she really didn't want it to happen again.

As it was, she'd sent that clown Sorenson all the way to L.A. with Hunter's truck without clearing it with Hunter, and now she couldn't find a load out of there to bring them home. Unless she came up with some decent information on Blue Hills — and a load — pretty damn quick, Hunter was going to be pissed off. Good thing he was still tied up in Whistler. El looked at the big clock on the wall. It had been over two hours since she'd last spoken to Sorry. He had no cell phone. She had no way to reach him.

Her phone started to ring and she lunged for it. "Watson!" she barked.

"Hello, El."

Her heart sank. It was Hunter. What could she tell him? She decided she had no choice but to lie like a carpet.

"Hi, there, sweet-cheeks. What's happenin'? Are you still hung up in Whistler?" She tried to sound as if all was right in her world.

"What's the matter? You sound cheerful."

"Fuck off, Hunter," she growled.

216

"That's more like it. You had me worried for a minute there. To answer your question, I'm at home now, and not even under arrest. When do I get my truck back?"

El cleared her throat. "I can't find a load out of Redding. I've had to send Sorry a bit farther south."

"I thought you already had a return load lined up from Redding."

"Fell through. I'll get him back here as soon as I can with a paying load."

"That's all I can ask, El. And let me know just as soon as possible what his ETA is going to be. Looks like I might have to drive the runaway boy back to Calgary."

Yes! El figured that would give her a couple of days' grace. "You found the kid?"

"I've got a lead. I'm heading to downtown Vancouver to look for him almost as soon as I get off the phone."

"What about the killer?" she asked, hoping that Sorry's trip to Sylmar wasn't going to be in vain. She still wanted a chance to help solve the murder.

"The Mounties always get their man," he said.

"They got him?"

"Not yet. But they will."

El heaved a sigh of relief as she hung up the phone. It was time to get on the phone and call in some favors, if she still had any left, from some of the L.A. area freight brokers she'd worked with in the past. Maybe one of them could hand off a load that would get Sorry back on the road to home.

She'd called four or five of them with no results and fielded calls from two local shippers and three drivers when her phone began to ring again. This time it was the call she'd been waiting for.

"Whatcha got for me, Sorenson?" she asked.

"It was a fuckin' waste of time. Took me an hour and a half to track down Jerome again, and he wasn't happy to see me. He wasn't answering his phone — you were right, his number was in the phone book — so I had to find his house, and of course, he wasn't there. I hung out there for another hour until his wife came home and seeing me almost scared the shit out of the poor woman."

"Well, yeah. That's because you look like a bad-ass biker."

"That's because I *am* a bad-ass biker, bitch."

"And then?"

"I was wrong about Juan Valdez. His name is Hor-hay Vasquez."

"Hor-hay?"

"That's what Jerome said. And he drives for an outfit called Don Julian Transport in Industry. Now when do I get outa here?"

"Is that all you got?" The name on the truck didn't sound as important as El had expected. Well, she didn't really know what she'd expected, but she'd hoped that a bell would go off for her, and it hadn't.

"That's what you asked for, that's what you got." Sorry's normal high-decibel voice had gone up a few decibels. "Now where do I go?"

"I'm workin' on it. Call me back in an hour."

"Yeah, but... I'm parked here at a fuckin' McDonald's in Pomona. You want me back at the trailer?"

"Yeah. Go back to Castaic and call me from there." She hung up before he could give her any more lip, then immediately punched the button for another line, but there was no dial tone.

"Hello? Hello?" It was a woman's voice.

"Watson Transportation. What can I do for you?" said El. It didn't sound like any of her regular callers.

"Oh, hello. I'm looking for Daniel Sorenson. I believe he's working for your company. It's important that I get hold of him as soon as possible."

El cleared her throat. "I'm afraid I can't give out a driver's home number..."

"Oh, no. I can't wait for him to get home. I need to reach him now. I just called his home, and his wife gave me your number." The voice was mature, and calm in spite of the urgency implied by her words.

"The best I can do is have him call you, ma'am. I should hear from him in the next couple of hours, although with Sorry, you never know."

"Well, if that's the only way, I guess. What did you call him?"

"Sorry."

"It's okay." A pause. "Oh. 'Sorry'. I see. Did you want my number?"

"Right. Go ahead."

"Please have him call his mother as soon as possible," and she gave El a number with a 530 area code, thanked her, and before El could ask her what it was about, she was gone.

El sat back and looked at the number she'd scrawled in the dog-eared notebook she always kept beside her phone. It was obviously urgent, and that usually meant bad news. The woman didn't sound ill, so it could be about Sorry's father. Something sudden, maybe a heart attack or a stroke. She just hoped that whatever it was wouldn't interfere with Sorry's ETA when she found him a load.

A load. She pulled her Rolodex closer and started flipping through the cards for the phone numbers of freight brokers in southern California. She'd better have a load lined up by the time she heard from Sorry again, or Hunter Rayne would have her hide.

Traffic for the Lions Gate Bridge was backed up almost to Capilano Road, and Hunter switched from the local news station to the country music station as the Pontiac inched forward. Only one lane of the three lane bridge was open to Vancouver-bound traffic, and the two lanes from North Vancouver had to merge with two lanes from West Vancouver into a single line. Toby Keith's Blue Moon song came on and it made him think about his ex-wife, and whether he really missed her.

No, he decided. It wasn't Chris that he missed — although he had at first — but what he really longed for was that sense of family they'd had, he and Chris and their two daughters. He missed being a part of an entity that came together at the end of a day, were interested in what the other parts had done that day and cared about what they planned to do tomorrow. Gord was right, though. He couldn't go back to something like that, not right now. He guessed he had more solo miles to travel before he was ready to become a piece of something bigger than his lonesome self.

When he reached the deck of the old suspension bridge, built by the Guinness (as in Irish stout) family in the late 30's, the traffic started to move. He always enjoyed the view from Lions Gate. The waters of Burrard Inlet stretched west toward the Strait of Georgia and Vancouver Island under the day's blue sky, and were populated with an assortment of small boats and rust-streaked freighters, one of which was just emerging from beneath the bridge deck. Then the Pontiac cruised between the living cedar walls of the Stanley Park causeway as it wound its way toward downtown Vancouver, where the tall cedars on either side of the roadway were replaced by walls of concrete and glass.

He debated whether to drop in on Joe Solomon first, and decided that his best bet was to drive past the pizza place and the Skytrain station, just in case the boys were in sight. At a stop-light, he pulled out his copy of the photographs and studied them to refresh his memory. Nathan was the taller, Adam had lighter hair. He could see some of Ken in the boy's facial features, and he wondered if the boy resembled his dad in other ways. He didn't think his chances of finding the kids at this time of day were good, but he had to try.

He was right. He drove by as slowly as traffic would allow, but couldn't see anyone resembling the two boys panhandling in front of the station, and wouldn't have found space to pull over if he did. He knew he'd have to check out the area on foot. He found a parkade several blocks away on Richards Street that would still give him change from a ten dollar bill for a couple of hours' parking, and made his way back along the busy sidewalks, watching closely for familiar faces under the ball caps and hoodies that he passed.

There was a mix of people on the streets of Vancouver, ranging from well-dressed women in makeup and heels bent on a business destination to grimy vagrants with unkempt beards and crazy eyes drifting slowly along the walls as if they couldn't walk straight on their own. At one store front a beaten looking youth with a guitar sat behind a sign asking for change. The sign said 'hungry'. Hunter threw a dollar coin into the open guitar case and walked on. At a recessed service entrance smelling of urine, there was a bundle of rags and flesh snoring beneath a layer of cardboard. Perhaps it was safer and warmer to sleep during the day.

From October to March, Vancouver gets an average of 34 inches of rain, so a dry day like this one was a welcome change. But there's a price to be paid for sunny winter days. With no insulating cloud cover, the temperature can drop to well below freezing. It was hard to imagine that anyone would sleep on the city's streets by choice at this time of year. If Adam Marsh had any sense, he would jump at a chance to return home. Unless, of course, home was an even colder place for his young soul to be. Hunter couldn't believe that was the case.

He stepped inside the door of the pizza joint Joe had mentioned. A few heads turned his way, and the man behind the counter looked up from cutting a pizza with a rolling blade. Hunter didn't see anyone resembling Nathan or Adam, so he turned on his heel and walked back out to the street. Pedestrian traffic increased in the block in front of the Waterfront Skytrain entrance. It was an imposing historic edifice with a red-brick façade and a row of white columns, first built as a railway terminal in 1914. Now it served as a station for Vancouver's Skytrain and the SeaBus from North Vancouver, as well as the Western terminus for a new commuter train from the suburbs. The volume of pedestrian traffic made it an attractive place for panhandlers.

The main doors spewed out a trainload of new arrivals, drifting away and apart at varying speeds. There were a few knots of young men and women smoking cigarettes and talking in the rare afternoon sunshine in front of the building, and Hunter scanned them carefully for the runaways with no success. Inside the building, his luck changed. He saw a tall, dark-haired youth at the newsstand, counting out change for a chocolate bar. He waited for the kid to turn around, and when he did, Hunter approached.

"Nathan. There you are," he said, offering the kid a friendly grin. "I was hoping I'd run into you."

The kid stopped in his tracks and eyed Hunter warily. "Do I know you?" His hair looked unwashed and he had the beginnings of a patchy adolescent beard.

Hunter put out his hand and said, "Hunter Rayne. Adam might remember me as Sergeant Rayne of the RCMP, an old friend of his father's. Where is Adam, by the way?"

Nathan shrugged, ignoring Hunter's hand. "Haven't seen him," he said. He jammed both hands into his pockets, along with the Mars Bar.

Hunter frowned. "What do you mean, you haven't seen him? You were with him here last night."

"He went his own way last night, I guess. I haven't seen him since." The kid started to walk away.

Hunter grabbed the kid by the back of his jacket. "Whoa, chief. I'm not finished talking to you."

"Fuck off." He chopped at Hunter's forearm with his left hand to free his jacket.

Hunter grabbed the kid's wrist and twisted his arm up against his back, leaning forward to speak in his ear, soft and low, from behind. "I guess you didn't hear me say I was with the RCMP. I don't care what your plans are, I want to find Adam Marsh and you're going to help me. Understand?"

"Ow. That hurts. Let go of me."

"You mean, 'Let go of me, sir'." Hunter increased the pressure. He had a low tolerance for smart ass kids who showed no respect.

"Ow. Okay. Sir. Let go."

Hunter lowered the kid's arm but didn't let go until the kid turned around to face him. Hunter smiled at him, but his smile still carried a warning. "Where's Adam?"

"I don't know," said Nathan, rubbing his left shoulder. "I told you the truth. I haven't seen him since last night."

"Where?"

"Here."

"Exactly where."

"There." Nathan pointed to a bench near the Skytrain entrance. "He was sitting over there pretending to read a book."

"Pretending?"

"He was feeling crappy. He wanted to lie down, but he didn't want to get thrown out in the cold. Said he was going to pretend to be waiting there for someone."

"Where did you go?"

The kid shrugged. "Out."

"Out where?" Hunter said. His words were clipped and he scowled at the kid.

"I met this chick." He shrugged again, gesturing with his hands as if that would explain everything.

"Didn't you make plans to meet up again later?"

"With Adam? I figured he'd still be here when I got back."

"When was that?"

"This morning. But he was gone. I haven't seen him since."

Hunter took a deep breath and exhaled loudly. "Damn. Okay, you've been with him here for how long?"

"A few days."

"Where would he go? If you guys got separated, where would you expect him to go?"

"Here, dude," Nathan said, spreading his arms wide to indicate the cavernous interior of the station. He sounded exasperated. "I told you. I don't know where the fuck he is."

CHAPTER

FIFTEEN

The seminars on supply chain management were starting to wear thin, and Meredith found her mind drifting. As much as possible, she had watched the attendees enter the conference rooms for the first sessions after lunch. Then she had entered each of the four rooms in turn, and from the back door, scanned the rows of heads for dark hair on a tall man. In this, the room she'd entered last, she thought she had finally spotted him, so she took a seat near the rear door and tried to pay attention to the presentation on Tactical Capital Equipment Procurement so she'd have some subject matter to open the conversation with. But when the tall dark man turned around, he was a stranger. Where the hell was Brent Carruthers?

This afternoon was her last opportunity to make some kind of connection with him before the end of the conference. There was a final wrap-up to the conference scheduled for later in the afternoon, following an hour-long coffee and networking break when the seminars had ended. It was going to be difficult to buttonhole Carruthers in the main conference hall. It had become even more important to her client's interests that she get a good read on Carruthers before they headed back to Southern California. She thought back over her conversation with Tracy on the chairlift. Meetings. The blonde had said her fiancé was going to be tied up in meetings, which might have meant seminars, but also might not.

Meredith quietly gathered up her portfolio and let herself out of the room, making sure the door closed silently behind her.

A 'meeting' could be taking place in a private hotel room, or it could also be in one of the restaurants or bars. She made a thorough tour of the bars and restaurants in the hotel and found no sign of him. If he was holed up in a private suite, or somewhere outside the hotel, she was SOL. She decided to make the rounds of the four seminar rooms one more time before giving up, in case she'd missed noticing him, or if he had arrived late. Back in the presentation on Tactical Capital Equipment Procurement, Meredith was in luck. Or not.

Brent Carruthers was seated in the chair she herself had vacated just a short time before. Beside him, in what had previously been a vacant seat, with his left elbow hooked around a pair of crutches, was a grey-haired man.

"My father?" Sorry's gut felt like it dropped through a hole in his pelvis.

"I'm just guessing," said El. "Your mom wants you to call her, and she said it was urgent. What do *you* think it would be?"

Sorry's mind was already racing with the possibilities. Cancer. Like little Jerome's old man? That wasn't like an overnight thing, though, was it? He'd just seen Hank, and he seemed fine. Getting older, but okay. Something sudden. Most likely a heart attack, or maybe a stroke. "What else did she say, woman? Think!" Could it have been Sorry's fault?

"Chill, Sorenson. If she said something else, I wouldn't be guessing, would I? You got her phone number, so call her, you dickhead."

"I'm going back there."

"Wait, would ya. I've got a line on a load for you out of Torrance."

"Fuck the load."

"Just call your mom, would ya." El's voice was surprisingly gentle — for her — and if Big Mother Trucker was feeling sorry for him, it worried him even more. "You're jumping to conclusions. Maybe it's nothing. Call your mom before you go anywhere. No point losing money for nothing, you know what I mean?"

"Okay, okay," said Sorry. "I'll call her. But if it's something about my old man, I'm going to boot it back up the I-5. Now."

"Look, Sorenson. I've had to jump through hoops to get that trailer out of Torrance for you. The guy is going to get back to me any minute. Gimme a break and call me again as soon as you talk to your mom, okay?"

"Yeah. I'll call you," said Sorry, and hung up the phone. He emptied his pockets of change and not for the first time wished he and Mo could afford a cell phone. From what he'd heard, though, using them from outside the country was stupidly expensive and even Hunter used payphones when he was in the U.S. He dialed his mom's number and dropped in the requisite number of coins. There weren't many left. The phone rang. And rang. And rang.

"Of course," he said to himself. "Mom's camped out at the hospital." He looked at his watch. It would take him around nine hours, ten at the outside, to get to Yreka. If he left right away, he could be there before midnight.

Sorry slammed the receiver in its cradle and charged out of the restaurant toward The Blue Knight.

The first thing that crossed Hunter's mind when he found out that Adam had disappeared from the duo's usual haunts was that Adam had decided to go back home. He doubted that Adam could have come up with enough cash for a bus ticket to Calgary, so the sensible thing would have been for him to call his mother for money. But Helen hadn't called, and surely she would have let Hunter know. He thought it over as he headed for Joe Solomon's office in Gastown, dodging the tourists clustered around the old Steam Clock on Water Street. Joe's office was, perhaps ominously, situated two blocks east on Carrall Street, next to the historic Gaoler's Mews and within sight of Gassy Jack's statue.

Hunter climbed the narrow staircase to Joe's office and stepped into a small and homey waiting room. The receptionist was a diminutive woman of Asian descent. When he asked for Joe, she turned to look through an open door to her left, and Hunter saw that her upswept hair was held in place by a leather barrette engraved with a Haida raven.

"He's just on the phone," she said. "Give me your name and I'll let him know you're here as soon as he's free."

Hunter paced up and down between the entrance and a small window overlooking Carrall Street, pausing to study the passers-by each time he reached the window. He heard the receptionist clear her throat, and when he looked at her she was staring at him, with a slight frown. "Feel free to sit down," she said, nodding at a row of chairs beside the door.

Hunter took the seat closest to the window. He picked up a copy of the Vancouver Province newspaper, scanned the headlines on the first few pages, then tossed it back on the small table beside his chair. He could still see the opposite sidewalk from where he sat, and followed the progress of pedestrians from one side of the window to the other.

"You can go in now," said the receptionist.

Joe Solomon met him just inside his office door. "Hey, Hunter! Good to see you're still a free man." They shook hands and Joe motioned him to a chair, then pushed a stack of papers out of the way and hiked one hip up on the corner of his desk. "You're lookin' fit. Life on the road must agree with you."

After a few minutes of small talk, Hunter told Joe he'd found Nathan.

"You think he was telling the truth?"

"I can't be sure. I asked him to call me if he sees Adam, but I definitely don't trust him to do that. I don't want to say anything to Helen until I've had a chance to look for Adam. It'll just worry her more to know Nathan's lost track of him, too." Hunter shook his head. "He was feeling sick, so I'll start with the nearby hospitals, then check local shelters. I'll need addresses for them, though."

"I'll save you the legwork," said Joe, walking around his desk and reaching for his phone. "I'll call the shelters again. Most of them know me, so they'll be more willing to talk to me than you." He looked at his watch. "I've got a client coming in ten minutes, but I'll call you if and when I get any news."

Hunter kept his eyes peeled as he walked back to the parkade, but there was no sign of Adam or Nathan. He spent the next three hours, except for a half-hour dinner break at the White Spot restaurant at Cambie and 13th, visiting Vancouver's three hospital emergency rooms. It took more time to get through city traffic to each hospital, park where he could count on his car not being towed, and locate someone who had the authority and was willing talk to him than it did to get an answer to his questions.

"No. We haven't seen anyone by that name, or anyone who looks like the young man in the photographs."

He was just heading back to his car from the emergency room at the UBC hospital when his cell phone rang. It was already dark, and the temperature had dropped to just above freezing. It wasn't going to be a good night for the homeless. He flipped the phone open, hoping it was Joe with news of Adam, or maybe even Adam himself. It wasn't.

"I want to see you in my office at eight o'clock tomorrow morning."

It was Staff Sergeant Shane Blackwell, and he wouldn't take 'no' for an answer.

Meredith settled herself on a couch in the lobby of the Coast Peaks and watched the activity as many of the conference goers waited to board shuttle buses and rental cars bound for airports in Vancouver, Bellingham or Seattle. She was booked on a flight to LAX the following morning, but a lot of the purchasing professionals were leaving the hotel immediately following the last round of speeches.

Meredith hadn't had a chance to catch Brent Carruthers alone, nor in a situation that would permit her to engage him in anything more than superficial conversation. Now the conference was over. Her work here in Whistler was almost done, but she wasn't happy with it, and she had a sense that her client wasn't either. She needed to at least get more information on Carruthers to satisfy, not only her client, but herself. She knew from Tracy that Carruthers was staying until morning, and that he and Tracy had plans for a romantic meal and another night together before their departure.

"Tell me more," she'd said to Tracy as they waited in a lift lineup. "Are you going somewhere special for dinner?" Tracy told her they had reservations for 7:30 at the Chateau Grande Montagne. That meant they would be out of their hotel room for more than an hour, more likely two, allowing time to search through Carruthers' briefcase, if Meredith could find a way inside. She waited until the bellman was alone, and made her way to his desk.

"Quick question," she said, turning her head to watch a taxi stop outside, partly to give him less time to recognize her face. "What time is turndown on the third floor?"

"Sometime between 7:30 and 8:00," was the answer. She waved her thanks and walked away.

Hunter drove again past the Waterfront Skytrain station, slowing down until someone behind him honked their horn. He knew he had to tell Helen that Nathan had lost touch with Adam, but he dreaded making the call. He pulled into the same parkade he'd used earlier in the day, and walked down the cold streets, less populated now, to the station. He walked up and down the interior of the station, peering at the face of anyone resembling a teenage boy sitting on the benches or inside the fast food restaurants. Adam had been feeling unwell, and it made sense that he might have spent time in the men's room, but there was no public washroom that he could see.

He couldn't see any sign of Nathan, either, and wished that there was a way to contact him. A short, thin man in an olive green uniform was emptying the garbage containers, pushing a cart with spare garbage bags and cleaning supplies. Hunter approached him, and asked if there was a public washroom.

"Not here." The man scratched his scalp, behind his ear. "Only public toilet is in the Seabus waiting room. You gotta pay first to get in there, you know."

Hunter pulled the photos of Adam out of his pocket. "Have you seen this boy?"

The man took the fax from Hunter's hand and held it at arm's length. "Yeah. He's been here, off and on, for a couple days now."

"When did you see him last?"

The man shrugged. "Last night, I guess. I just come on shift, so couldn't've seen him today. Vagrant, right? He was tryin' to sleep on that bench. Maybe security chased him off."

Hunter thanked him and went looking for security. A heavyset man was standing near the Skytrain ticket vending machine wearing an orange and yellow safety vest with a Transit Security patch sewn on front and back. He unfolded the fax and held it out for the man to look at. "Seen this young man?"

"Yep. Seen both of them." He poked Adam's face with a gloved finger. "This kid was here last night, looked like death warmed over — all pale and shaky. Said he had to puke, so I let him go through into the Seabus waiting room to use the john."

"Where'd he go from there, do you know?"

"What you want him for?" The man swung around to watch a couple of teenage boys in black hoodies at the vending machine. They were going through their pockets, looking for coins. "Seemed like a nice polite kid."

"He's a recent runaway and his mom's worried sick about him. I'm hoping he's had enough of life on the street and ready to go back home." Hunter folded up the fax and put it back in his pocket. "Did you see where he went?"

"Might have taken the Seabus across to Lonsdale. Haven't seen him back out here, and he couldn't still be in the john."

"You sure?"

"C'mon, let's look." The big man led the way into the Seabus waiting room, and walked into the men's room ahead of Hunter. He tapped open one of the cubicle doors with his flashlight. "Not here. Figured as much."

"Thanks, chief. Appreciate the help." He pulled out his notebook, wrote his name and number on one of the pages, then ripped out the page and handed it to the man. "If you see him again, could you call me?"

"I'd check over at the Lonsdale Quay, if I was you." He saw the boys in black walking into the waiting room and hailed them. "Hey! Let's see those tickets, boys."

Hunter walked back out into the main station. Even if Adam rode the Seabus to the North Shore last night, that didn't necessarily mean he was still there. As far as Hunter knew, the boy had never lived in North Vancouver, and his buddy Nathan was on the downtown side of the inlet, so there was no reason for him to stay there. Adam could still be anywhere.

Hunter sighed and left the station for the cold streets again. It was the only lead he had for now, so he might as well follow it up. Besides, his home was on the North Shore anyway, although nowhere near the Seabus. Maybe the transit security on the other side had seen him. As he walked, feeling the cold hard sidewalk through the soles of his boots, Hunter calculated what time he'd have to leave in the morning to get to the Whistler RCMP detachment on time. If the weather held and the highway stayed clear, it would take him over an hour and a half, but at this time of year he should allow a good two hours. Snow or ice on the Upper Levels or the Sea to Sky could play havoc with traffic.

And why did Shane Blackwell need to see him in person? It hadn't been a friendly call, and the detective would offer no explanation. Hunter asked him if he had a new lead on Mike Irwin's killer, and the answer was, "Just be here," with an ominous implication of 'or else'.

Hunter couldn't help but speculate that he was back on the suspect list.

Meredith put the finishing touches on her makeup and tucked a strand of blonde hair behind her ear. Her wig wasn't exactly the same color as Tracy's hair, but she didn't intend for the maid to get a good enough look at her to tell. She wore tight jeans, tall beige leather boots, and a new sweater from the downstairs boutique, something she felt Tracy would be quite comfortable wearing. To be on the safe side, she had gone to the hotel lobby well before seven o'clock and browsed through the racks of brochures near the concierge desk, keeping an eye on the front door until she saw Brent and Tracy step outside toward a waiting taxi.

Then she hurried upstairs, scooped the outfit that she'd selected off her bed, and with the speed that came from long practice, transformed herself into an approximation of a wealthy young California blonde. The hard part was yet to come.

Now she had to lurk inconspicuously in the vicinity of Tracy's hotel room, waiting for the turndown maid. Several times during her wait she had to pretend to be on her way somewhere to avoid attracting the attention of guests leaving or returning to their rooms. Each time she would round the corner and take the elevator up or down one floor, then come back by the stairs, waiting in the stairwell until she thought the coast was clear. The fourth time, she saw the maid's cart parked just outside a door on the opposite site of the elevator, so she waited in the stairwell until the maid had entered the last room in the hallway where the elevators were located.

With the maid was out of sight, she snuck down the hall to the vicinity of Tracy's room. Just as the maid rounded the corner with her cart, Meredith pulled on the door handle as if she were closing it, then dropped her hotel key into her purse and turned her face away to rummage inside the purse. She pulled out her cell phone, punched in some numbers and walked in the direction of the elevators with the phone to her ear, giving the maid a friendly wave as she passed. She pushed the elevator button, but didn't get on when it arrived. Instead, she waited at the corner, peering around it so she would know when the maid had entered Tracy's room.

This was the most critical time; she breathed deeply and evenly to calm herself, then walked quickly down the hallway to the open door of the room. The maid was in the bathroom, making sure there were fresh towels. Just as she stepped out, Meredith breezed past her, saying "My God, I've got to hurry or I'll be late. I don't know why he couldn't have called me earlier," as if to herself, then "Thank you," to the maid in a sing-song voice, her inflection as close to Tracy's as she could make it, "Please make sure you close the door tight on your way out, would you? I'm going into the shower." She shut the bathroom door behind her, turned on the shower, and waited for the maid to leave.

Minutes later, she turned off the shower and listened at the door. When she heard nothing, she opened the door cautiously and checked to make sure the room was empty. She figured she had at least an hour, but the sooner she could find something on Carruthers and get out of here, the better.

The king bed was neatly made with the top turned down, and small foil-wrapped squares of chocolate had been placed on two pillows. In spite of the maid's efforts, there were clothes piled at the foot of the bed and draped over the chairs, mostly Tracy's from what she could tell. There was a desk on the far side of the room, over by the window, and Meredith headed there first. A ThinkPad laptop was open on the desk, and a closed briefcase stood beside a wooden chair that had been pushed up against the desk. The laptop screen was black until Meredith pushed a key, then a Windows screen came up open to an email message.

Meredith laughed quietly. Either Brent Carruthers thought he had nothing to hide, or he wasn't computer savvy enough to take security measures with his laptop. She quickly scrolled through his email messages for anything that could relate to her client, or to Mike Irwin. She found several that might be of interest and pulled a digital Kodak out of her bag to capture them for further study. Then she began looking through the document files. He obviously had some proprietary inventory management software related to his current employer, but she had no reason to believe there was anything of value to her client within its files.

Carruthers had some drafts of correspondence in his document files. Most clandestine business 'arrangements' do not involve written contracts, given they are often unethical, if not illegal. However, she did find two draft letters that warranted a photograph for further study. The letters, it appeared, were the first drafts of requests for a proposal from potential suppliers. She also found a document file that contained his resume, updated within the past month, and one that was a cover letter for a job application. The file had last been updated on Saturday, the day of Irwin's murder, and addressed to Blue Hills Industries. After her conversation with Tracy, the application came as no surprise, but the speed with which Carruthers had created it did.

Meredith slung the camera over her shoulder, then lifted the briefcase from the floor and placed it on the bed. It had a combination lock on each latch, and they were both locked. She knelt down beside the bed and, with her ear close to the lock, began to slowly turn the three cylinders, one number at a time. It took several tries and fifteen minutes to open the first latch, and she looked at her watch before starting on the second. What if the lovebirds were in a hurry to get back to their hotel room? Was it worth the risk? She took a deep breath and started on the second lock.

First she tried the same combination that had worked on the first lock, but no luck. She began the tedious process of turning the cylinders and listening for the almost inaudible telltale click again. And again, a failed attempt and she started the process over. As she did, the sound of a woman's laughter came faintly from the hallway, then the sound of a man's voice, right outside the door. Meredith couldn't afford to stop and listen. She swung the briefcase back to its place under the desk and tucked the camera back in her bag. There was nowhere to hide except the closet near the entrance, and if that was Carruthers at the door, it was already too late. Her only chance was to meet them at the door, dodge her way past them, and run.

234

Most of the houses along Greenhorn Road were dark. Of course, it was almost midnight and the country bumpkins in Yreka couldn't stay awake past ten o'clock. Sorry eased the Blue Knight around the dark curves of the narrow road and pulled into the gravel driveway of the neighbors' farm. With any luck, their bedroom was around back and the headlights and rumble of the big diesel wouldn't wake them. His heart dropped when he saw the lights on at his parents' place. And there were two cars parked outside that he didn't recognize. All he could think was that friends had come to comfort his mother. He was too late. His father was gone.

He made his way down the neighbor's driveway and back up the one that led to his parents' house, not wanting to risk the hazards of mud and old machinery, or the barbed wire fence that separated the two properties. Besides, now that he was here, he wasn't in a hurry to confront the reality of his father's death and face his mother's grief. He climbed the steps to the kitchen door, and was startled to hear women laughing inside, his mother included. What the fuck? He squared his shoulders and banged on the door.

Footsteps sounded and the door opened inward.

"Dad!" Sorry took an involuntary step backwards, his mind scrambling to make sense of what he was seeing. His father stood there, swaying slightly, a can of Budweiser clutched in his left hand.

"Danny? Hey, folks! My son's here." He ushered Sorry inside, and draped an arm across Sorry's back, bony fingers hooked over his shoulder. "You didn't tell me he was coming, Momma. Come to celebrate my birthday, Dan? C'mon, Ed, get my Danny a beer."

Sorry did think about refusing the beer, but it didn't seem like a good time to explain about being a recovering alcoholic and besides, if there was ever a time he'd needed a beer, this was it. His mother rushed up and gave him a hug. "I'm so glad you got my message." He could smell the wine on her breath. She stood back, head tilted, and added, "I don't remember telling your boss about your dad's birthday party, but I guess I must've." Then she grinned and hugged him again.

He hugged her back, took a slug of beer, then said, "Is there anything left to eat?"

A plateful of cabbage rolls and six quick beers later, Sorry sat out on the back stoop with the old man after seeing the other guests off. They could hear his mother clattering in the kitchen as she tidied up. Sorry smoked a cigarette while Hank puffed sporadically on a fat Dominican cigar. The old man went on about a woman named Belle Sorenson — not a blood relation, he kept repeating — but Sorry wasn't sure if it was a real woman or a movie he was talking about, and wasn't interested enough to care. Hank leaned into Sorry now and then as he spoke. Sorry didn't think he'd ever seen him drunk before.

"Prettiest damn farm in Northern California," said Hank, waving his hand around, the tip of the cigar glowing orange as if fanned by a bellows. "Look at the sky, would ya. Ever seen the stars that bright? Are they that bright in Canada?"

Sorry paused for a swallow of beer before answering. He smelled horse shit, not a pretty thing to his way of thinking. "Depends how close you are to the city lights, Pop."

"Yeah? You live in the city?"

"Sort of." Sorry thought about the little bungalow in Surrey where right now, Mo and the kids would be snuggled in their beds, Doobie the Doberman guarding the hallway to the bedrooms like he always did at night, the old Harley tucked away safely in the garage waiting for spring. They were on a quiet street, but it wasn't far to King George highway and 24-hour-a-day traffic and commercial buildings with banks of security lights on tall poles. "Just a small lot, big enough for the kids to play in. And Mo plants a garden."

"Mo? Your wife is named Mo?"

"Simone." Sorry tried to make it sound French but he just succeeded in sounding like a Jamaican saying, 'See, mon?' He tried again, the accent on the second syllable, with more success.

"You promised you'll bring her and the kids down for Easter, now, remember?" Hank patted his arm. "A promise is a promise, okay, son? It will mean so much to your mother."

Sorry took a deep breath. In spite of the farm smells, the air was cold and fresh, and he could feel the cold of the concrete stoop through the seat of his jeans. "When I heard Mom had called, I thought you had died, Pappa." The old name from his childhood came out involuntarily. "I wished little Bruno had a chance to get to know his grandfather."

The old man looked into his face, his eyes shining. "I'd like that." Then something between a snort and a laugh. "Not dying, I mean." He nudged Sorry's arm. "About the boy, I mean. Little Bruno."

Sorry leaned into his father. "I know, Pop." He overhanded his empty beer can into the back of his mother's pickup where it rattled around briefly before going still. A horse snorted in the barn.

"Did you ever kill a man, Danny?"

"Whoa!" That sure came out of left field. Sorry was so taken aback he didn't know whether to make a joke of it or tell the truth.

"Bikers are a pretty lawless bunch, aren't they?" said the old man. "It used to keep me awake at night, thinkin' about you, what you were doing."

"I hurt some people, but only bums like myself. Most times they hurt me back." He reached over and grabbed his father's beer can, drained the last of it. "And I never hit a woman."

His father nodded, still looking up at the stars. "You're no bad seed. I can't believe I ever thought you were. That damn movie screwed me up, and Belle Sorenson having the same last name and all."

They sat in silence, smoking, looking at the stars and hearing the vast silence of the night with the odd thump from a horse moving around in the barn, until the door creaked behind them. Sorry turned to see his mother, clutching her housecoat closed, her feet huddled side-by-side in sheepskin slippers.

"Hank, your hip. Your poor seventy-year-old hip. Get up off that cold cement and come in to bed. Brrr, it's cold out here." She reached down and ruffled the old man's hair, and he brushed her hand away with a growl. "C'mon now," she said.

"Okay, Momma. We're coming in soon." Hank held up his cigar. "Just about done."

"Don't bring that stinky thing inside," she said. "I've made up a bed for you in your old room," she told Sorry. "Good night, Danny."

He got to his feet, swaying a little, and his mother stood on her toes to kiss him on the cheek. "I'm so glad you came for your father's birthday," she said. Then, "Why do you let people call you 'Sorry', Dan. It sounds like a sad kind of name, you know what I mean?"

Sorry shrugged. "No big deal, Mom. Just short for Sorenson is all." He didn't want to tell her that he'd been given the moniker when he was a prospect for the Cobras by some asshole of a senior biker gang member who was later shot by the police and good riddance to the sadistic fucker. At first he *had* found it a little demeaning, but later he got so used to it that he'd never thought to change it. He shrugged again, more to himself than his mother. Not worth the trouble to try to change it now.

Hank stubbed the cigar out on the side of the stoop, then held up a hand to Sorry. Sorry braced himself on the door jam and helped his father to his feet. Supporting each other, they followed his mother back into the house.

"G'night, son." The old man reached up and clapped his hand lightly against Sorry's cheek. He wasn't smiling, and the look on his face made Sorry feel incredibly sad.

Sorry watched his mother help his father up the stairs to their bedroom, then went back outside for one last cigarette.

CHAPTER

SIXTEEN

"What's up?" Hunter walked into Shane Blackwell's office and pulled a chair back, preparing to sit down. When he saw the look on Shane's face, he stopped short. "What's happened?"

Shane motioned him to sit. "Want to tell me why two new witnesses have picked you out of a photo lineup?"

"What?"

"We've had several witnesses come forward in response to our public request. Two of them said they were in the chairlift line around the same time as the victim on Saturday morning. They said that prior to reaching the lift, they saw a man stopped at the edge of a slope that leads to the Harmony Express, and he was putting on a black balaclava. They gave a rough description of the skier they saw putting on the mask, so we showed them a photo lineup of six men who might fit the description. You were one of them." Shane raised an eyebrow and looked pointedly at Hunter before continuing. "They both picked you."

"Impossible. I was at Tom Halsey's that morning."

"So you say. Too bad Tom can't confirm it."

"He didn't hear me leave, did he?"

"Tom says he can't swear to it that you didn't leave and return by the basement door."

Hunter exhaled loudly through his lips and rubbed his forehead. "Who are these people?"

"You know I can't tell you."

"I can appreciate your position, damn it. But they're mistaken." He frowned. "Mistaken or flat-out lying." He looked squarely at Shane. "What now?"

"I may be a fool, but I believe you. At some point, however, it won't be my call whether or not to arrest you. If any more evidence turns up, I may be forced to make a recommendation to Crown Counsel. If the press gets wind of this, you know there'll be a lot of pressure."

Shane didn't have to elaborate. The Mounties protecting one of their own — an active or retired member, it wouldn't matter — would create just the kind of story the public loved. Corruption and conspiracy always made great fodder for the news media.

"Were the witnesses connected in any way to Mike Irwin's circle of acquaintances? Why would they lie? Or why would they think they recognized me?" Hunter had to wonder if it was an attempt to point the police away from another suspect, or could it be someone Hunter had spoken to at some time, making his a familiar face. The third possibility was that whoever had been seen putting on the ski mask looked a lot like him. Would this rule out the possibility that a woman had committed the murder? Not necessarily, he decided. How many skiers might decide to put on a balaclava on a cold, snowy day? The witnesses could have seen someone else entirely who might not even have boarded the Harmony Express that morning.

Shane shrugged. "My hands are tied."

"You know how unreliable eyewitness testimony can be," said Hunter.

"Hey, it's not me you'd have to convince."

Hunter nodded. The police might know it, the lawyers might know it, but it could sound pretty convincing to a jury.

"So now what?" Hunter asked again. "Why am I here?"

"For the record, you're a person of interest and you've come in voluntarily for questioning." Shane picked up a notebook and slid a pen into his shirt pocket, then stood up behind his desk. "Colin's got the interview room set up. We'll pick up a coffee on the way."

It was after ten a.m. when Hunter left the Whistler RCMP detachment, feeling exhausted in spite of three cups of coffee. They'd gone over his relationship with Alora, his interaction with the victim the night before the murder, details of his whereabouts on Saturday morning, all properly documented and videotaped, and finally Shane admitted that the witnesses who picked him out of the photo lineup hadn't been sure it was Hunter, only that it looked something like him.

He shivered as he sat in the Pontiac, waiting for the engine to warm up and the fog to disappear from the front windshield after brushing a thin layer of fresh snow off the rear window with his bare hands. He'd been up at five thirty for a shower and a quick breakfast before leaving his North Van suite in darkness to head up the Sea to Sky to Whistler. There had been fresh snow on the highway north of Squamish, and the road surface was slick, so the drive had required his full concentration. The police interview was icing on the cake.

Waking up to the alarm this morning he'd still had Adam Marsh on his mind. He hadn't found the boy in or near the Seabus station on the north side of the inlet, and he'd arrived home to find another worried message from Helen asking him to call as soon as he had any news. He'd decided against calling due to the late hour, but would have to break the news to her today. First, he wanted to connect with Meredith Travis again to see if she had anything new that would help clear him once and for all in the Irwin murder. There was no answer on her cell phone, so he decided to look for her at the hotel.

"I'm sorry, sir. Ms. Travis checked out early this morning." The clerk was preoccupied with something on a computer, and went back to her keyboard without waiting for a response from Hunter. He thanked her and turned away. He would have to try to reach Meredith later, after she had arrived back in L.A. He was only too aware that the entire suspect list — except for himself — had now left the country, and his chances of pinning down the killer were evaporating.

He felt as if nothing was working in his favor, and hoped that a phone call to El Watson would change his luck. The phone rang seven times before she picked up.

"Watson!"

"What's the latest on my truck, El? When's Sorry due back?" He was in no mood for small talk.

"Hang on a sec." El disappeared as quickly as she'd come and he was left on hold, listening to Shania Twain for what seemed like at least five minutes.

"Okay, here's the thing."

Hunter rolled his eyes. This couldn't be good news.

"I think he's in Yreka."

"You think?"

"I haven't heard from him since yesterday morning. I was trying to line up a load for him farther south, but he got an urgent message from his mother. I guess his dad was in rough shape, because Sorenson freaked out and wanted to head straight there. I told him to wait, but you know him." She grunted. "Doesn't take direction well, you might say."

"You got a number for him there?"

"Yeah."

"So phone it."

"You phone it. I don't want to call and ream him out if his dad just kicked the bucket."

"Have you got a load for him or not?"

He heard her sigh. "I'll call you right back." And she hung up.

Hunter drove into the Village to find a deli so he could grab a sandwich. El's call came just as he was waiting for his change.

"Best I could do for him was a load in Eugene. He's already done 1100 empty miles, so what's another couple hundred..."

"What! How far south did you send him?" Hunter almost dropped the phone trying to juggle the change and his deluxe roast beef sandwich. He was aware that all the heads in the deli had turned in his direction. "Who's paying the fuel for those empty miles? I sure as hell can't afford it." He stuffed the sandwich in his jacket pocket along with the change and headed back outside.

He could hear El working her calculator before she finally agreed to give up her percentage on the load to Redding, as well as the load from Eugene. "My bad," she said. "I don't know what I was thinking." She promised to call Sorry at his mother's and try to get him back on the road as soon as possible. "Call me again later", she said, and hung up.

Hunter sat in his car with the engine running and the heater on full blast, eating his roast beef sandwich. The deluxe part consisted of wilted lettuce leaves and pale, crunchy tomato slices. A slice of roast beef fell out and landed on the floor between his boots.

"This is definitely not my day," he muttered as he put the car in park and headed back to the highway.

El Watson leaned back and closed her eyes. She had so little information for Hunter from Sorry's expensive detour that she was afraid to tell him about her attempt to help his investigation. Don Julian Transport. Jorge Vasquez. That was all Sorenson had come up with. What good could that information possibly be? Now it was going to cost Watson Transportation the percentage on two loads and Hunter had to be wondering how she could make such a stupid mistake.

The only thing left was for her to see if she could find anything out about Don Julian Transport in Industry, California. She knew several brokers in Southern California. It was worth the cost of a few more telephone calls, although she was beginning to think that she was chasing a wild goose. Or following a red herring; wasn't that what detectives called a false trail? She started thumbing through her rolodex cards again, pulling out two of them by the time the phone began to ring.

"Watson!"

"Hi, El. I'm ready to go. Got something for me?"

"Sorenson. Where are you? What happened to your dad?"

"He's at work. Old bugger was totally shitfaced last night, but out the door at his usual time this morning." His voice faded, but she could make out what he was saying. "Any of that meatloaf left, Ma? It would make a great sandwich."

"He's not sick?"

"My dad? Nah, he's fine. My mom threw him a surprise birthday party is all."

El felt her temperature start to rise. Two loads with zero income, a good load in Torrance that she'd wheedled out of another broker lost, Hunter pissed off, and it was this clown's fault because he'd decided to go to a birthday party without telling her.

"You drove six hundred empty miles for a fuckin' birthday party?" she said between clenched teeth.

"Hold on, woman," he bellowed back at her. "You're the one who told me my father was sick."

She could hear a woman in the background say, "She did?"

"I said *maybe*, you jerk. I told you to *call* your mom, not drive six hundred miles to see her in Hunter's truck. You know how much that's costing me?" She lowered her voice and added, "I just might take it off your check."

"You mean Hunter's check. Let's just see what he has to say about it."

El knew she was SOL. Sorry would tell Hunter everything and it would all boil down to her own fault. "I had a load for you in Torrance. You shoulda stayed in L.A."

"Well, I'm here now. You got a fuckin' load for me here or do you want me to drive Hunter's rig home empty?"

Now a woman's voice said, "Danny, that's no way to talk to your boss. I don't want to hear language like that in my house."

El heard Sorry apologize to his mother. It figured that he wouldn't apologize to El herself. "Yes, I've got a fuckin' load for you. Write this down," she said, and gave him the address and directions to the shipper's warehouse in Eugene. "Can you be there by four o'clock?"

It took him a couple of minutes to find something to write on and get all the details written down. "Got that?" she said.

"Yeah, I got it. Be there by four. See you in the morning."

"Listen, Sorenson. Call me once you're loaded. Tonight, okay? I don't want any more surprises, hear me?"

All she heard back was a click.

The luggage was slow in coming. Meredith stood by the baggage carousel with her carry-on roller bag, watching the metal panels slide by, waiting for the sound of suitcases sliding off the conveyor belt. She turned on her cell phone and checked for messages. There was only one.

"Meredith. This is Hunter Rayne. Give me a call."

She erased the voicemail and put the phone back in her pocket. She didn't need anything more from him. She was sure that the police had nothing to tie her to the murder, and the trucker had nothing to contribute to the investigation she was doing for her client. If he really wanted to talk to her, he could call on his dime.

She had been relieved to find that neither Brent Carruthers nor his fiancée Tracy were booked on her flight to LAX. In her blond wig and at the speed she'd brushed past them last night, apologizing with a French accent for being late with the clean towels, they might not even have recognized her. Even if they had, as far as they knew, her name was Stella Clark and she was from Raleigh, NC. They would have found that nothing was missing from their hotel room, so if they suspected a break-in, police and security weren't likely to waste any manpower on finding her. She wasn't afraid of Carruthers anyway; it was only his connection to Cordero that worried her.

She thought about Todd Milton, who worked for Blue Hills' biggest competitor and had talked to her about 'purchasing espionage'. He had shared a table with Mike Irwin and Dave Cordero at the Chateau Grande Montagne the night before Irwin was killed. Todd was somehow connected to Cordero, and Cordero was now connected to Brent Carruthers, who considered himself a 'shoo-in' for the late Irwin's position at Blue Hills. There was something going on that would affect her client — she was sure of it — and now she just had to figure out the details.

Just what had gone down between Milton, Cordero and Irwin? Could Irwin have threatened to expose one or both of them? Had he upped the ante to an unacceptable level? Or had he gone back on his word, taking the bribe but not fulfilling his part of the 'negotiated' deal? She doubted that she would ever get useful information directly from Cordero — he had already seemed suspicious of her — and she might have burned her bridges with Carruthers, but Milton was still a viable source of information. She checked her wallet to make sure she still had his Cameron-Watts Aerospace business card. A dinner date wouldn't be out of line.

She was just putting her luggage in the trunk of her Mustang when her cell rang. It was the trucker calling from Canada.

"What else can you tell me?" he asked.

"Sorry," she said. "Since we last talked, I wasn't able make contact with anyone else associated with Irwin in Whistler, and I'm pretty much out of the picture now." She closed the trunk, and walked around to the driver's door. "I'm done with your investigation, and as far as I know, the detectives handling the case aren't interested in me anymore either."

"I wish I could say the same thing."

"Oh?" When he didn't answer, she couldn't help but smile. Even better that the detectives had their sights on someone else. "I'm sure you'll be fine. Don't you cops watch each others' backs?"

"If you find out anything else that might help, let me know," he said.

"Of course."

She ended the call and threw the phone on the seat next to her. "Of course, I won't, I mean," she said to herself as she started the engine. "Ten four, good buddy, you're on your own."

It was time for Hunter to make the call he'd been dreading. He dialled Helen's number, hesitating before he pressed the last digit, wondering if there was some way he could find some better news for her first. He heard the ring signal, then her almost desperate 'Hello'.

"Helen, it's me. Have you heard from Adam?"

He wasn't surprised when she said she hadn't. "Have you seen him? Is he okay?"

"No, I haven't seen him, but last night I talked to a few people who have." He didn't want to tell her that one of those people was Nathan. He didn't want to tell her that her son had been sick, so sick that he'd looked for the boy in all the local hospitals. "So we now know he's here and roughly where he hangs out, so it's just a matter of time before I connect with him."

"Oh, thank God! And you'll bring him home, Hunter? You said you'd bring him home."

Hunter remembered very well the promise he'd made to her, and the promise he'd made to himself looking out at Howe Sound. "Yes, Helen, I'll bring him home."

Hunter was once again on the Sea to Sky highway, heading south from Whistler. There was nothing more he could do in Whistler to discover Mike Irwin's killer, no suspects or people connected to Irwin were left in the resort community, no reasonable way to find clues on the mountain. He'd just hit a brick wall with Meredith Travis, the only effective link he had to the victim's business world, and now all he could do was wait for the RCMP detectives and their U.S. connections to do their jobs. He wished he could convince himself that there would never be enough evidence for Shane to recommend charges against him, but the unnamed witnesses from the ski hill, combined with Tom Halsey and the other witnesses who had seen his altercation with Irwin the night before in the piano lounge, just might be enough for the Crown Counsel if they felt pressure from the media.

Sorry was still in California, so his truck wouldn't be back until tomorrow at the earliest, and El hadn't yet guaranteed a load for him out of Vancouver. As much as he'd like to spend some time at home — just doing the things a man has to do when he lives alone, like laundry, bookkeeping, paying bills, checking in with his family, catching up on his sleep — he felt compelled to go look for Adam Marsh for the remainder of the day.

He turned on his car radio to catch up on the news. It wasn't good. The forecast was for a strong cold front. The cold of the night before was only going to get worse, and the news pointed out the serious risk the below-freezing temperatures would hold for the homeless in Vancouver. On the positive side, it could force more homeless into shelters. Additional emergency shelters were being set up, which might result in a call saying Adam Marsh was hunkered down in a church basement.

Once again, Hunter was looking out over the waters of Howe Sound as he made his way south from Squamish to Horseshoe Bay. He tried to recapture the powerful and positive feeling he'd had on his last drive, but his thoughts kept returning to Adam and what could happen to a sick and vulnerable boy in a big city. He decided that his strategy today would be to park on the North Van side of the harbor, do a walkthrough of the parking lots and the stores at Lonsdale Quay, search the adjacent Seabus station, then board the Seabus and travel over the inlet to the Vancouver side. Once there, he would search the Seabus and Skytrain station on that side, and seek out anyone who might have seen Adam since yesterday evening.

It was almost one o'clock before he reached the foot of Lonsdale in North Vancouver and found a space in the parking lot beneath the Lonsdale Quay. Although it was warmer in the parking lot than out on the street, he knew that he was more likely to find the young runaway inside the heated shopping area, so he took the elevator up to the mall itself. The mall was brightly lit and lined with colorful stores and kiosks selling everything from children's toys to jewelry to art prints, as well as delicatessen items, books and more. He headed straight for the men's washroom, making use of the facilities himself, then checking thoroughly for any sign of Adam, but there was no one in the room except himself.

There were stores and service counters running the length of the mall, with a central section of stores and kiosks as well, so it would be easy to miss the boy if he were walking around. He scanned a group of tables near the elevators with no success. There was more than one eating area — two small food courts featured several food service counters adjacent to a shared section of tables and chairs — and Hunter worked his way slowly from the one nearest the elevators toward the largest at the far end of the mall. He glanced into each of the stores along the way, occasionally brushing past shoppers carrying packages or dodging around baby strollers. He showed Adam's photo to the woman in the news stand and at two of the food counters, including one that sold pastries and other baked goods.

"Yeah, I seen him," said a girl with a purple stripe in her hair and a stainless steel stud in her nose. She was making change for two white-haired ladies who had bought cinnamon buns, freshly baked from the smell of them. "But he looked kind of sick. He bought a hot chocolate a couple hours ago."

Hunter's pulse quickened. Maybe his search wasn't as hopeless as he'd sometimes felt it was. "Did you see where he went?"

The girl shook her head, but said "Try the food court. They don't chase kids outa there if they've bought food."

Farther down the mall to his left, the space opened up to an eating area filled with tables and chairs. It was surrounded by floor-to-ceiling glass windows overlooking the waters of Burrard Inlet. To the east, a large boat sat serenely between docks, rocking almost imperceptibly. Seagulls perched on pilings blackened with creosote. Several tables were occupied by two or three people, most of them busy eating lunches from disposable plates. One couple shared a noodle and vegetable dish, deftly picking up pieces of broccoli and baby corn with chopsticks.

There was a lone person at a table in the corner, where the two walls of glass windows joined. On the table were a dirty paper plate and a crumpled napkin, along with a tall paper cup. The person at the table had his head down on one arm, so all Hunter could see was a tangle of sandy hair. It certainly could be Adam. Hunter walked over and stood beside the table. The boy was wearing a heavy jacket, badly stained in places. He smelled of unwashed hair and a trace of vomit. Hunter cleared his throat, but the boy didn't move.

He put a hand on the boy's shoulder and shook him gently. Still no reaction. "Adam?"

A barely audible moan.

Hunter spoke louder, his hand squeezing the shoulder through the quilted jacket. "Adam Marsh? Is that you, Adam?"

The boy's head raised slowly. His eyes looked sunken and were barely open, mouth slack. His forehead was pale but his lips and cheeks were red. He had a stainless steel stud in one nostril. "Hunh?" He didn't turn his head.

"Adam. Look at me. Are you alright?"

The boy turned his head slowly toward Hunter, eyes mere slits. "Dad?" he said, his voice barely more than a croak.

Hunter's heart lurched. "It's Hunter, Adam. Hunter Rayne."

The boy closed his eyes and slowly lowered his head again. Hunter reached over and felt the boy's forehead. He was burning up.

Lions Gate Hospital was only a few blocks up Lonsdale, and Hunter briefly considered carrying the boy to his car. He knew, however, that the boy would get attention faster if he arrived at the ER by ambulance, so he pulled out his cell phone and dialled 911. He told the dispatcher that he'd found a very sick boy, verging on unresponsive and unable to walk. "The International Food Court at Lonsdale Quay," he told them. "I'll be watching for you."

"I'm getting help for you," he told the boy. "You're going to be okay."

The boy raised his head again. "No," he said. "I'm fine." The boy put both hands on the table as if to help himself stand, but Hunter's hands on his shoulders kept him in his chair.

When he was sure the boy had given up trying to stand, Hunter brought up Helen's number on his cell phone. "I want you to tell your mom you're going to be home soon."

The boy frowned, and his eyelids fluttered. "My mom?"

Hunter pocketed his phone. It was probably best to wait until the boy was safely in the hospital and the doctors had a chance to assess his condition. "We'll call her as soon as you're feeling well enough to talk. How long have you been sick?"

The boy shrugged and lay his head down again. Hunter sat beside him, his hand resting lightly on the boy's arm, until the EMTs arrived. He hadn't seen Adam since he was about nine and didn't really know the boy, but felt a surprising rush of tenderness as he watched Adam's back rise and fall with his breaths. Ken's son. Ugly memories of Ken's death rose to the surface. He heard again Helen's panicked voice when he'd answered the phone. "My God! Oh my God! Ken has shot himself. Oh, Hunter, come… the blood… my God. I can't… Please come…" He had gone to her, and to confront what had once been his best friend, an image that still haunted his nights, even on far distant highways.

At first the approaching sirens seemed to belong to the past, but Hunter shook his head and got to his feet. He went to greet the EMTs as they entered the mall from the hotel entrance to guide them to the sick boy.

Although he objected and tried to push them away, the EMTs were able to get Adam to lie down on the stretcher, and once he was prone, the boy closed his eyes and relaxed with a sigh as they strapped him in. Hunter walked behind the stretcher to the ambulance, and when Adam was safely inside, promised to meet up with them again in the emergency room.

By the time he arrived at the ER, they had already moved Adam out of sight of the waiting room and triage window. Hunter went to the desk and gave them as much information about Adam as he could, but held off on giving them Helen's phone number. "I'll call his mother," he said. "Can I see the boy? I'd really like to talk to the doctor first, so I can reassure her he'll be alright."

They told him to take a seat, they'd call him shortly. He wanted to pace the waiting area, but settled for walking the perimeter of the room as best he could, as if he were inspecting the walls and doorways, trying to stay out of the way of patients and visitors.

"Mr. Rayne?"

The doctor was a young woman who didn't look much older than his daughters. She wore a white coat over what looked like a uniform, and had white clogs on her feet. Her hair was in a tight ponytail, and her voice was all business. "You're the boy's uncle?" she asked.

Hunter explained the situation briefly.

"I really should be talking to his next of kin," she said.

"I'm the only one he's got here, for now. I'd like to be the one to break the news to his mother. She doesn't even know I've found him yet."

The young doctor frowned. "I can't make a definite diagnosis yet, but it could be very serious. We'll be moving him to the isolation unit as a precaution. We don't need him spreading whatever it is he's got to other patients. For now, we've got him on IV fluids, and it may be that he'll respond to antibiotics but we won't know whether it's bacterial or viral until his blood work is done. We can't risk waiting for the results."

"It's just a bad flu, isn't it? He hasn't been eating well, and probably spent the night outside." Hunter hoped he was right, but already knew it was worse than that. Kids don't get that confused with an ordinary flu.

"It's *bad*, but I doubt that it's *just* a flu." She sounded irritated, her tone condescending.

Hunter drew his head back with a frown, but cut her some slack. He knew it was never easy to deliver bad news. "How long before you know?"

"I can't tell you. If he responds to the antibiotic he could be out of the woods by morning. If not..." She looked down at the floor, then back up at his face. "Okay. Look. He's got signs of a rash. Your young friend may have meningitis or meningococcal septicemia. Mortality rates are high. If I were you, I'd tell his mother to book the first flight here."

CHAPTER
SEVENTEEN

Hunter went straight home. He eased the Pontiac down the driveway into his usual parking spot, relieved to see that his landlord's car was in the carport. Instead of going downstairs to his own suite, he knocked at the landlord's door.

"Oh, for heaven's sake," said Gord as he opened the door. The old doctor's eyebrows wiggled above the frames of his bifocals. "You lost your key?"

"I'm here for a consultation, doctor," said Hunter.

Gord bowed from the waist and ushered him inside. "Coffee? Or beer."

Hunter hesitated briefly before answering. "I think I could use a drink."

He stood at the plate glass window in the living room, looking out at the tall cedars at the foot of the yard and the stretch of steel grey ocean visible between them. The cat came and rubbed up against his shin, but he wasn't in the mood to pet her and risk her fangs and claws.

Gord walked in a couple of minutes later with a small tray containing two mugs of beer and two shot glasses of rye whiskey. "You look like you could use more than just a beer," he said, setting the tray on the teakwood coffee table. "Come. Sit down."

Hunter sat on the chartreuse sofa and Gord settled into a purple chair with teakwood arms. The cat appeared from under the coffee table, threatening to jump on Hunter's lap, but Gord intercepted her and tossed her gently out of a sliding glass door onto the sundeck before sitting back down.

"Where's John?" asked Hunter.

"Library," said Gord. "Now what's this about? Have you got some symptoms you're worried about?" He raised his shot glass. "Cheers."

They both sipped, and Hunter felt the warmth of the whiskey slide down his throat. "CC?"

"Crown. My Christmas present to me." He smiled at his shot glass as he set it down.

"It's not me that's sick," said Hunter. "I've been looking for this boy, son of an old friend, who ran away from his home in Calgary. I found him this morning." He gave Gord as many details as he could think of: how Adam had behaved, how he looked, and what the ER doctor had said. "I guess I'm looking for some good news here. I hate to think the worst."

The old doctor looked grave. "I can't diagnose someone I haven't seen. Best I can do is give you a best case and worst case scenario. Okay?"

Hunter nodded.

"Best case, your young friend has the flu. Because of his living situation, the combination of vomiting, diarrhea, fever, and lack of proper care, including adequate food and fluids, has led to him becoming severely dehydrated. That can result in weakness and confusion. The rash? Maybe fleas or something he's encountered in his travels, not related to his illness." He paused, watching Hunter's face. "In that case, his prognosis *could* be full recovery in a matter of days. However, severe dehydration can also lead to organ damage, especially the kidneys."

Hunter winced. Even best case could be bad. "And worst case?"

Gord shook his head. "Like the ER doctor said, meningococcal septicemia or meningococcemia could quickly turn fatal. Meningitis is more common in youngsters like him, since adults seem to build up an immunity to the bacteria over time. The same bacteria that causes meningitis by multiplying in the spinal fluid ends up getting into the bloodstream. It's essentially blood poisoning. If antibiotics are started soon enough and the bacteria aren't resistant, it's possible the boy could make a full recovery, but it'll be touch and go for a while."

"I have to call his mother. Do you think I should tell her to fly out from Calgary?"

Without hesitation, the old doctor said, "Absolutely, and the sooner the better."

Hunter took a deep breath.

"Think about it. If his condition is fatal, you'll have to live with the thought that you didn't act in time for his mother to see her son before he died. You wouldn't want that on your conscience, would you?"

Hunter snorted softly. "You got that right."

He already had enough on his conscience when it came to Helen Marsh.

"It's about fuckin' time," Elspeth roared into the telephone receiver. Maybe she could deflect any criticism Hunter might have for her handling of Sorry's trip to California by going on the offensive. "You were supposed to be back at work on Sunday night. It is now fuckin' Thursday. You threw my road schedule for you totally out of whack."

"Good morning to you, too, El. Where's my truck?"

"I'm expecting Sorenson to pull into the yard any minute now. When'll you be ready to head out? I've got a couple of loads coming up this afternoon." She was surprised at his hesitation. "You're not ready to go?"

She heard him suck in his breath. "There's been a... an unfortunate development. You know that kid I was looking for?"

"You found him?"

"Yesterday afternoon. Right now he's in an isolation ward at Lions Gate Hospital with possible blood poisoning. I just called, but the hospital won't tell me anything. Evidently his mother's there now. She must've flown in last night but I haven't heard from her since I broke the news to her yesterday."

"Jeez, Hunter. You bust your ass trying to find the kid for her and she can't even call you to tell you how he is?"

It took him a few seconds to respond, and when he did his words were clipped. "Her son might be dying, El. She's got more important things than me on her mind."

"You coming back to work or not? Have the cops still got you in a bubble?"

Again, a pause. "I'll be there within the hour."

Hunter struck out for Watson Transportation's warehouse on Annacis Island before the end of rush hour. Sitting in the traffic bottlenecked at the Second Narrows bridge was better than sitting around the house, waiting to hear from Helen. She had no cell phone, but he would have expected her to use a payphone from the hospital. He could only assume that Adam's condition hadn't improved and that she was totally consumed by concern for her son. He hoped it wasn't worse.

After his conversation with Gord the previous afternoon, he had immediately called Helen and told her about Adam. He didn't sugarcoat the news. He was a parent himself, and knew she would want the truth. She had thanked him, but was in a hurry to end their conversation so she could book a flight. He had asked her if she would need a ride from the airport, and her answer was, "If I do, I'll call you." Keeping his cell phone handy so he wouldn't miss her call, Hunter caught up on his errands. He did laundry, brought his bookkeeping up to date, paid bills, picked up some groceries, and ate some store-bought lasagna. He fell asleep watching Jay Leno. Helen never called. He only knew of her arrival from what the hospital told him over the phone in the morning. He'd asked if he could visit the ward, but the answer was a definite 'no'.

When he pulled into the yard, he saw The Blue Knight had already arrived and its trailer had been unhooked. He parked his car and climbed the steps to El's office. She was on the phone, as usual, and Sorry was leaning on the counter leafing through a newspaper.

"Hey, bro," he said. "For what it's worth, at least I brought your truck back safe and sound."

"What do you mean by that?"

Sorry rolled his eyes. "Looks like you and her," he nodded in El's direction, "barely broke even on the deal. And I'm going home with less than I figured on."

El gave him the finger without even looking up at either of them.

Hunter rubbed his forehead and recited an old mantra inside his head: *tomorrow will be a better day, tomorrow will be a better day*. But tomorrow he would still be a murder suspect, and tomorrow Adam Marsh could be dead. No. *Tomorrow will be a better day.*

"I can send you back to California this afternoon," said El as she hung up the phone. "I've got a load for Downey. You gonna take it or should I call one of my teams?"

Hunter held up his hand, signalling her to wait while he thought it over. Blackwell hadn't told him to stay in the country this time. He could stay here and stew about his situation, or be on the road earning some much needed cash to cover his expenses. It didn't take him long to decide. "I'll take it."

"You got it. A loaded trailer will be ready to pick up in Port Kells by two o'clock." El reached for another ringing phone. "Have your truck ready to pull outa here at one. Watson!" He'd been dismissed.

"Gimme a lift home?" said Sorry, closing the newspaper. It was the morning's Vancouver Province. He slapped the closed newspaper with his hand. "I see they've got a warrant out for your arrest."

Hunter was heading for the door but stopped in his tracks. "Let me see that."

"Hah ha!" roared Sorry. "Just kidding. Whoa! If looks could kill..."

Hunter shook his head and turned around again.

"Wait, Hunter." Hunter heard footsteps thudding down the steps behind him. "Hey! How about we go get some breakfast on the way?"

They didn't have to wait for a clean table at the Denny's on Scott Road. They took a booth against the wall, and the waitress brought over a pot of hot coffee before they'd even settled in. Sorry ordered bacon and eggs with pancakes and a side of sausages, and Hunter ordered a Denver omelette. It actually felt good to be with someone who would carry the conversation and take his mind off the past few days.

"So tell me about the trip," he said, as if Sorry needed prompting.

"Just peachy," said Sorry, pouring sugar into his coffee. "Hey, it was fuckin' weird, you know? Remember we were talking about my dad? I hardly think about him for months — maybe years — then you and me talk about him, and the same night I come across these two runaway kids from Minnesota and it makes me think about him, and then my driving time is up and where do you think I am? Fuckin' Yreka, my home town."

"You saw him, your dad? El said he was sick."

"Fuckin' El. She was thinking with her big mouth. Turns out it was his seventieth birthday and here I was, pedal to the metal on the way back, thinkin' my old man was dying and when I get there he's half wasted drinking beers with his friends. And this is where it gets really weird." Sorry hunched forward over his coffee as if he were about to share a secret.

"We're sittin' outside having a smoke late at night and he starts talkin' about this woman named Belle Sorenson. She was some kind of a serial killer and they called her the Black Widow. She kept inviting unsuspecting dudes out to her place to marry her and then she'd drug them and butcher them and feed them to the pigs." He shuddered. "You ever hear of her?"

Hunter frowned, trying to place the name.

258

"It was in Minnesota, I think," Sorry continued. "My old man kept saying, 'no blood relation', but I think it freaked him out that she had the same name as us, and he was talkin' about seeing a movie about a bad seed or something that had to do with this Black Widow, and then he brings up Marlon Brando, that fat actor from the Godfather who bought the island, and the biker gangs. Somehow he connected that to me when I was a kid and he asked me if I'd ever killed anybody. He says, 'I'm sorry, Daniel' — my dad calls me Daniel. He thought I was a bad seed, but now he's changed his mind, and all of a sudden it's like we're bosom buddies."

Hunter had to wait for Sorry to take a sip of coffee before he could get a word in edgewise. "Hell's Belle?"

"What?"

"Belle Gunness. Hell's Belle. If I remember right, she was thought to have killed over twenty five people. I think she lived in Chicago. That's probably who your dad was referring to."

"She killed her husbands, right?"

"Husbands, or would-be husbands, I think. Your dad thought you were a serial killer?"

"My guess is he thought all bikers were bad dudes who raped innocent women and tortured puppies and kittens. But after all these years of acting like he hated me and wished I was dead, now he's made me promise to bring Mo and the kids down for Easter. What do you think of that?"

Hunter leaned back to let the waitress set down his breakfast. "I'm happy to hear it. That's how it should be."

"Yeah." That was all Sorry said until he'd cleaned half his plate. When he came up for air, he said, "And I haven't told you about my adventures in Sylmar and Pomona yet."

"Sylmar and Pomona? That's close to L.A. What were you doing there?" A light went on. El had said 'farther south'. Sylmar was where Mike Irwin used to work. He sighed and leaned his forehead on his hand, his elbow propped on the table. "El sent you to do some detective work, didn't she?"

Sorry nodded, and mumbled a 'yeah'. His mouth was full again.

Hunter went back to his omelette and the waitress breezed by the table to top up their coffees.

A few minutes later Sorry's plate was finally empty and he pushed it to the end of the table. He doctored his fresh coffee and took another sip, then leaned back with a satisfied sigh. "Like I was sayin'," he said, raising his eyebrows as if to ask Hunter if he wanted to hear more.

Hunter nodded, finishing off his last piece of toast.

"El had me do some kind of a stakeout at this company called Blue Hills. The place had pretty good security. Can't get in or out of the lot without the security guard opening the gate. Somebody's payin' off somebody there when it comes to the shipping contract is my guess, because it seems the shipper made a deal with one guy, an operator named — oh, shit, I wrote it down in that notebook you keep in your truck — Jerome something, out of Pomona, little black dude, and then the shipper blows him off to give the contract to another outfit that Jerome figured had gang ties." He paused. "So what do you think?"

"You talked to this Jerome?"

Sorry nodded. "After a little hand-to-hand combat, yeah."

"Explain that, please."

Sorry launched into a detailed account of Jerome throwing something into the competitor's truck, himself following Jerome's rig down the highway and getting pulled over by the California highway patrol, then being attacked with a tire iron in a parking lot in Pomona. Then El sent him back to find Jerome again to ask him something he'd forgotten to ask him the first time. "So the big news is that the outfit that took over the job was called Don Julian Transport from Industry, if that rings a bell. The driver's name was Hor-hay Vasquez. Mean anything to you?"

Hunter rubbed his chin. "Jorge Vasquez of Don Julian Transport. No, it means nothing to me except…"

"Except?"

"Don Julian sounds vaguely familiar. Do you think it's a Latino name, maybe Mexican?" He remembered what Mike Irwin's wife had said about the man who'd sold Mike the boat. "Industry is on the east side of L.A. Must be a good hour's drive from Huntington Beach when the traffic's light." He shrugged. "Might mean nothing. It gives me something to work on, though." Hunter hadn't been planning to do any investigating while he was in L.A., but it might turn out to be a productive way to spend his off hours. Industry was only about twenty minutes up the 605 from his drop in Downey.

"I don't know what you're talking about, but did I give you a lead? I gave you a good lead?" Sorry blew on his finger nails and buffed them on his shirt.

"Better than nothing. Not sure if it's worth the diesel fuel but it *is* something."

"Aw-right!"

Sorry held his hand up for a high five and Hunter met him half way across the table. "Let's get you home. I've got some packing to do. You're buying, right?"

Sorry patted his pockets then shrugged apologetically. "I'll gladly pay you Tuesday…"

Hunter shook his head. "Okay, Wimpy. Let's go."

It was still daylight when Hunter crossed the border into Washington State and accelerated onto the southbound I-5. The highway opening up in front of his windshield and the steady hum of the big diesel were just the antidote he needed after the stresses of the past several days. The smell of stale cigarette smoke in the cab had faded, so he rolled up his window, settled back into the driver's seat of his Freightliner and felt himself relax. Life already looked a little brighter. After all, the boy he had been looking for had been found and, whether or not Hunter had heard from her, his mother was now at his side. At the thought of Helen, he reached over and checked his cell phone to make sure it was on, since he usually turned it off when he was on the road. You never know, in California he could find a new lead on who might have killed Mike Irwin and why. If he was lucky, the case would be solved in the next few days and he would be free to get back to his simple and solitary life.

He thought about what Sorry had said in relating the story of his visit with his dad, and the elder Sorenson's reference to Belle Sorenson Gunness, the Black Widow. Her crimes came to light early in the 1900s. He couldn't recall the details, but knew that she was one of the most prolific, if not *the* most prolific, female serial killer in history. A female murderer. Hunter shook his head. He was sure that Mike Irwin had definitely not been the victim of a female serial killer.

But then Sorry had gone on to describe his so-called stakeout at the company where Mike Irwin had worked. The change of carriers for product moving out of the Blue Hills factory must have been something that was put into play either immediately before or immediately after Mike Irwin's death. Hunter wished he'd gotten more cooperation from Meredith Travis during their last conversation, because he'd had no real opportunity to investigate the victim's business relationships himself. Perhaps if he made the effort to meet with her in L.A., she would be more forthcoming. At some point, if he continued to be a suspect, he might be forced to hire her himself.

He had been on the I-5 for less than an hour and was just nearing Lake Samish when his cell phone rang. He picked it up and flipped it open with his thumb, then held it to his ear and said, "Hello."

Static. Then, "Hunter?" It was a woman's voice.

"Helen?"

More static, then what sounded like "… he says Adam is…" and then nothing.

The Blue Knight had obviously entered one of the many dead zones along the highway. Hunter gave it thirty seconds or so, then flipped the phone closed and threw it on the passenger seat. He thought better of it, reached over to pick it up again, and pushed the button to turn it off. If she called back, she could leave a message and he would retrieve it when he was somewhere with a stronger signal. He could only hope the news was good.

Hunter drove until just after two a.m. and parked at the rest stop just south of Hornbrook. There had been snow flurries on the Siskiyou Summit and he was tired from concentrating on the climb, not to mention he had used up all of his allowed driving hours since leaving Watson Transportation's yard. He was now on his ten hour break and a good sleep was in order before he went searching for a hot breakfast. After a quick visit to the facilities, he locked himself inside the cab and polished off a sandwich and pint of milk that he'd picked up at his last fuel stop. By the time he crawled into his down sleeping bag in the truck's sleeper, the air inside had already started to cool off. He was just drifting off to sleep when he realized that his cell phone was still turned off and sitting on the passenger seat. Too late now. It could stay there until morning.

CHAPTER

EIGHTEEN

Hunter made good time on the second leg of his trip. He grabbed a hot breakfast and a coffee to go at the Pilot in Weed, then kept driving south, past the exits to the Napa Valley and the San Francisco Bay area, until he reached one of his favorite meal stops in Santa Nella around sunset. He parked his rig at the truck stop and headed across the road to Andersen's for dinner before fueling up and getting back on the I-5. By ten on Friday evening, he'd crossed the Grapevine Pass and pulled in to park for the night at the Castaic truck stop. He couldn't take a chance on finding a safe parking place closer to the consignee's warehouse in Downey. Morning traffic through Los Angeles wouldn't have been much fun on a weekday, but it was Saturday so Hunter figured it wouldn't be so bad.

That morning he had retrieved a message from Helen. "I have booked a motel room, but am spending most of my time at the hospital. I'll try to call you again later." The only thing that told him about Adam's condition was that it was serious enough for her to spend most of her time nearby. He couldn't call her back, so he would just have to wait for another call.

He had to make the delivery too early to allow him to consider doing much else beforehand on Saturday morning, other than a shower at the truck stop and a quick breakfast. The delivery was routine, with none of the problems that typically complicate a driver's day. No miscommunication about delivery time, no locked gates, no angry receiver, no damaged freight when the trailer doors were opened. He was grateful for that, and was able to pull away from the consignee's dock without undue delay. If he planned to spend some time following up on the murder investigation, he was going to have to find a safe place to drop the trailer and secure it until he was ready to hitch up again. He called El.

"Delivery's done," he said. "Have you got something else lined up for me?"

"Yup. Hang on," and he was on hold, listening to the Vancouver weather forecast. It was raining there, no surprise. In the L.A. basin it was overcast but dry, a comfortable sixty-eight degrees.

Roaming charges on his cell were a killer, but he was parked on the side of a road in Downey and didn't want to set off in any direction in relatively unfamiliar territory until he knew where his truck would be needed next. Fortunately, El was back on the line in about thirty seconds.

"You've got two choices. You can drop that trailer today and pick it up with a load of packaged plastic products on Monday morning in San Bernardino, or get six skids of machinery Monday afternoon in Buena Park. The machinery can be a through trip to Fort McMurray if you want. What's your pleasure?"

"Not before then?" A parked truck doesn't pay the bills.

"It's the weekend, sweetcheeks. Make up your mind now, because I'll be making the same offer to Ray Nillson in five minutes and you'll have to take what's left."

Hunter opted for the load out of San Bernardino, taking down the information in the spiral-bound steno notebook he kept on the passenger seat. It would involve more empty miles and a couple extra hours of driving time, but it suited him better in other ways. Not only would he be able to leave the trailer there, the San Bernardino pickup would put him back on the road early on Monday. Although traffic was lighter at night and drivers could generally make better time, Hunter always preferred to drive during the day if he had a choice.

He checked his LA freeway map, then made his way to the 605 enroute to the San Bernardino freeway.

As he passed the exit for Pomona, he wondered if it would be worth his while to seek out that driver Sorry had mentioned seeing at the company where Mike Irwin had worked. He'd just noticed the name and phone number Sorry had scrawled in his notebook, and decided to at least try to contact him by phone. Less than an hour and a half later, he had dropped the trailer and pulled into the I-10 Truck Stop in Rialto so he could order some lunch and make some calls.

"Jerome here." The man's voice was soft and pleasant.

"Hello, Jerome. My name is Hunter Rayne. I'm doing some investigation on behalf of the Royal Canadian Mounted Police into the death of a tourist from California. I understand you might have some information about the victim's place of employment and was hoping I could ask you a few questions."

"You kiddin' me? Who you talkin' about?"

"You've hauled freight in the past for Blue Hills Industries, is that right?" Hunter kept his tone polite and professional.

With some hesitation, the man said, "That's right. The dead guy from there?"

"How long have you done business with the company?"

"Couple years." The man's voice became less hesitant. He said he'd known the shipper personally and they'd gotten along well. The shipper had given Jerome all the freight he could handle for delivery within the state of California, up until a few days ago.

"So the shipper was the one who made the decision?"

"Used to. As long as there were no complaints about the rates or service and his boss was okay with it, you know what I mean? And he was."

"I understand there was a recent change there. What do you know about it?"

There were a few seconds of silence, then the driver's tone changed to one bordering on belligerent. "Hey. You talkin' to that big dude looks like a Viking was hassling me couple days ago?"

"I expect you mean Dan Sorenson. Yes." Hunter decided to make Sorry sound legit. "He's been doing some undercover work for us."

"Yeah? That dude looks more like a biker than a cop. Sure was glad he didn't want to hurt me. He's a brute." He exhaled loudly. "Anyway, last week my shipper friend there was told he had to give all the California loads to this other outfit. He said he couldn't help it, that he couldn't call the shots no more."

"Did he say why?"

"He said that the manager had decided he wanted to control the shipping costs, but there was some talk that he was getting money under the table, you know what I mean?" Hunter heard him sniff.

Hunter smiled. El was right. Drivers loved to gossip and could be a great source of information as long as you took everything they said with a grain of salt. He encouraged Jerome to talk until he'd pretty much run out of things to say about Blue Hills. It confirmed what Hunter had already suspected. If the staff suspected Mike Irwin was taking bribes, it was very likely that the company's executives did too. That would certainly be a motive for hiring a private eye, but hardly a motive for murder, unless that was how the company's executives did business.

"You say you only did deliveries for them, Jerome? Do you know who handled the inbound freight?"

"Yeah. Same bozos who took my freight away."

"You've been very helpful. I hope you get the freight back, Jerome."

"Thanks, man. Good luck to you, too. Hope you find your killer."

After a call to the Whistler RCMP detachment and a brief discussion with Colin Pike, Hunter hung up the payphone and found a free table in the truck stop restaurant to order lunch. He wanted something fast, so he ordered a ham and cheese sandwich with soup and a coffee. If he wanted to cover all the bases in this murder investigation, whatever his hunch was, he had to follow up any leads he could. Before he left California, he had places yet to go and people yet to see.

His first destination was over an hour away: a building on Hollywood Boulevard. He was able to park the Blue Knight at a small shopping mall a few blocks away and he walked past shops and restaurants to a small apartment building not far from the Hollywood Freeway. It was what he would consider a character building. Old but attractive, unobtrusive, fronted by retail stores and a coffee lounge, not where you would expect to find a successful private eye, but he guessed that was the point. He had opted not to call first, but knew from his talk with Colin Pike that Meredith Travis worked out of an office in her home. He buzzed her apartment.

"Yes?"

"Hello, Stella. I have some information you're going to find useful. Can I buy you a cappuccino? It's warm enough to sit outside." He grinned in the direction of the camera, guessing the CCTV was available to tenants.

"Give me five minutes," was the terse reply.

Hunter pulled out a chair at one of the cafe's sidewalk tables, facing the archway to the apartment building. A few minutes later, Meredith emerged wearing hip-hugging jeans and a dark grey hoodie, her hands jammed into its pockets. She kept her eyes on his as she pulled out a chair for herself and sat down.

"You call this warm?" she said.

"Weren't you just on a snow covered mountain?"

"You expect it there. This is LA. Where's my cappuccino?"

"I guess I'll have to go inside to order."

She shook her head. "Just talk," she said. "Fast."

"I'm sure it's not news to you, but rumor has it Mike Irwin was abusing his position at Blue Hills Industries. I'm guessing that's why you were hired to watch him."

"You said you had some information I'd find interesting." He saw the muscles of her jaw bunch.

"A company by the name of Don Julian Transport muscled their way onto the loading dock at Blue Hills. I'm suspecting a connection between them and your friend Cordero."

She nodded. "That could be."

"You know more about what was going on at Blue Hills than I do. You were investigating him prior to the conference at Whistler, and I know you were undercover at the conference to find out more about his connections outside the company. Can you speculate on just what it was that Mike Irwin was doing to make himself a target for murder?"

Just then a casually dressed young woman in a black apron arrived to take their order. Meredith ordered a mocha. Hunter took this as a sign that she was willing to spend a little time there, and he ordered a regular coffee for himself.

"Off the record — if the police need a witness, I'll deny I ever said it — Mike Irwin was playing with fire. He was taking advantage of his position in charge of purchasing to sell favors to suppliers. I suspect he started small and didn't get caught, so he started getting careless. Getting fired — and possibly sued — was going to be one of the consequences, but it looks to me like he welched on a deal and made somebody angry. A very dangerous somebody."

"Cordero?"

She shrugged.

"How does Todd Milton fit into the picture?"

"That's something I'm still working on, but given he works for Blue Hills' biggest competitor, I don't doubt that he's involved somehow. By the way — and again, you didn't hear it from me — it turns out Brent Carruthers has applied for Irwin's job."

"You think he's a plant?"

She shrugged again.

"What else aren't you telling the police, Meredith?"

She sat back and raised one eyebrow.

"You're good at your job," he said. "You're smart and skillful, and creative when you need to be. I don't believe you lost sight of Mike Irwin last Saturday morning." He leaned forward, one elbow on the table. "You followed him to the ski hill and you saw him get on that chairlift."

Meredith's lips played briefly with a smile. She looked down at her lap and rubbed one cheekbone with her fingertips, but said nothing.

"Publicity is bad for business, I get that," he continued. "This won't go any farther than Hollywood Boulevard. I won't tell anyone where I got the information, or even that I've seen you again, but I want to know who you saw get on that chairlift with Irwin, every little thing."

She took a deep breath, pressing her lips together and looking at the sky. Then she looked directly at Hunter and said, "Keep in mind that I was watching Irwin, planning how to get on a chair close enough behind him that I wouldn't lose him at the top, but not so close that he would begin to notice my presence." She paused, watching a white panel van back into a parking spot across the street while a motorist behind it leaned on the horn. "There were two chairs between us, meaning seven or eight people in the line ahead of me. I didn't pay much attention to whoever got on the chair with him. They didn't get there together, though, I know that. He was alone, and I didn't see him ski with or speak to anyone from the time he left the hotel."

"At least you could tell if it was a man or a woman," he suggested.

She shook her head. "I wish I could tell you for sure. My impression was that it was a man, but I wouldn't swear to it."

"Did you see anything on the way up the hill?"

"Snow. The snow was heavy enough that I could barely see the chair in front of me."

"And at the top?" He nodded his thanks to the server as she set their coffees on the table.

"I was getting ready to get off the chair, but out of the corner of my eye I saw a man riding the chair back down. I turned for a quick look and from the ski clothes I figured it could be Irwin, but my chair was just arriving at the top and I couldn't be sure." She shrugged. "Of

270

course, when I started searching for him at the top of the chair, I realized I'd lost him and that it could have been him riding the chair down. It occurred to me that he'd noticed me and was thumbing his nose at me all the way down." She picked up her mocha and took a cautious sip, then licked away a thin line of whipped cream along her upper lip.

Hunter stirred some sugar into his coffee. "Did you follow him down?"

She shook her head again. "Then he'd know for sure, wouldn't he? I figured I'd pick him up again as soon as I could."

He nodded.

"So who do you think killed him?" she asked.

"I'm still trying to make all the puzzle pieces fit. I'm just not feeling comfortable with the business angle. That kind of thing goes on to some degree in every industry, and seldom leads to murder. In spite of what looks like an execution-style killing, I'm beginning to suspect the motive was more personal than professional. One of the major pieces is missing, because I'm not totally sold on the real motive yet. On some level, I'm hoping that my hunch is wrong." He took a sip of coffee, still keeping his eyes on her face. "So you don't think the other skier was a woman?"

She raised an eyebrow. "Your lawyer friend?"

"Is that who you suspect?"

"To tell you the truth, I don't really care who did it so I'm not going to waste any time thinking about it. No." She stirred the whipped cream topping into her coffee, then licked off the spoon and set it on a napkin. "I do care on some minor level. Maybe I'm being catty, but I'd like to see her get nailed for it. Some lawyers think they're smart enough to maneuver around the law." She paused to sip at her coffee. "Besides, if it was personal, she's got one of the biggest motives."

"One of them?"

"Duh."

Hunter smiled. Duh, indeed. When it came to motive, Mike Irwin's unhappy wife might have had the biggest motive of all. "Did you see Kelly Irwin that morning? She said the grandparents took the kids to McDonald's, so she went for a long walk. Alone."

Meredith sniffed. "Along with 'I went for a long drive', that's got to be one of the weakest alibis in the book. No, I didn't see her. Not that I'm aware of, anyway, but I wasn't looking for her that morning, was I?"

Hunter took out his wallet and tucked a ten dollar bill under his empty cup. "You're right. No one with any sense would use an alibi like that," he winked at her, "unless it happened to be the truth."

"Right," she said with a laugh. "You realize, of course, that could be exactly what she wants you to think."

After he left Meredith Travis, Hunter had the rest of Saturday and all day Sunday before the shipment in San Bernardino would be ready for pickup. Usually when he had a layover, he would take short sightseeing trips if he could afford the fuel, or else find a good book and hang out at the truck stop, spending time in the restaurant or the drivers' lounge when he wasn't resting in the truck's sleeper bunk. This time, he was on a mission to find out as much as he could about, or from, anyone connected with Mike Irwin.

He gave some serious thought to how he should approach Alora Magee. Things had ended awkwardly in Whistler, to put it mildly, and although he had no intention of pursuing a relationship with her, he was going to have to talk to her. Her behavior troubled him, or more accurately, the motivation behind her behavior. He thought it reasonable that he had offered to reschedule his meeting with John Irwin in order to take her to dinner, but she had taken what he thought was unwarranted offense at the fact he hadn't planned to spend the entire evening of her last day in Whistler with her.

Why had she seemed so eager to find an excuse to end it with him? He replayed their conversation, as near as he could remember it. Was what he did really so unforgiveable, had she simply over-reacted, or could it be that he had outlived his usefulness? Had he really been set up, as the private eye suggested? He hated to think he had misjudged Alora so completely, but a homicide investigator had to be thorough. She would not be happy to hear from him and he expected to get flak from her, but he would have to set aside his pride and ask if he could see her again.

The woman had been the victim of a stalker, so staking out her apartment would no doubt backfire. The solution would be to visit her office. Lawyers were a dedicated bunch when it came to billable hours, so he wouldn't be surprised if her firm's office was open and active on a Saturday afternoon, and that she was at work, catching up after her vacation. He decided that was his best bet.

It was after two thirty by the time he parked his tractor at a small mall in Sherman Oaks and walked across Ventura Boulevard to the building housing her law firm. The law office was on the fourth floor of a concrete and glass tower, and he checked his reflection before opening the glass door to the building. He had on clean jeans and an only slightly wrinkled cotton shirt, blue with narrow white stripes. He thought he looked respectable enough, although he knew he was no 'sharp-dressed man'.

The receptionist, a young woman wearing a grey suit and who wouldn't look out of place in a fashion magazine, was clearly a professional and gave no indication that his appearance was inferior to that of the firm's usual clients. He asked her if Alora Magee was in her office.

"Do you have an appointment?"

"No, she's not expecting me. Please tell her it's Hunter Rayne."

A moment later Alora emerged from an office down the hall. She wore tailored black slacks and a blouse of a satiny yellow fabric that somehow accentuated the amber of her eyes. She looked good. Hunter felt an unexpected twinge of regret that things hadn't worked out between them. "Thank you, Rebecca," she said to the receptionist, then motioned with her head for Hunter to follow her. She didn't smile or offer her hand.

Hunter echoed her 'thank you' to the receptionist with a smile and followed Alora.

Once inside the office, Alora closed the door behind him and remained standing, her hand on the knob.

"What do you want?" she asked.

Hunter glanced around the office before he replied. There was a low black filing cabinet and credenza, plus a couple of framed abstract prints on the wall. A large desk with several files open on its surface was between him and a tinted glass window; one chair was pulled out behind the desk and two chairs faced it. Beyond the window he could see nothing but a high overcast sky.

"I realize you want to put Mike Irwin behind you, but it may not be that easy," he said. "The detective in charge of the case still considers you a prime suspect — you and me both, in fact. I'd like nothing better than to forget the whole thing myself, but I'm trying to be proactive here. If I can find evidence pointing at the real killer, you and I can get on with our lives without worrying about a knock on the door and an escort to jail early one morning."

"That doesn't answer my question. Why are you here?" She dropped her hand from the door knob and leaned against the wall behind her, arms crossed over her chest.

"If you'll answer a few questions for me, I'll be on my way."

She nodded, but said nothing.

"Last time I spoke with Kelly Irwin, she indicated that you and she did not — do not — have an attorney-client relationship. Is that correct?"

Alora nodded again.

"So whatever she said to you during your time together at Whistler is not privileged information. Is that correct?"

She took a deep breath and rubbed the bridge of her nose. "Ask your questions. Depending on what they are, I may or may not answer you. If I feel that I am betraying her confidence, well, I'm not under oath and I'm not obligated to tell you anything. You're not even a cop."

He had to smile. "That's right. I'm just a truck driver." He gestured toward the two chairs in front of her desk. "I won't be here long, but that doesn't mean we can't sit down."

She moved away from the door, hesitating at the chair next to him, then walked around the desk and took the chair on the other side. She slid it forward, closed the file that was open in front of her, and placed her elbows on the desk.

Hunter cleared his throat as he sat down. "As you probably know, sometimes an insignificant detail can create a tiny wedge that breaks open a criminal case. I do intend to speak with Kelly Irwin again, but I'm hoping your powers of observation and intuition will shed some light on her behavior. Did Kelly say anything to you about the last time she saw her husband?"

Alora frowned. "Give me a minute," she said, leaning back and closing her eyes. "I need to think about that."

Hunter sat silently. Was she trying to recall her conversation with Kelly, or was she considering her strategy? He had to take what he could get.

"She told me that she didn't say goodbye to him that morning. She heard him getting ready to leave, but she pretended to be asleep."

"Did she say why?"

"She didn't have to. As much as she now says she loved him, she hated the bastard. She was also afraid of him. Don't forget, I've been there."

"Then what did she do?"

Alora's pursed her lips. "Funny. I didn't ask her — why would I? — but she made a point of telling me that she got the kids up and dressed and took them over to their grandmother's, then went out by herself for a long walk in the snow."

"Why do you think she made a point of telling you that?" He thought of Pierre Elliot Trudeau's long walk in the snow the day he made the decision to resign as Prime Minister of Canada. A major life-changing decision.

Alora shrugged. "Maybe she felt it had some kind of cosmic significance. You like to think that when someone close to you dies, you'll feel something, somehow, before you hear the news." She looked right at Hunter as she spoke.

Hunter looked away. He knew what she was talking about. On his way to their home after Helen had discovered Ken's body, he'd had a hard time believing Ken could have died without Hunter receiving some kind of psychic message. From who or what, he didn't know.

"You never doubted that she actually did go for that walk?"

Alora leaned back, looking more relaxed than she had since his arrival. "You think she could have killed him?"

Hunter wondered if her relaxation was a sign of relief that his questions pointed to another suspect besides herself. "You don't?" he asked.

"I think, if I were in her position, I would want him dead," she said, "but do I really think she has the jam to kill somebody?" She shook her head. "If she were tough enough to kill him, I'd assume she would have been tough enough to leave him before it came to murder."

"As tough as you are, you mean?"

She didn't reply, but she looked him in the eye and, for the first time that day, he saw her smile.

CHAPTER
NINETEEN

Sunday morning at the Rialto truck stop dragged. Hunter was restless, wishing he could do something — anything — to get information that could solve Mike Irwin's murder, but the people he wanted to speak with now were in Seattle. He considered looking up Dave Cordero but he decided he didn't have enough information or the credentials to interview or even approach the man successfully. He didn't have access to police databases or research sources, but maybe he could find at least some information at a library. He asked one of the truck stop employees and she told him that the best and closest library open on a Sunday would be at the University of California Riverside. It took just twenty minutes to get there on the freeway but it took him another half hour to find the right place to park and make his way on foot through the maze of buildings to the Rivera library.

His first search was for anything that might enlighten him about Don Julian Transport. A business directory told him that it was located on Don Julian Road. Hunter rubbed his chin and remembered that he hadn't shaved. So, he wondered, did the name Don Julian have a Mexican connection? Don Julian Road ran northwest to southeast through the primarily Hispanic city of La Puente, east of L.A. Next he looked for Cordero's company, which he remembered Meredith saying was somewhere south of L.A. He couldn't find anything at all on Dave Cordero, and no obvious connection between Cordero and Don Julian Transport. Nothing came up on Todd Milton, either, but that was no surprise.

"Does the name Don Julian mean anything to you?" he asked one of the librarians, an older woman who reminded him slightly of Jessica Fletcher from the TV series 'Murder She Wrote'.

"Only Don Julian Alvarado," she said. "A character in the Hornblower series."

Hunter hit the side of his head with the heel of his hand. "Of course. El Supremo. That crazy Spaniard." He had borrowed the book from Gord, his landlord, who had the whole series of C.S. Forester novels. So Don Julian looked like a dead end. He thanked her and was about to walk away, but it was still Sunday and he still had hours to kill.

"While I'm here," he said, turning back to the librarian, "how about Belle Sorenson, or Belle Gunness? Have you got anything on her?" Sorry's mention of her had piqued his curiosity.

"I happen to be a big fan of true crime myself," said the Jessica Fletcher look-alike with a smile.

Hunter laughed. "I wouldn't exactly call myself a fan," he said.

The librarian frowned, then punched something into the computer. "I should be able to refer you to a couple of books. I know there was also a movie inspired by Belle's story. Did you ever see *The Bad Seed?* The mother of one of the main characters was a female serial killer based on Belle, except in the movie she went to the electric chair and no one knows for sure what happened to Belle. In fact," she looked at him over her reading glasses, "rumor has it that Belle ended up in California."

"A recent movie?"

"Mid-fifties, I think. Black and white. The little girl almost won an Oscar."

"Little girl?"

"The bad seed. Her poor mother got the idea that she'd somehow passed on her grandmother's murderous tendencies to her daughter, so she tried to kill the child and herself. Kind of a weird ending. They both survived. You'll have to keep an eye out for it on late night television."

"I will," said Hunter, just to make her happy.

She eventually directed him to a book in the stacks. It was called *Belle Gunness: The Lady Bluebeard.* Hunter settled into a chair near a window with his reading glasses perched halfway down his nose and began to read. Belle had carried out most of her murders in Indiana, not Illinois but he'd remembered partly right: she'd killed would-be suitors as well as her husbands. She'd also killed her own children. He shuddered.

After skimming through the book, he still wasn't sure why Sorry's father would have felt a need to mention her to his son. The only connection he could see was the name Sorenson, which was the last name of one of her husbands. He decided not to bring it up again with Sorry. His relationship with his father was precarious enough. One detail of Belle Gunness' story struck him in relation to Mike Irwin's murder. Revenge. Some psychologists suggested that Belle was exacting revenge on men as a result of being badly beaten by a rich boyfriend when she was only seventeen.

He looked at his watch. When he got back to the Rialto truck stop, he'd give himself that overdue shave, maybe catch a hockey game in the driver's lounge — only possible now because football season was over — or maybe a movie, then have an early dinner and read himself to sleep.

As much as Hunter liked highway driving for a living, those layover days on the road sometimes made him wish that he were home.

Elspeth was looking for a piece of paper one of the drivers had given her with what he called 'an awesome lead on backhaul from the Yukon'. ("I get a commission, don't I?" he'd said.) She was rifling through a messy stack of papers on her desk Monday afternoon when she came across the two Rolodex cards that she'd pulled out after hearing from Sorry about Don Julian Transport.

"What are the chances?" she muttered. Not good, in a city the size of Greater Los Angeles, that the two Southern California freight brokers she knew well enough to ask would know anything significant about a small trucking outfit in the City of Industry. She was on the verge of slipping the cards back into the Rolodex file, then decided it was about time one of her attempts to help Hunter paid off. All she had to lose was a few minutes of her time, and a few dollars worth of long distances charges.

The first call was a bust. "What? Who? Never heard of 'em. Gotta go." The guy hung up before she could squeeze in another question. She knew what her drivers would've said. *Taste of your own medicine*, or something like that. Oh, well. She dialled the second broker and found herself on hold.

She was just about to hang up when Matt Yost at MY-way Freight Services came on the line. "Yo, Mattie," she said. "Greetings from the Great White North."

"Wassup, bitch? You buyin' or sellin' this time?"

"Neither, bro. I'm looking for information on an operation in your 'hood."

"Hit me."

She gave him what she knew about Don Julian Transport. When he didn't respond right away, she thought she'd struck out again.

"I crossed paths with them a couple a times lately. Aggressive sons of bitches. The drivers are Latino thugs, not sure if they're Puerto Rican or Mexican, but best guess is Mexican. Don't quote me, but I think they've got some kind of extortion thing going. You know, could be anything from 'give us the contract and we'll give you a cut' to 'give us the fuckin' contract or we'll break your fuckin' legs' kind of thing."

"Anybody you know get hurt?"

"None of my regulars. I tell my guys to stay clear of them. They tried to bully one of my customers, but he took my advice and told them to take a hike. When push came to shove, they backed off. Still, my advice is, stay away, mama. Don't let 'em rope you into anything."

"Don't worry. I'm particular about who I do business with. Listen, Matt, while I got you..." she began.

"I knew it," he said. "I just knew it. You got a driver in SoCal and you need a load north, am I right?"

"Moi?" she said, in her Miss Piggy voice. She would need a load soon, but didn't want to ask for one now. "Just wanted to say, I got a couple of loads shaping up here for next week if you need backhaul."

"That's a first! I got no drivers up that way right now, but I'll keep it in mind."

El hung up the phone with a shiver of excitement. She had something for Hunter, at last! "Now we're cookin'with gas, Pete!" Peterbilt looked up at her from his doggie pillow, which was big enough for a dog four times his size, then tucked his nose under his tail and went back to sleep. El went to the lunch room and pulled a can of Coke out of the fridge, popped the top, and took a couple of big swallows. Then she settled her butt back in her big swivel chair and dialled Hunter's cell number.

Around sunset on Monday, Hunter was at the Flying J truck stop near Lodi. He hadn't managed to get away from the plastics warehouse in San Bernardino until almost eleven o'clock so he'd grabbed a Subway sandwich on his way out of town and was now ready for a break. After dinner, he could get back on the road and drive another four hours or so north, wait out his ten hours of off duty time at the Pilot truck stop in Weed, then be back on the road by about nine o'clock Tuesday morning. That was, of course, barring delays with traffic or any kind of mechanical breakdown. He'd been lucky lately, with his truck, and did his best to make sure the old Freightliner stayed healthy.

There was space at the pumps, so he pulled in to fuel up before parking his rig and heading to the restaurant for something to eat. He sat at a booth by the window. Whoever had been there before him had left a copy of USA Today on the seat, so Hunter picked it up and glanced at the headlines, then left it folded on the table. He ordered a steak with fries and gravy, aware that his daughters would be horrified at his choice if they were there, but he was too hungry to care. He knew they would scold him for not eating more vegetables, so when the waitress returned to set down his coffee, he asked for a side of onion rings.

After putting cream and sugar in his coffee and taking a sip, he pulled his cell phone out of his jacket pocket, about to turn it on and check for voicemail, then thought better of it. Roaming charges came straight off his bottom line. There was a payphone at every table for the convenience of truckers, so he called El on her 800 number.

"Make it quick. I'm standing in the lineup at the Colonel's," she told him. "Did you get my message?"

"No. What's up?"

"I'll give you the details when you get back. What time do you expect to pull in?"

"When do you need me?"

"Get your beauty rest Wednesday morning, sweetcheeks. See me in the office around noon, and you can make the delivery in Port Kells yourself anytime after one o'clock. I'll have a load to Winnipeg for you Thursday morning, if you want it. That work for you?"

Hunter said it did, and El said, "Five pieces of chicken and a large fries with gravy, please," as she hung up on him.

Next he retrieved his voicemail. He listened to the message from El, and a message from his daughter, Lesley, suggesting they 'do lunch' on Saturday if he was around. He'd have to call her back for a rain check when he got home, and tell her he'd be in Winnipeg on the weekend. He preferred the north-south run to travelling east in the winter, but he couldn't turn down a load. The Coquihalla highway across the Coast Mountains could be treacherous during a snowfall, and the passes over the Rocky Mountains were unpredictable. Temperatures of minus thirty degrees Fahrenheit weren't uncommon on the prairies, and he usually had to keep his engine idling to keep both himself and The Blue Knight from freezing during the night.

No further calls from Helen. His mind conjured up an image of her silently weeping at her son's bedside, and he realized it was an image from the past, when she had sat holding her husband's lifeless hand. Hunter took a deep breath and tried to concentrate on what was outside the window of the truck stop restaurant, under the lights.

He saw a mini-van pull up, and a woman dressed much too lightly for the temperature here at nightfall — she must have come from the desert — emerge from the passenger door, slide open the van door, and extract a young child out of its car seat. The child was blonde and wore shorts and little yellow sandals, so he thought it must be a girl. A young boy aged four or five jumped down from the van and the woman grabbed him by the shirt before he could walk away, and she made him take her hand. A man, also in shorts and with a backpack slung over one shoulder, appeared from around the other side of the van. He took the youngest child from the woman's arms, the little girl leaning into his shoulder as he settled her on his arm and kissed the top of her head, and the four of them walked together toward the restaurant. Again, Hunter found himself thinking about days past, a different life that seemed so long ago, when he was part of a young family.

His own girls were now young adults, and he was so far away from them most of the time that if anything were threatening them, he wouldn't even know, let alone be able to do anything to protect them. That ate at him when he let himself think about it. He wondered if he would feel differently about a son. Young men are usually their own worst enemies. A father would have to hope that he'd done his job well enough to ensure his son would make the right choices in life, but Hunter didn't think he would worry as much about protecting a son as he worried about his daughters. Is the mother more responsible for the behavior of a daughter? If so, his ex-wife Christine had done a good job.

Can a father, then, be held responsible for the behavior of his son? Or hold himself responsible? He couldn't help but think about Sorry and how his father had been disappointed in him. Had the older Sorenson actually been more disappointed by his own failure as a father? And what about Adam Marsh? Had his tormented father not only caused his wife and son the devastating pain of dealing with his suicide, but also doomed young Adam to travel the wrong roads for the rest of his life?

The little family from the mini-van, still moving as a single unit, arrived at a booth opposite Hunter's table. Hunter watched as the woman pulled some clothing from the backpack and handed it to the man before starting to put a hoodie on the little girl. The man shepherded the little boy back toward the restaurant entrance, in the direction of the men's room. Just as Hunter's meal arrived, the boy and his father, now in long pants and sweatshirts, came back to their table. The boy stared at Hunter while he waited for his father to position a booster seat, so Hunter smiled at him. The little boy grinned back before he clambered up on the bench and into the booster seat.

Hunter opened up the copy of USA Today and tried to concentrate on the news as he worked on his steak. He wasn't unhappy with his present life. After all, he had chosen to remain alone, hadn't he? Yes. It was the best thing for him right now.

The little girl at the next table started to giggle at something her father said, and Hunter's heart ached, just a little more, for days gone by.

Kelly had finally managed to get Correna to fall asleep. The little girl had napped too long in the afternoon and was wide awake, chattering to her mother long after brother Jordan had dropped off to sleep on the other twin bed a few feet away. Kelly had lain beside her daughter, stroking her hair gently and admonishing her to whisper. Correna had whispered loudly at first, with an animated face and frequent hand gestures, then more softly and slowly. At last her eyes had fluttered, then closed, and she fell silent except for soft breaths that puffed against Kelly's cheek.

Kelly carefully moved away from her daughter, tucked the quilt close around her, and sneaked out of the room. She went to her own bedroom — the room that had been Mike's and still held his old sports trophies on a shelf and team photos on the wall — but she wasn't ready to go to bed and it was certainly not an atmosphere that she felt comfortable spending time in. As soon as the estate was settled, she would have to make plans to sell the house in Pasadena and buy a new home for herself and the kids, somewhere that they could create new memories and escape from old ones. She didn't know yet whether that would be in Southern California or in the Pacific Northwest, or maybe somewhere entirely new.

She made her way quietly down the stairs. She could hear the television still on in the den, and suspected that either Beth or John would still be there watching, but when she looked inside, the couch was empty. She was about to enter the kitchen to make some camomile tea when she heard Beth's quavering voice coming from that direction.

"Oh my God, John. How in God's name did it ever come to this?"

John's voice, low and soft. "We've had a good run, my love. We've known many who never had the good times we've had, or who've had to endure worse. You and I — and Michael —we've had our turn. Now we've got to do what's best for Jordan and Correna."

"Yes. Yes, that's the most important thing. Oh, John, sweetheart. You've always been my rock."

"Not so, my love. You've been mine."

Kelly heard Beth's soft sobbing and imagined John would be holding her.

John spoke again. "Let's go upstairs to bed now, in case Kelly comes back down. We don't want her to see us crying again, do we?"

"I couldn't face her right now, with what I know."

Kelly backed away silently, went to the den and sat down on the couch. She flipped the channels, not to find something else to watch, but to alert her in-laws to her presence. Her heart was thudding against her breastbone. What did Beth mean, *I couldn't face her now, with what I know?* Kelly felt suddenly alone in a house belonging to strangers.

They stopped at the doorway to the den, John's arm around Beth's shoulders, hers around his waist. Beth's face was averted. "There you are, Kelly," said John. "Kids asleep?"

She just nodded, trying to read his face. She couldn't summon a smile.

"Good night, sweetie," said Beth.

Kelly said good night back to her.

"Have a good sleep," said John. "We'll see you in the morning."

Kelly remained seated on the couch, staring at the floor. She muted the television, but could hear nothing more from her in-laws. What was it that they knew?

Kelly no longer wanted tea. She didn't want to watch television, and she didn't want to go up to Mike's old room to bed. She turned off all the downstairs lights and climbed slowly up the stairs. In her room — Mike's room — she undressed and put on a flannelette nightgown, then went to the kids' room.

She had tried to hide how she felt about Mike, and how destructive he was to the lives and souls of her and the children. She loved Beth and John, and she wouldn't hurt them for the world, but she was a mother, and children always came first. After midnight some time, or maybe after one, she fell asleep snugged up against Correna, under the My Little Pony quilt.

CHAPTER
TWENTY

Hunter arrived just south of Seattle during afternoon rush hour. There was a light rain falling, and the temperature hovered just a few degrees above freezing. He pulled his rig into a highway rest area a few miles north of Tacoma and turned on his cell phone, then looked in his wallet for a piece of paper torn from a notebook. This time it was worth the roaming charges to make a call.

A woman answered, and Hunter asked to speak with John.

"Who's calling, please?"

"Tell him it's an old friend who's just arrived in town from California."

There was a slight hesitation, then, "Just a minute. He's been napping. I'll see if he's awake."

When John came on the line, Hunter identified himself. "I'd really like to talk to you, John. I'd come over to the house, but that's not so easy with a forty-eight foot trailer in tow. Is there somewhere not too far off the I-5 that I could meet you, somewhere I'd be able to park my rig?"

"I've been wondering if I'd hear from you. I could meet you at Northgate Mall, it's only about ten minutes from here. Give me half an hour. Park on the east side, near 5th Avenue. What color is your truck?"

Hunter asked for forty-five minutes. "Rush hour, I'm afraid."

It took him a little over the forty-five minutes. It was almost dark when he pulled up, and the rain had started alternating with a biting sleet. He saw a Dodge van parked by itself along the east side of the parking lot, and pulled to a stop nearby. John got out and walked over, shoulders back, seemingly oblivious to the cold rain. Hunter rolled down the window and invited him to climb inside.

The older man settled himself in the passenger seat, his leather bomber jacket glistening with streaks of rainwater. "Nice," he said. "Always wanted to drive one of these things myself."

"It's never too late."

"It is for me." He smiled sadly, looking out beyond the dash at something Hunter couldn't see. "I'm dying. I only have a few months left, at best."

Hunter nodded, his eyes fixed on the steering wheel. "I'm sorry to hear that, but not surprised." He had left the engine idling for heat, and the dials on the dash illuminated the inside of the cab with a subtle glow.

They were both silent for a moment, then Hunter said, "What would you say if I told you that the RCMP have found a couple of witnesses who say that I was the man on the chair with your son?"

The older man drew in a deep breath, then let it out slowly. "I'd say they were mistaken."

"Why, John?"

"Why do they think it was you? You're probably a little bit, or maybe a lot, like the man who killed my son." He turned to look at Hunter, and when Hunter didn't respond, he said, "But that's not what you mean, is it?"

Hunter shook his head.

John sighed. "I have no reason to hide it from you any longer. Beth knows. My wife is a highly intuitive woman, and a strong one. She knew somehow that I was dying, but waited for me to give her the news on my own time. Last night, I was shocked to find out that she also somehow suspected I had killed our son. I didn't have to tell her why." He paused, stroking the dash with the long, knotted fingers of one hand. "I guess you're pretty intuitive yourself. You must've been one hell of a detective. How did you guess?"

"I didn't, at first. I looked at several possibilities, several people with motives, and I began to think that the person who had the best motive was your daughter-in-law, Kelly. The love a mother has for her son can eclipse the love for her husband, even a good, kind man, never mind one who is abusive."

John nodded sadly.

Hunter continued, "I didn't want to believe she was capable. If he were alive, I might have suspected Kelly's father, your best friend."

"Scott. I promised him I would look after her."

"And you couldn't do that without saving her from your son."

"I thought about helping her get away, get a divorce, hide from him. But I knew he would track her down, just like he keeps finding and tormenting Alora."

"There's more to it than that, isn't there, John? You feel responsible for your son's behavior. What he did to Alora, what he was doing to his wife and children. When did you decide?"

"Hard to believe that such a horrendous act was determined by impulse and opportunity, but it was. I've always kept an old service revolver in the van when my wife and I travel. I forgot to take it out, and I guess the Canadian border guards didn't think to check for one. It's not as if we looked like criminals when we crossed the border. Fortunately, the guard wasn't close enough to smell the alcohol on Mike's breath." He smiled weakly. "Our last visit with Mike in California was no picnic, but on the drive to Whistler, it was clear that his behavior was seriously endangering the mental and physical health of Kelly and the kids. He got so angry with Kelly and myself when we suggested he not drive, even his mother was shocked at how brutal he'd become. She was crying silently in the back seat. I should never have let him drive and I'm ashamed of myself for backing down. I rationalized that although he'd been drinking, he wasn't actually impaired, and I guess I didn't want his rage to escalate. That just proved to me how his behavior could cow a person, even an ex-Marine. What would that do to a sensitive six year old?

"The icing on the cake was that incident with Alora — the first time I saw you. It was then that I started to think about...uh...putting him away." He snorted softly. "Putting him away. Away where he couldn't do any more harm. I didn't have the time left to fix him, so I had to take responsibility for what I'd created and un-create him."

"A bad seed," said Hunter softly.

John looked at him sideways, his left eyebrow raised. "Yes. A bad seed. Funny you should say that. Beth used that term last night." His shoulders slumped, and he put up one hand to cover his eyes. "It does nothing to ease her pain. It's a nightmare for her. They refer to guilt as a burden, and it truly is. At moments I feel so crushed by it I can barely take a breath."

Hunter felt an almost overwhelming sense of tragedy. Taking a life was wrong. John was wrong in killing his son. Hunter had always believed that a man guilty of murder should be brought to justice. Killing in self defence or defence of others could be considered justifiable homicide, but that was for a judge and jury to decide in court, not a truck driver in a shopping mall parking lot. In court, Hunter knew, John would be found guilty of premeditated murder. But he felt tremendous sympathy for the man and couldn't help wondering, if he were in John's position, would he have considered doing the same thing?

"That toast," he said. "When we had a drink together, you gave a toast, in Latin."

"Non Sibi Sed Patriae," said John. "Not for self, but for country." He sucked in his breath, almost convulsively. "I killed my little boy." His voice faltered. "Sometimes it seems like just last year that I taught him how to throw a football, taught him how to cast a line and catch a fish. Beth and I were always so proud of our little man; he was strong and brave. I loved my son and I would have gladly died for him." He paused. "But something went wrong. Terribly, terribly wrong."

John put his fist to his lips and was silent for a moment before he continued. "I have to keep reminding myself that no matter what happens to me, how much it hurts Beth and myself, it was for the greater good. For Kelly and those two little kids."

Hunter cleared his throat and broke the silence that followed. "You must be a good skier."

"Used to be. Following Mike just about killed me, to tell the truth. I told Beth I was going for a walk, but I tailed him right from the hotel. If he hadn't been rusty and a little out of shape, I never could've kept up with him. After... When I'd skied back down to the Village, I got back to the hotel as soon as I could and lay down, waiting for the call." He stared through the windshield into the darkening sky a moment before continuing.

"If I hadn't had the gun, it wouldn't have happened, at least not then. It was as merciful as I could make it. He didn't know it was coming, and death was immediate. Like flipping a switch." He sighed. "The pain is reserved for those of us left behind. I know they're better off, even Beth, because she'll be spared the heartache of seeing poor little Jordan go through hell. I fervently hope it's not too late for the boy. But there is still the pain of loss, grieving for what used to be or what could have been. For Beth and I there's also the pain of failure, the worry that if we had been better parents, our son could have turned out different. And maybe I was wrong. Maybe if he'd had the chance, Mike would have changed."

Hunter knew nothing he could say would help. Listening was the best thing he could do for the man, so he remained silent.

As if reading Hunter's thoughts, John continued. "It's such a relief to talk to someone about it. A friend. I still miss Scott, Kelly's father. It sounds corny, but when I knew I was dying, I started to think about what we'll say to each other when we meet on the other side in a few months. After the drive up to Whistler, I could imagine him saying, *What have you done to protect my little girl? You let her marry that son of yours and now the bastard is making her life hell, destroying her self-esteem and killing the spirit of my little grandson. I trusted you and you let me down.* He gave a short, self-conscious laugh. "I couldn't let that happen. No matter what the price, I just couldn't."

"And there *will* be a price," said Hunter.

The older man nodded almost absently, then reached inside his jacket and pulled out a sealed envelope. "A signed confession," he said. "My lawyer has a copy as well." He handed the envelope to Hunter.

"Where's the gun?"

"Somewhere on Whistler Mountain. It's in the letter. I tried to describe the place as best I could, in case it's needed to corroborate my confession, but I was so tired and I don't know the names of the runs." His voice trailed off.

In the pale light from the dashboard dials, Hunter could see the older man's eyes close. His face was haggard, suffused with a profound weariness.

"I had hoped this would never have to become public, but I can't chance someone else taking the blame for what I've done. I didn't want Beth to know, but now that she does, I am still dreadfully afraid of what the publicity will do to her, and both the knowledge and the publicity to Jordan and Correna. Kelly, too. Is there any way that this could be kept just between us if no one else is charged?"

Hunter ran his hands lightly along the underside of the steering wheel, considering what John was asking of him. He understood John's fears. It crossed his mind that he could hold on to the confession until someone — perhaps himself — was arrested for the murder. Would justice be served by putting a dying man in jail? But he'd been a cop too long to let himself withhold the information from the detectives.

"I can't promise you anything," he said, "but I truly wish I could."

Hunter parked the Pontiac in front of the exit doors at Lions Gate Hospital. He was early, and stayed at the wheel of his car in case he was asked to move. He'd just come back from Whistler, where he'd met with Staff Sergeant Shane Blackwell. The detective had visibly struggled with Hunter's request.

"You know it won't reflect well on the detachment, if the public thinks we're just letting a murder case go cold. The local media will be after us every slow news day," Shane had said.

"You're big tough guys, you can take it. Jordan Irwin is a little kid, already beaten down by his bully of a father. He doesn't need to know that he was the reason that his beloved grandfather killed his own son. As for John Irwin, he's not trying to escape justice as much as he's trying to spare his family further pain. He's a good man who served his country well, and he's dying. Soon. Let him die surrounded by his family and not in a prison hospital."

Shane had sighed mightily, but folded up John's letter and tossed it in a file, then put the file beneath a stack of papers on his desk. "Go away," he said. "I have work to do, and there are never enough hours in my day to get all this…," he gestured at his desk, "…all this crap cleaned off my desk."

The day was cold, although not nearly as cold as it had been in Winnipeg, and the sky was a brilliant blue above the dark waters of Howe Sound as Hunter drove back down the Sea to Sky highway. Hunter felt his spirits lift, although he had already begun to grieve the loss of his new friend. He had called from Whistler to give John the news, but Kelly had answered the phone. She told him that her father-in-law was out making arrangements for his impending move to a nearby hospice. "Beth wanted him to stay home until the end, but he said he doesn't want Beth's house to be tainted by memories of his dying days. Did you want me to give him a message?"

"Just tell him his Canadian friend called," was all he had said.

Hunter had spoken to Helen on the telephone when he got in from Winnipeg the night before, but he hadn't yet seen her or Adam. She told him she'd booked the two of them on a flight home to Calgary.

"I could take you by car," Hunter had said.

"No. The long drive would be too hard on Adam. The doctors say he'll need some time yet to recuperate at home."

So Hunter had volunteered to take the two of them to the airport. He looked at his watch, then at the automatic doors. He could make out figures approaching the doors from inside, one on foot, pushing the other in a wheelchair. As the doors opened, he popped open the trunk, then stepped outside the car and went around to open the two passenger side doors.

He looked up to see a very pale Adam Marsh being helped out of his wheelchair by a man in a sky blue hospital uniform. The male nurse helped Adam get settled into the back seat, and Hunter bent down, one hand on the roof of the car, the other resting on the boy's shoulder. "Hi, Adam. You're looking a hundred percent better than last time I saw you."

The boy smiled weakly. "Thanks. I feel like shit."

"You're going to be fine, kid," the male nurse shot over his shoulder as he pushed the wheelchair away.

"Remember me?" asked Hunter.

"Yeah. Well, I know who you are. You're my middle name."

Hunter grinned. "You got it. They make you take out your stud?" He pointed at his own nose.

The boy nodded glumly. "They *said* it got lost."

"Where's your mom?" Hunter turned to look back at the doors, watched the nurse and wheelchair disappear inside.

"She said she had to pick up her suitcase and stuff, but I saw her go into the can. I guess she wanted to fix her face." Adam closed his eyes for a moment, then opened them again as he put his left hand on top of Hunter's. "Thanks, eh. They say you're the one got me to the hospital, and if it wasn't for you I prob'ly would be dead."

"You'll live to play guitar again." Hunter was hoping that Adam had more than that to look forward to, but he wanted to see the boy smile again. It worked.

"I never could play guitar worth shit," said the boy. "Besides, I'd rather play drums."

"Drummers are all crazy."

Adam's smile broadened. "So, what's your point?"

Just then Hunter felt a warm hand on his back. He straightened up and turned around to face a vision from his past. Helen was hatless, her fawn colored hair loosely framing her face, and the brown

294

suede coat she wore was open at the throat. A backpack and a soft-sided suitcase sat beside her on the asphalt. At the moment he first saw her face, Hunter couldn't smile, and he couldn't speak.

"Hello, Hunter," she said, and reached for his hand.

THE END

ACKNOWLEDGEMENTS

As solitary an occupation as writing is, there are always thanks due to the many people who help create a work of fiction. First and foremost, I owe my late husband, Jim Donald, for getting me started and providing the inspiration for the character of Hunter Rayne. I am also eternally grateful to my father, who supported and encouraged me from the start. He passed away in March of 2012 at the age of 93, and is sorely missed by those who loved him.

Thanks to fellow Rainwriters including Ed Griffin, Bob Mackay, and Paul Burgoyne for their feedback during my time with the group, and especially to Loreena Lee, who volunteered to help edit the manuscript. Thanks also to Sergeant Peter Thiessen of the RCMP for helping with questions related to the Whistler detachment, and to Laura Gallant, the Public Relations Coordinator for Whistler Blackcomb for information relating to the ski lifts.

I hope readers will forgive any errors I may have made in geography or description, and keep in mind that in I have taken literary license when I felt the story would be better for it. The Chateau Grand Montagne and the Coast Peaks Hotel, like many elements of the story, are products of the writer's imagination.

Thanks once again to Chris Hunter and Steve Johnsen for the wonderfully atmospheric cover and for their ongoing support. Thanks also to my partner, the irrepressible French Canadian cowboy, Gilbert Roy, for his patience while I spent hours each day on 'that damn computer' instead of outdoors enjoying our Langley farm. Above all, a huge thank you to all my readers, especially to those who have taken the time to give me feedback or post reviews. Your enthusiasm for my mysteries gives meaning to how I spend my working days.

ABOUT THE AUTHOR

R.E. Donald is the author of the Hunter Rayne highway mystery series. Ruth worked in the transportation industry in various capacities for over 25 years, and draws on her own experiences, as well as those of her late husband, Jim Donald, in creating the characters and situations in her novels.

Ruth attended the University of British Columbia in Vancouver, B.C., where she studied languages (Russian, French and German) and creative writing to obtain a Bachelor of Arts degree. She currently lives on a small farm in Langley, B.C. She and her partner, a French Canadian cowboy named Gilbert Roy, enjoy their Canadian Horses (Le Cheval Canadien) and other animals.

Also by R.E. Donald in the Hunter Rayne highway mystery series:
Slow Curve on the Coquihalla
Ice on the Grapevine

For information on new releases visit
redonald.com or **proudhorsepublishing.com**

Made in the USA
Charleston, SC
30 December 2016